# FAMILY
# SECRETS

## Jayant Swamy

VISHWAKARMA
PUBLICATIONS VP

# FAMILY SECRETS

1st Edition Published in India by Vishwakarma Publications in October 2020

© **Jayant Swamy**

ISBN - 978-93-89624-50-2

**Disclaimer**
This is a work of fiction. Names, characters, places and incidents are either the product of the author's imagination or are used fictitiously and any resemblance to any actual person, living or dead, events or locales is entirely coincidental.

**Published by:**
**Vishwakarma Publications**
34A/1, Suyog Center, 7th Floor, Gultekadi Marketyard Road, Giridhar Bhavan Chowk, Pune: 411037, Maharashtra, India.
Mob.: 9168682200
Email: info@vpindia.co.in
Website: www.vishwakarmapublications.com

Cover : **The Book Bakers**
Typeset and Layout : **Vishwakarma Publications**
Printed at : **Repro India Ltd., Mumbai**

*Dedicated to Mummy*

*You taught me how to live. I am yet to learn to live without you*

*My mission in life is not merely to survive, but to thrive; and to do so with some passion, some compassion, some humor, and some style (Maya Angelou)*

# Acknowledgements

F*amily Secrets* is a work of fiction. All characters are figments of my imagination. Yet, like most fiction, the genesis can be traced to family folklore, that was revealed to me, relating to the extra-marital alliance of a particular patriarch many many decades ago. When this lady, the patriarch's daughter, found out about a half-sister to whom she had lost her father's love, what did she feel? How did she deal with the sense of abandonment and betrayal that may have haunted her for the rest of her life? What was her frame of mind when the half-sister went on to become a renowned doctor while she herself was destined to be a homemaker, despite her aspirations to become a lawyer? These questions troubled my sensitive soul for days. *Family Secrets* was born thereafter. A fictional story of two half-brothers. Who face-off under totally different circumstances. I delve deep into their mindsets, motivations and machinations.

Gratitude brings me joy. It takes a team larger than a village to get a novel published. Gratitude is all I have to offer them. Gratitude was not put in my heart to stay there. Gratitude is not gratitude until I give it away. And here I go.

Suhail Mathur my literary agent, for reposing faith in me, championing my novel and spearheading the marketing campaign. Vishal Soni and the Vishwakarma Publications team for publishing *Family Secrets*. The Book Bakers for cover design. Sneha Bawari and Jyoti Sharma for editing magic.

Madhuri the first-ever reader, for invaluable inputs around court procedures. Debra, Pratik, Sandhya, Syed and Varun, my early-readers. Alex, Bonnie, Joshua, Rob and Shweta, my writing group brigade. Ritika, Shesh, Ganesh, Hema, Jake, Ketaki, Nandini, Ravichandar, Sangita, Shinie, Vikrant, Shoba and Srikanth, for valuable suggestions.

Vidhya, for humouring me, listening with patience, and quality-checking critical decisions. Ahan, for offering me social media insights and understanding me like no one else can. The Universe, for bestowing grace and bringing it all together.

# Contents

Book 1

# 1985: Siddhartha & Abhimanyu

# 1.

# The Heist

"Honey, it is time to go." Siddhartha looked in the mirror one last time to make sure his beard and turban were firmly in place and slipped his arms through the sleeves of a navy-blue blazer. The tall frame and broad shoulders he had inherited from his father could pass him off as a North Indian.

Sadhana, his petite wife, giggled. Dressed in a yellow and gold salwar-kameez that accentuated her portrayed pregnancy, her pixie-like face perfectly made up and a zari dupatta draped over her hair, she looked every inch the North Indian woman that she was not. Sadhana had willingly sacrificed her wedding sari to get the salwar-kameez stitched – they had both agreed on the need to look well to do, if not rich.

"Loveleen Kaur, you look lovely." Siddhartha whistled. "I, Sunny Singh, love you." Those were their aliases for the assignment.

Traveling through the bumpy roads of Bangalore in a rickety auto rickshaw, Siddhartha put his arms around Sadhana protectively and drew her closer. She was one of the few good things that had happened to him in a life otherwise filled with failure, rejection and misfortune. She had supported him unconditionally during the sixteen years of their marriage. They were really two of a kind. *We like the same things, do everything together, like those proverbial peas in a pod.*

It was the day before Deepavali, the festival of lights. Even at eleven in the morning, there were people everywhere, buying clothes and sweets, flowers and fireworks and above all, the customary gold and silver articles in veneration of Lakshmi, the Goddess of wealth. Amidst the ceaseless noise of bursting crackers, the auto warrened its way through the pot-holed streets of central Bangalore towards M. G. Road, the pride of downtown.

M.G. Road was closed to vehicular traffic due to the exceptional crowds it attracted during the festive season. After paying off the auto driver, Siddhartha and Sadhana trudged through its length, passing in front of shops selling books and clothes, antiques and carpets, the gleaming Orange Computers Institute, an ice cream parlour and the swanky Hotel Zyatt, to arrive at their destination, Aradhana Jewellers. A robust security guard with a bushy moustache and glistening rifle stood outside the showroom.

Siddhartha had surveyed the jewellery showroom during his past visits. The lower floor, which displayed gold and diamond jewellery, was the focus of their plan. Siddhartha held a nervous Sadhana by her forearm as they entered the brightly lit showroom, jam-packed as expected. Playing the part of the demure housewife to perfection, Sadhana kept her head bowed and her face partially covered by the dupatta.

Gleaming glass-topped cabinets displaying jewellery occupied the bulk of the space adjoining the far wall as well as the left and right walls. Salespersons stood behind the locked cabinets, carefully displaying the wares to customers. More shelves filled with jewellery, lined the walls behind them.

There was a rectangular island counter about a foot and a half high in the centre. Sitting in comfort on thick mattresses spread along the four edges of the island, customers could examine their purchase options at leisure. Track lights on the walls of the showroom and chandeliers hanging from the ceiling ameliorated the allure of the displayed wares. There were no windows on any of the three walls.

Siddhartha and Sadhana walked towards the manager's cabin adjacent to the door through which they had entered. The cash counter was located beyond the manager's cabin, followed by a landing area and a spiral staircase. Squished between the manager's cabin and the cash counter was a parrot green door. Siddhartha was aware what lay behind that door – the electric room, a tiny bathroom and a utility area.

The manager's cabin was filled with people. Siddhartha and Sadhana stood by the door patiently, until the manager, an elderly man with a gaunt face, could finish attending to the customers seated in front of him.

Siddhartha hoped he would not run into any of his business associates. While the chances of anybody recognizing him through his disguise were slim, he did not want to be remembered for any reason.

"I am Sunny Singh, the owner of Bobby Travels." Siddhartha addressed the manager in his gruffest voice. "I need assistance to buy a diamond necklace for my wife." Sadhana pulled the dupatta tighter around her lower face, barely stifling her laughter.

The manager, whose name was Mathur, threw measuring looks and assigned them to Vimmy, a traditionally dressed saleswoman in charge of the diamond counter for the day.

Making way through the crowded showroom, Vimmy led Sadhana and Siddhartha to the far-right end of the showroom. Opening the partition door, she took her position behind the glass cabinet and locked the partition door from her side.

Siddhartha and Sadhana stood on the opposite side and surveyed the diamond ear studs and pendants displayed inside the glass-topped cabinet. "Look for small and valuable diamonds, one carat and above." Siddhartha had coached Sadhana, the previous night.

An attendant placed a small stool in deference to the pregnant Sadhana and requested her to sit down.

Siddhartha tugged at his turban. It was time to put their plan into action. Sadhana would have ten minutes to do what she had to do. "Count to 120." Siddhartha bent down and whispered in her ear. His bald head was a messy canvass of sticky sweat under the tight turban.

Sadhana adjusted the dupatta over her bump and focused her attention on the jewellery display.

Siddhartha turned around and slowly inched his way through the milling crowds, towards the parrot green door. Loitering near the door, he looked in either direction. No one paid him any attention. Customers were intent on striking the best bargains; salespersons focused on notching up maximum sales. Had someone asked, he would have said he was looking for the bathroom.

Siddhartha slipped on a pair of skin-coloured gloves that he pulled out of his blazer pocket and waited. When he saw a woman in a pink dress and pink high heels trip and fall, near where Sadhana was sitting, he opened the parrot green door, closed it behind him and made his way to the electric room. He could only hope things were moving along exactly as he had planned, back at the counter. If not, he hoped Sadhana would remember his instructions, to adopt Plan B as he had told her.

◆

Seated on the stool, Sadhana had counted to 120 as Siddhartha had instructed. Tapping the glass-topped cabinet at several places, she asked Vimmy if she could inspect those jewellery sets more closely.

Vimmy told her that she could take out only one or two sets at a time.

Sadhana's eyes followed Vimmy's actions as she extracted a set of keys from underneath a neighbouring desk, unlocked the glass cabinet and brought out a single jewellery box. As she examined the glittering diamonds, Sadhana's fingers worked behind the protection provided by her dupatta, to remove a linen bag attached to the inner lining of her layered kameez with a Velcro strip. Sadhana soon returned the diamond set to Vimmy, and pointed a finger towards several sets in the farther end of the cabinet.

When Vimmy busied herself to go through the steps of putting back a set and taking out another two, Sadhana turned around on her stool so her back was to the counter. Clutching the linen bag in her left palm, she looked at the oncoming flow of people – couples, older people, families with children, groups of women, one or two single men. Be they rich, poor or middle class – everyone purchased gold and silver for Deepavali. On spotting a single woman in a pink dress balancing precariously on pink clogs as she weaved her way in, Sadhana slyly stretched out her right leg as if mitigating a cramp.

The next instant, the woman in pink had tripped and fallen, her pink purse flying across the floor. At the same time, as unobtrusively as she could, Sadhana let loose the mass of zirconia crystals contained in the linen bag.

Chaos followed, as the diamond-like crystals scattered themselves all over the showroom floor. Customers seated on the mattresses around the island counter were the first to dive after the crystals. Just as Sadhana turned around to face Vimmy who was taking out the diamond sets for her, the showroom lights went out. Two battery-operated lantern-lights turned themselves on, casting a dim and ominous glow.

In the semi-darkness of the windowless showroom on a sunny afternoon, the crowd had gone berserk, stomping across the floor, making a grab for the rolling crystals in a bid to gather as many as could be held. The security guard closed the front door shut. A salesman made an announcement requesting the customers to stay inside the showroom and stay calm. Manager Mathur was beckoning somebody to call the electricity company to attend to the fault.

Sadhana clutched her stomach and looked at Vimmy, as people thronged all around her. Making a retching sound, Sadhana half closed her eyes and rotated her fingers around her head.

Vimmy stopped what she was doing. Opening the partition door, she pulled Sadhana over to her side of the counter and propped her on a chair. A pregnant woman on the verge of fainting never fails to gain human sympathy, especially from another woman.

"Water please." Sadhana leaned back against the wall. "Sugar."

Vimmy must have panicked, for she frantically shouted out the names of her co-workers for help. No one came, all of them caught in the maddening crowd that stampeded around the glittering crystals, mistaken for real diamonds.

Eyes half-closed, Sadhana held her breath as Vimmy removed the key from the cabinet keyhole, dropped it into the top drawer of a hidden desk and dashed out.

In the semi-darkness, Sadhana opened the drawer and extracted the key. Standing up and leaning against the glass counter, she twirled the key and opened the cabinet door. Picking up every alternate box of jewellery one by one, she slipped each one of them into the pouches sown securely underneath the layers of her kameez.

Sixty seconds and there was no sign of Vimmy. Two more battery-operated lights had turned themselves on and one of the alarms had begun to beep.

When Siddhartha had miraculously materialized in front of her, Sadhana clutched her belly, gave him a slight nod; locking the cabinet door, she returned the key to the drawer.

◆

The security guard had opened the front door to let in the electrician and closed it back immediately. Pandit, the boyish salesman with the long mop of hair, was escorting the electrician towards the electric room. Making strong strides through the crowd, gently dragging Sadhana with him, Siddhartha slowed his pace, not wanting to run the risk of being recognized. *Thank God Pandit was not in charge of the diamond jewellery counter today!*

No zirconia crystals remained on the floor any more. Having locked up the jewellery counters, the salespersons were appealing to the customers to stay in one place until the lights came back on. Mathur was gesticulating angrily at the woman in pink, who in turn had turned ballistic, hell-bent on convincing him that she was not the one who had strewn the crystals.

When Siddhartha and Sadhana arrived at the front door, the security guard refused to heed Siddhartha's plea to let them out. Out of the corner of his eye, Siddhartha could see Vimmy making her way, back to her counter, a jug of water in hand. Mathur was escorting the shrieking woman in pink, to his cabin. Siddhartha could hear him say something about escalating the situation to his boss.

"Sir we have an emergency," Siddhartha called out to Mathur. Sadhana clutched her stomach and swooned. Siddhartha tightened his grip around her. "Please give us permission to leave. I don't want to lose our baby." He appealed to Mathur. "We have nothing to hide." He pointed at Sadhana's hands. "She has not even brought her purse."

Mathur looked at them, a look of indecision dancing on his face.

"Your security guard can check me." Pulling out his wallet and a cheque book from his pant pocket, Siddhartha overturned the empty pockets of his navy-blue blazer.

The lights chose that exact moment to come right back on. Siddhartha cursed.

Several customers swarmed Mathur, asking for permission to leave the showroom. A beleaguered Mathur ordered the security guard to unlock the door only for the Sikh couple, and walked on to his cabin with the woman in pink.

Vimmy was calling out after Sadhana. The security guard was unlocking the door.

*Has Vimmy discovered the missing diamonds?* A petrified Siddhartha could barely breathe as he stepped out into the blazing afternoon sun, his arms encircled around a shaking Sadhana.

◆

Breezing into the air-conditioned foyer of Zyatt, the swanky hotel next-door, Siddhartha and Sadhana made their way up two flights of stairs exactly as they had rehearsed the day before. The second-floor bathrooms, they had determined, were the quietest.

"I am upset that the woman in pink got blamed for spilling the diamonds," Sadhana said, when they had reached the landing.

"That is exactly what worked to our advantage." Siddhartha retorted, as they headed in opposite directions.

Siddhartha walked over to the men's room. Removing his beard and turban, he washed his olive face with running water and mopped it dry. Opening the door of the cupboard under the washbasin, he groped for the white and black plastic bag he had left there the day before. Removing his blazer, he placed it inside the bag along with the beard and turban and exited the men's room.

Sitting on a sofa in the second-floor lobby, waiting for Sadhana to appear and expecting to hear a police siren any moment - he wondered what was happening back at Aradhana Jewellers, even as he mentally congratulated Sadhana for having the presence of mind to relock the cabinet door and restore the key.

When Sadhana appeared before him, clad in the thin churidar-kurta that she had worn underneath the yellow and gold ensemble, her hair bound in a ponytail, she too carried a white and black plastic bag in her hand. Scrubbed free of makeup, her face was pale and sullen.

Siddhartha peered into her bag, reaching inside with his right hand, and digging through, until he could feel, among the folds of the clothes, the pouches containing the jewellery boxes. "There, there, there," he said aloud, as if to assure himself of the existence of the booty.

When the two walked out of Hotel Zyatt arm in arm, Siddhartha carrying two plastic shopping bags, the neighbouring jewellery showroom was teeming with people. If anyone was looking for a well-to-do North Indian couple, there was no way they would have guessed the nondescript man and woman walking away to the other end of M. G Road were they.

Hailing an auto, Siddhartha was glad he had decided against using their car. It would not only have proved a parking nightmare but also slowed down their getaway. Somehow traveling by auto assured greater anonymity, and gave them a greater sense of freedom under the stressful circumstances. Siddhartha and Sadhana huddled together within the cosy confines of the auto, as the incessant crackling of the Deepavali fireworks on the roads, accompanied by the billowing smoke, drowned out any guilt that might have tried to overpower them. Neither spoke until they had reached the haven of their rented flat on the twelfth floor of a residential high-rise in North Bangalore.

◆

"Honey, you were marvellous." Siddhartha kissed Sadhana on the cheek as she extracted the little jewellery boxes from the pouches of her kameez and arranged them in the locker attached to her steel almirah. Two black and white plastic bags lay strewn on the floor of their little bedroom.

"Once an actor, always an actor," she said.

That is how he had fallen in love with her – on seeing her on stage, playing the role of Cinderella, in a dance ballet. She had only been nineteen, a good ten years younger than he was. She had not changed much in the sixteen years of their marriage, notwithstanding the permanently etched melancholy in her eyes – ever since losing their young daughter, Pinky, to leukaemia some years ago.

"I can't believe it," Sadhana said. "Everything went like clockwork."

"The proof of the project lies in the planning," he grinned. "That is my mantra."

"You are a genius."

"Genius or madness, this is where I got the germ of the idea." He bowed with mock reverence in front of a book displayed on the mantel. *If Tomorrow Comes by* Sidney Sheldon. "The details are mine, though. I adapted an incident from the book to suit the Indian ethos."

Siddhartha was a voracious reader. As much as he had resented his father for what he had done to him and his family, Siddhartha had inherited his father's sense of style and proficiency in the English language.

"I was paralyzed," Sadhana said. "I expected the emergency lights to come on and the alarms to go off as I stole the boxes."

"I talked to some electricians after our earlier visit. To learn how to disconnect the wires and disable the alarms. Their main UPS is primitive. It only supports the two lights that came on first. I had drained the charge of the secondary back-up which supports the alarms."

"Technical. Boring." She crinkled her nose and emptied the remaining contents of the plastic bags onto the bed.

"The trick was to do just enough damage to deactivate everything for a few minutes without raising the suspicion of vandalism."

"Why did you make me steal every alternate box? Why not every box?"

"It probably got us a few extra minutes to getaway. The saleswoman may not have realized at first glance that a theft had occurred."

"You are right." Admiration had seeped into her eyes. "We might have been caught if I had gone after every box."

"That idea was original. It was not written in the book." Siddhartha picked up his navy-blue blazer and searched through the pockets. "Where is my Parker pen?"

"Your pockets were empty when you pulled them out before we left the showroom."

"Shucks. I must have dropped it in the electric room."

"Won't we get caught?" There was panic in her voice.

"No fingerprints." Siddhartha pointed to the gloves lying on the bed among the other contents of the bags.

"Your father's name was engraved on the pen."

"No proof it belongs to me. I bet my father's ignoble son has a whole set of pens with the same name engraved on them."

"At least you took precautions." She sighed.

"The best of con artists, leave a clue behind, no matter how well-planned they are." Siddhartha grinned. "I am but a novice."

"There goes my pregnancy." Sadhana picked up the deflated air pillow from the bed and tossed it into a wick hamper.

"Nothing beats the sympathy a pregnant woman, garners."

"God willing, it could have been real," Sadhana winced.

"God, if He exists, has never helped me." Siddhartha gave her a gentle hug.

Sadhana had suffered two miscarriages after the birth of Pinky and taken them in her stride at the time. However, after the devastating death of Pinky, she had become desperate to become a mother again, but not met with success. "Tell me the truth. You dropped the pen in the electric room, on purpose." She had switched back the subject hastily. She was still in denial in matters concerning the death of their daughter.

Siddhartha picked up a ballpoint pen and positioned himself in front of the locker. Opening each box within the locker, he examined the contents and recorded his notes on a writing pad. Most boxes contained two diamond studs and a pendant. A few boxes contained a pair of studs only. He could not wait to sell them and pay off his debts. The panacea for all their financial problems? "Twenty-one boxes. At least twenty-five lakhs." He whistled after toying with his calculator.

"Higher the carat size, greater the value." A wide-eyed Sadhana repeated what he had taught her.

"I want you to keep one diamond set for yourself."

"I was waiting for you to ask."

"You can pose as a rich woman on our next assignment."

Sadhana sifted through the slew of sleek boxes in the locker. "Like this?" She held out an open box with a heart-shaped pendant and pear-shaped ear studs.

"As they say, diamonds are forever."

"For me, only our love is forever." Sadhana sealed his lips with hers.

Siddhartha closed his eyes. Did his sense of elation stem from his love for Sadhana or the satisfaction of conning his father's ignoble son? Siddhartha shuddered. He hoped it was not the latter.

It had all begun three months ago. Or had it? It may have begun the day he was born. A day later than his father's ignoble son.

●●●

# 2.

# Genesis

*August 10, 1985*

"Members of the board request your august presence at the annual conference of the Bar Council of Mysore, on August 10, 1985 at the grand new auditorium of the century-old Town Hall in the heart of Mysore. To commemorate the golden jubilee of its inception the bar council will felicitate illustrious lawyers produced by the state over the past decades. The conference will be followed by cocktails and dinner ...." Siddhartha's face had acquired a happy glow as he read and re-read the personalized invitation.

The day of the conference, dressed in a dark grey suit, Siddhartha sat amongst the audience and watched the compere, a budding actor called Nalanda, invite the first lawyer onto the dais. After Nalanda had read aloud a synopsis of the lawyer's achievements, the Chairman of the bar council presented a memento to the lawyer; the lawyer then made a brief speech addressing the audience.

Siddhartha was eager to collect the award on behalf of his father Vikramaditya – an honour being bestowed on him three years after his demise. Siddhartha touched several times the coat pocket where he had placed a small card with mnemonic notes for the speech he had rehearsed – a glorious tribute to the father he had revered. Words heartfelt, that had remained unspoken during an entire lifetime, would discover an avenue for expression today, he promised himself.

"The next awardee of this evening, the late Mr. Vikramaditya," Nalanda announced, "Was the most prominent lawyer in the state, as early as the 1930's and 1940's. Educated at Oxford, Mr. Vikramaditya had established a profitable practice in Mysore and in Bangalore. He specialized in property law and women's rights to inheritance as related to the Hindu Undivided Family, also known as HUF. Legally knowledgeable and pragmatic, equitable yet compassionate, a passion for social welfare was the cornerstone of Mr. Vikramaditya's professional success."

Siddhartha's heart had swelled with pride. How he wished Sadhana could have been with him – but the invite had precluded a wife.

"To receive the award on his behalf I call upon Mr. Vikramaditya's son . . ." Nalanda paused. Members of the audience were clapping in a studiedly polite rhythm.

Siddhartha got up from his seat and started walking down the aisle, towards the dais.

"Bangalore's business baron, Mr. Abhimanyu and his respected mother, Rani Gayatri Devi – wife of the late Mr. Vikramaditya..." Nalanda was looking at the front row. "Owners of the illustrious Aradhana Conglomerate..."

Legs wobbling and head reeling, Siddhartha stopped his descent.

A tall, fair-complexioned man in a tailored suit, and an elderly woman who wore a bejewelled tiara, had ascended the dais.

*I am the legitimate son of lawyer Vikramaditya. My mother was Vikramaditya's wife – legally wedded and socially sanctioned.* Staring at the well-lined face of Rani Gayatri Devi – the woman who had displaced his mother in the life of his father – Siddhartha tried swallowing the bitter bile regurgitating in his mouth. Thankfully, he could not see Abhimanyu's face, shielded as it was from his line of sight, by the lectern.

Feeling helpless, Siddhartha held on to the banister. While he had always known about his father's 'other family in Bangalore' – that is how the mother-son duo was referred to in hushed tones within the joint family in which Siddhartha had grown up – this was the first time in four and a half decades that he was seeing them in person. Siddhartha had become aware at a very young age that this 'other family in Bangalore' had gotten the lion's share of his father's wealth, time and attention.

Turning around, Siddhartha lumbered up the aisle as quickly as his body could beat gravity, and got back to his seat.

Though their interactions had been infrequent and distant, in his heart of hearts, Siddhartha cherished a deep regard for his father. Whenever he visited Mysore, Vikramaditya had always stayed at Panchsheel Villa, the large house in the western part of the city. Siddhartha and his mother

Sulakshana, and Vikramaditya's aged parents, were the permanent residents of Panchsheel Villa. Siddhartha also had four sisters, who had all been married even before he was born, and lived in smaller towns near Mysore. They had been frequent visitors at Panchsheel Villa, along with their husbands and children.

Blessed with a happy-go-lucky nature, Siddhartha had experienced no emotional voids, despite the lack of a full-fledged father's attention. Until he was ten years old, Siddhartha's grandfather had fulfilled the need for paternal affection. A true Sthithapragna[1] as he liked to call himself, his grandfather had taken a keen interest in Siddhartha's upbringing and imparted his knowledge of the Ramayana, the Mahabharata, and the Buddha Charita Manasa. After the death of his grandfather, Siddhartha learned to fend for himself both intellectually and emotionally. Having tumbled upon his father's collection of English classics, he had developed a keen interest in English literature.

Siddhartha stared ahead vacantly. The Chairman of the bar council had presented the posthumous award – a rosewood panel with silver inlay – to Abhimanyu. Compere Nalanda had handed over the microphone to Abhimanyu.

The first time that Siddhartha had set eyes on his father's ignoble son, was on the front page of a local newspaper. Abhimanyu had bagged the President's Gold Medal for graduating from the Delhi College of Economics. Filled with a sense of abhorrence at the sight of a handsome Abhimanyu grinning ear-to-ear, Siddhartha, who must have been twenty years old at the time, had tossed the newspaper into the fireplace.

"My father is my hero. I worship him unconditionally." On the dais, Abhimanyu touched the rosewood memento to his chest. "Rani Maa understood him like no one else did."

Siddhartha shuffled his butt in the constricted seat. *My father was my hero too. Even I worshipped him unconditionally. You stole my inheritance. Your mother stole my father from my mother.*

"Vikramadityaji constantly received public accolades for his legal successes." Rani Maa had taken over the mike. "Yet he was shy of the limelight. He did not like to publicize the Good Samaritan side of him, though he actively promoted several social causes. At home, he was a doting husband and a devoted father. Abhimanyu continues to live in the

---

[1] Self-actualized individual

Bangalore house his father gifted him on his first birthday." Her diction was impeccable.

Siddhartha was appalled; neither the organizers nor the mother-son duo had acknowledged him or his dead mother Sulakshana or his four elder sisters – all members of Vikramaditya's 'first' family. Their existence had not just been ignored, but denied. Pulling out the mnemonic card from his coat pocket, Siddhartha shred it into pieces, stuffed the pieces into his mouth, and chewed on them until his saliva had ingested the pulp.

"Vikramaditya-ji resides in my heart. I continue to talk to him as I did for the past forty-five years. The only difference is .. .." Rani Maa's oratory was flawless.

"The year was 1942." The mike was back in Abhimanyu's hand. "I was barely two years old when my father decided to enrol me in Bangalore's prestigious Bishop Cottons School. . ."

Siddhartha watched the audience watch the mother-son duo with captive fascination as they went on to narrate anecdotes from the life they had shared with Vikramaditya.

"I, me, myself ... leading businessman ... profits, winner, wealth ..." The incessant stream of Abhimanyu's arrogant chatter was unbearable. Placing his sweaty palms over his searing ears, Siddhartha closed his flaming eyes.

The influence of his grandfather's tutelage had engendered in him a sense of acceptance with the way things were. 'Desire is the root cause of sorrow. Follow in the steps of your namesake, who became Gautama Buddha. Be detached from materialistic pleasures.' That is what his grandfather had taught him. Complicity, he had learned, was a virtue. Would he have been more ambitious and hence more successful, had he grown up under the sphere of his father's influence, like this man on stage, Siddhartha wondered.

"... My ancestors were the rulers of the Malnad kingdom. This heirloom is a vestige of my royal lineage. It was handed down to me by my father, and I shall pass it on to my son Abhimanyu one day." Siddhartha opened his eyes. Rani Gayatri Devi held in her hand, the bejewelled tiara that had adorned her top knot.

When Abhimanyu and his mother had exhausted their repertoire of stories for the evening, the Chairman offered the customary vote of thanks and invited them for an exclusive sit-down dinner with the council members. Nalanda announced that a buffet dinner was in order, for the rest of the audience.

The lines leading to the buffet tables were endless. People milled around with no sense of urgency. Lackadaisically making his way through the crowds, Siddhartha had found himself face to face with his adversary.

Their eyes may have met for the fraction of a second – both men were the same height, although Abhimanyu with his head held high and nose sticking in the air, appeared taller. There was no acknowledgement from either side. Yet Siddhartha was certain, Abhimanyu had recognized him, for, Siddhartha was a spitting image of their father Vikramaditya, albeit with a complexion that was a shade darker.

The aroma from the buffet table was inviting. Siddhartha inhaled deeply as he joined the tail end of a long line. The line inched along aimlessly. Greeting family friends and business associates of his father only increased Siddhartha's agitation. Their intentions may have been honourable, but the unspoken sympathy he thought they offered, was debasing. Forcefully piling his plate high with his favourite dishes from the festive spread, he walked out into the well-lit garden and sat down at a lone table under a chinar tree decked with yellow lights.

Siddhartha had lived at Panchsheel Villa all his life. Vikramaditya had taken care of all household expenses. Even after Siddhartha completed his M.A in English Literature and joined the Mysore College as an English lecturer, Vikramaditya had given him an expense allowance. After marriage, when Sadhana had become an additional member of the joint family, Siddhartha's modest salary had primarily served as pocket money to meet her modest wants.

The fallacy of his own financial status and the irony of his fate had struck Siddhartha only after his father's death. Panchsheel Villa had been his only inheritance, even though Vikramaditya had been one of the most sought-after lawyers of his times. The rest of the wealth valued many times over, had belonged to Vikramaditya's illegitimate son Abhimanyu, right from the day of his birth. Why had his father, who was otherwise a fair and principled man, committed an act of such grave injustice? What had motivated him to will away all his wealth to the illegitimate son? Had his father never given thought to the financial fate of his legitimate son?

Plunging his silver spoon into the bowl of kheer with an uncharacteristic voracity, Siddhartha rolled his tongue around in his mouth, to savour the taste of the cream and almond delicacy.

When Siddhartha had received a sum of Rupees five lakhs, by being the primary beneficiary of his father's life insurance policy, he had quit his job at the Mysore College and embarked on his own business venture. Enthralled by the dramatic thrill and the creative possibilities offered by video gaming, he had decided to enter the business of running video parlours. And Vikrama Ventures was born. When a detailed appraisal of the project had revealed the inherent riskiness of the venture, Siddhartha had tacked on a trading business, mostly video equipment and accessories, in a bid to generate steadier streams of revenue.

Having been an English lecturer for over twenty years, Siddhartha neither possessed business experience nor technological expertise. Two whole years and Vikrama Ventures had accumulated huge operating losses; and debts had piled up.

The sumptuous dinner refused to whet his withered appetite. Siddhartha stuck his spoon to the mound of saffron flavoured rice and sat back.

Destiny had always favoured Abhimanyu. A flourishing business, name and fame, and most importantly, the love and wealth of their father – Abhimanyu had everything going for him. *If only I were born a day earlier? If only my mother had known about me sooner?* An inexplicably overpowering feeling that made his body burn, had engulfed him. Envy as an emotion had hitherto been alien to Siddhartha.

A seed had been sown. Siddhartha's imaginative mind provided fertile ground. Ideas germinated. His nurturing instinct spurred their growth. A single plan that would kill two birds – avenge Abhimanyu and resurrect Vikrama Ventures – had taken shape. Reconnaissance and rehearsals had started immediately thereafter.

●●●

# 3.

# Ray-Koy-Netre

*September 10, 1985*

"Project kick-off." Siddhartha manoeuvred the Fiat through the crowded lanes of City Central, Bangalore's popular commercial locality. "What did you find?" He turned to Sadhana sitting next to him.

"Two rings whose gemstones have fallen off. And that ancient brooch." She patted her purse.

Those were the last of his late mother's trinkets, which he had held onto out of a sense of whim. "May not fetch much. Maybe enough to get the car repaired. Visiting Aradhana Jewellers is a good excuse for a detailed reconnoitre, though. The first phase of my project plan. To make that *bastard* understand the meaning of suffering."

"Pray tell me what this ray-koy-netre means," she said. "Mr. English Professor."

"We will familiarize ourselves with the showroom layout. Get to know every significant nook and corner. A sort of preparation to set ourselves up for success." Siddhartha parked the car in a by-lane off M.G. Road. They would walk the few steps to Aradhana Jewellers. At five in the evening, the prominent jewellery showroom had just opened its doors. A security guard with a bushy moustache held the door open for them.

A full-length mirror welcomed them. Purple Kanjeevaram sari, long-sleeved blouse, elaborate hairdo, tinkling bangles and a huge bindi – 'the traditional South Indian woman look' that Sadhana had chosen, also made her look older than her thirty-five years. Siddhartha, clad in a crisp white dhoti and a starched white kurta, adjusted his wig. The adhesive underside was making his bald scalp itch.

"Makes me feel like I am back on the stage." Sadhana would not stop biting her lips. "You know acting is my first love."

"I thought I was your first love." Siddhartha chided her.

There were few customers in the store, most of them seated on the mattresses around the island counter. The lights in the manager's cabin were out. The showroom supervisor was setting up his paraphernalia behind the cash counter.

"We are looking to sell some family trinkets." Sadhana addressed him, her hands folded. This was no different from acting on stage.

"Please wait," the supervisor said. "Pandit should be here any minute."

Siddhartha and Sadhana sauntered around the showroom, scrutinizing the well-lit jewellery cabinets, and making mental notes of their content. Pretending to look for the bathroom, Siddhartha strayed towards the landing area between the manager's cabin and the cash counter, and slipped through the parrot green door, to the area beyond.

Having explored the electric room, when Siddhartha came back to the main area, Sadhana stood at the foot of the spiral staircase, a young man with a long mop of hair, next to her.

"My name is Pandit." The young man flipped his mop. "The work area is upstairs."

Siddhartha and Sadhana followed Pandit up the staircase, to an open landing laden with showcases displaying silverware and steel racks crammed with files. Accounting staff sat around a large steel table; heads bent over thick ledgers. Pandit led them into a workroom and seated them on a mattress.

Pandit brought out a tray from the wall cabinet and sat down on a small mat facing them. Slipping on a pair of gloves, he picked up a magnet from the tray and held it over the three trinkets. Nothing happened. "No iron, no contamination," he announced.

Next, Pandit rubbed the brooch on a slab of slate. Picking up the green bottle labelled *concentrated acid* from the tray, he applied a drop on the slate, at the exact spot where the brooch had left a trace. There was no observable change. "Pucca. 22 carats." He handed the brooch back to Sadhana. "Concentrated acid causes no visible reaction if the gold is 18 carats or higher."

"Did you use Aqua Regia?" Siddhartha recalled an article he had read in preparation for an English class for science students. "The term literally means royal water. Because it can dissolve gold."

"We jewellers use a contaminated version," Pandit said. "Because pure Aqua Regia cannot be stored. The fumes are corrosive." When he repeated the test for one of the rings, there was a slow sizzling sound, and the trace on the slate disappeared. "Must be 14 carats." Pandit made another trace with the ring and added a drop from the other green bottle, labelled *dilute* acid. There was no reaction. "Confirmed. 14 carats. If this trace had also dissolved, I would have suspected the ring is not made of gold."

"As they say, the acid does not lie," Siddhartha said. "That is how the term 'Acid-test' must have originated."

Conducting the same series of tests for the second ring, Pandit confirmed it was 14-carat gold as well. "We have to go back downstairs. So, I can weigh the items and tell you their value." He got up.

"My foot has gone to sleep." Siddhartha remained seated. His brain was spinning. There was a way to convert the reconnaissance into a profitable mini-venture. It would also be a warm-up for the heist. The mere thought of conning his father's ignoble son a little extra warmed the cockles of his heart.

Sadhana had followed Pandit out. A minute later, Siddhartha got up and wrapping the two acid bottles in his handkerchief, dropped them into his kurta pocket. Opening the wall cabinet door, he selected two green bottles off the shelf and placed them in the tray, to replace the ones he had removed.

When Siddhartha came down the spiral staircase, Sadhana was sitting on a stool near the cash counter. His head bent, Pandit was counting out the money for them.

"We will be back next week," Siddhartha said. Pandit was a gem. Meticulous but naïve, efficient and talkative – giving them all that information without the asking. "You do know everything around here."

"Two thousand four hundred Rupees." Pandit handed over the cash to Siddhartha. "Please recount."

◆

"I can finally get the jalopy repaired." Siddhartha patted his pocket. After they had exited Aradhana Jewellers.

"I feel a little more confident now." Sadhana hit him playfully with her purse. "To be your full-fledged partner."

"Is there anything else we can sell?"

"Why? Is the ray-koy-netre not over?"

"We must do a rehearsal of sorts. A mini-con before D-day. After all, practice makes perfect."

They had walked past the Zyatt Hotel. Sadhana stopped in front of the next building – Orange Computers Institute. "I want to go in here."

Smiling acquiescingly, Siddhartha followed her in.

The air-conditioned lobby, furnished in grey and orange, looked sleek. A posh-looking receptionist welcomed them and ordered them refreshments. An articulate counsellor took them around the institute on an educational tour.

Siddhartha watched Sadhana's melancholic eyes light up, as she latched on to every word uttered by the counsellor with an unquestioning faith.

Sadhana had been fascinated by the advent of computers in business. Not having a formal college education had always been one of her biggest regrets. Following her parents' death, Sadhana had joined the Prabhat-Kala drama troupe straight from high school. Her innocent looks and emotive versatility had earned her a steady stream of secondary roles in popular dance ballets.

The one time she played Cinderella, because the lead actress was sick, was when Siddhartha first set eyes on her. Transfixed by her elfish charm and evocative eyes, he kept going back to the theatre, day after day. The plays may have been different, but the petite girl had a significant supporting role, each time. At the end of five days, he had shyly invited her to lunch and been pleasantly shocked when she had accepted. The year was 1970. In sleepy Mysore, by any stretch of imagination, dating was not the norm.

They were married a few months later. Sadhana had willingly drawn the curtains on her acting career, content to play the role of the respectable daughter-in-law. Their daughter, Pinky, was born a year later and Sadhana had turned for her, a nurturing mother, doting teacher, and trusted friend all rolled into one, a role she had cherished for ten beautiful years.

Pinky's death changed everything. The regret of having missed a formal college education paled in comparison; first to the bigger regret of losing Pinky and then to that of not conceiving again.

The tour ended back at the reception. "The institute charges twelve thousand rupees for the diploma program in computer studies. An eight-month course and a three-month project. Placement assured." The counsellor had handed them a glossy brochure.

◆

Siddhartha had made the last turn into the mud road leading to the residential high rise in North Bangalore that housed their rented flat and parked the car in the narrow adjunct space. "I know what we can sell," Sadhana said as they rode the birdcage elevator to their twelfth floor flat. "Our darling daughter's wedding trousseau."

"Are you sure?" Siddhartha grasped the metal frame. He could still feel the steely coldness of the shrivelled body he had held that disastrous day, five years ago. The day he had stopped questioning the existence of God; and proclaimed with wholehearted certainty that God did not exist. Leukaemia had been the diagnosis but it had come too late. Grandpa Vikramaditya had egged the doctors to perform a bone marrow transplant, but Pinky had left them before the assessment could transpire.

"Pinky gave us ten beautiful years. The memories will be with us forever." On entering the flat, Sadhana headed straight for the bedroom.

Following her in, Siddhartha flopped down on the bed. Pinky had been a gifted child, almost a prodigy. Adept at making friends and holding court under any circumstances, she was participating in debates and quiz competitions even before she turned eight. Grandpa Vikramaditya was her role model. On her ninth birthday, she had made a declaration that she would grow up to become a criminal lawyer. Siddhartha had seen in her a beacon that would elevate their status beyond the pinnacles of Abhimanyu's success and had even fantasized secretly, that his father would reverse his testament and bequeath his fortune to Pinky.

"It is time to move on." Sadhana had laid out several coloured boxes, that she had taken out of the steel almirah, on the bedside table.

"22-carat gold?" Siddhartha opened the boxes one by one. Sadhana had started a collection of neo-modern jewellery the day Pinky was born, and added to the collection every year, on Pinky's birthday. After Pinky's death, she had held on to it for sentimental reasons, spending many a fateful day staring at the jewellery or fondling them. He was glad that she was finally keen to come out of the shadows and plunge into a new career.

"14 carats." She handed him the weighing scale she had fetched from the kitchen. "Can you estimate what it is worth?"

"I can get you double whatever it's worth." Siddhartha pulled out the two acid bottles from his kurta pocket and placed them in the lowest drawer of the dresser. Nothing would give him more pleasure than conning that bastard.

"Have you been plotting again?" She tousled his hair.

Siddhartha weighed each piece of jewellery in the coloured boxes and punched numbers into his calculator. "Anywhere between fifteen thousand and sixteen thousand rupees," he announced.

"I only need twelve-thousand." Sadhana clutched the Orange Computers brochure to her bosom.

"What if I buy you a personal computer?" Siddhartha held out his arms. "Since I will be getting us double that amount."

"I will love you for the rest of your life." She walked into his arms and locked her lips over his.

◆

*September 25, 1985*

It was a gloomy afternoon, when the rains would not stop lashing the city, that Siddhartha and Sadhana revisited Aradhana Jewellers. They wore their traditional South Indian garb as before, except that Siddhartha's white dhoti-kurta ensemble was more wet than crisp and Sadhana's sari was pink. Sadhana carried a small suitcase that contained the ten coloured boxes.

The guard saluted them with a smile, which did not please Siddhartha who did not want to be recognized or remembered. There were few customers in the store at that hour. Most salespeople were at lunch. Pandit, once again welcomed them. "We are not going upstairs this time." He led them towards the island counter.

Sadhana and Siddhartha settled down on the mattress as Pandit set up the paraphernalia. Siddhartha breathed easy only after he had spotted in the tray laid out by Pandit, two green glass bottles that looked exactly like the ones he had taken.

Sitting cross-legged opposite them, Pandit surveyed the array of coloured boxes with the fervour of a hungry man invited to taste a sumptuous wedding feast, and set to work immediately, starting with running the magnet over each piece of jewellery with tender care.

Siddhartha took out a large handkerchief from his pocket and dabbed his lips. A cue for Sadhana to tug at the old-fashioned string of black beads around her neck. The next minute, the little black beads had spread all over the white mattress.

"That is so inauspicious." Sadhana looked like she was going to cry. "For the mangalsutra black beads to snap like this."

"Stupid superstition." Siddhartha clucked his tongue.

"Let me collect them for you." Veering his attention away from the testing tray, Pandit swooped down across the mattress.

Making way for him, Siddhartha slid to the edge of the mattress, and stealthily swapped one bottle in Pandit's tray for an identical bottle he had carried in his kurta pocket.

Testing resumed after Pandit had filled the loose beads he had scooped into a little bag and tied its mouth.

Siddhartha watched with heightening anticipation as Pandit rubbed each piece of jewellery on the slate and applied a drop of concentrated acid. Each time Pandit stated '22 carats', Siddhartha mopped his forehead with his handkerchief. Good news. The item was going to fetch them double its worth.

It had stopped raining. Bipolar weather predicted. Siddhartha remembered the headlines in that morning's newspaper as a cool breeze hit them.

Pandit had completed the acid-test for the contents of all ten boxes. He placed the jewellery in the weighing tray and punched the numbers into his calculator. "Rupees thirty-one thousand eight hundred and eighty." He wrote on a scrap of paper.

"Can you round it up to thirty-two thousand rupees?" Sadhana took the paper.

"Of course. I can add another five hundred rupees if you will take a cheque."

"We prefer cash today," Siddhartha said hastily. "My wife is registering with Orange Computers next door. Today is the last day for payment." A dash of truth helps even a con become credible.

"I need your name, address and contact number," Pandit said.

"Ragini and Ranga Shankara. This is our address." Sadhana handed him a visiting card. 'Trident Technologies. 434 Cunningham Road. Phone No. 23578.' A few days back, while visiting the Cox Town Press for a business meeting, Siddhartha had surreptitiously pocketed a pack of visiting cards which probably belonged to a real customer that had placed an order with the press to get them printed.

◆

"No more acid-tests for us." Walking out of the showroom, as they turned the corner, Siddhartha pulled out the bottle he had pocketed a little while back and chucked it into the garbage dump.

"Did we really need all that rigma-roll?" Sadhana pouted. "You were so tense."

"You mean rigmarole. Remember, we are doing this for much more than mere money."

"Mere money! I only hope you don't abandon me like your namesake and start doing tapas[2] and call yourself Gautama Buddha," Sadhana said. "You have to explain to me again how we got double the money."

"On our last visit, I pocketed both the acid bottles from Pandit's tray. At home, I did some re-engineering. I emptied the contents of the bottle labelled *concentrated acid*. I poured the dilute nitric acid from the other bottle into it. Today, I switched Pandit's bottle containing concentrated acid with the one I carried."

"Genius! So, it contained dilute nitric acid, even though the label said *concentrated acid*."

"You cracked it. The 14-carat gold showed up as 22-carat. Making us a profit of sixteen thousand rupees."

They had reached the Fiat. Sadhana opened the door on the driver side. Siddhartha hopped into the passenger seat beside her.

"Hooray! I get to join Orange Computers and buy my own computer." Her eyes shining, Sadhana pressed the accelerator pedal and slid the car into the traffic.

Siddhartha rolled down the car window and let the breeze play on his face. It made him happy to see Sadhana happy. It was the only pleasure in a life where he had little to rejoice. *I can only play with the cards dealt to me. His eyes turned moist.*

---

[2] penance

◆

**October 10, 1985**

Research, reconnoitre and rehearsals were complete. Siddhartha had budgeted an outlay of ten thousand rupees to purchase a bagful of zirconia crystals for the D-day and had devised a little ruse to pay for them.

Dressed in a well-pressed corduroy suit and maroon brogues, clutching thick books to his chest, Siddhartha entered Primrose, the multi-cuisine restaurant inside Holiday Inn, and chose a table near the entrance. He was a guest speaker at that day's conference and preferred to wait in the restaurant until it was his turn. That was the story he gave the waiters.

Credit cards had become increasingly popular. While not all retail establishments accepted them, five-star hotels did. Watching the goings-on at the restaurant, Siddhartha deduced that on an average, three in ten customers paid with a credit card. The waiter would take the card to the billing counter in a plastic folder, and a clerk would call the card company for approval. Once approved, the waiter brought the plastic folder back to the customer for signature. Customers who signed the receipt and carefully pocketed their card did not interest Siddhartha. Those that forgot to take the card with them – because they were in a hurry or engaged in a conversation or plain careless – would form Siddhartha's target set.

It was almost two hours before Siddhartha had spotted his first opportunity – two talkative executives who had maintained a running commentary on contemporary cricket, had left their cards behind. However, by the time Siddhartha had gathered the courage to slither to the table, they had remembered and returned.

The next person to leave behind a credit card was a woman. Siddhartha did not budge. Flicking it meant that Sadhana would have to purchase the zirconia crystals. He would not involve Sadhana in more risky activities than was necessary.

Siddhartha continued to keep vigil. The restaurant had turned empty. There would be a lull until the dinner-crowds arrived. Should he leave and come back another day? He would give it one more chance. Yawning from the tedium of pretending to read random books, he got up and wandered around.

Familiarity fosters freedom. Siddhartha casually flipped open the plastic folder on a nearby table. A hundred rupee note nested in it – a tip for the waiter. No card. He moved to an adjacent table and repeated the act; the folder was empty. He walked across the length of the restaurant to the farthest corner.

"Forgot your credit card?" He heard a booming voice. A dapper man whose badge read 'Restaurant Manager', was holding out a Citibank card.

Siddhartha glanced at the name on the card. *I can pass off as Govinda.* Thanking the Restaurant Manager, he had pocketed the card, and made a rapid retreat from the restaurant.

◆

Siddhartha's research had taught him that credit card companies took at least 24 hours to trace a lost or stolen card. During the course of the same evening, Siddhartha visited three different jewellery stores in three separate localities. Each time he purchased a packet of zirconia crystals using the Citibank card belonging to Govinda. On reaching home, Siddhartha cut the card into small pieces and struck a match – extinguishing any possibility of getting caught.

Siddhartha then consolidated the zirconia crystals from the three packets into a thin linen bag which Sadhana would attach to the inner lining of her yellow and gold kameez with a Velcro strip, in preparation for the D-day. "Countdown begins." He had rubbed his hands together in anticipation. "For our date with Aradhana Jewellers. On the day before Deepavali."

●●●

# 4.

# Ignited Cinders

*November 11, 1985*

Sitting in the penthouse tower of Lakeview Terrace, a high-rise in the heart of downtown Bangalore, staring at a Lotus 1-2-3 spreadsheet on the green-lit screen of a brand-new desktop computer, business baron Abhimanyu could not stop preening. Aradhana Conglomerate had attained a major milestone. Gross revenue for the year had crossed Rupees fifty crores. Retail sales of all six divisions – refrigerators, television sets, soaps and cosmetics, silks and suiting, gemstones and handicrafts – were booming in the metro as well as mofussil areas.

Abhimanyu pressed the print button to take a snapshot and preserve the milestone for posterity. His vision would continue to transform Aradhana and propel it to newer heights. They were on the verge of obtaining the license for producing polyester yarn. Groundwork for commissioning the manufacturing plant had started. Preparation for launching an issue of convertible debentures and preferred shares to the public was in full swing. Aradhana's revenue would reach the Rupees One hundred crores mark before the turn of the decade, of that he was certain.

Abhimanyu rotated his chair on its axis and stared at the colour portrait on the credenza. Rani Maa, his revered mother, widely recognized as Mysore state's first successful lady-entrepreneur had pioneered the parent firm. In 1942, on Abhimanyu's second birthday, she had set up Aradhana Enterprises, a firm, trading in gemstones and silks, and inducted him as partner through a trust.

After graduating from the Delhi School of Economics and acquiring a post-graduate degree from the London School of Economics, Abhimanyu's corporate journey at Aradhana Enterprises had started at the age of twenty-two. When, within three years, Aradhana Enterprises had emerged as the country's top exporter of gemstones and silks, Rani Maa had promoted him to the position of General Manager.

Continuous diversification had been Abhimanyu's strategic thrust. Over the years, he had transformed his mother's modest firm into the gigantic Conglomerate. Rani Maa had stepped down from the mantel of Managing Director when she had turned sixty, and remained in the wings as Chairman. It was after the death of her husband, Vikramaditya, that she had announced full retirement from active business and shifted base to Mysore to live at Indigo Castle, the ancestral mansion she had inherited from her royal family.

Abhimanyu patted the portrait of his mother lightly with his fingers. Rani Maa was currently on an extended tour of Australia and Singapore.

The clock struck twelve. It was time to leave for the weekly luncheon with the board members of Ascot Bank. Abhimanyu picked up the folder that contained the five-year strategic plan he had formulated for Aradhana Conglomerate. While confident that it was robust, he was eager to discuss it at the luncheon, to see if any of the others, each a stalwart in his own right, would pick any holes in it. Abhimanyu loved challenges, especially if they would boost the chances of his own success and translate into higher revenues or profits, or both for his business. Aradhana was not only his passion but also his destiny.

Picking up the Armani sports coat from the back of his revolving chair, Abhimanyu stood up. The tall French-style windows covering three of the four walls of the penthouse offered him a panoramic view of the bustling buses and careening cars thronging downtown. The continual noise of bursting crackers reminded him that Deepavali had arrived.

He opened the door of his air-conditioned office and stepped into the foyer, where Veronica, the rotund middle-aged woman who had been his personal secretary for the past decade, chipped away at the day's invoices and receipts. He and Veronica were the only two people in the penthouse tower – the offices and cubicles of all other employees were located on the first four floors.

"I presume you are organizing the customary Lakshmi Pooja tomorrow for Deepavali," he said, approaching Veronica's desk.

Veronica nodded her head in the positive and picked up the ringing phone.

"Thank you for keeping the tradition going even in mother's absence." Abhimanyu was about to walk towards the elevator when he saw the agitated look on Veronica's face and took the receiver from her.

There had been a melee of sorts at Aradhana Jewellers following a break in the power supply. Mathur, the manager of the showroom, was on the phone. The woman responsible for causing the commotion refused to own up and threatened legal action. Customers remained locked inside the showroom for security reasons.

"We have to be at Aradhana Jewellers immediately." Abhimanyu returned the receiver to Veronica. "Ask Varun to join us. Cancel all my meetings for the day."

◆

Seated in the chauffeur-driven Toyota with tinted windows, Abhimanyu briefed Varun and Veronica of the situation they had to bring under control. M. G. Road was within a mile from Lakeview Terrace. A curious crowd had collected in front of Aradhana Jewellers when the trio alighted from the Toyota. Varun rapped on the closed door to announce their arrival and the security guard opened it wide enough for the three of them to file in.

The brightly lit showroom was a study of unbridled chaos. Irate customers were engaged in arguments with showroom staff or in deep commiseration amongst themselves. Members of the showroom staff ran around valiantly trying to appease the wrath of the customers.

"I was walking up to the diamond counter when someone tripped me." A woman in a pink outfit and pink high heels accosted them. "Nobody came to help me. When I got up, I saw shiny crystals rolling everywhere. People were scrambling to grab them. Instead of finding the real culprit, Manager Mathur has been blaming me." She recited in a single breath.

"If you did nothing wrong you have nothing to worry." Loosening his tie, the lanky Varun stepped forward. Varun, who had earned the tag of Abhimanyu's blue-eyed boy, was the manager in charge of corporate planning for the Aradhana Conglomerate.

"You have to believe me." The woman clutched at his arm.

"Let me get to the bottom of this." Varun led her over to the island counter.

◆

Abhimanyu and Veronica trooped into Manager Mathur's cabin. Abhimanyu glared at Mathur. "Do you know what is missing?"

Mathur blabbered something about having to check with the sales staff.

"Find out. Come back with a list of whatever is missing." Abhimanyu issued his first command. "And be discrete. I don't want the customers to panic."

A harassed-looking Mathur rushed out, closing the cabin door after him.

Veronica, who had spread her paraphernalia on a side table and called the Bangalore Electricity Company, reported that there had been no power shutdown in the M. G. Road area.

"The power outage was part of the burglary then." Abhimanyu looked at her. "Connect me to the DCP." Abhimanyu golfed with the District Commissioner of Police every Friday at the Bangalore Club. While this did not make them bosom pals, the shared activity offered Abhimanyu certain privileges, of which instant access to the DCP's private number was the foremost.

The DCP promised to dispatch the local police to investigate the burglary. There had been two other thefts in the area over the past month and each time they had discovered that somebody had disconnected the power lines. A gang of vagrants from a neighbouring state were the prime suspects.

"Make sure the police officers are in mufti." Abhimanyu was keen to keep the incident under wraps. "I do not want a robbery rumour to diminish our reputation."

◆

When Abhimanyu ventured out of Mathur's cabin, the scene on the showroom floor was in deep contrast to the one he had witnessed earlier. Peppy music filled the air. The showroom staff looked more relaxed attending to the customers. Customers seemed calmer as they went about their selections. Even the irascible woman in pink was examining whatever trinkets she was seeking.

"There was a power outage a little while back." Microphone in hand, Varun addressed the customers, "We have been warned that thefts have been reported at other locations under similar circumstances. While we trust each one of you and have not noticed anything amiss, we must follow our security procedure. The doors will remain locked until further notice. We must search your belongings. We will do so respectfully when you leave. We appreciate your cooperation."

*I have never been wrong with my judgment.* Abhimanyu looked at Varun with admiration. Ambitious and hardworking, with an MBA from a prestigious institute, the twenty-eight-year-old Varun was the youngest employee to report directly to Abhimanyu.

"Please continue with your shopping." Varun added. "We regret the inconvenience. As a token of goodwill, we have ordered refreshments."

"We have to do our own investigation." Abhimanyu apprised Varun of his conversation with the DCP after he had switched off the mike.

◆

Varun herded a sullen-faced Mathur and a traditionally dressed saleswoman into the cabin and closed the door.

"What did you find out?" Abhimanyu addressed Mathur from behind the desk.

Mathur stated that Vimmy, the saleswoman standing next to him, had determined that several sets of diamond jewellery were missing.

A sobbing Vimmy, haltingly described how she had locked the counter and then gone to fetch sugar water for the pregnant woman who had fainted. On coming back, agitated customers had surrounded her and bombarded her with complaints. By the time, she could free herself from them, the couple had vanished. She had immediately taken inventory. Twenty-one of the forty-six boxes in her counter were missing. They all contained diamond sets of one carat and above. She had verified that the contents of the remaining twenty-five boxes were intact.

Varun stood leaning against the wall next to Abhimanyu. "Sir, the cost of the missing jewellery is between eighteen and twenty lakh rupees." He held out his calculator. "The sales value is higher, around twenty-five lakh rupees is my guesstimate."

"Where is this woman now?" Abhimanyu thumped the desk.

In a faint sounding voice, Mathur admitted that he had allowed the pregnant woman who was on the verge of fainting, and her husband to leave, fearing an emergency. He had not suspected her at that time.

"Whatever you did was the height of carelessness," Abhimanyu yelled.

Mathur mumbled incoherently and bowed his head even lower.

Veronica, who continued to work at the side table, had offered the shaken Vimmy a glass of water. A more composed Vimmy informed them that every alternate box inside the counter was missing while the rest were intact.

"I suspect a conspiracy." Abhimanyu turned to Varun. "I am certain the diamonds were stolen by the couple that absconded."

"A very intelligent couple." Varun nodded his head in concurrence. "They picked the boxes in a pre-determined pattern after tripping the pink woman and deliberately scattering fake diamonds to distract the public!"

"Sound hypotheses but no proof." Abhimanyu's unibrow furrowed involuntarily. "There must be a way to track this burglar couple and retrieve the jewellery."

Vimmy nervously held out a pink leather case and stated that it had fallen where the pregnant woman was sitting.

Varun opened the case and dangled the pink sunglasses it contained. "This is not a clue. It can only belong to one person – pink suit, pink heels, pink purse, pink watch. . . That lady is innocent."

"I will send for you later." Abhimanyu waved his hand dismissively at Vimmy and Mathur. "Keep this confidential. Do not let the customers panic."

"Please apologize to the lady in pink," Varun told Mathur. "Give her a twenty percent discount on whatever she purchases."

"What next?" Abhimanyu turned to Varun after Mathur and Vimmy had exited.

"I am going to check on the electrician." Varun dashed out.

◆

There was a knock on the door. The security guard entered the cabin, followed by two hefty men, who introduced themselves as the plainclothes officers dispatched by the DCP.

Abhimanyu briefed them about the situation. "Find that pregnant woman and her husband," he commanded. "You will find the loot with them."

The security guard shared one additional piece of information. That the couple had gone towards the posh hotel next door.

◆

"The electrician just left." Varun was back in the cabin. "He told me that several wires had been severed and the UPS battery was drained of charge. Obviously, someone deliberately tampered with them."

"That confirms our hypothesis," Abhimanyu said. "The power outage was created by the crooks."

"Pandit, one of our salesmen was supervising the electrician," Varun said. "He wants to speak with you. He won't tell me what it is." He flicked his finger and thumb.

Pandit entered the cabin. "Sir, I found this on the ledge of the electric room." Bowing reverentially, he placed a Parker pen on the desk. "If the electrician had seen it, he would have taken it."

*Why does the pen look familiar?* Abhimanyu pulled out a pair of reading glasses from his pocket and examined the pen. Puzzled on finding his father's name, he opened his leather valise. His own Parker pen with the engraved name of Vikramaditya was right there.

Abhimanyu turned to Varun. "This pen belongs to whoever orchestrated the power outage and the theft."

"I guessed as much," Varun said. "The absconding couple is our strongest link."

"Can you recollect anything about a pregnant woman who fainted?" Abhimanyu signalled Pandit to occupy the chair in front of him.

Pandit nodded his head in the negative. "Her face was covered. I heard her husband talking to Manager Mathur though. He spoke pure English like a foreigner."

"What did he look like?" Abhimanyu asked.

"Tall and lean. A typical Sikh with a beard and turban. About your age."

Abhimanyu clenched and unclenched his fist. *A tall man my age who speaks chaste English and owns a gold-plated Parker pen with the name of my own father, can only be Siddhartha. The beard and turban are for disguise.*

Abhimanyu's father, Vikramaditya, had owned a set of twelve Parker pens that he had brought with him from London in the 1930's. Keeping one pen for himself, he had gifted Abhimanyu the remaining eleven pens, on his eleventh birthday. Siddhartha must have inherited that one pen after Vikramaditya's death. Abhimanyu was certain that his eleven pens were all intact.

"Tell us everything you can remember," Varun said to Pandit.

"I did not interact with him today. I was upstairs. For some reason the Sikh reminded me of another man who had cheated the showroom last month. That man had worn a dhoti and kurta. No beard or turban. That man and his wife sold 14-carat gold jewellery for 22-carat prices."

"How did that happen?" Abhimanyu growled.

Pandit, who seemed to be enjoying the spot of limelight, gave them an animated description of the South Indian couple's visit. "I don't know how, but someone switched the acid bottle."

"Corporate was not informed of this incident," Varun whispered to Abhimanyu.

"Sack Mathur." Abhimanyu covered his mouth with his palm and leaned towards Varun. "Lack of integrity and lax controls."

"Last month's man also spoke pure English." It was apparent that Pandit had started believing he was junior Sherlock Holmes. "The same couple may have deceived us both times. Had I been at the island counter today I would have recognized them."

"Can you recognize them if you see them again?" Abhimanyu asked Pandit.

"The man, Yes." Pandit flicked his mop. "Not so sure about the woman."

"We will find out." Abhimanyu turned to Veronica. "Can you send for the photo album from the Town Hall conference?"

The Bar Council of Mysore had posthumously felicitated his father, Vikramaditya, a few months ago. Abhimanyu and Rani Maa had been special invitees at the conference and received the trophy on Vikramaditya's behalf. Siddhartha had also attended the conference. The photo album was a personal memento from the Chairman of the bar council.

Varun asked Pandit to return to his sales counter. "I will send for you once the photo album arrives."

◆

The security guard was back with a complaint. Press reporters had congregated outside the showroom and were pestering him to let them in on the scoop.

"Get me the Secretary of the Press Club," Abhimanyu said to Veronica.

"Let me deal with the reporters outside." Varun dashed out. "A few hundred rupees should do the trick."

"The press is creating a nuisance at our showroom," Abhimanyu said on the phone, as soon as Veronica had connected him. "While we deal with an internal matter, a routine security protocol, following an unscheduled power shutdown. Stop hounding us. Make sure that neither the newspapers nor television give us unwanted publicity."

The Secretary of the Press Club, who was no more than a business acquaintance of Abhimanyu, was evasive in his reply. He expressed his unwillingness to curtail the freedom of the press.

"Nothing that is happening here is detrimental to the public interest." Abhimanyu's tone was authoritarian. "Freedom of speech is not a universal licence granted to the press to spread false rumours, sully the reputation of my business and obstruct justice. If you do not cooperate, I will consult legal counsel immediately and sue for disruption, defamation and libel."

The Secretary of the Press Club caved in, promising that he would not permit the publication of any news that was unsubstantiated. Doordarshan, the nation's solitary television channel, would not bother to cover such minor incidents due to paucity of staff, he assured Abhimanyu.

"If there is anything newsworthy, I will personally request you for coverage." Abhimanyu dangled the customary carrot before ending the call.

◆

Varun leaned against the wall and watched Pandit flip through the album that an office assistant from Lakeview Terrace had delivered.

Abhimanyu paced the length of the cabin. When he was alive, Vikramaditya had compartmentalized the two halves of his family life efficiently. The palatial Manyata Manor in Bangalore, where he lived with Abhimanyu and Rani Maa, was his primary residence. The few days he was out of town, to manage his law office in Mysore, he stayed with his first family.

Neither Abhimanyu nor Rani Maa ever had any reason to meet Vikramaditya's first family, not even on their annual sojourn in Mysore, when they stayed at Indigo Castle, the ancestral mansion that belonged to Rani Maa's royal family. Their high society life and business-related schmoozing had never intersected with the middle-class roots and traditional customs of Vikramaditya's first family. Yet, at the bar council conference, Abhimanyu had recognized the man lurking diffidently in the shadows; as much as he hated to admit it, Siddhartha bore a close resemblance to their father.

Pandit pointed to a tall bespectacled man with receding hair standing amidst a group of people in a couple of photographs. "I think it is him."

Varun borrowed an eyebrow pencil from Veronica and added a beard and turban to one of the pictures of the man. "Now?"

"100 %." Pandit gave him a thumbs-up.

"Whatever was discussed here is top secret. Understand?" Varun signalled Pandit to leave.

Abhimanyu rotated the glass paperweight with such force that it bounced off the desk. He could not fathom why Siddhartha had done this. It came as a shock to him that Siddhartha, whom he had always thought a loser, might be the mastermind behind such a sophisticated heist. "I will talk to the DCP about the man in the photograph and his link to the burglary." He handed the album to Veronica.

"Now that we have found the crook, there is no need to hold up the customers. The front door can be unlocked." Varun bounced out of the cabin.

"Make sure every customer gets an additional ten percent discount," Abhimanyu called out after him.

◆

Abhimanyu dialled the DCP's private number. "The burglary was not pulled off by the same gang that you referred to. An English-speaking gentleman in disguise and his female partner who pretended to be pregnant, orchestrated a power outage, created a public distraction using fake diamonds, and absconded with expensive diamond jewellery of high carat value." Abhimanyu briefed the DCP on the groundwork and the cerebral sleuthing he had indulged in.

The DCP listened attentively and commended Abhimanyu's powers of deduction.

"I have reason to believe the crooked gentlemen in question, is none other than Siddhartha, the other son of my father," Abhimanyu stated. "I expect you will have him arrested within the next forty-eight hours."

The DCP was unwilling to arrest Siddhartha without any proof or evidence.

"I have his Parker pen here. You can get the fingerprints analysed," Abhimanyu persisted.

The DCP agreed to the fingerprint analysis but refused to arrest Siddhartha until they had undeniable proof.

"I will incur losses to the tune of Rupees twenty-five lakhs, if you do not catch the thief." Abhimanyu banged the phone down in exasperation.

◆

The clock had struck three. Abhimanyu gingerly bit into the mint and cheese sandwich Veronica had ordered from the restaurant at Hotel Zyatt.

"The customers are delighted with the discount offer." Varun was back. "Most of them are picking up an extra trinket for the price of the discount. Deepavali after all."

"That was my strategy." Abhimanyu beamed at Varun. "We need to talk to that saleswoman now."

His protégé, whom he had trained to operate on the 'your wish is my command' principle, had immediately dashed out to fetch Vimmy.

*Varun is not my son. He cannot inherit Aradhana.* Abhimanyu turned wistful for the briefest moment. While he had no plans of retiring soon, he would have loved to groom a successor only if there was one.

Abhimanyu's daughter Simi, who was eighteen years old and studied in the twelfth grade, was not inclined towards anything business. Her interests centred around shopping, partying and holding never-ending phone conversations with her friends. Neither did she have a clue on what she wanted to do with her life nor was she willing to listen to her illustrious father. She had taken after her mother whom she twisted around her little finger.

Abhimanyu wiped his fingers with a paper napkin and picked up the steaming cup of coffee Veronica had placed before him.

Varun was back. An obviously petrified Vimmy followed him into the cabin and stood cowering.

Abhimanyu did not ask her to sit down. "I understand you have been with Aradhana for ten years. I will give you one more chance, only because you are honest. You will forego your Deepavali bonus for this year, though."

Vimmy had tears in her eyes as she thanked Abhimanyu profusely for his kindness.

"Learn to be alert at all times." Abhimanyu waved her out.

"I thought she would lose her job," Varun said to Abhimanyu, after Vimmy was gone. "The same way as Mathur."

"Mathur is not running a tight ship. I do not trust him to run my showroom anymore. Vimmy was an anonymous pawn in the bigger scheme of things." *Now that I know who is behind this, I will make him pay.* "Being successful is all about taking timely action and knowing when to be rational and when to be ruthless." Abhimanyu looked at Veronica and Varun as a king would look at his subjects. "It has taken me twenty years to grow a Rupees fifty lakh business into a Rupees fifty crore business. Less than the time it took my mother to build a Rupees fifty lakh business from scratch."

"May I ask you a personal question, Sir?" There was earnestness in Varun's voice.

"You may." Abhimanyu smiled on catching Veronica tug at Varun's shirt in a bid to caution him. She knew from experience; Abhimanyu did not tolerate personal questions from the staff. "To answer it or not is my prerogative."

"Who is the man in the photograph you identified as the crook?"

"Whoever he is, he will be brought to book." Abhimanyu's tone was unintentionally stern. He did not intend to discuss the identity of his half-brother with a subordinate. "Now if we can resume business. The showroom needs a more high-tech alarm system .. .."

"I will get three quotations." Varun poised his pen against his notebook. "And send you the evaluation."

"Train the showroom staff not to talk about the incident, neither amongst themselves nor with the customers," Abhimanyu said. "News of the burglary must remain a secret. Words loosely used are more dangerous than loose bullets. Drill that into their heads. Or Aradhana will lose the trust of its customers."

•••

# 5.

# Phone Off

*November 12, 1985*

The day after the heist, the sun had barely risen, when Siddhartha and Sadhana left for Mysore. Sadhana's suitcase filled the boot of their Fiat. Stashed in the suitcase, was a felt-lined box made of lacquered wood, containing the twenty-one sets of diamond jewellery. The previous night, after Sadhana had removed the diamond sets from their original boxes imprinted with the Aradhana logo, Siddhartha had mutilated the boxes beyond recognition with a sledgehammer and dumped the pieces in garbage.

Siddhartha leaned back in the passenger seat and scoured through the morning's newspapers, as Sadhana steered the car on the Bangalore-Mysore Highway. Surprisingly, despite the prime location of the showroom, the theft had not made it to the front page of any of the newspapers. *The bastard has used his influence to preserve his reputation.* Only the *Deccan Herald* had deigned to report it, relegating it innocuously to an inner page. In a selfish way, Siddhartha was relieved that the incident had not garnered much publicity.

It was ten o'clock when Sadhana and Siddhartha arrived at Panchsheel Villa. That the two-storied house was in shambles was an understatement. Not just the paint, even the cement underneath had peeled off in several places, showing red brick. The wood of the doors was rotten. In one of the corners, the roof had fallen in. The one-time garden was a jungle of weeds and wild grass.

Siddhartha possessed dreams of remodelling Panchsheel Villa, and restoring its lost glory. Despite all his financial travails, he was not prepared to sell the house, his solitary inheritance as the son of Vikramaditya. He was not willing to rent it out either; for fear that the lessee would somehow usurp it.

No sooner had Siddhartha and Sadhana stepped inside, hauling the suitcase on its wheels, then Laxman informed them that a very important sounding man had called. Laxman, a roly-poly lad of twenty-four was the grandson of Siddhartha's eldest sister. Since his parents had lived in remote parts of eastern India, Laxman had practically grown up within the folds of the joint family at Panchsheel Villa and completed his education in Mysore. Having developed an emotional affinity for Siddhartha and Sadhana, he continued to live with them even after graduating from college.

Ever since launching Vikrama Ventures, Siddhartha and Sadhana spent more time in Bangalore, staying at the rented flat during that time. Laxman had become by default, the designated caretaker of Panchsheel Villa, a role he relished with palpable abandon.

Sadhana went into the kitchen to rustle up a quick brunch.

Siddhartha, along with the suitcase, entered the drawing-room on the ground floor that used to be Vikramaditya's office and closed the door. Having put away the lacquered jewel box in a safety locker of the old-fashioned vault that had once stored legal documents, he was lounging lazily on the divan when the phone rang.

"Mr. Siddhartha?" A crisp feminine voice, most likely a secretary, enquired.

"I know you are behind this," a booming masculine voice stated, quickly thereafter.

*Abhimanyu.* Siddhartha felt scared for a moment. *Will my father's ignoble son get me arrested?* As he held the receiver to his ear, he remained silent.

"I found your Parker pen," the voice boomed. "Return the jewellery you stole, or I will send the police after you. While you and I do not consider each other family, to my misfortune, everybody else does. It is a terrible association for me, considering the excellent reputation I enjoy."

*What a pompous snob. Does he honestly believe he owns me, and I will dance to his every tune?* Siddhartha reclined on the divan, holding the phone to his ear.

"Make me an unconditional promise. That you will never harm me or my business ever again," Abhimanyu demanded.

"I don't know what you are talking about," Siddhartha said.

"Who else but you would possess a gold-plated pen engraved with the name of Vikramaditya?"

"You." Siddhartha smiled to himself.

"That pen belongs to you," Abhimanyu said.

"False accusation." In a strange way, Siddhartha felt glad that Abhimanyu had surmised that he was behind the theft. *The bastard must feel the pain. The same pain I carry with me.* "You took away everything that was mine, even before I was born. Would you spare me a mere pen?"

"I know I am right," Abhimanyu said. "As always."

Siddhartha jumped up. "Proof?"

"Do as I say. Return the jewellery."

"Check the pen for fingerprints," Siddhartha sniggered.

"Do not antagonize me."

"The fingerprints are yours. Undeniably." Siddhartha chuckled to himself at the thought of Abhimanyu seething with impotent anger.

There was silence on the other end.

"Did you stage a theft to implicate me in a crime I did not commit?" Siddhartha questioned his nemesis.

"I neither have the time nor the intent to harm you or anyone of my own accord. If you attack me first, I never fail to retaliate, though." Abhimanyu's voice alone could have singed Siddhartha's ear if the two had been in the same room. Siddhartha moved the receiver farther from his ear. "Wait and watch what happens. Every time, without exception, it is I who wins." Abhimanyu had disconnected the phone before Siddhartha could mouth 'Goodbye'.

●●●

# 6.

# Ascot Bank

*November 11, 1985*

"Wait and watch what happens. Every time, without exception, it is I who wins." Abhimanyu handed the cordless back to Veronica as soon as he disconnected.

Siddhartha's chutzpah infuriated him, fanning the forgotten fires of humiliation he had endured at the time of his father's death. Despite being the elder son, societal traditions had denied Abhimanyu the freedom to pay his respects to his father's dead body. On the contrary, the rights bestowed on Siddhartha had been undisputable and infinite. Siddhartha was the son assigned to perform the funeral rites and preside over the memorial services.

The 'first family' had not bothered to inform Abhimanyu or Rani Maa when Vikramaditya had suffered a massive heart attack during his stay at Panchsheel Villa and subsequently passed away. Abhimanyu had heard the news from a family friend. Since protocol dictated that they maintain a distance from the 'first family', the mother-son duo had to desist paying homage to the man they had both worshipped unconditionally.

Abhimanyu picked up the daily sales report Veronica had placed on the desk. Truth and nothing but the truth. He had told Rani Maa about the burglary when she called him last night from Singapore. She was leaving for Australia and staying there through December, fulfilling her dream of celebrating Christmas in summer.

The news had not particularly perturbed her. "Incidental losses are a part and parcel of any successful business. You should install those closed-circuit televisions in the showroom," she had said. Abhimanyu had not revealed the identity of the suspect. He feared that she might genially coerce him to forgive Siddhartha – because of her devoted respect for Vikramaditya.

The sales report failed to bring a smile on his face despite the stellar performance of his sales staff. Abhimanyu cast it aside.

'Did you stage a theft to implicate me in a crime I did not commit?' The audacity of Siddhartha's offense caused his blood to surge and his head to throb. That blackguard must be arrested. It was time to call the DCP on his private line.

The DCP was apologetic. The police officers had interrogated the managers of Hotel Zyatt and confirmed that a North Indian couple had breezed into the lobby. They had scouted every floor, conducted surprise checks on a sample of rooms under the guise of a routine review, and pored over the registration records. However, they had not been able to trace the couple.

"What a flop show. What came out of the fingerprint analysis?"

The DCP stated that the only fingerprints found on the Parker pen were those of Abhimanyu and Pandit the salesman. The pen might as well have belonged to Abhimanyu – not only were his fingerprints plastered all over it but also his father's name was engraved on it.

"The smart-Alec must have worn gloves or wiped the pen clean before dropping it in the electric room. Just arrest him."

The DCP re-asserted his unwillingness to seize Siddhartha in the absence of concrete proof. While the police had interrogated Pandit, his claims were too tenuous for any further action.

"The police force should be more efficient." Abhimanyu put forth several arguments to sway the DCP's decision.

The DCP remained resolute. Neither he nor his officers would breach the boundaries of the rulebook.

Abhimanyu took several deep breaths. "Try putting yourself in my shoes." Playing the victim card was the last resort. "How would you feel.. .."

Though the DCP responded with empathy, when he grudgingly admitted admiration for the conman for pulling off a professional job, Abhimanyu banged the phone down. To hell with the police force. He would take the matter into his own hands. Vikrama Ventures – was that not the name of Siddhartha's video business? What a big blot on their father's reputation. Abhimanyu could only wish Siddhartha had chosen another name.

Two years back, Siddhartha had approached Ascot Bank with a loan application for his video business. Vikrama Ventures – the name is what had caught Abhimanyu's attention. Abhimanyu had reviewed the application and discovered that the project plan was flawed. It failed to consider the financial impact of several critical factors like exorbitant customs duty on the import of video machines, the impending component of luxury tax on video gaming, and the rapid obsolescence of video equipment.

In Abhimanyu's assessment, these factors would increase operating costs and consequently the working capital needs, beyond what the plan envisioned. Breakeven would take three years or longer rather than the eighteen months projected. While Abhimanyu had rejected the application for long-term financing, he had sanctioned a portion of the working capital loan, in accordance with the bank's policy guidelines.

Acting on a hunch, Abhimanyu called Shetty, the manager of Ascot Bank. "Send me the list of overdrawn loans and overdraft defaulters. Immediately."

In the early 1980's the-then Chairman of Ascot Bank, having noted the phenomenal success of Aradhana Conglomerate had invited Abhimanyu to head the bank's board in an advisory capacity. This had given Abhimanyu, who held a post-graduate degree from the London School of Economics, a legitimate avenue to apply his avant-garde vision and shape the bank's investment policies within the confines of the closed-economy model adopted by India.

There was a tap on the door. Veronica entered to place a file on his desk. "A delivery boy just dropped this off. It is from Ascot Bank."

Perusing the contents of the file, Abhimanyu experienced a sinister delight. Siddhartha's floundering company featured prominently at the top of the list of defaulters. A review of its current financial state proved that his own judgment of the project plan was accurate. *I will annihilate the blackguard on my own.* Abhimanyu loosened his Dior tie. He had found a legitimate pathway to tighten the noose around Siddhartha's neck.

◆

### *November 25, 1985*

"The bank's profits for the last few quarters were squeezed. Loan repayment defaults are on the rise and the bank is writing them off as bad debts."

Abhimanyu addressed his fellow members of the board in the conference room of Ascot Bank. "Small and medium-sized businesses are the principal defaulters. Reason?" He looked around the table, at the six bank officials and two industry bigwigs who comprised the board, before continuing. "Given our current norms, small and medium-sized businesses end up availing working capital loans much larger than what they can service. Main culprit? Working capital turnover ratio."

Abhimanyu went over to the whiteboard that covered the wall opposite the window and wrote down a series of formulae.

Current assets = Inventory + Customer receivables + Cash and bank balances

Current liabilities = Vendor payables + short term payments

Working capital = Current assets – Current liabilities

Working capital turnover ratio = Annual Sales/ Working capital

"Working capital, a crucial ingredient to run a business, is the money available for spending on operations after paying off its bills," he explained. "The working capital turnover ratio analyses the relationship between money used to fund operations and the sales revenue generated from these operations. Simply put, it measures how efficiently a business uses its working capital to generate sales."

Abhimanyu opened a thick binder titled *Ascot Bank: Working Capital Policy and Norms*. "Page 24. Ascot Bank has currently set this ratio at '3' or higher for assessing the financial health of small and medium-sized businesses making working capital loan applications. The bank then finances 75 % of the working capital needs for businesses meeting this norm. As most of you have figured out, this means that the bank commits to financing three months' sales if it approves the working capital loan. Questions?" Abhimanyu looked at his fellow members.

There were murmurs and side conversations at the table but no one asked him any questions.

"While the norm is low enough to benefit customers in obtaining higher financing, it does not accurately reflect their ability to service the loan on an ongoing basis. Large inventory pile-ups, slower collection of customer receivables and payment pressure from vendors, compounded by lower credit ratings, cause these firms to suffer a perennial paucity of funds. Consequently, they stop repaying their working capital loans. Businesses that default for five or six quarters generally do not recover, forcing the bank to write off the loan as bad debt." Abhimanyu returned to his seat.

Shetty, the Manager of Ascot Bank, stood up to distribute copies of the proposed amendment to the members of the Board. "Based on the above analysis, the loan policy has been amended to incorporate the new norms recommended by Mr. Abhimanyu. Ascot Bank will raise the acceptable norm for the working capital turnover ratio from 3 to 6 for small and medium-sized businesses. Under the new norms, the bank will only finance one and a half months' sales, henceforth," Shetty announced.

A burst of applause ensued. The board's approval for the amendment was unanimous.

"The higher ratio will lead to greater efficiency. Loan amounts we sanction will be more conservative, improving the ability of the businesses to service them, and reducing the incidence of bad debts over time. Ascot bank's profitability will bounce back." Abhimanyu affixed his signature and passed the document to the next board member.

There was a smug smile of satisfaction on his face. This move would give him the weapon to counteract the humiliation of the heist. Ascot Bank would revoke the working capital loans of top defaulters immediately. Vikrama Ventures, with a working capital turnover ratio as low as 2.4, would be among the first set of casualties. Loss of working capital financing would bruise daily operations; cash flow would get progressively worse; breaking-even would remain a distant dream. Liquidation would be the only recourse. It was a solitary masterstroke that would hurl Siddhartha down the path of his own decimation. *The blackguard will regret the day he decided to take me on.*

•••

# 7.

# Vikrama Ventures

*November 25, 1985*

Siddhartha drove his Fiat through the heart of the city, passing in front of the Mysore Palace, and entered the commercial arena off Albert Victor Road. Having parked the car in front of an ancient building, he climbed the narrow staircase and entered a spacious veranda. Irwin Shah, the owner of the building, was a minor-league jeweller, whom Siddhartha had known off and on, ever since he had been a client of his father.

"I want you to evaluate this." Siddhartha held out a worn-out suede box containing a pair of diamond ear-studs and a matching pendant.

The taciturn Irwin Shah weighed the jewellery items on a small scale and brought out a magnifying lens to examine the diamonds.

During the past two weeks, Siddhartha had visited nineteen small-time jewellers in Mysore and the surrounding mofussil areas, each with a single set of the heist jewellery. Each jeweller had heard the same sob story that he would give Irwin Shah. Whether it was the cloak of confidence, he projected or the reputation of his father – Siddhartha had succeeded in selling the diamond set at each store for its fair value.

"This is the last gift from my father to my wife before he passed away. It is unfortunate, but we can no longer retain it." Hoping his face looked morose, Siddhartha removed his glasses and wiped them with a handkerchief. Partial truth was a relatively safe and easy outlet. "My business is suffering losses, and we are forced to sell the jewellery."

The story did not fail to hit its intended target – as it had at the previous nineteen stores. There was no reason, the affable words of the suited and booted Siddhartha, son of a respectable lawyer of his times, should have sounded incredulous.

When he heard Irwin Shah's valuation verdict – blue diamonds of the best quality, worth two lakh rupees – Siddhartha suppressed a smile. He would have kissed Irwin Shah on his cheeks had he known him better. This was indeed the most expensive set of the lot. Most of the sets had fetched him between one lakh and one and a half lakh rupees.

Like his predecessors, Irwin Shah tried to dissuade Siddhartha from selling the jewellery, offering instead to safe-keep the diamond set as collateral and advance a loan of one and a half lakh rupees.

"Thank You, my friend." Siddhartha clasped Irwin Shah's hand in a show of genuine gratitude. "I think it is best to sell." He described how loan sharks had hounded him, in the face of mounting debts.

Irwin Shah offered to write a cheque for two lakh rupees.

"The loan sharks will only accept cash." Siddhartha knew by now that most jewellers preferred to transact in cash – which is what he was counting on – neither party wanted the transaction recorded in their books.

Irwin Shah counted out one lakh and ninety-six thousand rupees, explaining there was a two percent cut when he settled in cash.

Siddhartha pocketed the money without a flinch – that was standard practice. Some jewellers had deducted as much as five percent. "At least I have the satisfaction of selling it to a good friend like you, who I know will not take me for a ride. Ciao."

*If only Vikrama Ventures had shown this magnitude of profit!* The roads were deserted. Driving back home in the moonlit night, Siddhartha conjectured how he would utilize the monetary harvest he had reaped. The proceeds from the sale of the twenty sets of jewellery totalled a little over twenty-seven lakh rupees.

Vikrama Ventures owed sixteen lakh rupees to private moneylenders who had advanced ten lakh rupees for the import of electronic video machines at 24 percent interest. When he had started Vikrama Ventures, none of the nationalized banks had agreed to provide the long-term financing required to purchase video machines and other equipment, forcing Siddhartha to approach private money lenders for the money. While Siddhartha had known that he would pay compound interest, what he had not known back then was that the interest compounded monthly.

Vikrama Ventures owed a little over four lakh rupees to a loan shark who had financed the payment of customs duty. It was sheer bad luck that the government had slapped customs duty on additional categories of electronics in the same month the video machines and equipment had arrived at the port. Siddhartha had run from pillar to post to raise money and clear customs. The terms laid down by the loan shark were obscenely unfavourable; but the parlours could not have operated without the video machines.

Siddhartha wanted to pay at least three lakh rupees towards the working capital loan with Ascot Bank, which he had overdrawn way beyond limits. Ascot Bank was the only bank that had deigned to sanction him a working capital loan, even though, because of his poor credit rating, only to the extent of fifty percent of his requirements.

Siddhartha brought the car to a halt in front of Panchsheel Villa and honked. He would buy a brand-new car for fifty-five thousand rupees – the modern day Maruti was a sexy car. The remaining money, a little over three lakh rupees, he would invest in fixed deposits in Sadhana's name. God forbid, something untoward happened to him, that money would benefit her.

Laxman, who came running to open the gate announced that the manager of Ascot Bank had called, requesting that Siddhartha meet him in person before the end of the week.

◆

*December 1, 1985*

Siddhartha had driven down to Bangalore to meet with Shetty, the manager of Ascot Bank. "I was going to ask for a meeting myself."

"The purpose of this meeting, Mr. Siddhartha, is to discuss the status of your working capital loan that remains overdrawn beyond its limits." The light-eyed Shetty would not meet Siddhartha's gaze. "Your father was one of the earliest customers of Ascot Bank. He had established a longstanding relationship of trust and loyalty with the bank. That was the guiding factor in approving your working capital loan when you first came to us . . . .."

Siddhartha barely listened, as he sorted through the contents of his maroon briefcase.

". . . The bank has observed repeatedly, that Vikrama Ventures is not able to service the working capital loan. Interest due is heavily in arrears. The accumulated balance in the overdrawn loan account is. . ."

"Rupees six lakhs twelve thousand and thirty-three." Siddhartha placed a large envelope on the table, making Shetty gag mid-sentence. The envelope held notes of varying denominations – 100's, 50's, 20's, 10's and even a few 5's – culled from the monies received from disparate jewellers. "This money will bring down the balance of the overdraft to two lakhs ninety-two thousand. Well within the loan limit of three lakhs."

Shetty silently opened the envelope and with some struggle started counting the bundles of soiled notes.

Feeling elated for doing his homework and appearing business savvy, Siddhartha pulled out a slim document *VV Project Report 1986-88* from his briefcase. He had come fully prepared to make an official request to extend the loan limit. After paying off the debts he held with the private moneylenders and loan sharks, he had gotten the financial projections of Vikrama Ventures updated. Additional funding would help him turnaround Vikrama Ventures within the year and head up the highway of profitability.

"Rupees three lakhs twenty thousand." Shetty had organized the counted notes by their denomination and clipped them. He pressed the buzzer and handed over the cash to the clerk who appeared and instructed him to deposit it into the Vikrama Ventures loan account.

"My balance sheet just got cleaner. And my cash flows healthier." Siddhartha placed his new project report in front of Shetty. "Vikrama Ventures now qualifies for a higher overdraft limit as per your bank policy. I am making an application for Rupees five lakhs."

"We have declared changes to our banking policy." Shetty pressed the buzzer one more time. "The bank's working capital norms are stricter."

An attendant appeared with a freshly typed letter. Shetty signed the letter and handed it to Siddhartha.

"I ask and you sanction?" Siddhartha quipped. "This is a first."

"I advise you to read the letter." Shetty did not smile. Nor did he meet Siddhartha in the eye.

"What the f . . ." Siddhartha bit his tongue as his eyes scrolled through the verbiage. "I just streamlined my cash flow and paid off all my arrears." He got up from the chair. "You cannot pull the plug on me."

"The Advisory Board just approved a policy change."

"Will you at least let me retain the current limit?" Siddhartha kneeled on the ground so his eyes were level with those of Shetty sitting across the desk. "I promise to make prompt interest payments going forward." He hoped his squeaky voice did not give away his desperation. "I will not exceed the loan limits ever again."

Shetty looked out of the window. "The bank gives you a grace period of 30 days to repay the outstanding balance of two lakhs ninety-two thousand rupees. From this moment onwards, you are not allowed to avail further credit from the account."

"This is so goddamned unfair. You cannot revoke the overdraft." Siddhartha frowned. If word got out, no other bank would touch Vikrama Ventures even with a barge pole.

"I cannot flout bank policy," Shetty said.

"A change in policy so you can lynch me?" Siddhartha rubbed his sweaty hands on the thigh of his denim pant.

"We have to adhere to the norms dictated by our Chairman."

Siddhartha stood up. "May I speak with your Chairman?"

Shetty shook his head in the negative. "Mr. Abhimanyu, our Chairman, and economic advisor, is a busy man."

*Abhimanyu is the Chairman of Ascot Bank!* Siddhartha's fingers clawed and crumpled the letter he held in his hand. *The bastard is doing this to ruin me.*

"Please acknowledge the cancellation of your overdraft account as of January 1 1986." Shetty proffered his pen. "The account stands frozen with effect from today."

Siddhartha stared blankly at the letter. 'I neither have the time nor the intent to harm you or anyone of my own accord. If you attack me first, I never fail to retaliate. Every time, without exception, it is I who wins.' Abhimanyu's phone threat seared his ears.

"If your repayment is not received before December 31, 1985, the bank retains the right to confiscate your current assets," Shetty said. "Rupees two lakhs ninety-two thousand."

Siddhartha smoothed away the wrinkles on the sheet of paper. If this rigmarole was part of Abhimanyu's ploy to make him own up to the heist, he would not give him an added advantage by flouting a banking rule. *People who live in glass houses should not throw stones.* With one brisk stroke, Siddhartha signed on the dotted line.

"We appreciate your cooperation." A fake smile plastered Shetty's freckled face. "Do you wish to avail of our advisory services for a fee? You can learn how to lower your inventory, quicken collections from customers and space out your payments to vendors."

"Fuck you," Siddhartha muttered under his breath, sending a spray of spit towards Shetty's tie.

"Here is the bank counterfoil for the cash you deposited," Shetty handed Siddhartha a white envelope, "And a copy of your last bank statement."

A spent Siddhartha literally dragged his feet out of Ascot Bank.


Four hours later, back at Panchsheel Villa in Mysore, Siddhartha unlocked the ground floor vault to count and reorganize the remaining cash one last time. There would be no fixed deposit for Sadhana. That money he had earmarked would have to go towards repaying Ascot Bank. His anger morphed into depression.

*If Abhimanyu had not been born a day too soon, if he had not usurped what rightfully belonged to me . . . if things had not happened the way they did – my life would not have been the fucking mess it now is.* Siddhartha shook his head vigorously, in a bid to rid himself of the image of the conceited Abhimanyu that haunted him.

What had motivated Vikramaditya to rob Siddhartha of his inheritance and grant it to his bastard son? Had Vikramaditya done it out of volition or from coercion? Siddhartha had not had the courage to ask his father the question when he was alive. His mother had never had the courage to give him an honest reply when she was alive. Siddhartha would never know the agony of that truth, ever.

Even as Siddhartha sorted through the bundles of cash in the locker and put them into separate envelopes depending on the purpose, the happy family photograph of yore, adorning the wall opposite, smiled back at him. Seated next to Vikramaditya, surrounded by her four daughters, his mother looked peaceful, almost divine.

As far back as he could remember, she was a gentle and simple soul, eternally engaged in running the house and attending to the needs of others, never with a grudge or a frown, always with a smile on her face and a song in her heart. 'Sulakshana' her very name meant a woman with virtuous characteristics. What had motivated his father to arrogate the rights of this noble woman and offer them to a selfish manipulator?

'I was an uncrowned beauty queen of royal blood with British Education.' The image of Gayatri Devi's ivory face laughed haughtily.

Siddhartha continued to stare at the black and white photograph, which he had learnt dated back to a few years before his birth. As far as he was aware, Indian law did not recognize polygamy. His father had never divorced Sulakshana, so she was his legally wedded wife. Yet, Rani Gayatri Devi had paraded herself as Vikramaditya's wife and enjoyed societal sanction of that status for forty-five years. Did the law have no value in Indian society? Siddhartha failed to fathom the fallacy. What about moral values? Were they worthless too?

Gayatri Devi was the only living soul who knew the answer. Siddhartha sighed as he stacked the cash filled envelopes back in the vault. He would never learn the truth behind his torment.

●●●

*Book 2*

## 1939: Rani Gayatri Devi

# 8.

# Enigmatic Lawyer

April 1939. Gayatri Devi opened the almirah in the dressing room, extricated a sheaf of papers from a large folder and popped them into her purse. She pulled out a cash box from behind the clothes and unlocked it. The cash box always contained one thousand and one rupees. Leaving behind the one rupee – it was bad luck to empty out the cash box – she stuffed the remaining notes in the pouches of her purse.

As she closed the almirah, she could not resist studying her appearance one last time in the dressing-table mirror. Her ivory face emitted a healthy glow. She bit on her naturally rosy lips to make them rosier and resisted a strong temptation to adorn her smooth forehead with a vermillion dot. Allowing herself a single spray of an exotic perfume instead, she draped a layer of the baby pink sari over her head and pinned it at her right shoulder, with a silver brooch.

During a time when women were confined to the kitchen and denied an independent existence outside the shadow of their husbands or fathers or sons or brothers – Gayatri Devi rode to Lawyer Vikramaditya's office in the family Bentley chaperoned by a mere chauffeur.

"Welcome Mrs. Devi. My pleasure." The gentleman immaculately dressed in a tweed suit and a bow tie, held the chair for her. His shiny black hair combed back in pompadour style was greying at the temples.

Despite her royal lineage and occasional interaction with the local aristocracy, Gayatri Devi had met few people like him. Digging into her purse, Gayatri Devi watched out of the corner of her eye, as the sinewy Vikramaditya went around the leather-topped desk and occupied his lawyer-chair. "You have to help me get justice." She handed over the papers.

"That is my duty." Vikramaditya's lucid eyes looked straight back at her.

*Was the sheen in his eyes, appreciation?* "My husband died last year."

"Condolences." Vikramaditya's eyes scanned the papers. "Your husband was part of a joint family that is immensely wealthy. He left no will. His uncles and cousins refuse to recognize his share in the joint family property and have disowned you . . ."

"None of that is written there, but it is all true." Gayatri Devi bit her lower lip. "For a moment, I felt you were clairvoyant."

"Clairvoyant? I am not sure what that means."

"Sorry. I thought you would know. After all, you are foreign-returned."

"I am sure you were educated by a British governess." His face broke into a smile.

"True again." Gayatri Devi took out a small fan from her purse and waved it across her face. *I hope he does not notice I am blushing. I do not want him to think I am flirting.*

"Coming back to the point, I deal with property-related cases day in and day out. The details may be different but the basic issue remains the same," he said.

"We had been married for ten years." Gayatri Devi readjusted the single strand of pearls on her neck as if she were missing the heavy mangalsutra society no longer allowed her to wear. "We had no children. My husband, a sensitive and caring man, contracted severe pneumonia."

"When did it happen?"

"Five months back." Tears pricked at the edges of her eyes. "We were on a holiday in Shimla. He was only thirty-three."

Vikramaditya glanced at the calendar on the wall. "He died in 1938. The law then is on our side." He pulled a hardbound book from the bookcase and placed it on the desk. "This Act was passed recently. It amends the Hindu Law and gives better rights to women."

*The Hindu Women's Rights to Property Act 1937.* Gayatri Devi looked at the bold letters. "Does that mean I can claim maintenance?"

"Much more. If a man dies leaving an interest in a Hindu joint family property – as in your case – his widow shall have the same interest in the property as he himself had."

"Equality at last." She smiled. For the first time since her husband's death, she felt protected. By the handsome lawyer. By the warm confines of his office. By the laws of Indian society. From the world, at large.

"You will have limited interest known as the Hindu woman's estate and have the same right of claiming partition of a male owner," he explained.

"May I ask for another favour?"

"The changes are sweeping." Vikramaditya, caught in the throes of legalese seemed oblivious of her question. "This Act gives better rights to women. Men like your husband's uncles and cousins abound in Indian society. The Act is the outcome of dissatisfaction expressed by a large section of society." He opened the book as if he had proclaimed his own verdict.

"I need another favour." She folded her hands Namaste style. "My father-in-law died five or six years ago. My mother-in-law lives in the same joint family under dire conditions. Can she get her share of the property as well?" *I hope I did not sound greedy. If she gets her share, being her sole beneficiary, I will inherit it all someday. It may sound selfish but I am only coveting what is lawfully mine. Why should I let those wicked men inherit what is rightfully not theirs?*

"That is noble of you. Even to ask," he said.

"My father has roots in one of the lesser-known royal families of Mysore. He raised me to be an independent woman. Thanks to which I could walk out of the joint family set-up when I faced hostility. I now live with my father. Unfortunately, my mother-in-law is too meek to stand up to the menfolk." *Why am I telling him all this?*

"Unfortunately, your father-in-law died before this Act was passed."

"She is a kind woman. I wish she too could get justice."

"If your share is substantial, she can come live with you," he said.

Gayatri Devi toyed with the pearl bangle on her wrist. *I am not even thirty years old. I have a full life to lead. If the law is not with her, she will stay in that joint household.* Her eyes furtively sought to obtain different perspectives of the attractive man sitting opposite her – as he alternately pored over the hardbound book and the sheaf of papers.

"I should say you are well organized," he said, several minutes later.

"My husband was meticulous. I do not understand these things so well."

He placed the sheaf in a paper tray. "A few records are missing. My staff can get them from the Registrar's office."

"I have brought a thousand rupees." She reached for her purse. "Advance remuneration for the case."

"I have never lost a case." Vikramaditya rang a bell on the wall near him. "Truth always wins. That is how I ensure justice."

A middle-aged man with a thick ledger materialized, counted the money, and wrote her a receipt.

"Thank You, Mr. Vikramaditya." Gayatri Devi held out her hand. *Why did I do that? To touch him? No. To show him I am modern. Yes. In many ways, we are equals.* Vikramaditya's large leathery palm clasped her soft ivory palm. She almost took a step back as if to counter the magnetic force of attraction that had erupted.

◆

Ensconced in the Bentley, Gayatri Devi felt like a frisky kitten. The warm breeze from the tree-lined avenues bathed her face and neck. When they drove past the Cantonment Club, she wanted to ask the chauffeur to take her there but desisted – she did not want to become fodder for gossipmongers. Especially not now, when she had just found out she would get a real share in her husband's family property, in lieu of mere maintenance.

She wished she had a real friend. Growing up, her aristocracy had set her apart. The other girls had been in awe of her, but they had little in common. After marriage, the upper-class women she befriended at the Cantonment Club had remained mere acquaintances. She had not gone there since her husband's death – society expected her to play the part of the grieving widow whether she liked it or not. None of the women had bothered to look her up either.

The Bentley entered the driveway of Indigo Castle, her father's dilapidated mansion. The pale walls of the mansion glowed an orange-pink, reflecting the haze above the horizon cast by the setting sun blazing like a ball of burning fire. Parking the car in the portico, the chauffeur held the car door open. A maid opened the front door. Gayatri Devi walked straight into the dining room where the housekeeper had laid out jam sandwiches and English tea.

Gayatri Devi had not paid her staff their salaries for the past month. The next month's salaries would soon be due. Then there would be the groceries and the medicines. Not to forget the car's petrol expenses. Her bedridden father's bank balance was depleted. She had paid the lawyer their entire cash reserve. On a whim. Otherwise, the money could have funded household expenses for several months.

The money she had paid Vikramaditya was an investment. Yet, how would she survive the next few months? She had not asked Vikramaditya how soon she would get her share of the joint family property. She had wanted him to perceive her as a grieving widow, not a gold-digger.

Sipping the English tea, Gayatri Devi picked up the newspaper. The Indian National Congress had denounced Nazi Germany. Gandhi and Sardar Patel had refused to join the Second World War until the British declared independence. The British Raj was adamant against decolonization in the middle of a war. Subhash Chandra Bose had broken with the Indian National Congress and contemplated an alliance with Japan. The gory details scared her. She threw the newspaper across the room. The maid scurried by and picked it up.

Vikramaditya. She could sense his strong masculine aura all around her. When would she see him next? Court cases generally took months, even years. Gayatri Devi looked at her palm. The memory of his firm fingers clasping them sent a chill down her spine. She got up to do her sadhna[3] hoping the dulcet notes of Ananda Bhairavi[4] would impart to the melancholic Indigo Castle a whiff of well-deserved cheerfulness.

◆

Next morning, Gayatri Devi sat near the foot of her father's bed and waited for the nurse to finish feeding him arrowroot biscuits dipped in warm milk.

"Mother's locker is bare," Gayatri Devi said as soon as the nurse had left the room. "What happened to her jewellery?"

"Why do you need them?"

"We have to sell them."

"I already did that. Immediately after her death."

---

[3] music practice
[4] classical tune

"Where is the money then?" Gayatri Devi closed the bedroom door, not wanting the staff eavesdropping on this conversation.

"It has been spent. For living expenses."

"Your bank accounts either have a minimum balance or an overdraft." She pulled out several passbooks from her purse and held them over his head.

"I know that. My body may be paralyzed, my mind is not." He started coughing.

There was a perfunctory knock on the door. The nurse stepped back into the room to attend to him.

Gayatri Devi went to stand near the window. The day she lost her husband was the day her father met with his accident. It was mostly of his own doing. Inebriated after hearing the news, he had driven off the road in a drunken stupor, totalled his Buick and ended up paralyzed. His gift of speech was all he had left; a boon when he felt reminiscent; a curse when his mood was bilious.

Once the nurse had given him medicine, his cough subsided. The nurse left the room again, closing the door behind her this time.

"Baby, my funds started dwindling after your marriage."

Gayatri Devi stifled a sob. Baby. An endearment he had not used in a long time. Her life as a teenager had been the proverbial bed of roses. A morning swim; lessons with a British governess; an evening game of tennis; horse riding and ball dances over the weekend; she had it all.

"Your wedding was the most talked-about event that year," he said.

"Why in the world did you overspend?" Celebrations for ten days. Expensive gifts to the guests. The bands, the music, the lights. "I had not wanted any of it." Gayatri Devi flung the passbooks across the bedroom floor.

"To maintain our prestige."

"Father, I have to run this household." Her tone rose in anger.

During the ten years of her marriage, she had lived on the Rajvamsh family estate, a fleet of cars and a retinue of servants at her disposal. Her time was spent organizing lavish parties, vacationing at exotic places, and designing ensembles for both sets of occasions. Menfolk managed the money, which had flown freely. As long as her husband was alive, nothing that she wanted had ever been denied.

"I started selling the investments after your marriage. Then the deposits. After your mother died, I sold her jewellery too."

"What do I do now? I have nothing valuable of my own – save for the pearl trinkets I wear. All my jewellery was confiscated . . ." She cursed her husband's uncles and cousins, their sisters and wives. Silently and Ceaselessly. "I wish I could take up a job. But no one will employ me." Her tone was vicious. Like her father was somehow responsible for the norms of Indian society.

Hearing no response, she turned around. Her father's eyes had filled with tears. He was a helpless invalid. "Forgive me." Overcome by remorse, she walked over to the bed and laid her head next to his.

"There is one last thing I still own." He patted her cheek.

"I will not sell *that*." Stepping back, she said with authority.

"My grandfather and his ancestors were the ruling kings of Malnad. My father was a crowned prince but never the ruling king. Our kingdom was invaded and annexed by the Rajah of the Corner Province in 1872." His tone had taken that faraway quality she so loved, whenever he recounted those lost days of glory. "I was neither a ruling king nor an heir to the throne. You won't remarry. Our lineage shall end with you."

The bejewelled tiara. She sat down. He was right – there was no need to retain it. There would be nobody to inherit it. Indian society frowned upon widow remarriage. She would be the last surviving member of the Malnad family. She was lucky her father was not conservative like her dead husband's family that mandated widows shave their head. "Where is it?"

"Bring the cash box."

"The box is empty. Except for the token one rupee note."

"Father knows best." There was a weak smile on his tired face.

Feeling like a carefree little girl all over again, Gayatri Devi ran up the stairs and fetched the heavy cash box.

"Slide the bottom panel," he said.

A few failed attempts later, she had succeeded in deftly dismantling the false bottom to reveal a blue velvet box. Unclasping the box, she stared at the tiara-shaped crown she had not set her eyes on, in over a decade. Made of gold and encrusted with twelve octagonal blue sapphires and several diamonds, it had a huge oval emerald set in the centre. She knew by heart the inscription on the back. In Sanskrit. 'Satyam Shivam Sundaram'.[5]

"The tiara was gifted to my grandfather by a British nobleman – can't recollect whether he was an Earl or a Count. British law supposedly prohibited them from taking crown jewels out of Great Britain."

"What was the purpose of such a law?" These stories always fascinated her.

"It was enacted to prevent crown jewels from being pawned."

"Did this nobleman smuggle it into India then?"

"No. This tiara was created here in India. It was a replica of a real crown jewel he owned back there."

"That explains the Sanskrit inscription. Why did he give it away?"

"Impressed by the magnanimity of my grandmother or so goes the story."

"No details?" Gayatri Devi had always believed that she had English blood coursing her veins. May be her grandmother had carried on a secret affair with this nobleman.

"No details. It resulted in a public furore, though." His eyes twinkled. "You can take out a pawn loan on the tiara. It is not prohibited under Indian law."

"Mr. Vikramaditya is going to file a case to claim my inheritance. He thinks my share will be substantial." She was too preoccupied to appreciate his sense of humour.

"The tiara will fetch us a lot of money though," he said. "If only you will sell it."

"We need just enough money to tide us through until Mr. Vikramaditya wins the court case."

"I have brought you up to be an independent woman. You are not going to remarry."

Why did he keep saying that? She harboured no such intentions. "The day I part with the tiara will be the last day of my life."

"Don't say such things," he said.

"You reminded me that you brought me up to be independent. I have always wanted to be the first woman entrepreneur of Mysore state." She clutched the box to her bosom. Parting with the tiara, the only relic of their

---

[5] Truth, Divinity and Beauty

heritage, the harbinger of good fortune, was akin to discarding their royal status.

"Do what you think is right." He closed his eyes.

*No matter what happens I do not want to part with the tiara. I must find a way to keep it.* She would give her sadhna a miss. Gayatri Devi did not return to her bedroom. She summoned the driver instead. Minutes later, the Bentley was on its way to the crowded market area in downtown Mysore. The blue velvet box nested within the confines of her tote. The crown jewel would never leave her.

●●●

# 9.

# Crown Jewel

Gayatri Devi had gone ahead and made a pawn loan application to Brindavan Bank, offering as collateral, the coveted and controversial crown jewel her father owned. A month later, the bank invited her for an appraisal meeting. As she had expected, Brindavan Bank had requested renowned gemmologist Gupta, also the owner of the biggest jewellery showroom in Mysore, to conduct an independent evaluation of the collateral.

Prithviraj, the branch manager of Brindavan Bank, had set the stage for the evaluation in the bank's locker room. About twelve feet square in size, the locker room had numbered steel lockers stacked one above the other, along two perpendicular walls. A solemn-looking Gupta sat at the oblong table aligned against the third wall. Gayatri Devi leaned against the adjacent wall, the pallu of her beige sari draped over her head.

Locking the locker room door from the inside, Prithviraj placed a blank appraisal form on the table. Gayatri Devi handed him the blue velvet box.

Unclasping the box, Prithviraj took out the tiara and held it in the palm of his hands. "Satyam Shivam Sundaram." He read aloud the inscription on the back. His face puffed with pride – as if the mere act of holding it somehow sanctified him.

Gupta wiped his glasses with the corner of his dhoti and placed a set of lenses on the table.

"Are these Rangoon diamonds?" Prithviraj placed the tiara in the tray.

"The diamonds are from Golconda; the sapphires are from Burma." Gupta peered at the tiara using one of the lenses.

"I have never seen such a large emerald either!" Prithviraj leaned against the table's edge.

Gupta examined the tiara from all angles and made notes on the appraisal form.

Prithviraj watched his every movement with a hawk-like eye.

Gayatri Devi fidgeted. The cosy room was hot. Prithviraj's extreme inquisitiveness had caused her blood pressure to rise.

Finishing his examination, Gupta restored the tiara to its box and started writing on the appraisal form.

"I have failed miserably." Gayatri Devi let out a sudden sob. "Being born a Kshatriya, it was my duty to preserve the heirloom, the glory of our dynasty."

As both men turned to look at her, she pulled out a lace-edged handkerchief from her tote. Just as she was about to take it near her eyes, the handkerchief fluttered and fell to the floor, away from her. When she bent down to pick it up, the pallu of her sari slipped from her head.

Aware that the soft creamy skin of her neck and a part of her back below the hemline of her blouse, were exposed, she stood back up hastily, without picking up the handkerchief. As she tried to wind the pallu of her sari back over her head, Prithviraj whose burning eyes had taken in the scene, behaved exactly as she had expected. He advanced a step and bent down to pick up the handkerchief.

Gayatri Devi had all of fifteen seconds before Prithviraj's attention would re-focus on the table. Secure with the protection offered by the folds of her sari, she brought out a second box from her tote, switched it with the one in the tray on the table and dropped the original box into the tote. By the time, Prithviraj held the lace handkerchief before her, she was standing still, her sari draped back over her head. Silence followed. Gayatri Devi could hear every tick and tock of the Swiss watch on her wrist.

When Gupta handed over the completed appraisal form to Prithviraj, an audible whistle escaped Prithviraj's lips, his gaze riveted on the appraised value that stretched to tens of lakhs. *He knows the loan amount is paltry in comparison.* She wiped her wet brow with the edge of her handkerchief.

Prithviraj had taken the tiara out of the box. Passing it from one hand to the other, he peered at it. *I did not do this to go to jail.* Gayatri Devi looked at him fearfully. Could Prithviraj hear the scary beat of her scared heart? She took a deep breath. It only got louder. Prithviraj held the tiara up against the light. The pendulum of Gayatri Devi's heart swung to the other end and her heart almost stopped beating. She popped a peppermint into her mouth, hoping that sucking on it would calm her nerves.

"This is the first time my bank has received a crown jewel as collateral." Prithviraj closed the lid and placed the box in one of the lockers.

*I could not have pulled this off without your cooperation.* Gayatri Devi looked at Gupta with gratitude.

"Madam, your loan for ten thousand rupees is sanctioned." Prithviraj placed several documents on the table. "The amount will be credited to your bank account next week. The tiara will be safe with us."

Gayatri Devi clutched the tote tight with her left hand as she read each document and affixed her signature. The family heirloom was safe within its confines. It was only after she was inside the Bentley that she took the liberty to throw her head back and laugh heartily, recollecting her meeting with Gupta more than a month back.

◆

It was the day her father had suggested selling the royal tiara. Having given her sadhna a miss, she had visited Gupta's showroom in the crowded market area of downtown Mysore. Jeweller Gupta was one of her father's closest friends.

"Namaste Guptaji." She had given him the blue velvet box. "Please evaluate this for me."

"I know its value by heart. Twenty-four lakhs. The heirloom is priceless. Never sell it."

"Can it be copied?"

"I will not."

"I beg you."

"It is one of a kind. That is why it is valuable." He opened the box and stared at it. "An emerald of this carat size I have never seen. The sapphires are the deepest blue I have ever seen. They are costlier than the diamonds surrounding them. It was handcrafted more than a hundred years ago."

"It is a question of survival." Gayatri Devi briefed him of her financial condition. "I beg you." She prostrated before him.

"Stop," Gupta yelled and moved his feet away. "You come from a royal family. As a Kshatriya, you belong to a higher caste than me. What you did is tantamount to a sin." He rested his hands on his forehead as if in penitence. "You should not have fallen at my feet."

"I have to take a bank loan to tide over our finances. Until I get my share." She briefed him on the property prospects promised by her lawyer.

"Even if I can get a duplicate made at a reasonable cost, the loan it will fetch – roughly eighty percent – is paltry, a thousand rupees perhaps. Not enough to solve your financial problems, even if I do not charge anything for making the duplicate."

"You will perform the valuation using the real tiara." She was a woman with a plan.

"Then why do you need the duplicate?" Gupta stared at her with a puzzled look.

"So, I can do this." With legerdemain, she picked up the box with her right hand and swiftly switched it with the small purse she carried in her left hand.

Gupta started laughing. "The old rascal, did your father come up with the plan?"

"The tiara is the last symbol of our royal heritage. And a sign of our fortune. I do not want to lodge it with the bank as collateral."

"On one condition. What happens after the valuation is your responsibility. God forbid, you are caught, I will plead ignorance." Gupta extracted his pound of flesh. "The duplicate will be ready in a week's time. We will use low-grade gold alloy and artificial gemstones."

"You have my word." Gayatri Devi had not bent down to touch his feet this time.

●●●

# 10.

# A Day in Court

June 1939. Dressed in a grey flannel suit, sporting a black and white bow-tie, Vikramaditya stood at the lectern on the bar side of the airy courtroom.

"Until last year, the law excluded women from receiving a share in the joint family property. Succession was governed by the rule of survivorship. When a member of the joint and undivided family died, his share passed on to the surviving male members, the coparceners. The old law was of men, by men, for men. It did not consider fairness and equality where women were concerned.. .."

Seated at the plaintiff table, a hypnotized Gayatri Devi watched Vikramaditya make the opening statement. Predictably, she was the only woman in the courtroom.

The bank loan had solved her financial problems for the present, and the tiara was safe in the confines of her dressing room, where it belonged. Vikramaditya had made a fair estimate of the joint family wealth and her share in it. She had visited his office several times after the initial visit. The perfect gentleman, he always valued her opinions and treated her as an intellectual equal. She thought their interactions were refreshingly novel and respectfully energizing.

"The Hindu Women's Right to Properties Act 1937 gave a death blow to the old doctrine," Vikramaditya stated. "Thankfully the widow of a deceased coparcener of a Hindu Undivided Family will now have the same interest that her husband had while he was alive. Among other things, she has the right to claim partition . . ." Vikramaditya paused to pour himself a glass of water from the jug.

Sunlight reflected off the white-washed walls of the spacious courtroom. Gayatri Devi drew out the Japanese fan she carried. The summer day was sultry.

". . . The right to claim partition, as my client, the eldest daughter-in-law of the Rajvamsh family has decided to do," Vikramaditya continued. "Not by choice, but compulsion. Compulsion, because the fifteen male coparceners of the undivided Rajvamsh family, who continue to live the lavish lifestyle along with their wives and children, have evicted my client, Rani Gayatri Devi, out of the family mansion. With no qualms, whatsoever. Never for a moment did they remember that my client's husband, a male member of their own renowned family, through his business acumen and commercial expertise, had played a pivotal role in the accretion of the combined wealth of the family."

*He is forceful yet polite, logical yet empathetic.* Gayatri Devi tightened the pale green sari around her shoulders. While she did not venture the effort to meet their eye, she was vaguely aware of the presence of her dead husband's cousin, Raghu and one of his uncles, at the defendant table to her left.

"Denied of her rights in the ancestral property by the collective decision of these powerful men, how can this lone lady eke out a decent existence in our paternalistic society?" Vikramaditya cast a prolonged glance at the defendant table. "Your Honour, I implore you to grant justice, restore the dignity of this noble lady and establish a model case in the state of Mysore, so that no woman, rich or poor, shall have her rights violated henceforth."

Having concluded his opening statement, Vikramaditya came over to the plaintiff table and sat down on the chair adjacent to hers, discretely pulling it farther away, a bid to maintain respectable distance between them.

There was absolute silence in the courtroom. Disapproval? Probably. Envy? Possibly. It seemed like every single person was gawking at her. Gayatri Devi tilted her face upward as if in defiance.

The Judge tapped the table with his gavel. An elderly man with a walrus moustache, in a black coat worn over the traditional dhoti, approached the lectern. Speaking in chaste vernacular, Krishnakant, the defense lawyer, launched a strong emotional pitch upholding the values of the joint family and expressing respect for women who stayed within its confines.

"... A barren woman is an utter failure. She cannot discharge the maternal duties essential for the unity of a true joint family." He beamed at the spectators as if seeking their approval. "She is a curse. She contributes nothing to the growth and progress of the family. Such a woman does not deserve any share in the family property. What will she do with it anyway? A barren woman should be cut off without. . ."

Gayatri Devi noticed to her horror, that the men were nodding their heads in approval. Vikramaditya had raised his hand and gotten to his feet. Loud and clear, he was voicing strong concern over the vile statements and the derogatory tone of the defense lawyer. Gayatri Devi waved the little fan near her ear. She was glad Vikramaditya had chosen to sit next to her – it assuaged any feelings of rejection, in the scenario that was unfolding.

The Judge ordered the defense lawyer to adhere to court decorum and refrain from making pejorative references.

"The Hindu woman is only entitled to the Streedhan – gifts given to her by her parents, husband, friends and family, on or before her marriage. No matter what the law says, her inclusion into the confidential family matters depends solely on moral grounds. . ." Krishnakant stayed subdued until he finished the rest of his opening statement. He looked cryptically towards Gayatri Devi and Vikramaditya as if they were an unusual pair and walked back to the defendant table amidst thundering applause.

An orderly announced that the case of Rani Gayatri Devi Rajvamsh vs. The Rajvamsh Family would resume six weeks later.

"We need to meet." Vikramaditya turned to Gayatri Devi. "I have reviewed the records submitted to the court by the Rajvamsh family. Details of properties and other assets are very different from what I got from you. Some investigation is needed."

"I will ask my driver to follow your car."

◆

Gayatri Devi walked a few steps behind Vikramaditya as they exited the courtroom into the garden outside. The Bentley parked right next to Vikramaditya's Austin, refused to start. Vikramaditya insisted he would drop Gayatri Devi home. "Perhaps we can finish our discussion in the car."

Seated in the back seat of the white Austin next to Vikramaditya, Gayatri Devi was acutely conscious of the stares of the people in the courtyard, as the car weaved its way around the garden towards the road. She was sure conversations were coming to a standstill as people gawked at the gutsy lady driving off with the attractive gentleman.

His nearness was compelling, the aroma of his masculinity intoxicating. Gayatri Devi was glad she had donned her sunglasses. She did not want him to sense her true feelings.

Vikramaditya pulled out the statement of assets the defense lawyer had presented to the court. "I have compared this statement with our list. The estate, the summer bungalow, the orchards match up. A major item missing – the farmlands. ..."

"The farmlands are vast. Thousands of acres. My husband managed them, and visited them every month."

"Undisclosed."

"I used to help my husband with the accounts and administrative affairs."

"We have to prove their existence," he said. "Before the next hearing."

"What about cash, bonds and jewellery?"

"Liquid assets are mostly missing. Their list contains a third of what you shared with me." Vikramaditya placed the sheaf in her lap, his fingers inadvertently brushing against the side of her waist left partially exposed by her sari.

She loved the way her skin tingled. Reluctantly removing the sunglasses, Gayatri Devi pored over the list. "This is insane. They are obviously out to cheat me."

"Would your mother-in-law come forward and support your statement in court?"

"She will not step out of that house." Gayatri Devi stifled a snicker. "She fears the menfolk. They have forbidden her from talking to me."

"Let me submit a report to the Judge. Highlighting the discrepancies in the statement of assets provided by the defendants." He explained to her what would happen next, as the Austin continued to traverse the hot dusty avenues of Mysore.

The court would appoint a commissioner to independently procure, inspect and produce before the court, records such as notarized bank statements, title deeds and lease deeds, property assessment certificates, tax receipts et al. The court commissioner would conduct his own investigation and make recommendations on the division of the scheduled property. The Judge would consider the recommendations made by the court commissioner while pronouncing the judgment.

"In addition, it might be a good idea to do some inspection of our own." Vikramaditya knit and unknit his eyebrows. "And provide the evidence we collect to the court commissioner. It will speed up the proceedings. And strengthen our case."

"Prithviraj, the Manager of Brindavan Bank may be able to help us reconcile the liquid assets," Gayatri Devi said. *That joker is secretly in love with me.* She held back her tongue, not wanting Vikramaditya to think of her as brazen.

"Can we go to the bank now?" Vikramaditya looked at his watch.

Gayatri Devi smiled. She loved how he was quick to call for action. It was part of his charm.

"We can take a quick tour of the farmlands tomorrow. If you will accompany me," he said. "We can talk to the people who manage the farms, prepare notes and make lists. I will bring along my camera and take some pictures."

*Just the two of us.* Where would we spend the night? Gayatri Devi perched the sunglasses back on her nose and rolled up her side of the window. "The dust is pricking my face."

"I will ask Shamlal, our accountant to accompany us. If we start the journey early in the morning, we should be back by nightfall." Anxiety danced on his face.

"I will do whatever it takes to get my rightful share in my husband's property." Gayatri Devi removed her sunglasses. She wanted him to see the gratitude in her eyes. "We have to win the case."

◆

On arriving at Brindavan Bank, Vikramaditya a few steps behind her, Gayatri Devi led the way into the Bank Manager's cabin. She had to feign being oblivious of the people who stopped in their tracks to gawk at the elegant couple gracing the bank.

"Meet my lawyer." She introduced Vikramaditya to Prithviraj.

Vikramaditya signalled Prithviraj to close the cabin door. "We need some information. The matter is extremely confidential."

"Anything for our royal customer." Prithviraj switched on the table fan. "The bank is safekeeping the royal tiara."

Vikramaditya looked at Gayatri Devi quizzically.

"I gave it as collateral to get a bank loan."

Prithviraj was cloyingly polite – exactly as Gayatri Devi had expected. While he confirmed that the Rajvamsh family had rented several bank lockers, vouching for their contents was far beyond the scope of his authority. On conditions of confidentiality, he gave them handwritten statements listing the monies and deposits held by the Rajvamsh family at Brindavan bank.

◆

It was early evening when Vikramaditya dropped Gayatri Devi off at the portico of Indigo Castle – that time of the day when women in the neighbourhood indulged in idle gossip. Gayatri Devi was certain that inquisitive eyes and wagging tongues did not let the event go unnoticed. Once inside, the housekeeper and maid refused to meet her eye.

The nurse cast glances filled with aspersion at her when Gayatri Devi went to check on her father. Gayatri Devi sent the nurse away on an errand. As she held his withered hand in hers and apprised him of the day's happenings, she thought her father looked more peaceful than ever. "I need your permission to accompany Lawyer Vikramaditya and his accountant on a quick tour of the farms."

"You have staked your claim. Emerge victorious. People will talk. Ignore them." His body made a movement as if to bless her. "Dheergha Sumangali Bhava."[6]

It was a blessing given to married women, not widows. Gayatri Devi got up from the chair as if jolted. "How can you say that?"

"Baby, my body may be paralyzed my mind is not." A toothless smile lit up his well-lined face. "May Vikramaditya partner you and protect you. You have done the right thing by safeguarding the tiara. You will remarry. Your son will be the inheritor. He will rule over the business empire that you build."

Was he clairvoyant or plain delirious? Gayatri Devi patted his cheek and adjusted his blanket. It was with mixed emotions that she returned to her room, and started packing.

•••

---

[6] May you remain a married-woman for a long time

# 11.

# Father's Foretelling

Vikramaditya's car arrived at five o' clock the next morning to pick her up. Accountant Shamlal sat in the front seat with the driver. Vikramaditya held the rear door open and settled in the back seat with Gayatri Devi.

The first three farm visits were uneventfully successful. The supervisors were cooperative – answering Vikramaditya's questions and providing whatever information he requested. Vikramaditya made notes. Gayatri Devi clicked pictures of the farms and their boundaries.

The Austin chugged through the narrow mud roads and made its way through the dense surrounding greenery as they headed to the fourth farm. Vikramaditya continued to scribble in his notebook. "We have a pucca case to present to the Judge," he stated.

*You are my Messiah.* Gayatri Devi looked at him with pride from behind her sunglasses.

"Your husband, Ashoka, seems to have enjoyed great respect amongst the farm people."

*Ashoka.* Gayatri Devi clutched the seat beneath her with both hands. *We were happy together. For more than ten years. Yet in the ten months since his death, I have rarely thought of him. What was missing?*

The ride had turned bumpy. The Austin had suddenly turned wobbly. They had a punctured tyre. The driver swerved the car off the road to a full stop. Vikramaditya offered to help him change the tyre. Gayatri Devi retreated to the shade of a tree, with Shamlal for company.

"Kalinga farm." Vikramaditya announced their destination when they bundled back into the car.

Birds were chirping. The late afternoon sun had almost set. "Can we head home instead?" Gayatri Devi was worried about her father. "I have to be home before nightfall."

"We will," Vikramaditya assured her. "Kalinga farm is on the route home."

◆

Semi-darkness shrouded the modest cottage of the supervisor of the Kalinga farm. The entire family was lazing around in an open veranda surrounding the cottage. Seeing Gayatri Devi and Vikramaditya get out of the car, the women folk hastily collected the younger children and retreated into the house. The elder children remained standing in the veranda and stared at them. Two rustic men, almost identical, emerged out of the shadows.

"Namaste." Gayatri Devi took a step forward.

"Stop right there," the man in the red dhoti roared.

The farm supervisor had probably not recognized her in the semi-darkness. "It is me, your master's wife."

"Respectable women do not come to our doors." The man spat out the words.

Gayatri Devi cringed from their hostility. She had interacted with them several times in the past, along with her husband, and they had always been genial. "We need your help.. .."

"We will only deal with our master," the man said.

"Excuse me." Vikramaditya intervened. "As you are aware, your master is dead. We need a favour .. .."

"You pig .. .." The man in the red dhoti advanced towards Vikramaditya. The other man pulled him back. A woman had come out of the cottage and lit the lantern hanging from the awning. A dog was barking in the vicinity. The elder children who had stood staring, ran back into the house with the woman.

"Your master's wife has to get justice," Vikramaditya said. "Anything you can do to attest that the farm belongs to the Rajvamsh family will help her."

The two men looked at each other. The man in the red dhoti vanished into the trees behind the cottage.

"We will not rat on our masters." The other man stared at them, hands on his hips. "We are not traitors."

"We are not asking you to lie." Vikramaditya sounded conciliatory.

"Get lost or else ..." The man caught Vikramaditya's collar.

"Stop being rude and apologize." Gayatri Devi raised her voice. "This gentleman is my lawyer." She pried Vikramaditya away.

"Don't come here and tell me what to do." The rustic man spat at her. "Get out of here. *With your minda*[7] ... "

The dreaded word. Gayatri Devi froze. The worst public humiliation a woman could face. "Take me out of here," she turned to Vikramaditya, barely able to contain a sob.

"Don't talk nonsense or else ...." Vikramaditya pointed an angry finger at the rustic man and herded Gayatri Devi back to the car.

Gayatri Devi flopped onto her seat and closed the door. The barking had become louder and incessant. A monstrous form had leaped from the shadows. She screamed.

The two rustic men stood laughing as a barking dog pounced at Vikramaditya. In a show of great equanimity, Vikramaditya pushed the puny driver roughly into the car, hopped in behind him and locked the door shut. The dog pawed at the front of the car. The two rustic men started pelting stones and twigs at the car.

As Gayatri Devi and Shamlal raised the glass of the windows, Vikramaditya revved the engine, reversed the car, and sped out of the farm, instructing the driver, sandwiched between him and Shamlal, to keep a watch on the road behind them.

"That was brave, Mr. Vikramaditya," Gayatri Devi said when they were safely outside the boundaries of the farm. "Hope you are not hurt."

"The dog's teeth just grazed my hand."

"Is there a first aid kit in the car?" She could not disguise the concern in her voice.

After they had driven a few kilometres – stray houses and the occasional lights started to appear. Vikramaditya stopped the car in front of a building that looked like a post office. "We have another forty kilometres to go. But the petrol level is low."

---

[7] colloquial curse word for paramour

The driver informed them that there was only one petrol bunk on the way to Mysore and it was only open until six in the evening. Shamlal began hyperventilating.

"6.50 P.M." Gayatri Devi read the time on her watch in the glow from the street light. "The bunk will be closed."

Vikramaditya turned around and looked at Gayatri Devi. "One of my clients lives in an estate near here."

"Is there no way we can reach Mysore?"

"I am afraid not."

"What if they have gone out?" She could no longer control her anxiety.

"We will spend the night in the car then." Vikramaditya started the car.

The petrified driver had not offered to take over the driving.

◆

The guard of Panchavati estate recognized Vikramaditya instantly and opened the gates. Inside, Mr. Neeladri welcomed the disparate quartet warmly and introduced them to the rest of his family. Mrs. Neeladri served them a delicious dinner.

The Neeladri family retired early to bed. Their bedrooms were on the upper floors. Shamlal and the driver had been housed in the staff quarters in the annex. Both the guest bedrooms were on the ground floor. Vikramaditya and Gayatri Devi stayed back in the drawing-room, listening to the radio.

"Tomorrow the Rajvamsh family will hear about the ruckus. I am sure." Vikramaditya sat slumped in an armchair, nursing a gin and tonic, his eyes closed. He had borrowed a white dhoti ensemble from Mr. Neeladri.

Gayatri Devi flipped the pages of a newspaper in the dim light of the kerosene-filled lantern. "Did you get your wounds dressed?" She looked at him.

"Yes." When Vikramaditya extended his left arm out through the cloth covering his upper body, his finger brushed against the soft flesh of her bosom and poked her nipple through the housecoat.

Gayatri Devi almost let out a soft moan – it was as though a dose of warm brandy had doused her veins.

Vikramaditya opened his eyes and sat up straight. "I am sorry. I did not mean to.. .." He had tucked his arm back.

Gayatri Devi undid her chignon without looking at him. Her upper arm still tingled from the tickling touch of his hairy forearm. She could have spent the entire night brushing her hair, with Vikramaditya's loving gaze fixed on her. With the soft notes of classical music, the cool light of the waxing moon and the scented breeze from the garden, together casting a soporific spell.

"I need another drink." When the grandfather clock struck nine Vikramaditya stood up. "Should I get you something?"

Gayatri Devi stopped brushing her hair. "I thought you would never ask." By the time, he came back with their drinks, she had woven her hair into a braid. "Excellent." She swirled her tongue over her lip after taking a sip. "Thank you for adding fresh lemon to the gin."

"You are the first lady I am sharing a drink with." Vikramaditya sat down in the armchair. "In fact, I have never had a lady client before. It is a pleasure to have a client who can converse with me on most matters..." Thoughts locked away in his heart had found an outlet.

Vikramaditya looked relaxed for the first time since that morning. The shadow of a beard was appearing on his chin. Gayatri Devi had the strongest urge to run her own chin on his bristled cheeks, kiss his glistening lips and run her fingers across his hairy chest. She stood up and switched off the radio instead. Wishes were indeed horses! Beggars would ride. Pigs would fly. Crows would turn white. Fish would climb trees.

When she turned around, Gayatri Devi found herself staring into a carpet of black and silver hair matting an ebony chest. Vikramaditya stood so close that the hair almost tickled her nose. As she slowly pressed her face into the folds of the diaphanous cloth that partially covered the coveted carpet, strong arms encircled her. Rough lips bruised the silken softness of her face and shoulders. Leathery fingers ravaged the smooth firmness of her upper arms.

Gayatri Devi cast off the loose cloth covering his shoulders as her tongue searched for his nipples. The cold sweat of his burnished skin was the perfect antidote for her fevered forehead. Feeling Vikramaditya's fingers unbuttoning her housecoat, "The door..." she whispered.

"Closed," he murmured and tugged at the dhoti tied around his waist.

"Beautiful," her eyes had widened.

Even as the lantern cast a dull undulating glow on the walls around them, they sank onto the plush Persian carpet, to seek unity in ecstatic bliss. Once and forever.

◆

Everything went with clockwork precision the next morning. Vikramaditya's car exited Panchavati estate at nine o'clock sharp and after a quick stop at the petrol bunk, sped off in the direction of the fifth and final farm, where Vikramaditya collected more statements and documents to strengthen his case and Gayatri Devi took the customary photographs for proof.

If only this journey were endless! She slid her hand across the seat and gently gripped Vikramaditya's wrist. She was no longer a forlorn widow. Her body had never felt this alive. During the ten years of her marriage, Ashoka had never made her feel this vibrant.

Gayatri Devi pulled out her compact and examined her face. Her eyes glowed with excitement. Her thoughts would not swerve from the ecstatically blissful night they had shared. Vikramaditya had consumed her savagely, cuddled her tenderly and worshipped her body passionately. "Once is not enough." Before they retreated to their respective bedrooms in the early hours of the morning, he had tugged her hand.

The cloudy sky had given way to a light drizzle when the car reached its destination. She was home. Why was there a crowd outside? The driver had to honk several times before people reluctantly made way for the car. Several neighbours and some strangers stood in the garden. Her father's nurse stood in the portico.

How could the nurse leave her father all alone in his bedroom? Gayatri Devi got out of the car, ready to give the nurse a piece of her mind.

"We have been frantic, not knowing how to reach you," the nurse said before Gayatri Devi could open her mouth. "Your father was asking for you all morning."

*I know what this accusing harridan is going to say.* Gayatri Devi looked at her sternly as she walked towards the front door.

"He is gone," the nurse called out after her.

Gayatri Devi rushed up the stairs to her father's bedroom. Vikramaditya followed her. The clusters of people engaged in desultory conversations suddenly fell silent. Gayatri Devi collapsed by the bedside. Her father's face was immobile, his nostrils plugged with cotton. She was truly all alone in the big bad world. For the first time in her life, she wished she had a brother or sister or a child she could call her own.

Several people slinked away, casting sly glances at the couple. Only a few women remained to make their acerbic barbs. "Shameless." "Bringing him here?" "She was sleeping with the English gentleman when her father was dying." "He has brought dishonour on this family." Among them were the nurse, the maid, and the housekeeper.

"Stop talking nonsense," a spent Gayatri Devi commanded the three women. "Remember, *you* work for me."

"We can't work for a shameless woman." The three women stormed out of the house. With their packed bags. In a show of peculiar solidarity.

Neither Gayatri Devi nor Vikramaditya knew what to do next. No sooner did they come down the stairs, then the group of elderly men who stood around gossiping in the living room, converged upon them. A pelt of insults followed.

"Enough." Gayatri Devi folded her hands. "I have to take care of the funeral arrangements."

"You are a woman. You are barred from entering the funeral ground." The men had raised their voices. "You can do nothing without us, the community elders."

"I request you to stop harassing this lady." Vikramaditya's polite baritone transcended the fracas.

"Who are you to tell us? Neither her husband nor her brother." One of the men pulled at Vikramaditya's shirt collar.

When Gayatri Devi begged him to stop, he raised a hand in her direction. "You may sleep with him. To us he is an outsider."

Gayatri Devi walked to the centre of the living room. "Please leave my house at once." Her hands folded she hurled the words like an army general commanding the battalion.

"You cannot insult us." The men clamoured around her. The remaining visitors stood around gaping and gawking. It was the arrival of Jeweller Gupta and a small coterie of his friends, that ultimately saved the situation. "Please do not harass Gayatri. She is like a daughter to us. Respect her moment of grief." The words of the influential men, who had been friends of the deceased, changed the dynamics in the room. The so-called community elders crept away, as did the other visitors.

The coterie turned out to be a Godsend. During the next twenty-four hours, all prescribed Hindu rituals were completed and the emaciated body of the dead respectfully cremated.

◆

Gayatri Devi prepared herself to spend the night alone in the dilapidated mansion. In a way, she was relieved her father's suffering had ended. Picking up the tambura[8] for her daily sadhna, she opted to sing in the Todi[9] raga that epitomizes sadness, the notes causing complex emotions residing in the innermost depths of her soul to tumble out as rivulets of tears.

When the sound of a car screeching to a halt cut through the silence of the night, she put down the tambura and went to the window. Vikramaditya's Austin stood in the portico. Wiping away her tears, Gayatri Devi ran down the steps and let him in, without turning on the outside lights.

"Sorry to bother you at this late hour." Vikramaditya sat down on the sofa, handed her some papers, and offered his gold cased pen. "I have to file the report on the asset discrepancies with the court tomorrow. That way a court commissioner will be appointed immediately."

Gayatri Devi sat down next to him and signed the document. *Once is not enough.* She rested her head on his shoulder. "I feel so alone."

"You must be aware that I am married." His arm encircled her waist, kindling her warm body aflame in the humid night.

"I know that you have four daughters. Three are married. The fourth one is getting married, right? She just turned fifteen."

"What are you, a journalist?" There was a twinkle in his eye.

"Your elder daughter is in the family way. You will soon be a grandfather." She chided him as she rubbed his cheek with her own.

"I am almost forty years old," he said. "I was born at the turn of the twentieth century. Literally. On the first day of January 1900."

"You are my perfect English gentleman." She nuzzled the nape of his neck.

"I was in England only for three years."

---

[8] musical instrument used to support the melody of the singer
[9] classical tune

"Oxford-educated. Born with the proverbial silver spoon in your mouth?"

"On the contrary, I was born into a conservative middle-class family." Vikramaditya was in the mood to talk.

While studying at a missionary school established by the British, he had been fortunate enough to come under the influence of Father Fernandez, a highly-reputed scholar and the epitome of compassion. Vikramaditya, who had always dreamed big, had adopted Father Fernandez as his role model and diligently imbibed his values. Throughout his school years, Father Fernandez had bestowed upon him both academic guidance and financial assistance, without the asking.

Later, when Vikramaditya had become a successful lawyer, it was Father Fernandez who had brought forth the opportunity of specializing in Civil Law at Oxford University, along with attractive scholarship offers, giving him a readymade ingress into the world of professional education and a valuable stint in distant England. "I have been back in Mysore since 1930," he said.

"Stay with me." Gayatri Devi led him inside. "Don't go home."

Ensconced in the cosy confines of Gayatri Devi's bedroom, they had made love, not once but twice. While he had fallen asleep immediately, she lay next to him wide-awake. His square face was serene. *I want you to marry me.* In some corner of her heart was a yearning to bear this man's child.

She got out of bed and walked over to the window. The flame of the corner-lamp lit up her father's face in the photograph above. 'Your son shall be the inheritor of the royal tiara.' His words rang in her ears. He had seen the light of love in her eyes even before she had felt it in her heart.

◆

Vikramaditya became a regular visitor at Indigo Castle after that night. He arrived before dinnertime, heading there straight after work. Gayatri Devi would mix him his favourite drink and they would sit and talk in the sitting room until dinner was served. The driver's wife and daughter were the new maids of the household.

At the age of seventeen, Vikramaditya had topped the B.A. Honours class and become the first recipient of the newly instituted gold medal from the University Chancellor. His parents got him married to Sulakshana, a girl of their choice, considered well-educated, since she could read and write in Kannada and excelled in classical music.

During the next few years, Vikramaditya had gone on to do his Bachelor of Law, cleared the Bar exam, entered the legal profession, and established a flourishing career as a lawyer. In a span of seven years, he had not only acquired his own house but also become the proud father of four daughters. When the progressively burdensome family life had started to overwhelm him, fate had intervened, sending him to Oxford and helping him to break free, even if it was only for three years.

"Were you so lucky that there was no resistance from anyone in your family?" Gayatri Devi was intrigued.

"Neither my parents nor Sulakshana objected. Everybody else in the neighbourhood did. They blacklisted my family for letting me cross the seven seas and implicitly banished them from all social gatherings."

"Brutal!"

"After my return, I went through a full-fledged Prāyaścitta, the formal atonement ceremony, out of my own will and volition."

"You committed no sin. I thought Prāyaścitta was done to cleanse one's sins."

"It was performed for the satisfaction of the society. So that social contact with our family was restored. Otherwise, we would not have found alliances for my daughters."

"Did you ever consider settling in London?'

"Never. I braved society to go there and gain expertise that was not available here. My intention was always to help people here, to the best of my ability."

"Such as me?" She giggled.

After returning from his sojourn at Oxford, Vikramaditya had consolidated his position as the most prominent civil lawyer in the state of Mysore. Dedicated to the success of his profession with a single-minded determination, he had drifted further and further away from Sulakshana, who focused her energy on the onerous task of taking care of their daughters' needs and running the joint family household. There had also been a prolonged lull in their childbearing activity.

God's will or Abstinence? Gayatri Devi would have given anything to find out.

"Not having a son is one of the milder regrets of my life." Vikramaditya had confided in a rare moment of intimacy.

"Chauvinism?"

"Fascination."

"Is that a new word for male superiority?"

"I already have four daughters. Don't we all aspire for what we don't have?"

Fatal attraction? Loyal friendship? Undying love? Gayatri Devi pondered what it was that bound her and Vikramaditya together.

•••

# 12.

# Court Proceedings

October 2, 1939. Court proceedings had resumed.

"Rani Gayatri Devi, widowed a few months ago, recently lost her father. She has no brothers or children ..." Vikramaditya's baritone voice held the court captive as he summarized her situation one more time for the benefit of the court. "She has a right to maintenance that originates from the sacred relationship she shared with her husband, who belonged to the illustrious Rajvamsh family."

"The Hindu woman is only entitled to Streedhan." Krishnakant, the defense lawyer, rebutted.

"That was the old Hindu law," Vikramaditya said with authority. "To reiterate, under the 1937 Act and the concept of the limited estate, my client is entitled to other inherited properties. It is not a right to property per se but rather a right against property arising from her pre-existing right to be maintained as declared by the Supreme Court of India in Section 14 (1) and (2) of in the case of .. .." He went on to cite the excruciating details of a recent case of the law.

Gayatri Devi sat in the same seat she had occupied the last time. Agnes, her one-time governess, a prim and proper British woman in her fifties, sat next to her. Jeweller Gupta and another elderly man who had been her father's friend sat along the perpendicular edge of the plaintiff table.

"In August, a court commissioner was appointed to investigate the discrepancies between the list of assets provided by Vikramaditya, the plaintiff lawyer and the partial statement furnished by the defendants, the Rajvamsh family." Vikramaditya picked up a thick brown file from the lectern. "Here is a comprehensive list of all properties and assets owned by the Rajvamsh family and their estimated value based on the court commissioner's assessment."

Referencing the contents of the file, Vikramaditya presented a bird's eye view of the financial position of the Rajvamsh family and highlighted the huge gap between the court commissioner's statement and the partial statement. He clearly spelled out Gayatri Devi's share of the inheritance.

"Well done Mr. Vikramaditya. Eloquent and Succinct." The Judge's clipped commendation of her paramour's performance made her spirits soar. Gayatri Devi uncrossed her legs and sat up straight. She would have to take the stand next.

While she herself had been in two minds about it, Vikramaditya had insisted she take the stand. The Judge, who was due to retire within the year, was looking forward to a landmark judgment. Vikramaditya believed that the Judge possessed a progressive outlook and had opined that Gayatri Devi with her aristocratic roots, dignified demeanour and articulate speech could make a favourable impression on the Judge.

"I now invite the plaintiff, Rani Gayatri Devi, to take the stand." Vikramaditya had announced.

Head held high, the powder blue sari draped to cover her chignon, Gayatri Devi walked majestically to the witness stand. After the customary swearing on the Bhagwad Gita, Vikramaditya started his direct-examination.

"Your name?"

"Gayatri Devi Rajvamsh." Her eyes angled downward. "Wife of Late Ashoka Rao Rajvamsh."

"Where do you live?"

"No. 5 Indigo Castle, Maharaja Street."

"How long have you lived there?"

"Last ten months." Gayatri Devi lifted her head to find herself staring into the eyes of Raghu, her dead husband's cousin, seated at the defendant table. "I returned to my father's house after the Rajvamsh family banished me."

"What happened?"

Gayatri Devi placed her palms lightly over her ears. 'Bahishkaara' – Raghu's proclamation to ostracise her – reverberated in her head. Wading against the humiliating memories flooding her mind, she narrated her tale of pitiful widowhood to a court full of conservative and most likely, chauvinistic men.

No sooner had her husband breathed his last than his family had embarked on indoctrinating her into the arduous journey of a quintessential Hindu widow. They prohibited her from leaving the bedroom for an entire fortnight, until the ceremonial rites were completed. The women folk confiscated her jewellery and insisted on controlling her diet, allowing her a single meal a day, of rice and bland lentils. At the end of the fortnight, when the family collectively coerced her to shave her head and don nothing else but a coarse cotton sari, she had put her foot down.

"I could not tolerate the interference in a matter so personal." She looked up. "I am not even thirty years old."

The Judge's stare was impassive. Yet she found his kind eyes paternalistically reassuring and sympathetic.

"But things only got worse," she resumed. Though she had altered the way she dressed – tying her hair in a chignon and wearing simple saris, her refusal to get her head tonsured had bought her the wrath of the menfolk. Overnight, her erstwhile royal status notwithstanding, she had become the embodiment of familial dishonour. The family persistently insisted that she capitulate to their demands unconditionally and resign herself to a life of renunciation.

When she had not relented, a family meeting of sorts had transpired, where her husband's cousin, Raghu, had been the vociferous voice of the family. Raghu, who was a couple of years younger than her, had talked to her with the utmost disrespect, launching into lengthy tirades and accusing her of every evil tactic that he could think of. While her husband's uncles and cousins had subjected her to their toxic taunts and vituperative barbs, the womenfolk had remained largely silent, their inimical stares fixed on her. Since she did not wish to follow the diktats of society, the family had unanimously decided that she would be an outcast.

"I wanted to maintain my self-respect. I packed my personal belongings and left for my father's house." She cleared her throat once, and then twice. "My father passed away recently. I am now all alone." Majestically, Gayatri Devi walked back to her seat.

The menfolk in the courtroom remained silent. Agnes dabbed her eyes.

"The husband has a personal obligation to maintain his wife and if he or the family has property, the woman has a legal right to be maintained therefrom," Vikramaditya declared.

Agnes took the stand next. Citing several anecdotes, she portrayed Gayatri Devi as an obedient and conscientious student and a woman of high principles. "'G' is the daughter I never had." She dabbed a handkerchief to her eye and planted a kiss on Gayatri Devi's forehead as soon as she returned to their table. "God Bless."

Gupta, the last witness Vikramaditya called for the plaintiff, reminisced about his long association with Gayatri Devi's father, described their erstwhile royal status and expressed his trepidation over the impending state of penury that would befall Gayatri Devi if the court did not act fairly and promptly. "She is all alone. If even one of her three brothers had survived to care for her, I would not be worried. All her brothers died in the plague epidemic that struck Bombay city in the 1920s." He left the stand with a deep sigh.

"Under the current circumstances, since my client has no one to take care of her and no source of income for her subsistence, I request the court to expedite the decision to grant her a rightful interest in the family estate as prescribed by law, as well as maintenance expenses that are worthy of the family's financial stature." Vikramaditya rested his case.

◆

October 3, 1939. The public gallery of the courtroom was full. Defense lawyer Krishnakant stood at the lectern, twirling his walrus moustache, setting the stage for the chief examination of the defense witnesses. "Let us suppose that the said woman is the keep, I mean maintained by another man." He started off, in chaste vernacular.

'Keep'. Gayatri Devi felt her blood freeze. She tugged the cream-coloured shawl tighter around herself.

"Defamation." Vikramaditya appealed to the Judge. "I object to the defense lawyer's line of thought, Your Honour."

"Sustained."

Gayatri Devi could feel the warm blood flow through her veins again. With Vikramaditya to protect her, she had nothing to worry.

"Remarriage, conversion, and unchaste behaviour are held as grounds for disability to inherit," Krishnakant persisted.

"I am aware of the law." The Judge threw him a grave look.

"Thank You, Your Honour." Krishnakant's face broke into a crooked grin. "While the lady in question has neither remarried nor converted to another religion, she has indulged in unchaste behaviour."

"Remember to adhere to particulars relevant to this case alone and nothing else." The Judge waved his gavel.

A bevy of people – five men and three women – walked into the courtroom at that exact moment and occupied the chairs surrounding the defense table.

"My witnesses are here." Krishnakant let out a snort. "I wish to present evidence of the unchaste behaviour I just referred to."

"I don't think that is relevant." Vikramaditya was in front of the Judge.

"These particulars are relevant to this particular case, Your Honour." Krishnakant bowed deferentially to the Judge. "The plaintiff lawyer has to hear what my witnesses have to say first. Before brushing it off as irrelevant."

"Objection Overruled."

Gayatri Devi looked towards the defendant section through the corner of her eye. The three women were none other than the maids who had quit work the day her father had died. They were the only other Indian women to have set foot into the court. They were perceived as belonging to lower strata of society, socially speaking; which automatically exempted them from the mores of the middle-class. The same way as Gayatri Devi's aristocratic status did, and Agnes's Anglo-Indian status.

Vikramaditya had sidled to occupy the chair to her left. "This is all orchestrated." His jaw visibly clenched, he whispered, "I recognize three of the five men – they were the ones who assaulted me at your father's house."

His unctuous face gleaming with wicked glee, Krishnakant proceeded to unfold in front of the court, a veritable phantasmagoria.

The neighbourhood elders took the stand first, one of them functioning as a spokesperson. Gayatri Devi had gone gallivanting out of town with Vikramaditya while her paralyzed father lay ailing. The wanton woman had the gall to flaunt her paramour at a public gathering, after her overnight tryst. She had not only sullied her royal lineage but also brought dishonour to her dead husband's family. Several of her husband's nieces had attained marriageable age and would not have found husbands had the Rajvamsh family not disowned Gayatri Devi. This was the gist of the spokesperson's dramatic monologue delivered in Kannada.

*I am not going to cry.* Gayatri Devi wished she could pull out the sunglasses from her purse and perch them on her nose.

"That man's car arrives after dusk and leaves at dawn." The spokesperson pointed a finger at Vikramaditya. "Every day. Neighbours have seen it." The other men nodded their heads to register assent.

Vikramaditya was fidgeting so vigorously in his chair that her chair had started resonating in sympathetic motion. Gayatri Devi thrust her left hand into the inner folds of her sari – a violent attempt to refrain from reaching out for his hand. While that would have calmed him down, it would have ended the case forever.

Next, lawyer Krishnakant called on the three maids to take the stand. Gesticulating heavily, they all spoke at the same time. They had been loyal servants of Gayatri Devi's father. After the widowed Gayatri Devi returned to her father's house, things had changed. They worked for several months without receiving their salaries. Then Gayatri Devi befriended the angrezi[10] lawyer and they miraculously received all their dues in a lump sum.

His car picked her up every evening and brought her home late in the night. Unfittingly for a widow, she wore expensive silks and pearls, and used powder and perfume, when she went out with him and flirted openly. The day before her father died, she had gone off with him and not returned home even after midnight. Overcome with shame, her father died in his sleep. His death had unshackled her completely. It was an open secret that she was the lawyer's mistress. "Even talking about her obnoxious behaviour is a sin." They declared before walking back to their seats with bowed heads, not looking in the direction of Gayatri Devi, their erstwhile employer.

Raghu went next, narrating his own version of the sequence of events at the Kalinga farm. Vikramaditya and Gayatri Devi had behaved like lovebirds as they toured the farm. Vikramaditya had ordered the farm folks around and demanded access to the accounts. When the farm folks had sworn their allegiance to the owners and declined to share confidential information, he had thrashed them, threatened them with dire consequences and made away with the ledger. "That is how

---

[10] colloquial term for someone who is well-versed in English

the angrezi lawyer put together the statement of property." He made a swearing gesture in Vikramaditya's direction.

"Objection!" Vikramaditya sprung up from his chair. "The statement was prepared by the court commissioner, an independent party appointed to clarify the discrepancies."

The Judge agreed with Vikramaditya and reprimanded Krishnakant for not explaining the role of the court commissioner to Raghu.

After Raghu had returned from the stand, Krishnakant summarized the statements made by the witnesses and emphasized one more time that under the Hindu Women's Right to Property Act, a widowed daughter-in-law can succeed to the property or claim her share only if she remained chaste. If there was any questionable behaviour, she would forfeit her interest and her share would devolve back to the remaining heirs.

Was the momentary stillness of the courtroom an ominous foreboding? Gayatri Devi shuddered at the implications.

◆

October 4, 1939. It was the third day of the court session. Vikramaditya had zeroed in on Raghu for the cross-examination.

Having worn crisp white clothes and slicked his long hair back, troublemaker Raghu was trying to look respectable. Would he be able to keep his fiery temper and street language in control? Gayatri Devi hoped he would not. Cocooned between Agnes and Gupta, she felt secure.

"Name?"

"Mr. Raghunandan Rajvamsh."

"Profession?"

"Landlord."

Vikramaditya grilled Raghu, covering details of the farms owned by the family, those he managed personally and the acreage area of the significant ones.

Raghu's responses were far from satisfactory.

"My Lord," Vikramaditya turned to the Judge. "I request you to read the list of properties from the statement submitted by the court commissioner."

The Judge read out the names of the farms on the list, including their area in acres.

Raghu seemed agitated. He kept looking at the defendant table and gesticulating at lawyer Krishnakant.

Obtaining the Judge's permission, Vikramaditya showed Raghu a black and white photograph. "Do you recognize these two men?"

"They are the supervisors of Kalinga farm," Raghu replied. "You thrashed them and snatched the ledgers from them," he added.

"Does the Rajvamsh family own the farm?"

"Yes."

"The particulars of the Kalinga farm were not on the list of properties that His Honour read out a minute ago," Vikramaditya said.

"You must have purposely left it out of the list."

"Wrong. The court commissioner had to omit Kalinga from the list for want of proof. Your supervisors refused to cooperate."

"That is a bunch of lies," Raghu shrieked.

"The supervisors used violence to threaten the court commissioner and chase him away. The same tactic they applied to me and my client." Vikramaditya held up a second black and white photograph that showed the same two men with raised sticks and a huge dog that was pouncing at the Austin.

Raghu's body was visibly seething. Krishnakant was frantically signalling him to stay calm.

"My Lord, the witness is either lying or ignorant." Referring to his notes, Vikramaditya listed out the mismatches between Raghu's responses and the statement the Judge had just readout. "Despite claiming to be a landlord he can neither name the properties correctly nor reconcile the acreage area of the properties he named."

There was a mild commotion in the courtroom.

His face turning a bright colour that betrayed guile, Raghu launched into a pompous explanation of how they were a large family with several properties and paid several clerks to keep track of such trivial matters. "Why haven't you shown him our statements and lists?" he shouted rudely, turning to the defense lawyer. "What do I pay you for?"

The Judge brought the gavel down to silence Raghu and reprimanded Krishnakant once again.

"I am a landlord. My lawyer should argue with you." Raghu left the stand in obvious fury and rushed out of the courtroom. There were a few sniggers from the gallery. Krishnakant's slimy face no longer sported the stupid grin.

Gayatri Devi raised her eyebrows at Agnes. Ego had gotten the better of the crooked man into cornering himself further into the maze of his own lies.

The Judge had the final say before adjourning the court. "The evidence has established beyond a reasonable doubt that the statements and affidavits provided earlier by the defense counsel were false. The court will henceforth adopt the accurate details of assets provided by the court commissioner with one addition – an estimate for the Kalinga farm. The aggregated value shall form the basis for determining the share of interest and compensation to the plaintiff at the time of the verdict."

Vikramaditya looked more relaxed as he joined Gayatri Devi at their table.

"You stood your ground well," she said. "Especially the way you interrogated Raghu."

"You can share the credit – for having the presence of mind to click those pictures."

"I think Raghu has lost his credibility."

"That is not the crux," Vikramaditya said. "It is the morality angle being projected by the defense lawyer that worries me. Krishnakant is waiting to pounce on you. He will try to chew you horizontally when you take the stand for cross-examination."

"What if I don't take the stand? Can we request an exemption?"

"Not at this juncture."

"If I admit to our affair, we will lose the case," she whispered. "I will not be able to deny it either. Not convincingly at least."

"I do not want you to lie either. You will be under oath."

"We are truly caught between the devil and the deep blue sea."

"I love your chaste English."

They exited the courtroom separately and departed in their respective cars. Neither of them wanted to add fuel to the gossip surrounding them.

◆

October 5, 1939. The fourth and last day of court.

"Would you like to cross-examine any more witnesses?" The Judge addressed Vikramaditya.

"No, My Lord," Vikramaditya replied.

Lawyer Krishnakant sprang up immediately. "I call upon Madam Gayatri Devi, the plaintiff, for cross-examination."

Walking to the witness stand, Gayatri Devi felt her nervousness return. There was no telling to what lengths the abominable Krishnakant would go to vilify her. The previous night had been torturous. The dread of the cross-examination by the weasel-like Krishnakant had caused her nightmares.

"Do you know the gentleman seated there?" Krishnakant pointed towards Vikramaditya.

"Yes."

"Is he your relative?"

"He is my lawyer."

"What is your relationship with him?"

"He is my lawyer."

"Do you have any personal relationship with him?"

"He is my lawyer." She cast a glance of gratitude towards Vikramaditya. They had mutually agreed that while maintaining a dignified stance of cooperation, she would not fall into the trap of justifying or denying an allegation or a question leading to it.

"Has he stayed overnight at your house?"

Vikramaditya got to his feet with an objection. Just as snickers were emanating from the spectators, the Judge sustained the objection.

"Where were you on the day before your father's death?"

"We were on a tour of the farms."

"Was the plaintiff lawyer with you?"

"Yes. With his driver. And his accountant, Shamlal."

"Why did you not return home that night?"

"The car ran out of petrol."

"Where did you spend the night?"

"We were guests of Mr. and Mrs. Neeladri. At their estate."

"Did the plaintiff lawyer spend the night with you?" Krishnakant looked around the court with a vicious grin.

The spectators tittered.

Gayatri Devi strived to keep her face expressionless.

Vikramaditya was up on his feet again with an objection. The Judge sustained the objection and issued a severe warning to Krishnakant.

"Did you take the photograph of the pouncing dog?" Krishnakant had fired his next salvo.

"Yes."

"May I ask why?"

"I was scared."

"Were you angry?"

"Yes."

"May I ask why?"

"The farm supervisors refused to provide the statement of accounts. My late husband was their master. They were being disrespectful."

"What did the men say to make you angry?"

"They were rude." She felt faint. "I don't remember the exact words."

"Did they use bad language?"

"Possible."

"Yes or No?"

Out of the corner of her eye, she saw Vikramaditya approaching the Judge. "I don't know."

"Was the bad word hurled at the lawyer?" Krishnakant's leering grin was back.

In that instant, Gayatri Devi had realized the lawyer's real intentions. "I don't know."

"Did they call the lawyer m .. .?"

She closed her ears. "Last warning." The Judge's gavel had come down heavily on the table before Krishnakant could utter the dreaded word. "The defense counsel will be suspended from the court if there are any more attempts to outrage the dignity of a respectable woman. This court will not entertain the use of bad language in any form under any circumstances."

Looking stunned, Krishnakant hung his head down.

"The court apologizes to the esteemed plaintiff on behalf of Lawyer Krishnakant." The Judge looked kindly towards Gayatri Devi.

Absolute silence followed. Vikramaditya had returned to the plaintiff table.

Gayatri Devi cast a grateful look at him, for pre-empting Krishnakant's move and quietly appealing to the Judge. Vikramaditya had guessed, as she had, that Krishnakant's intention was to cast aspersions on Gayatri Devi's conduct, incite doubt on her character and scandalize the court, in a bid to take the focus of the case away from the value of the properties involved and the discrepancies brought to light.

"You may proceed with the cross-examination as long as you adhere to the facts and do not humiliate the witness." The Judge's tone was harsh when he re-addressed Krishnakant.

"No more questions." Krishnakant did not lift his hung head. "I will not be cross-examining any more witnesses."

◆

"India has officially joined the Second World War. Despite resentment over the British Raj, several lakhs of people have joined Britain and their Allies to fight Germany and Japan. However, the Indian National Congress led by Gandhi, Sardar Patel, and Maulana Azad, has not been consulted..." Gayatri Devi was listening to the radio when she heard Vikramaditya's car screech to a halt in the portico.

"Did you hear the news?" She asked as he entered the sitting room.

His face was cheerless. He sat down next to her on the green velvet sofa, lighted a cigar and stretched his legs. The previous day's proceedings seemed to have taken a toll on him.

"...The Nizam of Hyderabad has announced large donations to support the Allies. The other Princely States.. .." She switched off the radio and locked her gaze on Vikramaditya. "Do you think we will win the case?"

"I have never lost a case." His voice was deep and rumbling. Yet the tone was gentle, with no trace of arrogance. "I certainly don't want yours to be the first."

"Our proof was impeccable. The Judge ratified it. Even lauded you for it."

"The turn of events has me worried." He licked his lips and puffed at the cigar.

"We did not choose to fall in love." She had adopted the gentle therapist tone that she was so fond of, especially when she needed to boost her own confidence. "It was predestined."

"I feel responsible for getting you into this mess." He extinguished the cigar and set it in the ashtray. "There is one way we can salvage the situation. The court is on vacation. We have some time until the day of the verdict. December 1. We should not meet until then. That way the rumours will die a natural death."

He had reclined on the sofa. She rested her face on his chest, her burning lips delighting in the silken touch of his fur. His visits were the only bright spots in her bleak life. An eight-week separation was a small price to pay if they could win the case and be together forever after that. By then, people would find something else to talk about someone else; the court would have no grounds to label her unchaste, nor deny her rights to inherit her dead husband's rights in the estate.

Clinging to him, his warm breath on her face, she could feel the flow of his blood, in every artery, every vein. Maybe, it was for the best. During the hiatus, she would focus on completing the legal formalities associated with her dead father's estate. Vikramaditya would anyway be busy with the arrangements for his daughter's wedding.

Lying atop him, she swayed her body with a cultivated languor, until his body had begun to reciprocate and rock rhythmically, in soulful unison. The warm rays of the afternoon sun streaming in through the window singed her ivory skin. When the pinnacle of pleasure had sent her levitating into a zone of blessed bliss, she knew something had changed; though she knew not, what had changed.

•••

Book 3

# 1986: Siddhartha & Abhimanyu & *Rahul*

# 13.

# Izod Investments

*June 1, 1986*

Siddhartha strived to be a good businessman in the months following the retraction of the working capital loan. Overseeing the daily operations of the video stores and parlours, hiring the right talent to take charge of marketing and publicity, appointing a qualified chartered accountant to manage financials – Siddhartha concentrated his efforts on turning around Vikrama Ventures. He neither indulged in a con nor any swindle.

Yet, six months later, when he arrived at the office of his chartered accountant to review the financial results, Siddhartha was in for a shock. The vicious whirlpool of a perpetual cash crunch had become the inescapable nemesis of Vikrama Ventures. The absence of working capital financing for daily operations was the root cause. While Joshua had navigated Siddhartha away from greedy loan sharks, approaching a moneylending firm had been inevitable. Interest rates were still high at eighteen to twenty percent per year and costs had mounted unabated.

"Profitability has worsened; rather losses have mounted is a better way of putting it." Joshua, his chartered accountant, had not minced words. While revenue had remained flat, operating costs had escalated rapidly and revenue leakage at the video parlours was astronomical – dishonest customers invariably discovered ingenious ways of outsmarting the video machines. Maintenance and service of the video machines were also proving to be prohibitively expensive. Inventory of video accessories had accumulated, unable to compete with the newer models flooding the market. "Profitability is still the lesser evil," Joshua said. "Cash flow is your cancer."

"Joshua, tell me how I can close the stable door before the horse runs away," Siddhartha frowned.

"I am not sure I understand?"

"Sorry. I did not mean to sound like an English teacher. But that is what I am. How can I make Vikrama Ventures debt-free, before it goes bankrupt?"

"With a big bang infusion of funds for business operations."

"Sorry Joshua, I am not sure *I* understand."

"We should approach a venture capital firm for our financing. That is our only recourse .. .."

"Is that like a joint venture or do we sell off Vikrama Ventures outright?"

"Neither. Venture capital is a form of private equity. Venture capital firms invest in businesses that are in the early stages of their life cycle, in exchange for ownership stake – that is equity. They also provide strategic direction to the business. Vikrama Ventures is an ideal candidate, given its limited market history and the market potential of its technology." Joshua had assumed the mantle of a trusted financial advisor with overwhelming alacrity.

Siddhartha grit his teeth. This is not how he had envisioned it, when he decided to invest the proceeds from his father's life insurance policy. "We wouldn't have to do this if Ascot Bank had not cut off our working capital financing." Anger had steeped into his voice.

"A friend of mine has started a venture capital firm. We should approach him." Joshua placed a visiting card on the table. 'Harshavardhan. Managing Director. Izod Investments.'

◆

**June 10, 1986**

The sun was blazing hot. The roads were empty. Sitting in the pale blue Maruti car in the parking lot of Orange Computers, Siddhartha waited for Sadhana to finish her class. The new car was the only indulgence he had allowed himself. He had also taken out a life insurance policy and made Sadhana the beneficiary. That way, if something happened to him, she would not be in the lurch.

There was a spring and a bounce in her step, as she walked towards the car, dressed in an orange sari and a sleeveless blouse that showed off her smooth arms and slender neck, her straight hair in a free fall around her shoulders, her nails and lips painted orange. Siddhartha found himself falling in love all over again with his faithful wife of sixteen years. "A pair of stilettos and you can walk the ramp." He started the car as soon as she had climbed into the passenger seat.

"Project starts next week." Sadhana examined her face in the vanity mirror of the visor. "Exams in October. Then I look for a job."

"Harshavardhan, the Managing Director of Izod Investments, turned out to be a friend. From my college days." Siddhartha briefed his wife on the highlights of his meeting. Izod Investments was looking at expansion. Harshavardhan believed that video parlours were a booming business. He had offered to purchase Vikrama Ventures outright in lieu of the venture capital financing that Siddhartha had sought.

"Good news! Are you going to sell?"

Over the past few months, Sadhana's eyes had gradually lost their shroud of melancholy. The computer course had given her much more than a career option. It had given her a new lease of life, even making her more accepting of the fact that she may never be a mother again; she had confessed as much on turning thirty-six.

"The offer is lucrative," he said.

"You are too soft with people." Her tone indicated agreement. "You are not cut out for business. Not in the long-term."

"Exactly what Harsha told me. Meeting him was a boon."

"How long will it take?"

"The deal will be sealed in October. It's called an acquisition in corporate parlance. Joshua will start working on the financial analysis and other preliminaries right away."

"Will we be rich? Will you stop working?"

"More secure, financially speaking. We will get a substantial lump sum payment. I will have Joshua invest it for us. Shrewdly. We will retain a limited interest in Vikrama Ventures, and receive annual dividends."

"I want to pursue a career in computers," she said. "As long as this deal won't stop me from getting a job."

"I will go back to teaching."

"Liberation at last?"

"I will be liberated the day I make that bastard suffer." The ignominy he had endured at the bar council conference had not stopped haunting Siddhartha. *The one where they denied my mother's existence and mine.* The way Vikrama Ventures had suffered at the hands of Ascot Bank and faced financial ruin had only exacerbated his humiliation.

"I know you cannot forget." Sadhana stroked his forearm. "Can you forgive?

"This is not about revenge." He had traversed too far down the path to retreat. "The saga will end when I get justice." Words the mother-son duo had uttered on the dais buzzed in Siddhartha's head. '... Heirloom a vestige of royal lineage ... shall pass on to Abhimanyu .. ..' The sparkling tiara taunted him. "The bastard has faced no hardships. He is accustomed to having his way. He must understand what it means to lose what is rightfully his. That royal tiara is the only part of his fortune that he is entitled to own."

"You are planning to steal it! Say no, please. Say no .. .."

"Yes." His eyes were flashing. "Only to teach him a lesson. Taking that one thing away from him would be fair payback for the dark deed of arrogating at birth everything that rightfully belonged to me."

"I know I can't hold you back. No matter what you do, please be careful." Her eyes entreated him.

"The tiara is either in a bank locker or a vault. First, we need first-hand information."

"That we can wheedle out of his wife," she said.

"His wife?" Siddhartha's foot almost fell off the accelerator. Cursing, he switched to a lower gear. "Do you know her?"

"You and I have no contact with that family, but all my friends know we are related. They feed me the occasional gossip. Kalpana manages Aradhana Cottage Emporium. A high-end handicrafts store on Cunningham Road. Looks of a doll, with brains to match. That is what my friends say about her. Low self-esteem. Treated shabbily by her husband."

"You know so much about that bastard's family. And you never told me?"

"I did not want to rub salt into the wound?"

"You are becoming an expert in the use of idioms," Siddhartha smiled.

"Simi, their daughter, studies at Benson College. First-year B.A." Sadhana was on a roll. "I've heard she is pretty and pretty conceited."

"Like father like daughter!" Assimilating the information as he deftly navigated the Maruti through the chaotic traffic of Central Bangalore, Siddhartha's conniving mind raced faster than the car.

Benson College. He had worked there as guest faculty a while ago. *Hamlet* or *Macbeth* – a Shakespeare play was always an integral part of the first B.A syllabus. Teaching Shakespeare was his forte – he had done it for twenty odd years – at the Mysore College. It was a long shot but Simi could be the one-way ticket to laying his hands on the tiara. "I think I should meet the principal of Benson college. And find out if they need an English teacher."

"You have a plan, don't you?"

"An outline." Siddhartha grinned. "You know my mantra; proof of the project lies in the planning."

"Do I have a role?"

"A double role. One role entails befriending this doofus Kalpana. Before that, can we meet with your doctor friend, the one who runs L'Atelier?"

"Done. I will talk to Pallavi," she said. "The other role?"

"Make-up artiste," he said. An expert at doing her own makeup when she was an actor, Sadhana occasionally moonlighted for weddings and parties, to supplement their income stream.

"Now I am excited." She rubbed her cheek against his shoulder.

•••

# 14.

# Project Charter

*June 15, 1986*

A violet brocade sari that had belonged to her mother-in-law, hair piled high in a top knot, finely tweezed eyebrows over-drawn with pencil in the style of Hindi movie heroines – Sadhana would not have recognized herself as the woman breezing into Aradhana Cottage Emporium.

Before leaving their flat, when she had adorned her ears with the pear-shaped solitaires and looped the diamond pendant into the chain around her neck, the irony of where the jewels had come from, had hit her. Despite their hardships, Siddhartha had refused to sell the diamond set, calling it the only expensive gift he had ever given her. "It doesn't matter that we stole it. Should have rightfully belonged to us anyway." He had rationalized.

There were few customers in the emporium at ten in the morning. Sadhana was pleasantly surprised when the receptionist ushered her into the office of Kalpana, almost immediately. Was it because she looked like a rich socialite rather than a social worker?

"My name is Mrinalini. I represent L'Atelier, a social organization for the upliftment of local artisans." Sadhana laid out handicraft samples, mostly Mysore styled paintings she had carried in a fashionable tote. L'Atelier was a non-profit organization founded by Sadhana's friend, Doctor Pallavi, a gynaecologist by profession. L'Atelier adopted the cooperative society model, encouraging local artisans to become voluntary members, and negotiated competitive prices on their behalf.

Kalpana, dressed in a black salwar suit with red motifs, her throat and wrists adorned with rubies and her hair stylishly coiffured, examined the samples with minute interest and expressed genuine appreciation for the handiwork. "I love how the artist has emphasized the crowns adorning the goddesses." She rubbed a finger on the Gesso work. "Unique."

*Siddhartha, my love, we may have hit the jackpot.* He had requested Doctor Pallavi to specifically source such paintings as would remind Kalpana of the tiara. "We would love to become your regular supplier. You will be directly helping the poor artisans make a living." Sadhana was ready with her next move. A copy of the tabloid *The City Tab* that she fished out of her tote. It carried an interview of Abhimanyu where he had spoken about the heirloom. With a picture of Rani Maa wearing the tiara. "And Congrats. This is so impressive."

"Oh, that." Kalpana turned away. "I would love to source handicrafts from you. What are your terms?"

"Our goal is to maximize the price received by the artisans. No middlemen. We bring artisan handicrafts directly to you." Sadhana smoothed the page of the tabloid. "Have you ever worn the tiara? So pretty."

"We pay 50 % of the retail price. I hope you don't find our purchase price too low." Kalpana sounded apologetic. "Our overheads are high. Like running this air-conditioned showroom. And running advertisements on Doordarshan." Kalpana's fingers continued to rub the Gesso work on the paintings. "Never," she said softly.

"50 % is a fair deal. Especially since your retail prices are higher than other stores." Sadhana had done her homework on the pricing structure.

"You are so reasonable. Not at all greedy."

"Let me leave the samples with you."

"I have to obey my husband. But a handicrafts store is not all about money. It is also about taking care of the artisans." Kalpana was running a pen across the width of the tabloid page. Like she was crossing out her authoritarian husband. "Even my daughter has never worn the tiara."

She had struck a chord with the wife of her husband's nemesis. Sadhana felt optimistic. "Is that a royal tradition? That only married women can wear a tiara? Like the mangalsutra for middle-class women?"

"I am a married woman. He has never allowed me to wear it. Like I am inferior."

"Safeguarding something so valuable must be tough. In today's times." As always, Siddhartha's coaching and Sadhana's own acting ability made for a powerful combination. "The tiara must be locked away in a bank."

"Hell no, he trusts no bank. We had an electronic vault installed long back with all kinds of advanced features for security. We also have Gurkhas round the clock to guard the house."

That was a lot of information. Much more than she had anticipated. Sadhana continued to look at Kalpana with a 'butter-won't-melt-in-my-mouth' expression, nodding her head in a show of empathy.

"I have access to the vault. I have never used it. When I was younger, I craved to wear the tiara. Now, with my daughter grown up, I have lost interest." Kalpana abruptly pressed the intercom, like she had second thoughts about confiding too much; she instructed the receptionist to come and collect the samples.

"Call me when you are ready to order." Sadhana gave her a L'Atelier visiting card and stood up.

"I want to increase our purchase price. And benefit the artisans more. I will see how much I can," Kalpana said. "My husband may not approve but it is not as if my business made a loss or anything last year."

"Thank You Kalpana-ji." Sadhana felt sorry for the unhappy woman in front of her, fraught with unresolved issues with her rich and powerful husband. He did sound obnoxious. "For being so kind." The words were heartfelt.

◆

**June 16, 1986**

Seemantini Abhimanyu. *The daughter of the ignoble.* Siddhartha read aloud the name from the attendance register and scanned the sea of feminine faces in front of him for a response. A plump hand shot up; a round-faced girl stood up. Excessive makeup made her look older than her classmates – their median age was eighteen. Siddhartha was inexplicably disappointed that the girl did not resemble Abhimanyu.

"Call me Simi," the girl said with a firmness that suggested she was used to ordering the people around her.

Even as his tongue read out the names of the girls and his fingers recorded their attendance status in tandem, his devious mind revisited the project charter he had formulated. Sadhana's meeting with Kalpana had confirmed that the tiara was in Abhimanyu's residence, Manyata Manor. It was so well safeguarded that it was nigh impossible to steal it without hiring a professional safebreaker. Anyway, that was not what he had intended to do. Play up to the frail ego of Simi, and ferret out the tiara from the vault; that was the ploy he had zeroed on. With the unwitting patronage of her shallow mother. Subliminal suggestions. That was his mantra for Project Tiara.

"I am your English teacher," Siddhartha addressed the class. "Substituting for Ms. Saloni Singh for the next three months."

Right place. Right time. On contacting the principal of Benson College, Siddhartha had immediately landed a short-term assignment as a substitute lecturer. Coincidentally, Saloni Singh, the college's star English lecturer, had been in an accident and was bedridden for three months. Relying on his chaste English accent, an intimate knowledge of Shakespeare, and borderline Machiavellian tactics, Siddhartha had succeeded in his mission; to be assigned to the first B.A section in which Abhimanyu's daughter belonged.

"I give you one week, to assimilate *Macbeth* and form your opinions," Siddhartha addressed his class from the lectern. "Thereafter you will dissect every scene in class, not me. I advocate class participation and want everyone of you fully engaged. Until then, we will focus on English grammar. Today, as a preamble, we review figures of speech."

Some girls stared at their books attentively; some transacted personal businesses with an obvious obtrusiveness; others were plainly distracted.

". . . Here's the smell of the blood still. Not all the perfumes of Arabia will sweeten this little hand," Siddhartha read aloud. "Identify the figure of speech Shakespeare uses here."

"Synecdoche." "Wrong."

"Apostrophe." "Wrong."

"Hyperbole." "Correct."

Simi had not shown any interest in participating, he noted. It was best he did not call any attention to her, good or bad. He did not want her to report anything about him to her father. No matter what he planned, no harm would come to her. He was neither an embittered avenger nor a hardened criminal. Just a dilettante conman out to teach his half-brother a life lesson.

◆

Siddhartha was teaching two sections of first-year B.A students and one section of the second. None of the sessions were consecutive and he spent the time between sessions in the staff common room, catching up with fellow lecturers.

The cultural festival conducted by Benson College every September was the focal point of Project Tiara. Siddhartha's devious mind had outlined a course of action that would take him to his goal. As a first step, he had befriended Asha and Bina, the lecturers in charge of the cultural activities of the college.

"What play are you staging this year?" He went for the kill.

His seemingly innocent question had led to an overheated exchange between them. Asha was keen on staging Beckett's 'Waiting for Godot' while Bina felt that the student community would boo it out for being too abstract. Bina was willing to stage any of the romantic comedies written by a contemporary playwright but Asha was certain the principal would blast them for going overboard with populism.

"You cannot go wrong with Shakespeare." Placing a copy of *Macbeth* in front of them, Siddhartha had extolled the richness of its dramatic content and the virtues of its contemporary relevance, interspersed with colourful anecdotes laced with pithy wit and scathing sarcasm. At the end of the hour, Asha and Bina were unanimous in their decision to stage *Macbeth*.

◆

'In the context of Macbeth's soliloquy on the perils of being a king, write a treatise on modern emblems of kingship – crown, coronation jewels and sceptre – Replete with illustrations and samples.' Siddhartha had thrown open a take-home assignment to his class. To make them think. He told them. Legitimate. Except he also had an ulterior motive. To get to his project goal.

Reviewing the dissertations his students had submitted, he had felt elated. As expected, Simi had succumbed to his ploy and unequivocally claimed bragging rights. "In 1971, the Constitution of India withdrew official recognition of all symbols of kings and rulers, including titles and privileges. I am a descendant of the royal family of Malnad. No one can take away that birth-right from me. Royal emblems may be a thing of the past. Yet my father continues to be the proud owner of a crown jewel given to my great-great-grand-mother by a British General as a symbol of gratitude . . ." She had provided a coloured photograph of the bejewelled tiara and an interview of her family published in a local tabloid as illustrations.

Siddhartha chose three dissertations, of which Simi's was one, for class participation. He had cast the die. And was pleasantly surprised when the bunch of teenage girls behaved exactly as he had wanted them to, rather than have a deep discussion on Macbeth's soliloquy. Was he becoming the master of human psychology?

"The tiara can't be real."

"Read the interview of my father in last month's *City Tab*," Simi said. "You will realize how real it is."

"We will believe you when we see it!"

"Let me take my father's permission first. You can all come and see it." Simi stood akimbo.

"You are a fake princess. With a fake tiara." Sniggers.

"Bring the tiara to college if you are a real princess."

"I will bring the tiara to college before the end of this term." Simi had the last word.

"Asha and Bina are looking to cast for Lady Macbeth. I think you should audition." Siddhartha did not forget to feed Simi's ego before the bell rang. "Especially since you are a real princess." And smiled to himself at his sarcasm-laden remark. For Simi suffered from the Princess Syndrome. Arising out of a sense of entitlement. Constantly bragging about herself and throwing tantrums at the slightest pretext; showing scant respect for anyone except herself; treating others as if they were mere minions.

◆

Vikas, a tall and handsome senior student who was a great orator was the unanimous choice to play Macbeth. Several girls had auditioned for the role of Lady Macbeth and three were shortlisted. Simi was one of them.

"Who will be Lady M?" Siddhartha went for the kill yet another time. And made sure he was witness to another discussion between Asha and Bina. They were both on the fence on this one. On one hand, Simi had a forceful personality and was immensely popular among her peers, making her the natural choice to play the haughty and power-hungry Lady M. On the other hand, they found Simi's arrogance off-putting and were nervous about dealing with her tantrums.

Siddhartha wanted to make sure that Simi bagged the role. That was the crux of his project charter. "Simi belongs to a royal family. She owns a real tiara." He gave them the juicy details of what had transpired in class. Whether they were mere suckers for gossip or willing victims of his gift of the gab, at the end of the hour, Asha and Bina were convinced that Simi should play Lady M.

Siddhartha could only cross and uncross his fingers. It was as if the universe were colluding with him to make Project Tiara happen.

◆

Sadhana, in the meantime, had developed her camaraderie with Kalpana. Her Mrinalini avatar had been called into the emporium, and Kalpana had granted L'Atelier a handsome order for the supply of five hundred Mysore paintings over the course of the year, with a request for enhanced gold work on the crown jewels of the gods and goddesses they depicted. Kalpana had decided to brand it as the Tiara collection. She had finalized a slightly higher purchase price than what she had initially promised.

"It may have been more to spite her husband than benefit the artisans," Sadhana, who had a first-hand feel for Kalpana's equation with Abhimanyu, confided in Siddhartha. "Whatever it is, we should not look a gift horse in the mouth. Right?"

•••

# 15.

# Birth Secret

Rahul stood staring at Nayantara's immobile face. Peace had found a home in the delicate arch of her eyebrows and the inimitable smile on her lips. The sheet that covered her was as pristine as the soul that had just left the body. He was already missing his mother terribly. How would he spend the rest of his life without her? He was only twenty years old. She had taught him to live. He would have to learn to live without her.

Grief was overpowering. What was worse? Suffering or death? When his mother lay in pain the past few weeks and the doctors had given up, he had fervently prayed to God to end her suffering. Now that God had answered his prayers, he felt adrift. He regretted praying to God to take her away. What price would he pay for such a prayer? Would bad karma consume him?

A strong and powerful hand pressed his shoulder protectively. Rahul buried his face in his father's chest, his tears flowing unchecked. The soothing touch of Indraneel's fingers did not calm him down. When Maharaj, the cook, announced the arrival of the priest, Indraneel extricated himself from Rahul's grip.

The afternoon sun filtered into the spacious room. Rahul took his mother's cold hand in his palm. The last time he had held her hand, it had been warm. In fact, a little hot, for she had been running a fever. She must have known she had reached her end or she would not have told him the big secret of her life. He should have guessed; but he had simply believed she was delirious.

Indraneel re-entered the room with an elderly man, Shastriji, the only priest known to the close-knit Indian community in Vancouver. Shastriji was a Sanskrit scholar working in the healthcare department of the Canadian Government. He moonlighted as a priest to put his knowledge of Sanskrit to good use, making nominal money in the bargain, and accumulating loads of *punya* or to use the more popular but malaprop term, good karma. Shastriji's devotion stemmed from the heart – even a vacillating semi-believer like Rahul could see that.

Shastriji performed petty purificatory movements around the bed. A trio of womenfolk walked in and looked at the men expectantly. Putting a hand each on their shoulders, Shastriji escorted Indraneel and Rahul out of the bedroom. Behind the closed doors, the womenfolk would prepare Nayantara for her final journey to the funeral pyre.

The three men came down the stairs and sat down on the living room couches. Rahul accepted the teacup that Maharaj, the family cook, thrust into his hand, but refused to eat the arrowroot biscuits.

The silence was comforting. His father was noble. Rahul looked at Indraneel's furrowed face with heightened respect. Yet the man whom he had revered for twenty years as his father was not his father. How could that be? What had he not taught him? Cycling. Maths. Chess. Driving. Honesty. Integrity. Giving. Yes. Giving. That was the biggest quality Indraneel had taught him. Refilling his teacup from the teapot, a part of him wished his mother had not told him the birth secret.

The house was filling up with friends paying their condolences. Rahul felt even lonelier amongst the familiar and not so familiar faces.

"This should not have happened to you. Your mother was only forty-two." When three aunties and two uncles had slobbered all over him, mouthing the same cliché, Rahul could take it no more. Rushing past the arms and bodies that made half-hearted attempts to hold him back, he went up the stairs and locked himself in his bedroom.

The face that stared back at him from the mirror on the wall looked tired. He had not slept in twenty-four hours. His long hair was bedraggled. He did bear a passing resemblance to his mother. The commotion bothered him. His mother's body would burn on a funeral pyre in accordance with the Hindu rites of passage. He could endure none of that. He needed a retreat.

Entering the bathroom, Rahul opened the medicine cabinet and took out a strip of Ambien. Popping three tablets into his mouth, he held his mouth to the tip of the tap. Returning to the bedroom, he undid his T-shirt and jeans, climbed into bed in his jocks and wrapped the comforter around him.

Everything was going to be fine. When he woke up it would be night. All the people would be gone. It would be time for his mother's medicine. She would have miraculously come undead. What a glorious thought. Then as days passed by, she would inexplicably stop suffering. One day in the future, he would come home to the familiar smell of bisibele bhaat in the kitchen. Indraneel, she would tell him was his biological father. God willing.

Amidst his soporific daze, Rahul heard a banging on the door. He wanted to get out of bed and open the door. Why was his body not moving? Somebody was calling his name. He tried to shout back that he was sleeping. Why would no words come out of his mouth? The sounds became feebler and then faded away. Exactly as he had wished.

◆

When Rahul opened his eyes, the room was dark. The radio clock next to the bed showed 9:00 PM.

The house was silent. Nayantara's body was no longer in the house, he could tell. Was it not his duty, as her son, to have completed her cremation rights? Is that not what the Vedas – the holy scriptures of the Hindus – prescribed? A part of him was relieved – the thought of all those rituals was intimidating. Another part of him was sad – what if Nayantara had not entered heaven because of his imprudence? Had he subliminally shirked his duty by sedating himself?

Rahul reconstructed the last scene with his mother one more time. Somehow, he had not been surprised when Nayantara had revealed her secret. Had he known the truth somewhere in his gut? His memory was vivid. The details were hazy. She had told him to go through the arrays in her closet.

Rahul's grieving heart let out a fresh bout of wails, as he walked into his mother's bedroom. A place for everything and everything in its place. All the time. That is how Nayantara maintained the house. The closet was no exception. Everything was colour-coded. The hanging saris and dresses. The folded blouses and sweaters.

Rahul opened the array of drawers. Cosmetics. Jewellery. Trinkets. He rummaged through them all. He unlocked the mirrored door of a small vanity cabinet. It contained three items. A square glass box with a white metal lid. A little round box made from ivory. A slim grey wallet of fine leather. Rahul carried them to his room.

The glass box contained a platinum necklace and matching bracelet. As far as Rahul could remember, his mother only wore gold jewellery. Never platinum. Maybe there was a reason. The ivory box was empty. Rahul placed both boxes on his desk and unzipped the wallet.

A passport size photograph in black and white. Rectangular face, deep-set eyes, unibrow, aquiline nose, a dimple on one cheek ... The man was strikingly handsome. Rahul turned the photograph over. *Abhimanyu. General Manager. Aradhana Enterprises. Bangalore.* Written in royal blue ink.

◆

Indraneel was having a solitary supper when Rahul came down the stairs.

"Forgive me, Pa." Rahul seated himself at the dining table.

"Are you feeling better, son?"

"I fell asleep. I feel foolish."

"I did the needful. Exactly as Shastriji instructed me to do."

Rahul felt lighter. His mother had gone to heaven after all. There was no way she was in hell, not when blessed with such a kind-hearted husband. "Pa, have I let you down?"

"You are still young."

Rahul would have felt better had his father scolded him. Was Indraneel over-compensating for being his stepfather? Why had Indraneel and Nayantara not had another child? Infertility or choice?

Maharaj had brought him a plate of rice and curd.

"You have been the best father any son can ask for but my heart yearns for the man whose blood flows in my veins." Rahul said abruptly.

"Nayan and I made a deliberate decision not to have another child ..." Indraneel closed his eyes.

Trying in vain to swallow a morsel of food, Rahul wondered if Indraneel was a mind reader.

"... So, we would never have to risk putting you in any kind of anguish."

"I want to go to India. To meet my meet my r r r real father."

"If that is what you want, I will not stop you."

"I don't mean to hurt you, Pa." His throat was choking. "But I feel a strange pull."

"This is your house and will always be," Indraneel said.

Rahul was fraught with apprehension. He had blurted out his desire in an instant of impulse sans reason. Was he doing the right thing by abandoning Indraneel when they were both grieving? Rahul respected Indraneel as a parent and adored him as his role model. His perfect relationship with Indraneel was cerebral and emotional. Yet something was amiss. The bond of blood?

Rahul pushed his chair back and stood up. Right or wrong, he would meet his real father and discover for himself what his future held. Rahul walked towards the telephone with a renewed resolution, to call the travel agent and collect information on airfares from Canada to India before his vacillating mind ordered a retraction.

As he picked up the receiver from the cradle, realization struck. With his mother gone, he was running away from the pleasant memories Vancouver held for him.

●●●

# 16.

# Incredible Journey

*August 1, 1986*

The flight from Vancouver had landed at Bombay airport. An awestruck Rahul looked out of the window. Everything looked dirty and crowded. Yet he felt an exhilaration. A love for the land where his mother had conceived him? After clearing immigration and customs, Rahul collected his duffel bag and walked towards the taxi stand, continually warding off the touts hounding to help him.

The rising dust did not bother him. Seated in a taxi headed towards Andheri, he rolled down the window and inhaled deeply, savouring the flavour of Indian soil. Abhimanyu. Rahul repeated the name for the zillionth time and opened the wallet to look at the black and white photograph.

The taxi stopped in front of a tall apartment complex with colourless walls and freshly washed clothes hanging from almost every balcony. Did people not feel embarrassed drying their underwear in public? The lift in the apartment complex was not working. Climbing the four flights of stairs effortlessly, Rahul tapped on the door of apartment number 425. The Chakrabortys were family friends of Indraneel.

There was no response. He knocked harder. Still no response. He banged the door latch against the door. Another door opened with a loud creak – somewhere behind him. Rahul turned around and folded his hands Namaste style.

The elderly man who stood at the door of the opposite apartment told him that the Chakrabortys were out of the country. Their daughter and son-in-law living in Dubai had died in an accident; with three orphaned grandchildren to tend to, there was no news of their return.

Rahul thanked the man and walked back down. Except for the Chakrabortys, Indraneel did not know anyone in India. Indraneel was a second-generation resident of Canada. In the twenty-plus years of their marriage, neither Indraneel nor Nayantara had ever visited India. As a young boy in school, Rahul had pestered his parents to take him to their home country during summer vacations. The trip had never materialized. Nayantara's parents were dead and her extended family had cut off relations with her over a family feud.

Rahul checked into a nearby hotel. The dingy room was badly furnished. There was no television. Water from the geyser was barely warm. The tap water reeked of chlorine. The mirror was cracked. He showered and ordered room service.

A boy barely in his teens brought him a thali meal. Child labour. Rahul seethed with anger as he polished off the Indian curries one by one, accompanied by rice pulao and naan. He did not forget to tip handsomely, the teen who returned to pick up the empty plate grinning obsequiously.

A bored Rahul stepped out of the hotel and strolled down the street. The brushed denim jeans and indigo T-shirt that made him inconspicuous in Vancouver, segregated him from the multitudes of men around him in Bombay. Most of them wore dull brown trousers and colourless shirts.

The hot afternoon sun was setting. Rahul found himself surrounded by teeming crowds of moviegoers pouring out of a cinema hall where a matinee show had ended. *Ram Teri Ganga Maili* proclaimed the poster that depicted a plump heroine called Mandakini, coyly revealing her breasts through the wet white garb of a Himalayan belle. He remembered reading in a magazine on the flight that this was India's first film with actual nudity and had translated into rich dividends at the box office. Hordes of college boys stood in front of the posters staring and salivating as they waited for their turn to enter the cinema hall for the next show.

Rahul continued to walk past the cinema hall unaffected. With the Chakrabortys not around to help him, he had to fend for himself. It did not make sense to spend any more time in Bombay. Rahul pulled out the grey wallet from his pocket. If Abhimanyu was as big a business tycoon as his mother had thought he would be, there may be a way to locate him.

Rahul headed back to the hotel and approached the receptionist. There was only one flight to Bangalore every day and the next day's flight was full. The receptionist got him confirmed tickets for the day after and booked him on a Bombay sightseeing tour the next day.

◆

*August 2, 1986*

Seated in the upper deck of Bombay's famous double-decker bus, Rahul stared out of the window. An overflowing slum offset every skyscraper that spelled the economic progress of India's financial capital, reinforcing the existential dichotomy of the great urban sprawl. The roads were narrow and crowded; yet the traffic moved with a sense of purpose and urgency.

"Gateway of India is Bombay's most famous monument, built as an arch of triumph to commemorate the visit of King George V and Queen Mary. Ironically, after the British Raj ended, this colonial symbol became an epitaph: the last of the British ships that set sail for England left from the Gateway of India." He found the tour operator's command over English praiseworthy, though the accent was pronouncedly local.

The bus stopped and the tour operator herded the occupants down the steps behind the arch to a bobbing little motor launch for a short cruise through the splendid natural harbour. Even as his eyes absorbed the picturesqueness around him, Rahul's mind wandered.

Once he reached Bangalore, how would he find his father – his dead mother's one-time fiancé? In a tale that was straight out of a storybook, Nayantara, after her betrothal, had allowed Abhimanyu to sweep her away by his charm. On discovering the future of their relationship sealed, due to reasons her father refused to reveal, she had married the Canada-based Indraneel, whose proposal she had received.

On the rebound, probably, when she discovered she was pregnant with him. Rahul steadied himself as the motor launch whirred.

Nayantara moved to Vancouver after marriage. Nayantara neither contacted Abhimanyu nor set foot in India ever again. The doting Indraneel had turned out to be the right choice. She had fallen out of love with Abhimanyu and harboured no ill will. She had vowed to tell Rahul about his parentage after he turned eighteen but her courage kept failing. Until the eve of her death.

The short cruise ended. Rahul and his co-passengers headed back to the double-decker bus, which continued its pre-determined journey, to Chowpatty, Bombay's most famous beach. Screaming kids on ferris wheels and pony rides, lazy adults snoozing in the shade of stunted trees, astrologers who waylaid passers-by to make a quick buck, self-styled gymnasts and monkey shows – the overcrowded beach was a regular carnival even at noontime on a weekday. The tour guide insisted everybody try the famed bhelpuri – a spicy snack patented by Bombay.

The Prince of Wales's Museum, Flora Fountain, Taraporewala Aquarium, Mahalaxmi Temple, Haji Ali Dargah, Nehru Planetarium – after a lightning view of Bombay's most popular tourist spots, the bus arrived at Juhu beach. Despite the atmosphere of a bourgeois paradise – playing children, courting couples and rowdy adolescents – Juhu seemed like liberation to the restless Rahul, as he retreated to the haven of the Sun and Sand hotel.

The ocean waves roared in front of him. The sun was sinking into the sea in the distant horizon. The hotel patio lights were not yet on. The surrounding foliage cast menacing shadows. Sitting at a secluded table with a magnificent view of the coast, Rahul chewed on a paneer sandwich and washed it down with lassi.

Nayantara had been vague about the break-up. Her father had committed suicide soon after her wedding. Rahul guessed Abhimanyu had bowed down to family pressures. Probably, there was a nexus between the break-up and the suicide of Nayantara's father, Rahul connected the dots. While he felt an indescribable force to unite with his biological father, would Abhimanyu accept him as his son? And embrace him into the folds of his pre-existing family?

Hearing the tour operator sound the bus horn three times in a row, Rahul got up. He had taken three steps, when a tall jeans-clad gentleman who had jumped out from a first-floor French window, came rushing towards him. Before he could move out of the way, the man had crashed into him, making Rahul fall on his back on the grass lawn. Electro-magnetic waves passed through Rahul's body.

"Excuse me." The muscular gentleman lifted himself off of Rahul.

Rahul got up and shook the shards of grass sticking to his jeans.

"Hope I did not hurt you." The gentleman gripped Rahul's hand in a powerful handshake.

"Vinod Khanna!" Rahul recognized the gentleman. One of the top stars of Hindi cinema, Vinod Khanna had taken a hiatus from his superstardom and joined the Osho cult in Oregon for a while. Rahul had read all about him in the Indian tabloid published in Vancouver.

Vinod Khanna cupped Rahul's mouth with his right palm. "I don't want junta to recognize me," he whispered in Rahul's ears.

Rahul experienced another bout of invigorating electro-magnetism start at his lips and ears and rip through his body.

"You are my favourite hero," Rahul whispered back after Vinod Khanna had removed his palm. "Sorry. I did not mean to attract junta."

Nayantara had been an avid watcher of Hindi movies, getting a steady supply of video cassettes from friends visiting India. Rahul had occasionally watched them with her, because of their melodious songs or the good looks of the actors or both.

"My dates are messed up." Vinod Khanna flashed him a wide-toothed grin. "I am supposed to be shooting for three films at the same time. I am literally running away."

Rahul had a peculiar longing to touch the deep cleft in the actor's chin. Hearing the tour operator sound the bus horn one last time, he bid the good-looking gentleman a hasty goodbye.

The tour headed south to Marine Drive – the windswept promenade flanked by the sea and a row of art décor buildings, looped between the concrete jungle of Nariman Point, Bombay's own Manhattan, and the leafy green slopes of Malabar Hill. His emotions a unique mix of restlessness and excitement, Rahul looked out of the window distractedly on hearing the tour operator say 'Queen's Necklace'. The string of glittering streetlights did look like an enormous strand of imperious jewels.

Somewhere among them lay the abode of the superstar that had crashed into him and awakened feelings that were hitherto latent. Rahul's body revelled in the memory of the lingering sensation; his questioning mind turned momentarily sedentary.

◆

### August 3, 1986

The next morning dawned bright and beautiful. The flight to Bangalore departed at two o'clock in the afternoon. The two-hour flight was uneventful. Perusing the in-flight magazines, Rahul identified a five-star hotel in Bangalore for his stay.

Victorian-style architecture, air-conditioned lobby tinged with lavender reeds, smiling staff in sharp uniform – entering Windsor Manor, Rahul felt at home for the first time since leaving Vancouver. Ensconced in a room overlooking the swimming pool, he booked a trunk call to Indraneel and ordered room service.

"How are you holding up, son?" Indraneel's kind words created a lump in Rahul's throat. Giving his father an update of his travails, his heart yearned to go back to the man who had taught him life skills.

There was a soft tap on the door. A uniformed waiter brought in a trolley filled with choice South Indian dishes.

"I love you, Pa." Rahul ended the call.

As soon as the waiter left, Rahul uncovered the lid of the dish nearest him. The sight of bisibele bhaat brought instant tears to his eyes. Nayantara's favourite recipe. "Ma, I can't live without you," he bawled.

◆

Nayantara stands under a huge tree with bright green foliage and vivid vermillion flowers, her flame-coloured sari contrasting with the foliage and competing with the flowers as it flutters in the wind. Her hand toys with her platinum necklace. A platinum bracelet adorns her wrist. A soulful tune plays in the background.

A glowing figure in a star-spangled suit and shiny shoes appears on the horizon, holding a round ivory box.

"We are a match made in heaven." Nayantara holds out her left hand.

The man kneels in front of her and hands her the ivory box.

Nayantara opens the box. There is no ring inside. She bursts into tears.

"I will not marry you." He turns his back on her.

"I love you." She clutches the ivory box to her bosom.

"I love you too," he says. "I will not lie to you."

"I have some news . . ."

"I will not go against my mother's wishes." The man walks away.

"What about your child, our child?" she calls after him.

The man walks away faster and faster.

"If only you can hear what I have to say you may change your mind."
She sails through the air after him.

The man is out of hearing distance. He has heard her. He is not one to
change his mind.

The man's face looms larger and larger. He is strikingly handsome.
Rectangular face, deep-set eyes bordered by a unibrow, aquiline nose...
"I never stopped loving Nayan, the woman I abandoned. I want to see
the son I never parented. Come to me son. I love you. Come running to
me..."

"Dad I am coming to you." Rahul woke up with a start. It was mid-
morning. The telephone receiver was off the cradle and the bedside lamps
were on. The food ordered last evening was untouched.

The scene may have been straight out of a Hindi movie. Was it a
dream or an exaggerated replay of his innermost desire? Rahul picked
up the Bangalore Yellow Pages and hunted for a listing of Aradhana
Enterprises. Not finding one, he scoured the pages for all businesses with
Aradhana in the name.

There it was. Aradhana Conglomerate, Lakeview Terrace, Main Street,
Bangalore.

●●●

# 17.

# A 1965 Interlude : Match Made in Heaven

Abhimanyu was twenty-five years old when Rani Maa had inducted him to be the General Manager of Aradhana Enterprises, the business she had daringly established and zealously nurtured. Primarily engaged in the trade and export of silks and gemstones, the firm's gross revenue had touched Rupees fifty lakhs, at the time. Abhimanyu had come with his own vision. To transform the firm into a business conglomerate grossing Rupees ten crore in revenue, before the end of the 60's.

Diversification was his mission. Strategic fit was his formula. Manufacturing industries that showed promise at that time – textiles, beverages and consumer goods – were all under the purview of large-scale industrial houses. These industrial houses, in turn, needed distribution networks to market and sell their products. Which is where opportunities existed for medium-sized businesses like Aradhana. And Rani Maa was willing to make full-blown investments to establish the networks – Aradhana was not only cash-rich but also maintained excellent relationships with its bankers.

Except that Abhimanyu wanted to adopt an approach that was less capital-intensive. Doing any kind of business within the framework of the mixed economy – newly introduced by Prime Minister Nehru in a bid to move away from unbridled capitalism – required a licence. And, getting a licence was a long-drawn process with an unpredictable outcome. Instead, Abhimanyu had proposed that Aradhana enter into business partnerships with organizations that already had such licenses. Rani Maa had reluctantly reposed confidence in her son's abilities. And recommended two prospective business partners for evaluation: Sharma Associates and Gupta Industries.

Mysore-based Gupta Industries, a major player in the distribution of textiles, silks and gemstones, was a privately held company with an all-India presence. Santosh Gupta, the son of Rani Maa's family friend, Jeweller Gupta, was the owner. He had the reputation of being financially conservative.

Bombay-based Sharma Associates was a leading distributor of consumer goods and beverages with an extended reach covering the metro areas of Bombay, Delhi, Madras, Bangalore and Calcutta. Mohanlal Sharma, the Managing Director, was a first-generation entrepreneur and had the reputation of entering new businesses with relative ease.

Abhimanyu prepared detailed dossiers on both companies. Rani Maa invited the Gupta family and the Sharma family to the annual spring festival hosted by Aradhana Enterprises. Santosh Gupta brought along his wife and children. Mohanlal Sharma arrived with his exquisite daughter, Nayantara.

◆

Match made in heaven. Bangalore newspaper-headlines had proclaimed.

A successful businessman at twenty-five, the London-returned Abhimanyu had earned the title of the most eligible bachelor of Bangalore. Being the son of a former princess and an eminent lawyer only enhanced his pedigree. Nayantara was exquisite by any standard. Triangular face with raised cheekbones and arched eyebrows, bow-shaped lips framed in a perpetual smile, a peaches and cream complexion, and svelte figure. Moreover, her Hindi-movie-heroine-induced glamorous avatar – bouffant hairstyle, sequined saris and translucent lipstick – made her the perfect candidate for a trophy wife.

Whether it was the journalistic hullabaloo or the constant nearness of Nayantara's exquisiteness and Rani Maa's subliminal goading, by the time the festival ended, Abhimanyu was very much in love with Nayantara. Their whirlwind romance continued even after Nayantara returned to Bombay. Abhimanyu became a standard fixture on the twice-a-week Bombay-Bangalore flights that Indian Airlines had instituted.

The glitzy engagement ceremony was a foregone conclusion. Clad in a blue-green ensemble, her bouffant decked with the bejewelled tiara – the family heirloom that Rani Maa had graciously lent her for the occasion – Nayantara had looked ethereal.

Wedding preparations started in full swing thereafter. Nayantara became a permanent guest of Manyata Manor. Virginity was the best wedding gift a woman could give her husband, she had believed. "We are as good as married." Abhimanyu had enticed her. The engagement had given her the licence to consummate their love. Nayantara had relented, reluctantly at first, willingly thereafter.

◆

Project planning for a business partnership between Aradhana Enterprises and Sharma Associates was underway. A separate corporate entity would be set up for the joint venture. Sharma Associates would offer the services of their distribution network to cover the range of consumer goods that Abhimanyu had zeroed in on – cosmetics, soaps and detergents, and men's suiting. Aradhana Enterprises would put up the working capital.

Everything was smooth-sailing until Abhimanyu had reviewed the distribution contracts.

Why was the distributor commission under 10 %? Abhimanyu knew that the industry standard was around 16 %. The lower commission would adversely affect the projected revenue as well as breakeven. The joint venture would fail even before taking off. They could not afford that.

Mohanlal Sharma had handled the contract negotiations. Abhimanyu booked a trunk call to Bombay.

Sharma insisted that the commission rates were fair and reflected market value. He would re-negotiate them, after the joint venture had established itself and gained more credibility.

Sharma's glib talk aroused Abhimanyu's apprehensions instead of assuaging his concerns. Abhimanyu sought help from his business contacts and met with two of the bigger manufacturing houses whose products were up for distribution. The cat was out of the bag. Sharma had struck two-tier deals with each manufacturer using two separate contracts – one on behalf of the joint venture and the second on behalf of Sharma Associates. The second contract incorporated the difference between the industry- standard rate and the lower rate negotiated on behalf of the joint venture. This difference directly benefitted Sharma Associates.

Abhimanyu was livid. It was time to confront Sharma. Before that, he had to deliver the bad news to Rani Maa.

◆

"I will tear up the existing contracts and have new ones drawn up." Abhimanyu paced the length of his mother's office room. "I want to see the expression on Sharma's face when I do that. I will supervise every aspect of the joint venture myself. I will show him who the boss is. He will have no option but to report to me."

"Call the joint venture off," she said.

"Is that not like throwing the baby with the bathwater? Incredulous."

"Sharma has no integrity. We can no longer trust him."

"What happens to our expansion plan? All my hard work?"

"I did not say the project is off," she said. "Only the joint venture with Sharma Associates."

"How is that possible? If we call off the joint venture, we have no license and no distributor network."

"You are forgetting Mr. Gupta. He has both. With some additional effort, you can rework the project plan for a joint venture with the Gupta Industries."

"Now I understand." Abhimanyu looked at his mother with heightened respect. "We should always keep our options open." Then a thought struck him. "Maa, where does that leave Nayan?"

"Mohanlal Sharma will pay a heavy price for what he did."

"I hate to hurt Nayan." Abhimanyu placed a palm on his own burning forehead. "For no fault of hers."

"All or nothing," she said. "Indian marriages are always between two families."

Abhimanyu's heart was heavy when he retired to his bedroom that night. The weight of emptiness. He and Nayantara had together created pleasant memories. Nothing was forever, not even memories.

◆

"There will be no joint venture with Sharma Associates." Abhimanyu placed several black and white photographs of the signed contracts before Mohanlal Sharma. "The two-tiered rate structure was not part of the deal."

"You misused our trust," Rani Maa said.

The three of them sat in the air-conditioned comfort offered by the Sun and Sand Hotel in Bombay. Rani Maa had organized the meeting.

"This is a common business practice in distribution circles." Unequivocally confronted with undeniable proof, Sharma had chosen to be defensive. "It is not necessary to cancel the joint venture over such small matters." He launched into a series of convoluted explanations to justify why he had done, what he had done.

The mother-son duo listened. The more he talked the more obvious it was; his ways were devious.

"The deal is off," Abhimanyu said. "Our decision is final."

"Do not forget that my daughter is your would-be wife." Sharma flared up.

"Not anymore," Rani Maa said. "I am calling off the engagement."

"Match made in heaven. Please don't do that." The wily businessman had transformed into a fawning father. "We are a middle-class family. We will lose our respect in society."

"Our decision is final," Rani Maa iterated.

"Just because you belong to a high society family you think you can use my daughter when it suits you and throw her out when you do not?" The fawning father was now a threatening tyrant. "I know your history. I will ruin your reputation ..."

"I give you two options." Rani Maa held up her hand. "One. Explain to your daughter the engagement is off. How you convince her is your problem but you will not bad-mouth my son or me under any circumstances."

"Not possible," Sharma fumed. "I will make sure she becomes your daughter-in-law."

"Option two." Rani Maa pointed to the photographs. "Your daughter will see proof of how you betrayed our trust. I will explain to her that this marriage cannot take place on account of your impropriety. She knows my son is fair-minded. She also knows my decisions are final. Don't forget that she has lived at Manyata Manor."

The mother-son duo prepared to leave. The look on Sharma's face said that they had struck at his Achilles heel. Nayantara was unaware of her father's treachery.

"I will go with the first option." Sharma blocked their way as they got up to go. "If you pay me one lakh rupees as compensation for ruining my daughter's reputation."

"Mr. Sharma, please allow us to pass." Rani Maa looked around as if to beckon the hotel staff. "There will be no negotiation." She turned to Abhimanyu. "Can you arrange for Nayantara to meet with us?"

"Wait." Sharma moved away. "Give me 24 hours. I will let you know my decision."

"If we have not heard from you by tomorrow, we will choose option two. And come down to meet with your daughter." Her head held high, Rani Maa walked out of the Sun and Sand Hotel, her son following a step behind.

When Rani Maa and Abhimanyu reached Bangalore the same evening – an urgent message awaited them from Mohanlal Sharma. "Option one."

◆

"What do you think of Kalpana?" Rani Maa asked Abhimanyu, as they drove down from Bangalore to Mysore to finalize the joint venture with Gupta Industries.

"You mean, Gupta uncle's daughter? What about her?"

"When I selected the Guptas and Sharmas for evaluation as partners they fulfilled two criteria. One, their business standing. Two, they both had eligible daughters."

"Are you telling me to marry her?" Abhimanyu had not paid Kalpana any attention during the Nayantara chapter.

"I am asking you to consider the proposition. Kalpana has completed her graduation at Sofia College. She is sociable but shy. Mainly her mother's influence."

The car stopped in front of Indigo Castle. Rani Maa had converted her father's ancient mansion into a holiday retreat for Abhimanyu and herself. Vikramaditya did not stay there when he visited Mysore; he always stayed at Panchsheel Villa with his 'first' family.

"A joint venture may let us get ahead for a while. In the long run, combining the two businesses is the key to flourish. A merger of sorts."

Abhimanyu was tongue-tied. His mother seemed to think of everything.

"I will respect your decision, whatever it is," Rani Maa said. "I have invited Santosh Gupta and his daughter over. Meet her once."

When the father-daughter duo arrived, Rani Maa stayed with Santosh Gupta, reviewing the project plan and the contracts, while Abhimanyu took Kalpana, whom he found pleasingly pretty and quietly poised, on a tour of Indigo Castle.

Kalpana's favourite topics were dresses and accessories, Hindi movies and pop songs, and the who's who she was friends with, not necessarily in that order. She had no interest in her father's business; she was not in the habit of reading the newspaper; she had no views on the world economy. Abhimanyu soon got bored.

Talking to Santosh Gupta, Abhimanyu learnt that many top government officials were close friends of the unassuming man and that Gupta Industries had longstanding relationships with most textile manufacturers. Neither Kalpana nor her sisters possessed any aptitude for business. Santosh Gupta was looking out for young blood to infuse another lease of life to his stagnating business. He hinted at his readiness to hand over the reins to his future son-in-law, his eyes shining with anticipation.

◆

"Santosh Gupta and his wife are coming over to make an official proposal," Rani Maa told Abhimanyu at dinner. "What is your decision?"

"Kalpana is pleasant." Abhimanyu weighed his answer. "But she lacks the vibrancy of Nayan."

"She will make a good hostess," Rani Maa added.

"And we could be running a multi-crore empire in a few years." Abhimanyu's sharp mind was making financial projections.

"Santosh Gupta is trustworthy. His father was like family."

"We should talk to Appa. If he approves the match you can go ahead." He exchanged a knowing look with his mother.

"As luck would have it, he is in Mysore this week. I will send for him."

Abhimanyu grimaced. Sharing his father with his 'first' family was the only blot in an otherwise perfect life.

◆

Over the course of the next few months, the joint venture between Aradhana Enterprises and Gupta Industries had launched to a glorious start. Abhimanyu got married to Kalpana at a modest ceremony in Mysore. Followed by a cocktail party in Bangalore. Kalpana did not get the opportunity to wear the royal tiara on either occasion. Rani Maa had worn it herself.

Honeymooning with his new wife in the Swiss Alps, Abhimanyu did not remember even for a moment that Nayantara had offered him her virginity. As a wedding gift. There had been no wedding. What then had happened of her gift?

•••

# 18.

# Hello, Father

"What does the crystal ball say?" Abhimanyu asked Varun who sat across from him, in the air-conditioned comfort of the penthouse office.

"The auditors just approved the financial statements for the fiscal year that ended March 31. Revenue as you are aware, hit the Rupees fifty crore milestone last November and soared to Rupees fifty-four and a half crores for the fiscal year, surpassing all projections and expectations." Varun held out a computer printout. "Gross profit was twenty percent for the conglomerate, up by one percent from the previous year. Net profit was twelve and a half percent. The jewellery business, however, recorded a nominal loss. After we had to write off the cost of the stolen jewellery."

The heist was a blot that would always haunt him. Abhimanyu cursed under his breath. For the first time in the history of Aradhana, an established business unit had not recorded a book profit.

"I was saving the best for the last." Varun handed him a faxed document. "The license for the manufacture of polyester yarn has been approved. CRISIL has raised our credit rating to AAA. Our share prices will soon trade higher by 25 % to 35 %."

"A wonderful precursor for the upcoming debenture issue." Abhimanyu's face broke into a smile.

The intercom buzzed. "Sir, there is a personal call for you on line one," Veronica announced. "A young man from Canada."

"What does he want?"

"Says he will only talk to you."

"Let me take your leave." Varun placed several annual reports of competitor companies on Abhimanyu's desk. "Some business intelligence."

Abhimanyu waited until Varun had vacated the cabin to switch on the speaker. He would normally not have taken the call from a perfect stranger that Veronica was unable to screen. His business had transcended exciting milestones, and his mood was jubilant. He would get whatever nuisance this was, out of the way.

"Good morning, Sir."

The soft western accent perked up Abhimanyu. "How can I help you?"

"May I meet with you? I have a confidential matter to discuss."

"I am a busy man. We can talk over the phone. Now."

"If I could, I would. I have to meet you in person."

"I have a flight to catch." Abhimanyu thrust the annual reports Varun had left on his desk, into the topmost drawer.

"I only need a few minutes."

"My few minutes are very valuable." Abhimanyu shoved the drawer with his left hand. The drawer refused to slide back. "Shoot." He rattled the drawer with all his might.

"Excuse me, Sir?"

Asking the caller to hold, Abhimanyu deftly slid out the top drawer from its grooves and picked up the objects – three photographs – that were causing the obstruction. "For me, time translates to money." He said into the phone. Placing the photographs on the table, he found himself staring into the eyes of an exquisite woman – triangular face, arched eyebrows, bouffant hairstyle.

"Sir, please don't disappoint me. I have come all the way from Canada."

*Westerners were super-polite.* Abhimanyu held up the three photographs as if they were cards dealt to him in a game of flush. Nayantara posed alone in the first two while he stood to her left in the third. 'A match made in heaven.' 'An ethereal couple.' That is what the newspapers had called them.

"There is a secret you should know." The patient voice on the phone was persistent.

"Secret?" Abhimanyu did not even know anyone who lived in Canada. What possible secret would this boy reveal? "Who are you?"

"My name is Rahul."

Abhimanyu put the photographs back inside the drawer. Nayantara was a closed chapter. He did not believe in looking back; he had always looked ahead, without any compunction.

"I have with me a few precious things you gifted someone special." He heard Rahul say.

*What in the big bamboozled world was this?* He would not run the risk of some rumourmongering stranger from a foreign country going to press and kicking up a scandal. "I will spare you five minutes. In exactly twenty-five minutes." Abhimanyu redirected the call back to Veronica.

Reclining the chair, Abhimanyu propped his feet on the desk. *Nayantara. What had happened of her?* Having walked out of her life more than twenty years ago, he had rarely thought of her. Yet, he had preserved those three photographs. On the rare occasions, he came across them, as he had this day, they did not give him a soft ache in the heart. He looked at them with admiration, every time. Nayantara was exquisite and as English poets were oft to quote, a thing of beauty is a joy forever!

◆

Life always offers us options. Yet we can only make one set of choices in each situation. We will never know how things would have been, had we made a different set of choices. No matter what our choices are, human nature dreads in prospect and regrets in retrospect.

Dressed in a white shirt and indigo jeans, Rahul sat in the back seat of a local cab and chewed his nails. His duffel bag lay next to him. The poise he had posed on the phone had vanished. He had checked out of Windsor Manor. The hefty bill had exhausted his stash of traveller cheques. Rather boldly, he had made a unilateral decision to live with his newfound father, henceforth.

The cab dropped him off at the Aradhana Conglomerate address in downtown Bangalore. Veronica showed Rahul the way to Abhimanyu's cabin.

Rahul found himself standing in front of a U-shaped desk, behind which sat Abhimanyu, regal as a king occupying his throne, his stare fixed on Rahul, one end of his unibrow raised. The view offered by the bay window was spectacular. The morning sun filtered in through the vertical slits of the venetian blinds.

Abhimanyu looked at his watch and back at Rahul. "You have three minutes left out of your five."

Rahul feasted on his nails. Abhimanyu's classic good looks were intact. The grey at his temples and the lines on his forehead enhanced his grace. His deep voice was captivating, his speaking style commanding. Though he had rehearsed the scene several times in the last few days, Rahul was unsure where to begin. Delving in his pockets, he pulled out a slim grey wallet of fine leather and handed the passport-sized photograph to Abhimanyu.

"Where did you get my photograph?" Abhimanyu turned it over. "Aradhana Enterprises. This is twenty years old. You are not looking for a job, are you?"

Rahul rummaged inside his duffel bag.

"Your time is up." Abhimanyu flashed his Bulgari watch in Rahul's direction. "Maybe I should call security."

Rahul placed the square glass box and the round ivory box on the desk.

"Is this really the secret?" Abhimanyu opened the metal lid on the glass box. "Where did you get these?" He pulled out the platinum necklace and bracelet that lay inside.

"I inherited them."

"Don't talk in riddles." Abhimanyu locked eyes with Rahul.

Rahul watched intently, to catch a flicker of recognition. Would the jewellery bring back any memories?

"Tell me the truth." Abhimanyu fiddled with the two boxes and the contents. The expression on his face was inscrutable.

This was not how Rahul had envisioned the scene. He had expected Abhimanyu to recognize him instantly on seeing the mementos. "I am your son," he said with hesitation.

"Who?" Abhimanyu got up and came around.

"Your son." Rahul could feel the magnetic energy of his father's presence. He smelled nice. Versace Blue. Rahul recognized the cologne. Haltingly, Rahul gave his father a scattered narration of what his mother had told him.

Abhimanyu listened without interrupting. The telephone rang but he did not pick it up. "May her soul rest in peace." He closed his eyes.

"Nayan never told me she was expecting you." His voice was no longer commanding.

Rahul sat down. Would that have changed your mind? He wanted to ask.

"Where are you staying?" Abhimanyu asked. After what seemed like eternity.

"I just checked out of Windsor Manor."

"Are you going back to Vancouver?"

"I came here to live with you."

"If I say, no?"

"I will go back to Pa." Rahul shuffled his feet.

"You can come and stay with me. Be my guest."

"Will I be known as your son."

"No. Not now. I will decide when the time is right. Deal?" Abhimanyu's contorted face reminded Rahul of an athlete on the field, on the verge of victory. "Deal." Rahul bent down and touched his father's feet.

"Keep this safe." Abhimanyu had returned the boxes and the jewellery to Rahul.

◆

Sitting in the back seat of Abhimanyu's chauffeur-driven Toyota that zoomed down the empty streets of Bangalore in the bright afternoon sun, Rahul tried to draw Abhimanyu into a conversation on the nature of his relationship with Nayantara. He was keen to find out what had gone wrong.

Abhimanyu, who was leafing through the pages of The Economic Times, was categorical in his refusal to talk at length. "We made decisions that were appropriate under those circumstances. Going back and analysing them in the light of subsequent events is an exercise in futility. Hindsight yields nothing other than despair. My motto: No regrets."

Rahul turned his attention to the passing scenery. Abhimanyu was not particularly sentimental about Nayantara or their affair. *What is his motivation in inviting me to stay with him?* Unconditional love for his newfound son seemed unlikely.

The Toyota had entered the manicured grounds of a palatial house in one of the poshest localities of Bangalore. Amidst apple trees and orange trees, musical fountains and manicured lawns, next to an oval swimming pool of sparkling blue water, stood a tall building in pale pink sandstone, Manyata Manor.

The chauffeur held the car door open. The Gurkha rang the front doorbell. A uniformed servant boy who had appeared from within the house took charge of Rahul's duffel bag. Rahul trailed Abhimanyu by a few steps as they entered the foyer. A well-groomed woman and a plumpish teenager, were engaged in a private conversation on the plush settee. Neither paid any heed to the entry of the two men.

"My wife, Kalpana. Daughter, Simi." Abhimanyu introduced them to Rahul.

"Meet Rahul from Vancouver, Canada. The son of a friend. He is here for an internship." Abhimanyu introduced Rahul to them.

"Hi." Simi gave him a sterile stare and stalked off.

Kalpana instructed the servant boy to take care of Rahul. "I am off to an exhibition. Bangalore Art Gallery." She had barely glanced at Rahul before trotting out.

Rudeness or indifference? Rahul was too excited by the prospect of living with his father to be bothered by the behaviour of the mother and daughter duo.

Rahul was allotted the premium guest suite on the second floor of the main wing. His laundry was whisked away as soon as he was out of the shower. After a three-course South Indian lunch served by a uniformed butler, the uniformed servant-boy took Rahul on a guided tour of the four floors and three wings of Manyata Manor. The west wing housed a ballroom for entertaining guests and the north wing housed Abhimanyu's study, a library of books and records, and a game room, Rahul learnt.

◆

*August 5, 1986*

"You will intern at my office." On discovering that Rahul was a whiz with computers, Abhimanyu told Rahul the next morning. "I want you to help with all our office initiatives – running database queries, building spreadsheet models, and training Veronica in using word processing software."

Rahul agreed wholeheartedly. He was keen to win the approval of his powerful and authoritarian father, whose mere presence he found protectively comforting.

"Varun, my corporate planning manager, is on vacation. Otherwise, I would have appointed him as your mentor," Abhimanyu said, as they rode the elevator to the fifth floor of the Lakeview Terrace.

Veronica organized a cubicle for Rahul in the penthouse foyer area.

"Get us admission forms for Bangalore University's B.E Electronics course. Talk to Munimji." Abhimanyu's instruction sent Veronica scurrying to one of the lower floors.

Rahul was wonderstruck. It had been less than 24 hours since his arrival. And his father was already organizing admission forms to a four-year under-graduate course in Electronics Engineering. "In Vancouver, I was doing my undergrad in Psychology."

"In India, you must do as Indians do. Remember – one day you will run the Aradhana Conglomerate. First requirement, an Engineering degree."

"Dad, I am not good at Advanced Math." Rahul wanted to escape from the Engineering monster he had always dreaded.

"We call it Maths. I can afford the best tutors."

"What if I do my Bachelor's in Business instead of Engineering?"

"No. An Engineering degree lays the best foundation. After graduation, you manage one of our business divisions – Refrigerators or Televisions. Two years later, you do your MBA. The Indian Institute of Management, Bangalore is number one. Back to business after that. Before you hit thirty – I make you CEO."

*What a control freak!* This was not a plan. It was a fucking blueprint. Rahul switched on the computer. *A readymade heir to take his name forward. Is that my father's motivation for inviting me to live with him?* "First I want to be known as your son."

"You have to wait. Until circumstances are right. I cannot risk a scandal."

•••

# 19.

# A Matter of Honour

*September 1, 1986*

Play rehearsals were in full swing. The time Siddhartha spent in the common room and his close association with Asha and Bina had stood him in good stead, to keep a finger on the pulse of Project Tiara. Simi seemed serious about wearing the royal tiara. She had ordered a teal ball gown from Paris, to go with it. Asha and Bina planned to hold a dress rehearsal in the college auditorium.

It was time to bring in Sadhana's second role. "Do you have a professional make-up artiste?" Siddhartha had enquired.

Asha and Bina looked at each other and rolled their eyes. They were obviously not that well planned.

The same evening when Asha and Bina were at the bus stop, a petite woman slipped into the queue.

Siddhartha, who had chosen a vantage point within the college campus that gave him a partial view of the bus stop while staying hidden behind a cluster of trees, let out a low whistle. He would have a tough time recognizing his own wife!

Translucent makeup had toned the skin of her face and neck two shades lighter. Her eyebrows were thicker, eyelashes longer, lips fuller and cheekbones higher – Sadhana had painstakingly altered herself into the persona of Carmelita, the makeup artist. A short wig and a long floral dress paired with platform heels, completed the transformation. In her hand, Sadhana held a transparent box full of beauty products.

Siddhartha watched Sadhana strike a conversation with Asha and Bina. The two lecturers repeatedly pointed to the box in Sadhana's hand, as they carried on an animated three-way chat. Exactly as he had scripted the scene and rehearsed it with Sadhana the previous evening, he presumed.

The bus that would carry Asha and Bina to their destination had arrived. Sadhana stood waving until the bus disappeared.

"Success?" Siddhartha approached her with rapid strides.

"A trial run first. They asked me to apply make-up on the girl playing Lady Macbeth. At the dress rehearsal."

"Did they say anything about payment?"

"It will take me around four hours to apply makeup on the entire cast. I quoted eight hundred rupees."

"They may ask you to settle for a little less."

"I will accept reluctantly. No bargaining."

"You passed the test," Siddhartha gave her a high five and hailed a passing auto. "You look gorgeous. A real Anglo-Indian."

"It is the expensive wig. I am lucky Prabhat-Kala let me keep it."

"I want you to buy a more modern dress to go with your persona." The long dress was another relic from her acting days.

"I need some real cosmetics." She wiped her brow with the edge of her handkerchief. "To do the make-up. Do we have the money?"

"I will make a visit to the Holiday Inn. And scout for a credit card."

Horns blared all around them. There was a traffic jam on the flyover leading to North Bangalore. It would take them another hour to reach home. Though Siddhartha opened Jeffrey Archer's *A Matter of Honour* to the bookmarked page, the thriller failed to hold his interest for very long. His own life promised more excitement than any novel could offer!

•••

# 20.

# May Truth Prevail

*September 5, 1986*

"What do you think of Pooja?" Abhimanyu stood at the door of Rahul's bedroom.

Rahul, who sat at the desk, with the latest edition of Filmfare, his eyes riveted on the picture of a lean and muscular Jackie Shroff clad in a leather G-string, closed the magazine, and swivelled his chair around.

"Pooja's father is expanding his business overseas. He has invited us to the inauguration party in Goa." Abhimanyu had stepped into the room.

"I don't like Pooja that much. She is bossy."

"I want you to go."

"I would rather be with you," Rahul said.

The Bangalore University had delayed engineering admissions. The office initiatives kept Rahul busy. He had spent almost all his time with his father the last month. Every day, they had lunch together in one of the exotic restaurants of the Five Star Hotels that proliferated downtown Bangalore. In the evening, father and son bonded over a game of billiards or golf, at the Cantonment club or the Golf club. Returning from the club, they had dinner together at home. Abhimanyu on his part had never missed an opportunity to coach Rahul on the rules of business engagement.

"I promised to send you," Abhimanyu said. "You don't have a choice."

"How long is the flight?" Rahul could not hide his irritation.

"Indian Airlines does not operate any flight between Bangalore and Goa."

"How long is the drive?" Rahul could not hide his consternation. "I can't sit in a car that long. Not with the poor bathroom facilities. . ."

"Chartered private jet. Pooja's father is a crorepati, many times over. What you call a multi-millionaire."

"College may start next month. I must fill the admission forms."

"That should not take you more than an hour," Abhimanyu said. "Stop making excuses."

"Do I get back the same evening?"

"A couple of nights. You will stay at the Holiday Inn."

"I don't want to fall sick."

"Pooja will take good care of you." Abhimanyu gave him a friendly wink. "Make the best use of the trip."

Why was his father thrusting this bossy girl on him? *I must learn the art of asserting myself when dealing with him.*

"Buy new clothes. Formals. At the Men's Favourite Shop. Charge it to my account." Abhimanyu had departed.

*The Abhimanyu way.* Rahul reopened the Filmfare to feast his eyes on Jackie Shroff's buff body one more time. The television in the lobby was beaming the weekly song and dance program, Chitrahaar. Listening to what was a prayer song, Rahul felt peculiarly peaceful. 'Itni shakti hamein dena daata; Mann ka viswas kamzor hona; Hum chalein ek raste se humse; Bhool kar bhi koi bhool ho na'. He barely understood Hindi. He could only say a few sentences with a stilted accent. Yet his intuition told him that the song was an appeal to the Almighty for emotional strength.

◆

### September 13, 1986

Rahul sat next to Pooja in her father's private jet. The morning sun shone in the brilliant blue sky patterned with fluffy white clouds. There were about fifteen people in the plane –members of Pooja's wealthy family.

"I have never been to Canada or the US. When are you going back? We holidayed in Thailand last year and plan to visit Egypt this year. Last year I spent the entire summer in Australia. My aunt lives there..." Pooja suffered from verbal diarrhoea.

Dusky skin, bobbed hair, busty figure – Rahul surveyed her appearance through the corner of his eye. Pooja was attractive albeit a tad sturdy for his taste.

"Don't ever settle in India," she said. "Here, give me your hand."

Reading a girl's palm was an old trick used by boys so that they get to hold a girl's hand. Was there a gender reversal?

Pooja traced the lines on his palm with her painted fingernails. "Such long fingers. Very artistic. Don't ever become an Engineer or a Doctor."

"You are kidding. Anyway, I don't want to be an Engineer."

"You have an average lifeline. Sixty-seven years at best." Pooja's prophecy flow was unabated. "You will have several relationships. Three at least." She massaged his fingers lightly. "You will never not be in love."

"You don't really know this stuff, do you?"

"Poor darling." Pooja burst into peals of laughter as Rahul watched her with amusement. "See no lies. Hear no lies. Say no lies. Whatever." She traced imaginary lines around his eyes, ears and lips with her fingers. "Guess what?" Her hand came to rest on his upper thigh.

Rahul ached to feel a rousing in his loins. I need to do it once. *With a girl. Then there will be no stopping. I will know I am heterosexual.* "You want me to be your boyfriend?"

"No. idiot. I have met the man of my dreams." Pooja draped a scarf over her head and acted coy. "Anil Ambani has asked me out on a date. Our family dined with the Ambanis last week ... You do not know who they are? Oh, I forget you do not live here. They are the owners of Reliance Industries."

Rahul sighed. Pooja was dreaming of being a trophy wife to the scion of India's leading industrialist. Trying to score with her would be an exercise in futility.

◆

The party – a high society affair – was in full swing at The Holiday Inn's banquet hall. Rahul leaned against the wall and yawned. Nobody there knew him. None showed an interest in getting to know him. He tried to catch Pooja's attention but in vain. Clad in a western dress that silhouetted her sturdy figure, she was engaged in meeting and greeting the glitterati gracing the glamorous occasion.

Rahul drained the last drops of beer from his mug. The high density of people aggravated his claustrophobia. He was sweating profusely under the stiff shirt collar and the purple tie felt like a noose. He closed his eyes to shut off the light from the scores of chandeliers descended from the high ceiling.

"You." Hearing peals of laughter, he opened his eyes with a start.

"Chandni – this is Rahul. My friend from Canada." Pooja introduced him to a slender lass standing next to her. "Rahul – Chandni will be performing at our party today. And she has just signed her first film."

Rahul loosened his purple tie. "Hello, Ms. Heroine."

"It is a small role." Chandni smiled shyly and extended her hand. "Opposite Jackie Shroff."

Rahul held her soft palm longer than necessary.

The bright lights began to dim. A makeshift dais had made its appearance at the centre of the banquet hall. "Go." Pooja pushed Chandni towards the dais. The orchestra started playing a rock and roll number. Chandni started to dance. With astounding grace.

Rahul riveted his gaze on the gyrating Chandni. Clad in a sequined dress with spaghetti straps, she looked alluring under the strobe lights. The orchestra had changed to a fast-paced dance number. Several guests joined Chandni on the dance floor. She shimmered among them like a queen bee.

Rahul weaved through the dancing couples and approached her. The next song was a romantic number. Chandni caught Rahul in a tight embrace and swayed to the music.

"You are a good dancer." Rahul furtively looked down her tiny cleavage, and hoped she was eighteen or older. "What is your role in the movie?"

"Cabaret dancer." There was a naiveté in the eyes that stared back at him. The sparkling powder smeared on her cheeks added to the allure. "I wish the movie becomes a hit. I want to be Jackie Shroff Sir's heroine next time."

"Have you met him?" he asked.

"Not yet." Her soft silky hair caressed his cheeks and shoulders as she shook her head. As they performed a slow waltz, she pressed her tiny body into Rahul's crotch gently, her small breasts delicately brushing against his chest.

Rahul could feel the soft stirring in his loins languorously burgeoning into a pleasant pulsation. When the music and dance ended and they joined the other guests at dinner, Chandni continued to cling to him.

Neither had an appetite for the entrees. As they sat at the table pretending to eat and played footsie under the table, their eyes made visceral pacts on what they would do next. Before dessert could arrive, they had pulled off an inconspicuous exit and ridden the elevator to Chandni's room. Rahul had not wanted to go to his own own since Pooja was the occupant of the adjacent room.

As soon as she had closed the door behind them, Chandni made brisk moves – slipping off her gown and laying on the bed clad in a flimsy bra and panties, her lips and legs parted. The room was dark save for the glow from a lava lamp on the headboard.

Rahul removed his blazer and draped it on the back of a chair. The tie, shirt and vest followed suit. He unbuckled his belt and hesitated. The tentative state of his tented tumescence did not guarantee a satisfactory performance.

Rahul need not have worried. Chandni had sprung from the bed and joined him. Pulling down his pants with her slender fingers, she tore off his white briefs with her pearly teeth.

Rahul closed his eyes. Jackie Shroff's muscular body pervaded his mind; the G-string had come undone. Chandni's mouth encircled his turgescence. Rahul's testosterone rush overtook his fears as his hips gyrated in slow harmony ...

◆

### September 14, 1986

I *am no longer a virgin.* When Rahul opened his eyes, the sun streamed into the room. Chandni sat on the bed clad in a negligee and smoked a joint. She may have been feasting on his youthful nakedness – there was a glint of wicked glee in her eye. On seeing him awake, she stroked his lower body with her feet.

Rahul felt no sensation. Collecting his clothes from the chair, he went into the bathroom and locked the door. Was he heterosexual yet? Rahul doused his hair with clinic shampoo and rubbed it vigorously to rouse a rich lather. Maybe he should refrain from labelling himself one-way or the other. Sexuality was not binary. Or was it?

When he came out of the bathroom fully dressed, Chandni was spiralling to the beats of a song on the radio, Rahul's purple tie slung around her neck.

"You have done me a huge favour." Rahul picked up his blazer.

She stopped dancing. "I fell in love with you the minute I saw you."

"I will never forget you." He would never see her again. Rahul wanted to give her a gift. The only valuable he had on him was a small gold chain that had belonged to Nayantara. He did not want to part with that.

"You are so cute. And kind." Chandni picked up her joint. "I am sick of fucking all those old farts . . ."

"I want you to have this." Rahul pulled out a Mont Blanc pen from his blazer pocket.

"Not for me." Chandni shook her head. "The pen is bloody expensive."

"A small gift from me."

"Only if you let me keep this." She fingered the purple tie encircling her neck.

The tie was a gift from Indraneel on his eighteenth birthday, but Rahul did not have the heart to disappoint her. He let her keep both the tie and the pen.

Chandni stared at the pen. "What does RR stand for?"

"Rahul Roy."

"Gentleman. You are a real gentleman." Chandni embraced him. Her cheeks were wet. "The pen is precious. I will preserve it forever."

◆

It was early evening when Pooja's driver dropped off Rahul in the circular canopied driveway of Manyata Manor. All the musical fountains were on and the trees were covered with garden lights.

Rahul was glad to be back. He had missed his father or rather his overpowering presence. Going up the stairs two at a time, when he reached the second-floor loft, instead of going to the guest suite in the main wing, he headed towards the sky bridge, that led to the north wing, which was exclusively Abhimanyu's territory. Was he getting used to being told by his father what to do? Did that somehow make his life less complicated, taking the pressure off him from making his own decisions? Rahul was unsure.

The familiar smell of his father's study was comforting. Abhimanyu sat behind his desk reviewing legal-looking documents. After he had enquired about the Goa trip, Abhimanyu handed Rahul a folder. "Sign the forms for your college admission. I had Veronica fill them out for you."

Ignoring the veiled reprimand, Rahul opened the folder. His name was listed as Rahul Roy. Father's name was listed as Indraneel Roy. Abhimanyu's name appeared against the box for a local guardian. "Aren't we disclosing our relationship?"

"Not now."

*I hate lies.* "I want to be known as your son."

"You will. When I am ready. I will have to legally adopt you."

"Does it mean I will no longer be known as Pa's son . . .?"

"Yes."

Rahul flopped down on a nearby chair. As much as he wanted to be known as Abhimanyu's son, he was unprepared to relinquish the identity of the past twenty years. He did not want to hurt Indraneel for any reason.

"Get up and get ready," Abhimanyu ordered him. "There is a party tonight. To celebrate Kalpana's birthday. Several big shots will be there. I want to introduce you to them."

"As your son?"

"No." Abhimanyu's voice was stern. "Did we not just go through that? Dress properly. No jeans."

A sulking Rahul picked up the folder. "I will sign later."

"Give the signed forms to Veronica tomorrow." Abhimanyu stood up. "Don't forget again."

◆

Back in the guest suite, Rahul unbuttoned his shirt to the waist and switched on the fan full blast. Yet he felt suffocated. He did not want to wear formal clothes. He did not want to attend the stuck-up party. He did not want to meet pretty girls. He did not want to do Engineering. The list was growing.

Abhimanyu was demanding and authoritarian. He was also successful. *I chose Abhimanyu over Indraneel and entered his life, unannounced. Rahul stripped off his clothes and walked to the bathroom. I cannot disappoint him.*

His life in Vancouver had been carefree. He had enjoyed being the lazy bum. If his grades were average or above, Indraneel and Nayantara had let him be. They had never ever interfered with the choice of his clothes or courses or hobbies or friends.

Suede pants and the mock turtle neck sweater it would be. After an invigorating shower, when Rahul opened the door to the walk-in-closet, a whiff of Versace attacked his nostrils. Abhimanyu's signature cologne. Rahul froze. What would Abhimanyu have been doing in there? He looked around. Everything seemed to be in place – exactly as he had left it. Rahul kneeled and lifted the stacks of towels in the lowest drawer. The magazines with pictures of gorgeous men were gone! Including the Filmfare with Jackie Shroff in a G-string.

Rahul distinctly remembered stashing them underneath the linen before leaving for Goa. Was Abhimanyu spying on him?

◆

It was after eight o'clock when Rahul came down to the ballroom. Ivory and gold wall paper, wall to wall carpeting, antique chandeliers, overstuffed furniture, a carved piano in the far end – the ballroom was the epitome of clichéd opulence.

Abhimanyu welcomed the guests alongside a glamourous-looking Kalpana – the who's who of Bangalore – as he had called them. Simi and her friends stood in the centre of the ballroom giggling. Simi introduced Rahul as her father's business associate from Canada. After a few polite hello's – the boys and girls resumed their conversations amongst themselves. A bored Rahul walked over to Abhimanyu. He did not know anyone else at the party. The staff members with whom he interacted at Abhimanyu's office were not invited. The aristocracy did not socialize with the hoi polloi.

Abhimanyu introduced Rahul to the VIPs with a peculiar sense of pride. "The intern from Canada ... my friend's son ... my business protégé..." Every description except the one Rahul wanted to hear. Rahul had to check his tongue several times from calling him Dad. Abhimanyu Uncle... Mr. Abhimanyu ... Abhimanyu Sir ... sounded untruthful.

Uniformed waiters walked around serving hors d'oeuvres – exotic cheeses and olives, chili chicken and spiced paneer. The bar was overflowing with choice liquor from around the world and was managed by professional bartenders borrowed from the golf club. Several bottles of champagne had been opened and the corks sent flying. An event coordinator conducted party games, primarily for the children. A radio artiste played the piano.

Rahul stayed glued to Abhimanyu. Worried that his father had confiscated the magazines, he kept analysing his every word for tell-tale signs.

"Circulate." Abhimanyu hissed in Rahul's ears. "Pretty girls."

No way. Rahul slipped away. Back in his room, he looked for the magazines again, in the closet and the bedroom, but could not find them.

A seven-course sit-down dinner was being served when he returned. Sitting next to Abhimanyu, Rahul refrained from looking at Kalpana – her fuming eyes bore into him from across the table. What was she mad about?

Dessert was served to synchronize with the cutting of the cake at midnight. Kalpana blew away the single candle stuck in the middle of a three-tiered cake with exaggerated gusto and stuffed a piece in Simi's mouth.

◆

The last of the guests had left and the ballroom lights dimmed. Kalpana was giving instructions to the staff members who were in the process of cleaning up the place. Simi had retreated to her bedroom.

Abhimanyu and Rahul walked down the carpeted corridor leading back to the main wing. The dim lit walls with black and white family photographs from another era created an eerie sensation – like several generations of forefathers simultaneously watched them through a telescope. Kalpana trailed them.

"You might as well get used to this lifestyle," Abhimanyu said. "Many of my friends enquired about you. They are filthy rich. Some of them live in houses twice as big."

Rahul had no interest in the net worth of his father's friends. Abhimanyu's unending zeal for money never ceased to shock him.

The three of them walked through the winding hallway and arrived at an open foyer. Abhimanyu pressed the elevator button to take them to the upper floors. Rahul would have preferred to take the stairs instead but tagged along, not wanting to appear impolite. When the elevator reached the first floor, Abhimanyu and Kalpana got out. Rahul was about to close the elevator door and continue up to the second floor when he saw that Kalpana was holding the button on the outer wall, pressed.

"I have to talk to you and you." She looked from Abhimanyu to Rahul. "Now."

An obedient Rahul followed his father and his father's wife as they marched towards their master suite. He had never visited the first floor or the master-suite before. When he spotted a colour portrait of a regal-looking woman right next to the double Georgian door, he stopped, enchanted. "Rani Maa."

Abhimanyu and Kalpana entered their suite. Abhimanyu turned the lights on and adjusted the brightness. Kalpana unclasped her dangling necklaces, flung them on the bed and poured herself a goblet of wine.

Rahul continued to stand at the door of the suite. The décor was more modern than the rest of the house. A four-canopy bed was visible through the glass door leading from the living space to the bedroom. One wall of the suite led to the terrace balcony. On the opposite wall, adjacent to an alcove, three doors were ajar – giving a peek into what lay beyond – a clothes closet, a bathroom and a Jacuzzi.

"I want to know your real relationship with Rahul." Kalpana stood in the centre of the living space, one hand on her hip, facing Abhimanyu who sat on the settee, legs crossed and hands clasped behind his neck.

Rahul stepped in. Intuition told him, Kalpana had discovered the truth. The clock on the wall said it was three o'clock in the morning.

"Indraneel's son," Abhimanyu said.

"Lies," she said. "Your son."

"What proof do you have?" Abhimanyu's nostrils had flared.

"You will provide the proof. Wait until I contact my lawyer."

"Stop it. This is ridiculous."

"The way you treat him – he is the crown prince. Forget being nice – you don't have any time for Simi."

"That does not make Rahul my son."

Rahul took a step forward. Why was he not getting any nearer? 'Dad I am your son.' He shouted, wanting to be heard above their loud voices. Why did no sound emanate?

"You can prove that in court," Kalpana said to her husband. "I cannot risk losing even a part of our business, our money, our houses, to a boy who landed out of nowhere. Everything we own is not just yours. What I inherited from my father and added to the kitty was substantial. . ."

"Did somebody at the party poison your mind?" Abhimanyu's face was red.

"Are you accusing me of not having a mind of my own? The walls of this house have ears. I know the truth. Your denial, your anger ... After twenty years of marriage, I can tell. Born out of wedlock, to that witch." Kalpana glared at Rahul who now stood near her; and tossed the contents of her goblet at Abhimanyu. Her aim was so bad that the red drops only hit the beige carpet, forming a weird pattern that turned brown.

Rahul approached the arguing duo, clenching and unclenching his fists rhythmically. His heart was pounding. Truth. Nothing but the truth. In that split second, he had made his decision. "My mother was a respectable woman. I will not have anyone talk ill of her."

"All my friends remarked on the resemblance in your mannerisms," Kalpana screamed at Abhimanyu.

"They are saying these things out of spite," Abhimanyu said.

Why did they continue to speak over him? Had he not spoken loud enough or were they ignoring him deliberately? Rahul cleared his voice. "Nayantara, my mother, was dad's first love."

This time they had both stopped talking.

"My mother was a respectable woman," he said clear and loud. "Repeat, I will not have anyone talk ill of her. Like it or not, I am the son of Abhimanyu." Walking across to the alcove, he opened the refrigerator door and poured himself a glass of cold water. His heart had stopped pounding. He was proud of himself for speaking the truth.

"First love. A whirlwind romance." Kalpana's mouth had ejected copious quantities of saliva full blast at her husband. "Why the hell didn't you tell me you had slept with her? I would not have married you had I known."

"You answered your own question." Abhimanyu let out a loud laugh.

Rahul gulped the water. His identity had been disclosed. Even if it was only to one other person. Yet he felt no triumph.

"You cheated me." Kalpana screamed. "I will call the lawyer right now."

"At three in the morning." Abhimanyu guffawed and held out the cordless. "Here, use this."

She snatched it from him and dialled.

"You will be the one to repent," Abhimanyu sneered. "I always win. Remember what I did with Siddhartha. I made a change to the bank's policy and cancelled his loan. Eight months later, his business has collapsed."

Kalpana flung the cordless in Abhimanyu's direction. It thudded to the ground and started beeping.

"Had it hit me I would have called the police." Abhimanyu scoffed vindictively. "Clean case of assault."

*He is devoid of understanding. For the feelings of those that love him.* Rahul felt a nascent sense of hatred for his newfound father. Had Nayantara been treated the same way?

Kalpana sat down on the nearest chair and began to cry.

Tears, the last refuge of the vanquished? Still, Rahul felt sorry for her. She was not a bad person. Just diffident. Maybe because of the way her husband treated her.

"Go to your room." Getting off the settee, Abhimanyu commanded Rahul.

●●●

# 21.

# A Day to Remember

*September 15, 1986*

Rahul slept fitfully. In his dream, Nayantara was a Goddess who showered gold coins all over him. *Ma, I wish you had never told me the truth. I wish I had never left Vancouver. I wish you had never left me.*

When Rahul came down to the dining room at eight in the morning, Abhimanyu who was reading the newspaper greeted him as if nothing had transpired. *Dad lacks compassion.* Rahul gobbled up his toast and gulped his coffee. When a puffy-eyed Kalpana appeared, he did not look up; he was enveloped by a sense of guilt, for causing a marital rift. Indraneel and Nayantara had never had a confrontation of such mammoth proportions. Not that they did not have their tiffs – none had been as vindictive as the one he had witnessed the night before. The office was his best refuge. Rahul pushed his chair back and slithered towards the wall.

"Be at the ballroom," Abhimanyu said to Kalpana. "Six o'clock this evening."

"I have to attend my Rotary meeting." Kalpana picked up her cup of coffee. "Page-3 party after that."

"Suit yourself. The decision will be made in your absence."

"No! Don't do this to me."

"Rani Maa has called for the meeting." Abhimanyu folded the newspaper, removed his reading glasses, and got up.

"What was the need to get Rani Maa involved? Could we not have solved this between you and me?"

"You know the rules." Abhimanyu walked out of the dining room.

Rahul followed his father like a lamb following the sheep. It piqued his interest that Rani Maa behaved like a real queen and arbitrated decisions. He knew she was on a tour of Europe. Was she flying in only for this?

Riding in the air-conditioned Toyota, Rahul was pleasantly surprised when his father volunteered information. "Rani Maa retired some time back. She has been on extended world tours ever since. There are circumstances under which I seek her counsel and leadership like today. She is flying in from London solely for this meeting. She will fly back tomorrow and resume her tour."

The glint of pride in his father's eyes intrigued Rahul. *He may lack compassion but he is a devoted son.* Rahul's youthful mind was unable to grapple with the complex dichotomy.

"Rani Maa is extremely special. Make sure you give her no cause for complaint." Abhimanyu patted Rahul on the arm as the car entered the portals of Lakeview Terrace.

◆

Rahul spent an hour training Veronica on using the Mail Merge feature in the Word Processor. He had nothing else to do that day. He leafed through all the magazines in the lobby and watched cricket on national television. Abhimanyu was attending a seminar organized by NASSCOM, the organization that set public policy for the software industry, in the afternoon. Rahul was on his own for lunch.

Rahul walked around downtown Bangalore – his mind in a state of turmoil. He was relieved that the truth had revealed itself and his birthright proclaimed. Rani Maa would likely learn about it in the evening. Soon everyone would know him as Abhimanyu's son. It no longer sounded authentic. He had next to nothing in common with the man. That they shared their DNA was but a moot point.

Rahul weaved his way through the tightly packed crowds cramming the restaurants and ice cream parlours, department stores and movie theatres that adorned Bangalore's prime commercial arena. He could feel the singe of the tropical sun tanning his fair skin through his sunscreen. Nayantara would have agonized about his tan if she could have seen him now. She had always been proud of his fair skin.

South Indian or North Indian? Vegetarian or non-vegetarian? Rahul did not feel any pangs of hunger. He decided against having lunch. An ice cream would suffice – from the softy vending machine outside of Kabir's bookshop. Rahul immediately felt better. Kabir's rustic nearness would be satiating.

Rahul bought two ice cream cones from the vendor and entered the bookshop.

During the past few days, Rahul had been a frequent visitor at the bookshop. Kabir, the owner, a fair Kashmiri chap, who may have been a couple of years older than Rahul, was always in a mood for mindless banter – his dreams for his bookstore, his views on cricket, population growth in Bangalore – he had no dearth of topics or opinions. Rahul loved to watch Kabir talk – his good looks and playful mannerisms acted like a peculiar charm.

"Afternoon break time." Kabir closed the door and latched it from the inside. Rahul held out a strawberry ice cream cone towards Kabir and stared lasciviously at the hairy forearm and artistic fingers that sprang forth to grab it.

When Kabir sat down on the narrow couch in the centre of the bookshop, Rahul plonked himself down next to him. Kabir licked his ice cream and narrated the morning's goings-on. Rahul watched the animated Kabir with fascination, his own ice cream streaming copious tributaries of milk towards his elbow. Kabir's curly locks danced on his forehead. The light stubble on his cheeks glowed golden from the rays of the sun. His rosy lips rendered rosier by the strawberry ice cream glistened with pent up promises.

"How big is your house?" Kabir was never tired of asking Rahul about Canada.

Their hairy legs pressed against each other. Rahul could feel the heat from Kabir's body seeping through the thin material of his ethnic pant. His body temperature shot up.

"Someday when I have enough money, I will visit you." Kabir rubbed his leg vigorously against Rahul's. "You have a fever." Kabir thrust the remaining portion of the ice cream cone into his mouth and placed his palm on Rahul's forehead.

Dropping his half-eaten ice cream cone to the floor, Rahul grabbed Kabir's face and locked the parted lips with his own. Kabir did not resist, his quivering lips a willing sign of reciprocal fervour. Rolling on the thin rug covering the floor of the vast bookshop, the two boys laughed uncontrollably as they ripped off each other's clothes. Kabir strapped his knee across Rahul's torso, his hot lips kissing Rahul's nipples.

Rahul's slim body tingled when Kabir's throbbing tumescence pressed into his flesh through the thin fabric of his own underwear, even as hairy hands kneaded his delicate belly and rough feet travelled across his soft thighs. *This is what I always wanted.* Engulfed by a languorous daze, Rahul slipped both his hands inside Kabir's shorts for exquisite pleasures he had never experienced before until they climaxed simultaneously with unbridled gusto ...

"Let me drop you off before I reopen." Kabir was the first to get up.

Rahul reluctantly buttoned up his shirt and zipped up his jeans, over his soiled underwear. *This is what I always wanted.* His mind was at peace, as he climbed on the bike and hugged Kabir.

The two friends laughed uninhibitedly as the bike swayed down the main street. Rahul loved riding pillion – his body pressed forward into Kabir's, the wind blowing his hair into his face. When the bike had entered the precincts of Lakeview Terrace and come to an abrupt halt near the entry, Rahul's laughter stopped abruptly. Abhimanyu was walking down the steps. His face remained impassive as he hurried towards the car and got in without as much as a sideward glance.

Kabir parked the motorbike in a corner of the parking lot. Rahul alighted, immediately.

"I know where to find you." Kabir winked. "Rich people. Posh locality. Manyata Manor." He had put his hand across Rahul's waist.

"You dog!" Rahul kicked at Kabir's leg. "You have evil designs on me?"

"Same as you." Kabir's hand slipped lower and gently caressed the smooth roundness of Rahul's buns.

Rahul experienced another fleeting moment of inner tranquillity. "I am scared." He backed away.

"I will come over tonight."

"No." Rahul's body tingled with tabooed anticipation. "Wait until Friday." His words faltered.

"I can't." Kabir pleaded with his eyes.

"Friday is the Gurkha's day off. I can let you in. Nobody will know." Rahul wanted to keep his tryst with Kabir a secret from his father, who already suspected his predilection. Even otherwise, his father would have disapproved of Rahul's association with Kabir, who in his eyes, belonged to some lower strata of society. He had to do what he had to do, there was no need for his father to know everything he did, Rahul rationalized.

"See you Friday, then." Kabir kick started his motorbike, revved up the engine to full throttle and sped away.

◆

Rahul spent the rest of the day lounging around the office and daydreaming. Exactly at half past five, Veronica called an auto and instructed the driver to take Rahul back to Manyata Manor.

The concierge led Rahul to the ballroom in the west wing. Rani Maa, seated on a royal green settee placed in the centre, directed Rahul towards the single sofa to her right. Before sitting down, Rahul bowed at Rani Maa's feet — as his mother had taught him to do in the presence of his elders. Rani Maa — fair complexioned with a round face, her ears and fingers glittering artfully with minute diamonds, raised her right palm in a sign of blessing and looked at him indulgently.

Kalpana sat to the left of Rani Maa. The two women exchanged no words.

Rahul refused to meet Kalpana's eyes, sensing the livid fury aflame in them. He was not sure whether to make small talk or remain silent — Rani Maa's demeanour resembled that of a queen rather than a grandmother.

Rani Maa resolved his dilemma. She asked him all the questions. Have you eaten? What did you do in the office? Where is your father?

*She already knows I am her grandson.* That the autocratic Abhimanyu trusted his mother so deeply, once again intrigued Rahul.

Abhimanyu arrived a little later, directly from NASSCOM. He bowed at Rani Maa's feet before occupying the couch opposite the settee.

"I hear you want a divorce." Rani Maa looked at Kalpana. "May I ask why?"

"It is your son's fault." Kalpana sounded recalcitrant. "I will let him answer."

"Rahul is my son, born to my first love Nayantara," Abhimanyu said. "I want to adopt him legally. Kalpana is against the adoption. She wants a divorce."

Rahul squirmed. He did not want a piece of legal document wiping away his relationship with Indraneel. Would the world know him as Abhimanyu's son henceforth? That just did not feel right anymore. Because of the twisted circumstances under which it was unfurling?

"I did not know that." Kalpana draped her dupatta over her head as if playing the role of a dutiful daughter-in-law. "The adoption angle is news to me."

"Do you want the divorce?" Rani Maa asked Kalpana.

"Divorce or not, I do not want me and my daughter cheated out of our rightful share of the wealth because of this b b b ..." Kalpana pointed her fingers at Rahul.

"Mind your language," Rani Maa said. "Rahul is my grandson. The rightful heir to the Aradhana Conglomerate."

"Aradhana is big and successful today only because of its merger with my father's businesses," Kalpana said.

"If she wants a divorce, then I want a divorce." Abhimanyu gave a sarcastic sounding laugh. "What are your demands?" he asked his wife.

"Ownership of Manyata Manor. Fifty percent ownership in the Aradhana Conglomerate, for my daughter and me. A monthly allowance that takes care of my expenses, with cost of living adjustments every year. Two cars and all my jewellery."

"No," said Rani Maa. "You will not get Manyata Manor or anything else. Abhimanyu's father willed all his self-acquired property to Abhimanyu through a trust created even before the time of his birth. Everything belongs to Abhimanyu and will belong to Abhimanyu alone until he bequeaths it to the person of his choice." Rani Maa waved a legal looking document in Kalpana's direction. "According to this testament, you can stake no claim."

"Kalpana, your father's former businesses were maintained under a separate corporate entity called Gupta Industries," Abhimanyu interjected. "That was distinct from the original Aradhana businesses. If we analyse only the businesses under that entity, they show huge accumulated losses."

"You are cheating me." Kalpana shook her head. "Bunch of lies."

"Proof." Abhimanyu tossed some glossy looking reports onto a side table.

"Fabricated to suit your greed." Kalpana flung them back at him.

"Do not accuse my son of fraud," Rani Maa's tone was soft as silk. "Annual reports contain statutory financial statements filed with regulatory authorities and adopted at general body meetings attended by shareholders. If my son has falsified them as you claim, he would face serious consequences."

"You do not even know how to read a balance sheet." Abhimanyu glared at Kalpana. "No interest in business. That has always been your problem."

"Enough." Kalpana got up. "I will call my father's lawyer friend."

"Sit down," Rani Maa ordered. "I am the lawyer here. Ever since Abhimanyu's father married me."

"Without divorcing his first wife," Kalpana muttered.

Rahul clutched the arms of the sofa. Did that mean Abhimanyu was an illegitimate son in the eyes of the law? Was this streak of illegitimacy a family trait? Was he himself, the illegitimate son of an illegitimate son? Would he sire an illegitimate son too? Not possible. He would never be with a woman ever again. That ship had sailed.

"Irrelevant," Rani Maa said. "Divorce laws did not exist in India during those times. Your father-in-law married me with the consent of his first wife and his parents."

Anachronistic. Bizarre. Was Abhimanyu illegitimate or not? Rahul was confused.

"You are a fifty percent shareholder only in Gupta Industries." Rani Maa waved another document at Kalpana. "You do not have any rights to the rest of the Aradhana Conglomerate. Abhimanyu and I have the majority shareholding in all businesses."

If Rani Maa's eyes were drills, Kalpana would have had two burning holes on her cheeks by then, thought Rahul.

"You can keep one car. And I don't want your jewellery." Abhimanyu sounded condescending and triumphant at the same time.

"I don't want a divorce." Kalpana's volte-face did not come as a surprise.

"I want the divorce," Abhimanyu appealed to his mother. "Otherwise, I will not be able to adopt Rahul. She will always object."

Rahul was dumbstruck. He did not want to give up Indraneel. He had only wanted Abhimanyu to proclaim his birth-right to family and friends. He did not want a legal adoption. He could go back to living in Vancouver and visit Abhimanyu and Rani Maa once or twice a year. That was the ideal solution.

"Do you agree to the adoption?" Rani Maa looked at her daughter-in-law.

Kalpana remained silent.

"I want Kalpana's consent in writing." Abhimanyu was extracting his pound of flesh.

"Is that acceptable to you?" Rani Maa looked at her daughter-in-law again.

Kalpana's head moved enough to qualify for a reluctant consent.

Rahul marvelled, how deftly mother and son had put Kalpana in place. The proceedings were no longer amusing. Rahul fidgeted.

"You get the adoption document prepared," Rani Maa said to Abhimanyu. "Kalpana will sign it."

Rahul shuffled his legs. The sweat from his thighs was staining his underwear. He did not want to run any business. He just wanted to run away. *Please de-sanction the adoption.* He had to talk Abhimanyu out of the legal adoption that was in the offing. The thought of persuading the autocratic Abhimanyu was frightening. He would wait for the right opportunity. The next time they played billiards or shared a drink after a gruelling golf game, perhaps. Abhimanyu always won at every game and that inevitably got him into a good mood.

"There has never been a divorce in our family," Rani Maa said to Kalpana. "I appreciate your change of heart. For your own sake and that of Simi."

Kalpana apologized to Rani Maa for her inability to dine with them and walked out of the ballroom, but not before aiming a vicious glare at Rahul.

◆

Back in the main wing for dinner, Rani Maa asked Rahul to follow her. Standing in the centre of the white marble mandir, she closed her eyes and folded her hands. The sickly-sweet scent of incense sticks filled the air. Soft strains of a classical bhajan emanated from the stereo system.

Prostrating on the marble floor before the array of idols that represented the family deity, Rahul felt a soft ache spread through his chest. Living in an alien country for the past two decades, Nayantara, who hailed from a middle-class Indian family, had found great comfort in celebrating every Hindu festival she could. Decorating the mandir, organizing bhajan sessions, throwing open the house to guests, cooking traditional festive lunches were her favourite activities.

Rahul wiped a tear from his eye as he got up from the cold floor. He felt like a five-year-old every time he thought of his mother. He had an entire lifetime ahead of him, sans her serenely energizing presence. The inexhaustible repository of memories would somehow have to suffice.

"Prosperity to you, Little Prince." The regal Rani Maa planted a dainty kiss on his forehead, astounding him.

●●●

## 22.

# Subliminal Suggestions

The dress rehearsal happened at the actual venue; the college auditorium annexed to the main college building. Sadhana's Carmelita avatar had been invited to apply make-up only for Simi, ostensibly as a trial run. "Just a formality. Asha and Bina are bowled over by your charm." Siddhartha had given her the inside scoop.

"You have such fine skin." Sadhana's praise was genuine, as she worked on Simi's face. "I can see why Asha and Bina chose you for the role. You are so poised. Like a real queen." Sadhana smirked to herself this time. 'Feed her ego,' Siddhartha had coached her.

Most women cannot desist from confiding in their hairdressers and beauticians and Simi was no exception. "I am a real princess." She had filled Sadhana in on her heritage.

"You are so good, Carmelita." Asha gave Sadhana a thumbs-up.

"Friday evening. 5 P.M. Same place." Bina added.

"I have never looked more beautiful." Simi squealed, admiring herself in the mirror when Sadhana was done. "I am wearing my royal tiara that day." She showed Sadhana a photograph of the royal tiara, as she slipped into a teal ball gown. "I ordered this gown from Paris. Just for the banquet scene. Because it matches my tiara."

"Why aren't you wearing a tiara today?" Sadhana pointed to Simi's bare crown.

"It is a family heirloom. Very valuable. I am not mad to bring it today." Simi lashed out.

"You don't always have to wear the real one." Digging into the VIP makeup case she had acquired for Project Tiara, Sadhana took out an aluminium trinket studded with cheap rhinestones, another relic from her Prabhat-Kala days. "Wear this."

"That is so cheap." Simi threw a tantrum. "I cannot wear that."

"This is a full-dress rehearsal. You must wear one, so you look and feel like a queen. And get into the skin of the character." Asha and Bina indulged in considerable cajoling before Simi reluctantly agreed.

"You don't bring this on Friday." Placing the aluminium trinket around her crown, Simi almost spat at Sadhana.

Sadhana sat in the front row of the auditorium with a few other students and watched the play, her photographic memory recording key pieces of dialogue and storing them in its folds. The three girls playing the witches were outstanding. Vikas and Simi were mediocre actors. Nahar, a pimple-faced senior who played Duncan - the King of Scotland, was a sensitive actor but lacked presence. Sadhana herself had never acted in any Shakespearean adaptations. One of her mild regrets.

As soon as the play ended, Simi had appeared in front of Sadhana, aluminium trinket in hand. "Returned. With no Thanks."

"Keep it," Sadhana said. "And wear it on Friday."

"No way. Did you not hear me? I will be bringing the royal tiara."

"You say it is a family heirloom. Isn't it dangerous?"

"Who the hell are you to tell me what to do?" Simi erupted. "I will only wear my royal tiara. No cheap imitations for me."

The students watched silently. Some enjoyed the unfolding spectacle; others feared Simi's temper. Either way, none intervened. Asha and Bina were backstage restoring the props.

"The real one is too valuable." Sadhana switched to her most patronizing tone. "To bring to a public place."

"What is it to you? You are not my mother. When I say I will not wear it, I mean it." Simi snapped the aluminium trinket in two and handed the pieces to Sadhana. "Keep this. I win."

Sadhana stared at the pieces wordlessly, inwardly relieved that Siddhartha's reverse psychology tactic was working. Not having as deep an understanding of human psychology as he did, she was content to adhere to his coaching. The chances of Simi not bringing the royal tiara on D-day seemed slim.

"We heard what happened." Asha and Bina came running. "Please don't take it to heart. We will add two hundred rupees to your payment. To cover the damage."

◆

The same evening, dressed in a starched cotton sari, Sadhana's Mrinalini avatar made her third and final visit to Aradhana Cottage Emporium. Ostensibly with the first consignment of handicrafts. The receptionist escorted her to the door of Kalpana's office.

Sadhana was shocked at Kalpana's ghastly ghost-like appearance. "Should I come back another day?" There was a genuine concern in her voice.

"No. Sit. Sit." Kalpana examined the ten Mysore paintings that Sadhana had brought with her.

Another showdown with her husband? Or something more serious? Sadhana wondered. (She would never learn the truth, either about Kalpana discovering that her husband had sired an illegitimate son or the disturbing arbitration that Rani Maa had meted out the previous evening.)

"Let me show you something." Kalpana took out a box and stuck a sticker – depicting a crown-shaped logo in blue and green that cannily resembled the royal tiara – on the back of each painting. "Brand Tiara. First batch."

"Pretty," Sadhana said. "But you don't look very well?"

"Teenager problems." Kalpana rolled her eyes upward.

"There is no saying what a teenager will do," Sadhana assented.

"My daughter wants to wear the royal tiara this Friday." Horizontal lines had formed on Kalpana's forehead. "Without telling her father. I explained the danger. The tiara is worth forty or fifty lakhs. But she is very stubborn. She has promised to show the real one to her friends. Says she must maintain her prestige. On top of that, it seems some Carmel lady asked her to wear an aluminium one, at the rehearsal today. Now she is even more stubborn. I even offered to buy her a silver and turquoise tiara. But nothing doing. She never listens to me."

Sadhana could barely keep a straight face on hearing the reference to her alter ego. "My friend's daughter slashed her wrists. Because her mother forbade her from wearing diamond earrings to a friend's wedding." She felt sad lying to Kalpana, who had begun to treat her as a confidante.

"How old was this girl?" Kalpana leaned forward.

"Twenty." Sadhana made it up on the fly.

"Simi has also threatened to consume sleeping pills. I am scared."

"Tough decision," Sadhana said. "As parents, you can't give in to all their demands either."

"Simi is a responsible girl. Always takes good care of her things. She has never lost anything valuable. She wants the tiara only for three or four hours," Kalpana was mumbling. "Anyway, the tiara will belong to her only one day. Not to that b b b ... anybody else."

Sadhana sensed Kalpana had stamped her foot under the table. Was there something deeper that had caused Kalpana's outburst? (Sadhana would never learn that Kalpana's fear that Rahul would usurp all their wealth including the tiara, was going to play a vital role in her decision to access the vault.)

"Do whatever is right for your daughter, Kalpana-ji." Sadhana stood up. Having made subliminal suggestions as Siddhartha had suggested, she did not want to overstay her welcome.

"I have access to the vault. I will use it." The horizontal lines on Kalpana's forehead had lightened. "For my daughter's sake."

●●●

# 23.

# Tiara, Tiara, Tiara

*September 19, 1986*

The culmination of Project Tiara was within reach. Siddhartha could barely contain the butterflies in his stomach as he drove the blue Maruti towards Benson college. The late afternoon sun blazed right into his eye, making him squint.

The evening program would start with an Antakshari competition, followed by Shakespeare's *Macbeth,* and end with a song and dance tableau encompassing all Indian languages, captioned Musical Medley. Siddhartha had been informed right at the outset, that due to time constraints, only the first four acts of *Macbeth* would be staged. Though initially disappointed that the fifth and final Act, including Lady Macbeth's famous sleep walking scene, would be left out, it had helped him finetune his plan – that Simi would not be required on stage after Act three would come as a blessing in disguise.

Siddhartha had worn tan slacks and an olive-green shirt that would serve as camouflage amongst the campus shrubbery. A brown hat covered his baldpate. Large rectangular glasses, a false moustache and goatee had altered his face. Though his role was peripheral, he did not dare run the risk of a stray student or lecturer recognizing him. Coincidentally, his teaching stint at the college had just ended.

Would Simi bring the tiara? Would Kalpana have accessed the vault? Or would that bastard have voted them down? "We will find out," he said aloud.

Sitting next to him clad in a jade green dress, Sadhana's Carmelita avatar inspected the contents of the *VIP* makeup case on her lap. After the dress rehearsal, so pleased were they, that Asha and Bina had requested her to be the makeup artiste for the entire cast of *Macbeth* as well as that of the Musical Medley.

*I am making Sadhana commit a crime. What if she gets caught?* Siddhartha shuddered. Abhimanyu could go to any lengths in retaliation. "Honey, abort the plan?" He looked at her.

"Too late," Sadhana took his left hand in hers and kneaded his fingers.

"We are doing this to teach that bastard a lesson." He needed to hear his own voice. "If you sense any danger, we call it off." Siddhartha parked the car outside the college gate. There was no chance of anyone recognizing the blue Maruti – he had travelled by auto during his stint as a lecturer. "I will hover around until the designated hour."

"As you say, the proof of the project lies in the planning." Sadhana gave him a thumbs-up sign, got out of the car with the *VIP* makeup case and walked away on her platform heels, down the winding path leading to the auditorium.

No plan is perfect. Every plan goes haywire. What happens is always at variance with the plan. Yet the process of planning helps to think things through and catch snags that are not envisioned. Siddhartha had based his entire plan on the tenuous whim of a vain teen. Aided by liberal doses of subliminal suggestions of his own making. Having handed the baton to Sadhana, he trusted her ability to think on her feet and respond to circumstances as they unravelled. Had he believed in God he would have asked God to protect her. Just her. All he cared about, above everything else, was Sadhana's safety.

◆

The cultural program was being conducted in the auditorium annexed to the main building. A long and narrow passage connected the back of the stage to the two green rooms – one for girls and the other for boys – each with its own attached bathroom.

Sadhana trotted into the girl's green room and set to work. The Antakshari competition had just started on stage – Sadhana could hear the songs in the green room. She had completed applying purple makeup to the girls playing the three witches, when Simi breezed in, her best friend Lola lugging a suitcase on wheels behind her.

Asha and Bina stopped their agitated chatter and rushed to welcome the heroine of their play with loud remarks of relief. All the other girls surrounded Simi.

Lola placed Simi's suitcase next to a square table that was right underneath the window overlooking the passage. Simi unzipped the suitcase, freed a shiny object from the layered depths of a suede bag, and perched it on her forehead. The girls squealed and shrieked, in delight and in envy.

Twirling around, Simi stopped in front of Sadhana. "Now do you believe me? Royal. Real. No imitations for me."

"Enchanting!" Sadhana beckoned Simi to sit on the chair. The arrival of the object that was the objective of Project Tiara was a major milestone. Was this 'Half the battle won' or 'Well begun, half done'? She was not sure. Siddhartha's figures of speech could be confusing.

The other girls watched as Sadhana transformed the real-life princess into the drama queen of the day. After Sadhana had finished blow-drying Simi's hair and applied to her face, a dusting of powder commingled with glitter, Simi got up to change into her costume.

Sadhana proceeded to the adjacent room with her paraphernalia – it was the turn of the boys – Vikas (Macbeth), Nahar (King Duncan) and the one playing Banquo – to get their makeup done.

◆

After completing the boys' make-up when Sadhana came back into the girls' room, Asha and Bina were cajoling a hysterical Simi to stay calm. Once the showing off had worn off, the enormity of being in possession of the royal tiara had struck her.

On stage, the Antakshari program had ended. Asha and Bina herded Simi and the rest of the *Macbeth* cast out of the green rooms.

Sadhana set to work on the Musical Medley girls. She could hear the dialogue of *Macbeth* - Act one loud and clear. By the time the girls were all made up, Act two had ended on stage. Simi returned to the green room to quickly change into the teal gown for the banquet scene in Act three. "I will be back as soon as my role is done and change." Adjusting the tiara, she announced to no one in particular, before returning to the stage.

Sadhana hastened the Musical Medley girls to proceed to the side wings and wait their turn. She desperately needed the green room to be empty by the time Simi arrived to change out of her costume, at the end of Act three. She was not required on stage for Act four. Only the three witches and Macbeth were. This detail was at the core of Siddhartha's complex plan.

Sadhana proceeded down the passage, back to the boys' room. Nahar, whose King Duncan gets killed in Act two, was back in the green room and was showing off his polaroid camera. He seemed smitten by Sadhana's Carmelita avatar; 'that cute lady' Sadhana had heard him whisper.

Sadhana got worried when Nahar started aiming his camera at her and taking pictures. Siddhartha would not want any relics for posterity that would put them in danger. Lifting her elbow to shield her face, she requested Nahar to stop clicking, pleading shyness. She breathed easy only after Nahar apologized and left the green room.

Sadhana made sure the Musical Medley boys were all made up before Act three ended on stage. "I am going to watch Act four with the audience." Sadhana announced. 'Create your alibi.' Siddhartha had taught her. As soon as she saw a lone girl clad in a teal gown enter the girls' room next door, Sadhana stepped out of the boys' room, into the passage.

◆

The passage was poorly lit. Sadhana did not proceed towards the stage, as she had announced. She ducked left instead and remained in the shadows.

The door to the girls' green room was ajar. Simi stood at the square table, her head bent, the lone naked bulb shining directly on her face. Placing her suitcase on the table, Simi packed the royal tiara in its suede box and put the box inside the suitcase. Next, collecting her jeans and kurta she went into the attached bathroom to change out of her ball gown.

As soon as she heard the bolt of the bathroom door click, Sadhana entered the green room. Simi would be in the bathroom for the next five or ten minutes. Sadhana had to be done before that.

Shoot. Simi had locked her suitcase. Thankfully, it was not one of those combination locks. While Siddhartha had equipped Sadhana with a host of steel instruments for any eventuality, she was in dread of using them. Instead, extracting the key chain he had given her, she managed to have Simi's suitcase open in a matter of seconds. Developing the skill had taken her several hours of practice. Siddhartha had made her use the myriad keys on every suitcase and trunk they owned.

Sadhana took out the bejewelled tiara from the suede bag. She had only seen royal jewels on display at the Mysore Palace. She had not imagined in her wildest dreams, what it meant to own one. She placed the empty suede bag back inside the suitcase, locked it and took brisk steps towards the back door.

She was halfway down the green room when the lights had gone out. This was not part of the plan. The green room was in pitch darkness. Sadhana panicked. What if things went horribly wrong? She heard a splash of water from the bathroom. Simi could come out any minute. Taking a deep breath, she goaded herself to hold onto the wall for support and dragged her feet towards the back door. Sadhana could hear the thud of her own heart as she slid the bolt of the back door open. She had barely slipped out of the door into the shrubbery, when she heard Simi open the bathroom door with a loud noise. Sadhana latched the back door from the outside.

◆

Siddhartha, the master of the plan, stood a few feet away, against the granite wall that ran all around the back of the auditorium. His eyes gleamed in the moonlight, as he took the tiara from Sadhana. They could hear the wolf whistles emanating from the auditorium. The students were getting restless in the darkness.

Siddhartha removed his hat, placed the tiara high on his forehead and replaced his hat over it. The thick brown felt hat did an excellent job of concealing the tiara.

The lights chose to come back on at that moment. Siddhartha pulled Sadhana down and the two crouched under a shrub. Act four of *Macbeth* would resume on stage.

"I cannot go back into the green room," Sadhana said. "Simi has come out of the bathroom." Had the lights not gone out, she was to have gone back into the green room and out of the passage.

"Do you have your alibi?" he asked. "We can change the plan a little."

She nodded her head in the positive. "I will watch Act four with the audience."

"Turn the lie into the truth. I shall wait for you in the Maruti."

◆

Sadhana brushed the leaves off her green dress, adjusted her wig and walked around the auditorium wall farther up. Slinking into the auditorium through a side door, she slipped into an empty seat near the back.

On stage, the three witches were circling a hissing cauldron, chanting spells, and throwing rubbish into the stew. Sadhana found that watching Act four unfurl on stage was soothing for her distressed soul. As soon it ended, she prominently walked down the middle aisle almost up to the stage, and turned right at the fourth row, to go backstage and then make her way to the green room.

Students crowded the long passage leading to the green rooms. "Call the police." Sadhana heard Simi's caustic voice rising above the din. "What kind of loafer elements does this college allow? I cannot be in the same place as this scum." Making her way through the packed passage, Sadhana entered the girls' room.

Simi's suitcase lay open on the table, displaying the empty suede bag inside.

"My father will make sure the thief gets capital punishment." Simi screamed, as Bina tried to pacify her.

"Carmelita, we need your help." Asha rushed towards Sadhana. "Simi's tiara is missing."

"When did that happen?" Sadhana pretended to freeze.

"When the lights went out," Bina answered.

"Did you see anyone suspicious?" Asha asked Sadhana.

"I was in the audience when the lights went out. I was lucky to catch Simi's last scene in Act three." Sadhana repeated Lady Macbeth's last line of dialogue from that act. "You lack the season of all natures, sleep."

"If you had stayed in here and guarded my tiara all this would not have happened." Simi shouted at Sadhana. "What was the need for you to sit with the audience? You already knew my lines by heart."

"I am sorry. That was unfortunate." Sadhana walked towards the back of the green room, quickly wiping the back-door bolt clean with her handkerchief and drawing it in place, before entering the bathroom and making a show of washing her hands.

"Call my father. He always knows what to do." Sadhana heard Simi say, as she came out of the bathroom. She approached Asha and Bina. "I wish I could stay back and help, but I have to leave."

"Nobody leaves this place," Simi erupted. "Not until my tiara is found."

Sadhana emptied the contents of both her purse and the VIP makeup case onto the square table. "Take a look. I am not a thief," she said to Simi. "I live on the outskirts. I have to be home before it gets too dark."

Simi stayed silent, a foolish look on her face.

"We trust you Carmelita," Asha said.

"Thank you for giving me the opportunity." Sadhana stuffed her belongings back into the purse and the makeup case.

"We should thank you." Asha handed Sadhana an envelope.

"I apologize on behalf of Simi." Bina gave Sadhana a hug.

Sadhana felt as if her heart dipped itself in molten lead. Asha and Bina trusted her unconditionally. Saying an internal prayer asking God to forgive her for lying to them, she bid goodbye and headed out.

The moon was smiling in the clear sky. "Bye Carmelita." Sadhana climbed into the blue Maruti parked outside the gate.

◆

Siddhartha's hands shivered as he drove the blue Maruti towards downtown. The bejewelled tiara stayed concealed under his brown felt hat. *We have left no evidence to associate the theft with us. I hope.*

Next to him, Sadhana tore off her wig, wiped away the fairness makeup from her face and neck with cold cream and slipped out of her green dress; she had worn thin pedal pushers and a short top underneath. Reaching over to the back seat, she pulled out two black plastic bags and an overnight case. The wig went into one and the contents of the makeup case into the other. She stuffed the dress into the overnight case.

On nearing a garbage dump, Siddhartha slowed down the car and Sadhana threw away one of the bags. A few minutes later, he slowed down the car one more time and she got rid of the other bag. On reaching downtown, Siddhartha drove the car into the basement of Hotel Zyatt and parked it as close to the elevator as possible. Seated in the car, he removed his brown felt hat, along with the tiara; Sadhana locked them both inside her *VIP* makeup case.

The keys to their suite awaited them at the front desk. They would check out of the hotel at five in the morning and make an early journey to Mysore. Their packed trunks stayed in the trunk of the car.

Siddhartha and Sadhana spent a sleepless night in the air-conditioned comfort of Hotel Zyatt's deluxe suite. Siddhartha could not wait to reach Mysore and store the tiara in the old-fashioned vault at Panchsheel Villa. Every few minutes, he rubbed his left hand lightly over the *VIP* makeup case on the headboard. The loss of the tiara should make Abhimanyu understand the pain of losing what is rightfully his. And teach him to give up his exaggerated sense of entitlement.

"What will we do with the tiara?" Sadhana got up from the bed as soon as it was five o'clock.

"Worship it?" If Siddhartha had intended to sound humorous, he did not, even to himself.

"We can't sell it. Who can afford it anyway?"

"What if I tell you we will return it?" He looked at her tenderly.

"I promise to love you for the rest of my life."

"We will return it. I promise. Eventually."

•••

# 24.

# The Hunt

Abhimanyu's black Toyota came to a screeching halt at the entrance of Benson College. Commanding the driver to stay in the parking lot, Abhimanyu got out of the car. Lecturer Bina had called Veronica at the office and requested her to send Simi's father to the college immediately, telling her that an emergency had erupted and the situation was too sensitive for them to discuss over the phone.

Folk music blared from the auditorium as the college peon escorted Abhimanyu through a long winding passage and led him to the girls' green room at the back.

"What the hell ..." Simi was belting out an angry tirade that rose above the cacophonous chatter of the unruly student congregation around her. "The tiara ... the tiara ..." She ran towards Abhimanyu. "It has been stolen".

"Our heirloom?" The empty suede box lying on the table confirmed the sordid tale. Viscerally, Abhimanyu knew this was Kalpana's doing. Kalpana had allowed Simi to bring the tiara to college. He would mete out fair punishment to mother and daughter, but later. The time was not right to lose his temper. "Tell me what happened." He grabbed Simi's trembling arm. The volcano of her anger immediately condensed into a burst of tears.

"Please clear the room." The principal, a rotund man with a red face, walked in. The students herded out. Only Lola stayed back. Along with Asha and Bina who stood gaping like the proverbial deer in the headlights.

"Please tell us what happened." The principal turned to Simi.

"I locked the tiara in the suitcase and went to the bathroom to change out of my ball gown. When I was in there, the lights went out ..."

"When you came out, the suitcase lay open and the tiara was missing." Abhimanyu completed her sentence. Lights of a different sort went off in his head. *Was that blackguard behind this?*

"No." Simi said amidst her tears. "The suitcase was locked when I came back. I removed my makeup and opened the suitcase to stuff my things. I pressed on the suede bag. I wanted to make sure the tiara was there ..."

"The tiara was stolen when the lights went out," Abhimanyu said. "The thief was intelligent enough to relock the suitcase."

"I promised mother I will guard it with my life," Simi bawled. "I failed her."

Asking Lola to pacify Simi, Abhimanyu turned to the principal. "I need to make a phone call."

The principal led him to a little office room across the passage. When he was unable to get the DCP on line, Abhimanyu called the head honcho of the Bangalore police station.

Three police officers had arrived at Benson College within minutes. Abhimanyu signed an official complaint recording the theft. "Lockdown the premises, detain everyone, conduct a personal search," he ordered.

At first, the police officers refused to heed Abhimanyu's demand, citing a lack of evidence. Abhimanyu called Veronica and asked her to page the DCP and explain to him, the gravity of the situation. Abhimanyu's reference to the DCP probably scared the police officers; they agreed to make concessions and ordered additional reinforcements.

Fawad, one the three police officers, left to investigate the power failure. Shankar settled down for an interrogation. Ganesh went about inspecting the green room.

Abhimanyu watched poker-faced as Shankar made Simi re-narrate her side of the events and wrote copious notes.

"Who else was in the green room at that time? Anybody who is not here now?"

"Carmelita. The lovely lady who did the make-up." It was Nahar, the pimple-faced senior, who answered. He had snuck back in when the police officers had arrived. "She left after the last act."

Ganesh juggled the back-door bolt. "Latched from the outside. That is how the thief got away."

"Find this Carmelita and interrogate her," Abhimanyu ordered Shankar.

"Where can we find her?" Shankar addressed Asha and Bina.

The two women looked at each other. Neither spoke. Beads of sweat collected on Bina's forehead. Asha cracked her knuckles.

"Carmelita has not stolen the tiara," Asha said. "She emptied all her belongings before she left."

"And she went out of the front door," Bina said. "Not the back door. After bidding us all goodbye."

"Who hired her?" Abhimanyu's voice boomed above everyone else.

"We met her at the bus-stop," Bina said.

"Where does she work? Did you get any references?"

"She comes from a cultured family," Asha said.

"Do you have an address, a phone number?"

"She lives in the outskirts," Asha said.

"That is not enough information to find her." Abhimanyu paced the width of the small green room. "Did you pay her by cheque? Was it crossed? We can track her down when she encashes it."

Shankar and Ganesh stood gaping. Asha and Bina looked to the principal.

"Miscellaneous payments are made in cash." The principal gave an awkward laugh, an apology of sorts.

Abhimanyu shook his head in exasperation. *If they were working for me, they would be long gone. Cancel that. I would never hire such nincompoops in the first place.*

There was a knock on the green room door. Two constables – one man and one woman – had arrived. Officer Ganesh walked them over to the auditorium. The three of them would cordon off the side exits and station themselves at the main door of the auditorium. The program would be ending soon. The outpouring audience would form a single file and their belongings searched as they exited.

Nahar, who had been fiddling with his Polaroid camera, held up three photographs it had ejected, all taken while Carmelita was applying makeup. Her own hands obstructed her face in two of them. Only her silhouette was visible in the third. Nahar was a terrible photographer. Shankar inserted the photographs into an envelope.

"Track her down." Abhimanyu reiterated. "She makes me suspicious."

"Carmelita did not steal the tiara," Nahar said. "She was watching *Macbeth* when the power outage happened."

Lola who was consoling Simi corroborated Nahar. The lady in question had been in the audience during that time. She had walked out of the auditorium and come to the green room as soon as the play ended. By then, the tiara had disappeared.

"That changes the spiel of the investigation." Shankar looked at the faces of Asha and Bina. "Any of the girls who were in the green room could have taken it. Or the boys next door."

Nahar and Lola exchanged worried glances.

"Please do not cast aspersions on my students without proof." The principal implored.

"No electrician visited the college premises." Officer Fawad had come back – having completed his investigation in the electric room. "There was an outage in all of Benson Town. The Electricity Board restored the power centrally."

"Maybe the theft was not planned," Shankar said. "Someone just capitalized on the outage."

"Or the theft was planned and the power outage was unrelated to it." Fawad turned to Abhimanyu. "Do you have any enemies? You are an important man."

"One," Abhimanyu replied. "He operates alone. It seems unlikely he was behind this. Especially since the power outage was not planned."

Ganesh and the two constables had returned. They had finished searching the belongings of people leaving the auditorium. Nothing worthwhile had been unearthed that could even remotely be linked to the tiara, they reported.

"Very disappointing." Abhimanyu glared at the police team. "Send out a high alert. To catch whoever tries to sell the tiara. Offer a reward. Do whatever it takes. I want my tiara back."

The principal was hyperventilating. Asha and Bina were packing up. Simi and Lola were whispering among themselves.

"Our family honour is at stake." Abhimanyu looked at the sullen faces surrounding him. "I want everyone to take a pledge. That you will not leak the news of the theft."

◆

This was all Kalpana's fault. Back at Manyata Manor, Abhimanyu paced the length and breadth of the ballroom fervently. "Rani Maa will die if she comes to know the tiara was stolen." He glowered at Kalpana who sat hunched on the settee. Exhausted from the crying, Simi had gone to bed.

Apart from Abhimanyu and Rani Maa, Kalpana was the only person who had access to the instructions to open the electronic vault. Abhimanyu had allowed her this privilege not out of choice but as a contingency measure. The vault, a room measuring 20 feet by 20 feet, lined with safes and lockers and boasting of advanced electronic features and alarms, was the single repository of all their valuables and records. Kalpana normally did not handle the vault. The enormity of the action scared her.

"*You* gave her the tiara!" Abhimanyu grabbed Kalpana's trembling arm. "Why did you do it? You know it is priceless. And the only relic of our glorious past." His fingers dug menacingly into the flesh of her arm. "To spite me?"

"Go away." Kalpana who was downing her third glass of Shiraz, flailed her arms.

"I knew you were careless. I knew you were stupid." Abhimanyu could feel the skin of his back burn in exasperation. "Now, you have become wicked. The incarnate of some she-devil."

"Simi would have overdosed on sleeping pills if I had not given her the tiara. You may not, but I love my daughter." Kalpana banged her wine goblet on the marble-topped table with such brute force that the glass broke in her hands.

"You could have asked me. I would have found a solution. Why did you take the matter in your own hands?" Chastising her seemed pointless. Kalpana had been on the warpath ever since she had found out about Rahul. "From now on .. .." He started coughing.

"Here drink this." Kalpana brought her blood-stricken fingers towards his mouth. "You will feel better."

"Gross." Abhimanyu picked up her designer bag from the settee and held it as a shield. "You will have no access of any kind to any valuables in the house, anymore. Count yourself lucky, I am concentrating on finding the tiara. I will take care of you later. You will repent every moment you have spent wreaking vengeance."

"Hand me over to the police. If you have the balls." Leaving him holding the bag, Kalpana stormed out.

Abhimanyu summoned the butler. He needed a martini.

'The day I lose the royal tiara I will die.' The walls reverberated with Rani Maa's words. He did not want Rani Maa to know that the tiara was missing. Though this was not his fault, he was accountable for Kalpana's actions. Rani Maa had always held him to high standards and he had never let her down, ever.

Rani Maa would be back in Mysore for the festival of Dussehra. He had two weeks within which to restore the stolen tiara.

◆

*September 20, 1986*

Abhimanyu was poring over the morning newspaper the next morning when Simi came down the stairs.

"Forgive me, Dad, it is my fault." Simi's eyes reflected an innocence he had not seen before.

It was the first-time Simi had ever admitted a mistake. A sliver of kindness spurted inside Abhimanyu. Sipping his coffee, he goaded her to continue. The more she talked, the more he would learn about the fiasco. The more he knew, the better equipped he would be to unravel the mess.

"I begged mamma to give me the tiara. Mamma refused. She is afraid of you. I blackmailed her so she would give in. It was stupid, what I did. I understand the gravity now. I am Rani Maa's only grandchild. One day the tiara will be mine."

At least Kalpana had not yet told her about Rahul. "You had absolutely no business taking something that valuable to your college." He glared at her.

"I took it to save my prestige."

"What prestige?"

"Siddhartha, the English lecturer who taught us *Macbeth,* had given us an assignment on royal dynasties and emblems. The girls made fun of me when I told them I was a real princess ..."

Siddhartha? English lecturer? Abhimanyu threw the newspaper aside. Logic dictated this was someone else.

"... They taunted me no end. I had to show them the tiara and save my prestige."

"Siddhartha. What is he like?"

"Harmless."

"Description."

"Tall and bald. Your age maybe."

"From Mysore?"

"I don't know. His English is too good. His accent reminds me of grandpa."

"Let us go to your college." Abhimanyu got up from the settee. "Now." This was no coincidence. Logic be damned.

"Do you know him?" Simi asked.

"He may be the mastermind behind the tiara theft." Abhimanyu had never acknowledged the existence of a half-brother to his daughter. He was not going to do it now.

"Today is Saturday. The college is closed. Siddhartha Sir did not attend the college festival. I don't think ..."

"Call up your Principal ..." Abhimanyu handed her the cordless.

"Yesterday was Siddhartha's last day at the college." Simi fiddled with the cordless. "He was only a temporary professor."

Cursing under his breath, Abhimanyu called the DCP instead. And offloaded his apprehensions. "You have to stop this rampage," he added. "By arresting Siddhartha."

The DCP was not convinced. That Siddhartha had been a substitute teacher at the college did not automatically mean he had orchestrated a complex theft.

"What about that Anglo-Indian then?" asked the DCP.

"She is a sidekick. Arrest her," ordered Abhimanyu.

The DCP was sceptical. There was no evidence of a nexus to the theft. He would be failing his profession if he went around issuing arrest orders against innocent people.

"Why don't you issue a search warrant?" Abhimanyu was tenacious.

Not possible. The DCP could not authorize a search warrant unless there was concrete proof that the tiara was inside his house.

"I will file a personal complaint against him if that will help." Abhimanyu turned belligerent. "This heirloom is the prestige of my family."

The DCP requested Abhimanyu to be patient, assuring him that the police officers would pursue all leads to bring the culprit to book. Verifying the substitute teacher's credentials; tracking down the make-up artiste; interrogating the college staff; and most important, circulating an alert among trade circles to report to the police, all inquiries related to the royal tiara.

The déjà vu was nightmarish. Abhimanyu disconnected the phone. He did not trust the police force. Whatever the consequences, he had to find a way of getting Siddhartha's house searched and have the tiara restored. Before Rani Maa returned from Europe.

*The blackguard ought to be shot.* Abhimanyu picked up the coffee pot and flung it out of the window. Watching the porcelain pot smash to smithereens on the concrete floor, an idea crystallized in his mind. From it evolved a strategy that could force the issue of a search warrant.

An action plan was the next step. He could only think of one person who could formulate and execute the plan. Varun. Thank God Varun was back from his vacation. Why could Rahul not be like Varun? Then a thought struck him. Varun would mentor Rahul. Having Rahul assist Varun on the assignment was the perfect way to hone his leadership skills. Rahul should get started immediately.

Abhimanyu walked the length of the ballroom to the main wing and took the elevator up to the guest suite on the second floor.

●●●

# 25.

# To Be or Not to Be

Who was pulling the comforter away from him? Abhimanyu, or Indraneel? Was school not over? Did he have to catch a flight? Rahul tried to open his eyes. He felt peculiarly sated. And pervaded by Kabir's overpowering masculinity.

The previous night, Rahul had impatiently rushed through the ritual of dinner, his body throbbing in anticipation. On seeing the flashing lights of a motorbike outside, he had slipped out of a side door and employed an age-old ploy to distract the temporary watchman, who was filling in for the regular Gurkha, so he could smuggle Kabir through the grounds of Manyata Manor, into his bedroom.

The comforter on the four-poster bed had stared at them invitingly, glowing wickedly in the flood of moonlight. Having showered, brushed their teeth, and doused themselves generously with an exotic cologne, Rahul and Kabir had snuggled together under it for a night of enduring bliss – elegant hands kneading hairy bellies, hot lips planting imprints on rosy nipples, hungry fingers exploring exquisite nooks and crevices – doing things to each other that they once thought unthinkable.

This was so different from the night he had spent with Chandni. *I had been a mere spectator then. I am a willing participant now. I had abided by the shackles of society at that time. I have set myself free this time.* If heterosexuality is the norm, homosexuality is no deviation. Diversity is an integral characteristic of nature.

Where was Kabir? Why did he not feel the warmth of his soft body? It was morning? Rahul managed to pry his eyes open. Abhimanyu's angry eyes flashed back at him. Kabir stood at the foot of the bed, fully dressed, staring down at his own feet. Sunlight was trying to filter in through the closed venetian blinds. The bedroom door remained locked.

"Get up." Abhimanyu handed Rahul his blue robe. "We have a decision to make."

*Cold and clinical.* Rahul suddenly became aware he had no clothes on. Thankful for the thin sheet draped over his torso, he got up and slipped on the robe.

"Go down and request the watchman to let you out." Abhimanyu commanded Kabir. "Tell him you were in the library all night. Attending to minor repairs."

"You can't send him away." Rahul tightened the sash of his robe. "Kabir is my friend."

Abhimanyu ignored Rahul. "You will not meet Rahul ever again. You will not talk about last night ever." He almost pushed Kabir. "Go."

"Don't go." Rahul went after Kabir, who had reached the door.

"Listen to your father." Kabir gave him a furtive half-wink as he slipped out.

"I apologize for my father's rudeness." Rahul put his hand forward but Kabir had closed the door after him.

"You came to check on me." Rahul turned to Abhimanyu. "I know you found my magazines and took them."

"I had to use the duplicate." Abhimanyu waved a key chain in front of Rahul. "I am handling a delicate situation. I came to offer you an assignment.

"You have to accept me as I am." Rahul looked his father in the eye. "I am gay."

"Stop doing this. You experimented once. Now get over it." Abhimanyu sat down on the bed. "Start dating. Pooja or any other good-looking girl. You will forget all this. It is a phase .. .."

"It is not a phase." Rahul gripped the part of the chest over his heart with his right hand. His proclivity was congenital, not incidental. He desired physical and emotional intimacy with men, dammit. He wanted to protect another man; in turn, feel protected by him.

"Your adoption will be complete in three months' time. My lawyer is drawing up the papers. Once you turn twenty-one, I will get you married. To a girl of your choice. Listen to me. I will make everything right for you."

"No." Rahul nodded his head vigorously. "It has been established that homosexuality is rooted in biology and genetics and cannot be changed. Time magazine published a detailed article recently."

"Once you start college and make new friends everything will be different."

"I can show you a copy of the article." Rahul hoped that scientific information would help his analytical father understand him better. "It is nature not nurture."

"These are western concepts, not part of our culture."

Rahul walked to the closet, slipped on a pair of boxers, and flung his robe on the floor. "Human nature is the same everywhere. It does not depend on being eastern or western." He pulled on a pair of jeans over his boxers and got into the T-shirt he had discarded the previous night.

"If you want to live in India you have to forget all this." Abhimanyu stood at the closet door.

"Then I don't want to live in India."

"You came to live here."

"I want to be who I am."

"You wanted to be with me. I am adopting you."

"To hell with the adoption." The words came out harsher than Rahul may have intended.

Abhimanyu looked stunned. "You have gone too far. You landed at my doorstep. You wanted everyone to know you were my son. You made me antagonize my wife. Now you don't want the adoption?" Abhimanyu walked away and stood at the bay window.

"I did not mean to hurt you. I am sorry." Rahul went over and stood next to Abhimanyu.

"Think about the bright future waiting for you. The CEO of Aradhana."

"I cannot change who I am. Even for you."

"Take whatever time you need. Do not be rebellious. For the sake of a momentary attraction."

Rahul closed his eyes. 'Itni shakti hamein dena daata; Mann ka viswas kamzor hona; Hum chalein ek raste se humse; Bhool kar bhi koi bhool ho na.' His mind hummed the Hindi prayer, an appeal to the Almighty to restore his emotional strength. He had to live his life – out and proud. Abhimanyu may never understand him nor accept him.

"Don't antagonize me," Abhimanyu was shouting. "Be grateful, that I am offering you everything I have."

"I came here on a whim and disrupted your life. You treated me like the crown prince. I am grateful for that." Rahul went back into the closet. Dumping his T-shirts and jeans into his duffel bag, he scooped up everything that remained on the shelves, thrust them into it, and walked out. "I am going back. To Vancouver. To Pa."

"Enough of this childishness. Take your clothes back into the closet. That is an order."

"Can I make one phone call please? Long-distance."

"Don't disobey me." Abhimanyu's tone was vicious.

"I love you, Dad." Tears appeared at the corners of Rahul's eyes.

"I always have my way. You know that."

"Some things are not meant to be." Rahul bowed down and touched Abhimanyu's feet.

Abhimanyu did not bestow upon him the customary blessing. "If you will not listen to me, then we do this on my terms. I do not want to see you ever again. You will not contact me ever. You will not tell anyone you are my son. The world shall not know that we are of the same blood. You will never ever stake any claim to my wealth. Your rights to any inheritance, stand abolished."

"You have my word. I will give it in writing if you wish."

"Not necessary. Just return the college forms."

Where were the college forms? He had no use for them anyway. He had not even wanted to do engineering in the first place. Rahul looked at the desk. They were not there. He must have packed them with the rest of his belongings. He opened the zipper of his duffel bag and fished out the forms.

Abhimanyu tore the forms and dropped the pieces into the waste paper basket. "Get out. Before the others wake up."

"I don't have enough money for my return ticket. Can I make one call to Pa? Please?"

"No. We are doing this on my terms. For the last time – leave."

Rahul picked up his bag, unlocked the bedroom door and walked out. The Gurkha at the gate fetched him an auto. Looking back at Manyata Manor one last time, Rahul wished his departure had happened under better circumstances.

'Goodbye. Dad, I will love you in the same way as any son loves a father. You want me to be flawless. I have to be authentic. I choose authenticity over flawlessness.' He scribbled his thoughts on a note and gave it to the watchman. "Please give this to Abhimanyuji."

◆

"Get out of here." Kabir's eyes flashed with anger on seeing Rahul. He had just opened the bookshop. There were no other customers there yet.

"I am sorry for what happened earlier." Rahul placed his duffel bag on the floor and advanced towards Kabir.

"I don't want to see you ever again."

"I need help."

"Your big man scares me. He threatened me."

"I have left Dad's house. I am going back to Canada."

"Go away."

"I have nowhere to go. My money is running out. Allow me to make one call to Pa in Canada, so everything will be ..."

"Here a Dad, there a Pa. Lucky bastard. One father in each country." Kabir waved his duster at Rahul. It may have been unintentional – but the wooden handle poked Rahul near the eye.

"Fuck you." Rahul lunged towards Kabir.

Laughing viciously, Kabir ducked, came around from behind the counter and pushed Rahul to the ground, rolling him over and pinning him to the ground under him.

"Get off me." Rahul slapped at Kabir's face.

"I have a loft upstairs that I use for night-outs during physical inventory." Kabir's nimble fingers tickled Rahul. "I will let you stay there. If you pay me in dollars."

"I have no cash." Rahul laughed hysterically. "Consideration in kind only. But you can conduct a physical inventory first."

Kabir caressed Rahul's lips with his own. They may have stayed that way forever had the sound of footsteps not forced them to separate.

It was indeed large-hearted of Kabir to let him stay, after the shabby treatment he had received from Abhimanyu. Rahul smoothed his clothes and peered at his reflection in the glass door of the bookcase. *Forgive me, dad. I love you; I respect you but I cannot be like you. I must be true to myself.*

"This is all I have." Rahul walked over to the counter and waved the meagre contents of his wallet. "Can I call Pa first?"

"I am scared." Kabir made no attempt to take the money. "What if that big man lodges a police complaint against me?"

"You have nothing to fear from Dad. I have left him." Rahul's heart ached with sadness on Abhimanyu's rejection. His body felt drained from his tryst with Kabir the night before.

"I would not have stayed with him even for a day," Kabir said. "So strict."

"In all fairness, he treated me like a prince." Rahul did not want to give Kabir the power to rebuke Abhimanyu. "He is a conservative man. Won't accept my sexuality."

The bookshop got busy. Kabir walked away to attend to his customers.

Rahul booked a trunk call to Indraneel and sat down on a stool, comic book in hand. He would get to spend two or three days with Kabir, the object of his infatuation. The attraction would wear out by the time he was back in Vancouver. Kabir and he belonged to two different worlds. Their togetherness had no future. He could only hope Kabir would not create any unpleasantness when they parted.

The phone rang. The trunk call had come through. When was the last time he had called Indraneel? Not once the entire time he had lived in Abhimanyu's house. How could he have been so insensitive? "I am sorry for not calling you even once in the past few weeks," Rahul blurted.

"What happened?"

"I am in a mess." Hearing Indraneel's voice after a whole month had calmed Rahul's nerves. *I am facing the consequences of coming out to the wrong father.* "I can't discuss it over the phone." He would have a tête-à-tête with Indraneel after returning to Vancouver.

"Are you safe? Should I come down? Do you want to come back?"

"I am coming back to you, Pa. I left Dad ... I mean Mr. Abhimanyu's house in a huff." Rahul relayed his financial dilemma.

196 | Family Secrets

"I will courier a one-way ticket and some traveller cheques. Should I make a hotel reservation? To stay until you fly out?"

Aah Windsor Manor! Rahul was tempted. "If you buy a dozen greeting cards, I will give you one card free.. .." Rahul could hear Kabir charming a customer, probably grinning like the proverbial Cheshire cat. The fly of Rahul's jeans strained forward. "I am with a friend," he said.

"You have a place to stay?"

"I believe so." Rahul threw a glance at the spiral staircase.

"Can you give me the address for the courier?"

Pa lets me be. Rahul dictated the postal address of Kabir's book shop over the phone.

"Face your past without regret. Handle your present with confidence. Prepare for the future without fear. Bless you, son."

Rahul replaced the receiver reluctantly. Indraneel's parting shot restored his tranquillity. Like mother, like son. Neither of them was destined to spend their life with Abhimanyu. Rather, Abhimanyu was not destined to spend his life with either of them. Like Nayantara before him, Rahul would cherish the pleasant memories. The bitterness would fade away. *Indraneel is my father. Indeed, mother made the right choice.*

●●●

# 26.

# Games People Play

Abhimanyu took the elevator down to the master suite on the first floor, after making sure Rahul had departed. He had suspected all along that *Rahul was not attracted to girls; the bedroom scene had confirmed his suspicion. Rahul has not taken after me. He may be my biological son but he is who he is, because of his upbringing. It is too late to mould Rahul to be the son I always wanted.* Abhimanyu tore up the lawyer's draft of the adoption agreement that lay by his bedside.

Back to square one. Rahul no longer fit into the scheme of things he had in mind for the Aradhana Empire. There was no successor in the offing. *I enjoyed having a son while it lasted.* Abhimanyu beckoned his personal valet. The night-and-day-golf tournament at Nandi Hills would be the ideal remedy for his disappointment; by the time the tournament ended, he would be reconciled to going back to the way things were, before Rahul appeared on the scene.

Kalpana had moved out of the master suite after the big showdown over Rahul. Over the years, every time they had a major altercation, she had fallen into the rut of occupying the annex to the ballroom until their frazzled tempers cooled down or a social obligation cropped up. And then return to the master suite. This time, he would disbar her from sharing the master suite forever. Because of the unpardonable crime, she had committed – permitting their daughter to wear the royal tiara without his sanction.

Abhimanyu instructed his driver to halt at Lakeview Terrace, before proceeding to Nandi Hills. Hook or crook, retrieving the tiara from Siddhartha's house was Abhimanyu's topmost priority.

◆

"While no money can be withdrawn from a bank without the account holder's signature, anyone can make deposits into any bank account – there are no restrictions whatsoever." Abhimanyu raised one end of his unibrow. "Right or wrong?"

Abhimanyu and Varun were seated in the penthouse office. Like Abhimanyu, Varun worked on Saturdays. Sometimes Sundays too.

"Right," Varun said. "I figured that out when I was eleven years old. I used to run bank errands for my parents. Initially, I was intrigued that anyone could make a bank deposit. Then I realized it required real money. The chances of anyone committing fraud were slim. It would not benefit them in any way. Once, I asked a bank manager . . ."

Varun talked too much, like all smart people who knew very well they were smart. Abhimanyu raised his hand. "I know you know this. I will still say it. What I am going to tell you, is super-confidential. Our reputation is at stake. Though we are not doing anything illegal, it is in our own interest that no one else comes to know of it." He apprised Varun of what he wanted to be accomplished.

Varun almost let out a low whistle. "Five Lakh rupees is a lot of money to be depositing into someone else's account."

*The power of money will get me back Rani Maa's tiara.* Abhimanyu handed Varun a piece of paper on which he had pencilled a bank account number and the name of the account holder.

"V. Siddhartha. The same person who robbed Aradhana Jewellers last year," Varun said. "Am I allowed to ask a question?"

"As always I reserve the right to answer it or not." Abhimanyu smiled for the first time since the previous night.

"I have heard that Mr. Siddhartha is your step-brother. Is that true?"

Abhimanyu spun the paperweight on his table and watched it rotate. Where there is trust, there should be truth. Where there is truth there will be trust. "There is no smoke without fire," he said.

"If I may ask, what is the rationale for this entire exercise you just asked me to do? Family feud?"

Abhimanyu contemplated letting Varun in on the past evening's events, but he had to protect Varun if things went awry for any reason. "As the adage goes, for your own good, ignorance is bliss."

"Consider the assignment done." Varun pocketed the piece of paper. "I will contact my Alma Mater and put together a team. MBA students are always looking out for projects to meet their curriculum requirements."

"Don't go yet. I have another assignment for you. Please put together a dossier on Vikrama Ventures. Latest financial position. Market reputation. Allies and adversaries. Alliances and partnerships. I want everything." While getting the tiara back was Abhimanyu's immediate concern, he planned to take permanent measures to stop Siddhartha from being a cog in the wheel.

"How long do I have?"

"One week." Abhimanyu gave him a slim document titled *VV Project Report 1986-88*. "This can serve as your starting point. It is a few months old though."

◆

### *September 22, 1986*

"You will follow a pre-determined routine over the course of the next five days." Varun addressed five youngsters assembled in his office on the second floor of Lakeview Terrace, on a bright monday morning.

"Each of you will make three visits each day to the Benson town branch of Ascot Bank. At each visit, you will deposit a pre-determined amount of cash, between five and ten thousand rupees, always into the same bank account. You will record the quality of your interaction with the teller for each visit. You will discretely talk to other customers to get their perceptions of the quality of bank services. You will report to me at the end of each day."

The five find-outers as Varun had christened them – were current MBA students of his Alma Mater. Varun had lured them to conduct a market research assignment for Ascot Bank, ostensibly titled, 'Customer service coefficient and factors of correlation.'

"Go to the bank at different times from each other. Pick your teller at random. Avoid, to the extent possible, going to the same teller on a consecutive visit. Do not attract attention to yourself under any circumstance."

Varun produced a book of deposit slips he had obtained from Ascot Bank and guided each team member to fill them out. "The account number for depositing the cash is KA04M316. The name of the account holder is V. Siddhartha. I will personally supervise that you collectively deposit Rupees one lakh each day. Not a rupee more, not a rupee less."

Varun drew out a bundle of cash from his valise and distributed the sum of Rupees one lakh amongst them. "To be deposited today. Any questions?"

Several hands went up. Apprehensions centred on handling the large sum of money. Each of them would be depositing twenty thousand rupees per day – which was the equivalent of four or five times the salary a decent manager might earn in an entire month!

"Be confident." Varun pepped them. "We want the study to be representative of current banking experience. Treat this as a precursor to the jobs you seek, where you will deal with high-value transactions in some capacity or other."

The team members were curious about the identity of the account holder.

"It suffices to say that the account holder is closely connected to our firm," Varun said. "Some aspects of the project are confidential. Integrity is the biggest trait we are looking for. For the same reason, you cannot discuss details of the assignment with fellow students. Who here thinks they will not be able to abide by this condition?"

No hands went up.

"If you cannot abide, please be upfront." Varun was enjoying himself. "You can be doing something else and I can always find another student to conduct this study. I want to make sure this is as relevant to you as it is to our firm."

Total silence.

"Mounam sammati lakshanam," Varun said. "Silence is acceptance. You will abide by my conditions."

For the rest of the week, the five find-outers met at Varun's office each morning and wrote out their deposit slips for the day, after debriefing Varun on the previous day's happenings. Once Varun had distributed the money for that day's deposit, they would disband.

Friday evening, Varun congratulated the five find-outers on successfully depositing the targeted amount of five lakh rupees into the Ascot Bank account KA04M316. "Please submit a confidential report summarizing the findings. Do not forget to reflect the customer satisfaction coefficient derived from the regression analysis of key concomitant factors. Your due date is September 30." He presented them with a cheque dated October 1 for ten thousand rupees.

◆

**September 26, 1986**

"Mission accomplished." Varun placed a single sheet of paper on Abhimanyu's table. It listed the dates and the corresponding amounts, aggregating to Rupees five lakhs, deposited to Siddhartha's account at Ascot Bank.

"You are the cat that got the cream." Abhimanyu looked at Varun appreciatively.

The police investigation had been a complete failure. It had neither nailed Siddhartha nor uncovered the whereabouts of the tiara. As per the police report, meetings with the college staff had not thrown up anything suspicious. None of them seemed capable, either individually or jointly, to pull off such a complex theft, evidently devised by a devious mastermind, the DCP had concluded.

The Bangalore police had not talked to Siddhartha as initially promised. Since Siddhartha lived in Mysore, his residence was outside of their jurisdiction. The Mysore police would not pick up the case since the theft had happened in Bangalore, which was outside of their jurisdiction. In the absence of any concrete evidence suggesting an unholy nexus, both sets of police had not taken any further action.

Leave no stone unturned. That was Abhimanyu's motto. Getting five lakh rupees deposited into Siddhartha's bank account was the first part of his three-pronged strategy. He was getting ready to drop a bigger bombshell at Ascot Bank's board meeting.

"I want you to prepare a report on the risks associated with dormant bank accounts." Abhimanyu handed a bunch of files to Varun. "List out the measures banks can take to safeguard their interest. I need the report on my desk before tomorrow's board meeting."

◆

**September 27, 1986**

"Dormant accounts are a primary source of bank fraud worldwide." Abhimanyu, Chairman of the advisory board of Ascot Bank, addressed his fellow members – six bank officials and two industry bigwigs. "Accounts become dormant when they have not been operated over extended periods of time. Many people simply stop transacting but make no effort to close the account. Death of an account holder and the legal heirs being unaware of the account's existence is the most common cause. Then there are those who abandon ..."

Eight heads were nodding around the table.

"Many dormant accounts carry minimal balances. However, all dormant accounts expose themselves to potential fraud." Abhimanyu referred to the report Varun had delivered that morning. "At Ascot Bank, more than two hundred accounts have been classified as dormant. Based on recent analysis, some of them have showed sporadic credit and debit movements over the past few months. I have called for a detailed audit to rule out fraud."

Allowing the board members a few minutes to express their opinions and arrive at the protocol for kicking off the audit, Abhimanyu drummed on the table with his fingers. He was anxious to get to the next issue – part of his three-pronged strategy – the real purpose of the meeting.

Once the din of discussion had died down, "Gentlemen," Abhimanyu said. "There is another item on the agenda, a high value anomaly relating to a dormant account. Since this issue is more operational in nature, Manager Shetty will discuss it."

"Irregular spurt in activity was noticed in account number KA04M316." Shetty cleared his throat. "The account has been in dormant status for forty months. The balance was one hundred and twenty-one rupees. Since September 22, there have been eighty transactions in the account, all cash deposits, aggregating to Rupees five lakhs. Mr. V. Siddhartha is the surviving holder of this account, which he has held jointly with his father since 1968. The account became dormant after the death of his father."

Shetty passed photocopies of an account statement bearing a CONFIDENTIAL stamp to the board. "The large volume of relatively high-value deposits during this short period of time, all in cash, especially during the last week of the first half of the financial year, is cause for concern."

Resting his right elbow on the table and cupping his chin with his palm, Abhimanyu watched his fellow-members study the document whose contents he had architected from scratch.

Shetty tugged at his tie. "Under the reporting guidelines for suspicious activity, Ascot Bank is obliged to notify the Income Tax Enforcement Federation – deposits and withdrawals of amounts substantially higher than the transactions that the customer normally makes."

The board members talked amongst themselves in low murmurs. The Income Tax department was a sensitive subject for any meeting.

"I want the board to vote on the matter," Shetty proposed. "Any concerns?"

"Is this insider fraud?" Asked one of the board members.

"No," Shetty said. "Cash has been physically deposited into the account."

"Do the deposit slips indicate who made the deposit?" asked another.

"Unfortunately, no," Shetty said. "They all say 'Cash'."

"Should we not contact the owner to verify whether the deposits are bona fide?" Yet another board member queried.

Abhimanyu kept his eyes focused on the glass paperweight he was twirling. Anticipating such questions, he had instructed Shetty ahead of time how to handle them.

"The activity raises suspicion. Not saying the deposits are necessarily dubious," Shetty responded. "The vote however is for compliance with the Reserve Bank of India guidelines. For reporting transactions substantially bigger than those that the customer normally makes. If the transactions are bona fide, the owner has nothing to fear – the onus is however on him to explain the source and account for the revenue in his income tax return."

"Reasonable." "That sounds fair." The board members nodded their heads in a show of concurrence.

"The owner will also be notified as per bank protocol," Shetty added.

The vote was passed, seven to one. Abhimanyu stopped twirling the paperweight. Winning the vote was his best bet to reclaim his tiara. Shetty was set to submit his report to the Income Tax Enforcement Federation the same day.

◆

Back at Lakeview Terrace, Abhimanyu placed a confidential call to the DCP. It was imperative to expedite the income tax raid on Siddhartha's house. Abhimanyu was intent on pulling whatever strings were necessary to make that happen.

The DCP whose tentacles spread wide and maybe far, did not disappoint Abhimanyu this time. He promised that the raid would be orchestrated within the next three days.

Abhimanyu was certain that the income tax squad would find the royal tiara in Siddhartha's house. While Abhimanyu had never set his eyes on or his foot inside Panchsheel Villa, he was aware from random conversations with his father that a drawing-room on the ground floor that served as his office contained a sturdy vault for storing legal documents and records. Logical analysis dictated that, in his current impecunious state, Siddhartha would safe-keep the stolen booty there. That is what Abhimanyu was relying on.

◆

"Haul yourself here." Abhimanyu buzzed Varun. "With whatever updates you have on Vikrama Ventures." Having taken care of everything in his control to retrieve the tiara before Rani Maa returned from her tour, it was time to set in motion the long-term measures that would eradicate the menace of Siddhartha's unscrupulous antics.

Abhimanyu browsed through the contents of an ochre dossier that Varun had prepared. "Truly a horror-scoop." The financial position of Vikrama Ventures was worse than he envisaged. The spectre of bankruptcy loomed large. Vikrama Ventures would self-destruct in a month or two. He was almost convinced he needed to do nothing. Until he found the freshly typed page pinned to the back cover. Izod Investments, a venture capital firm, was in negotiation for the acquisition of Vikrama Ventures!

For once Siddhartha had used his intelligence in the right direction. "Varun, we have to act fast." Abhimanyu banged his fist on the table. "And seal a deal with Izod Investments. Before October 3."

"A strategic alliance can be a win-win for both." Varun's voice was steeped with excitement. "Izod is cash-rich and possesses financing experience. Aradhana would provide instant access to a wide customer base."

"You have obviously done your homework." Abhimanyu was glad that Varun was one-step ahead. "What kind of cash outlays, are we looking at?"

"Rupees 1.2 crores is my initial estimate." Varun consulted his notebook. "We can pitch for equal partnership. We have the liquidity to do so. Our treasury folks can make the funds available with a 24-hour notice."

"That's my boy." Abhimanyu found himself embracing Varun. *Why could not have Rahul been more like him?*

◆

*September 29, 1986*

Abhimanyu, through one of his business contacts, wrangled a private meeting with Harshavardhan, the Managing Director of Izod Investments.

Abhimanyu had read an excerpt of Harshavardhan's interview with India Today and been suitably impressed by his credentials. Harshavardhan had been a part of the team that had undertaken venture capital financing for Digital Equipment Corporation in Silicon Valley. 'Venture capital as an economic metric for innovation', a white paper authored by him, had been published in the Harvard Business Review. Arun Shourie, the renowned editor of *India Today*, had dubbed Harshavardhan the 'rising star on India's financing horizon'.

When Abhimanyu arrived on dot at the Bangalore Golf Club for the scheduled meeting, there was no sign of Harshavardhan. The club's reception however indicated that a confidential call awaited him.

"Sorry Mr. Abhimanyu, I have to cancel the meeting." Harshavardhan was the caller. "It's Monday morning."

"We can reschedule." Abhimanyu grit his teeth. Time was of the essence. Izod was on the verge of acquiring Vikrama Ventures. He had to avert that debacle. "Breakfast tomorrow?" he asked.

"I am busy."

"I can make myself free if you let me know when you are free." Abhimanyu rolled his eyes.

"I will call you later."

Abhimanyu knew for sure what that meant. "I had a business proposition."

"Make your pitch now," Harshavardhan said. "I can spare two minutes."

Abhimanyu's ears throbbed. No one had dared to treat him this way. "Izod investments is cash-rich. Which makes it an attractive target to corporate raiders who want to channelize your reserves for increasing their own market share."

"So?"

"I am proposing a strategic alliance between your Izod Investments and my Aradhana Conglomerate."

"Why?"

"Aradhana can protect Izod from corporate marauders. Diversification is our mantra. Izod can expand its customer base using our influence. You can consider ..."

"Stop!" Harshavardhan said. "Your offer is very selfish. A genuine business partnership is like true love. It happens only once in a corporate's lifetime."

"Sure. Consider Aradhana Conglomerate to be that perfect partner."

"No. I am not looking for an alliance now. When the perfect suitor comes along, I will know." Harshavardhan's clipped tone was followed by a polite click.

Aradhana is the perfect suitor. Now is the right time. Abhimanyu opened the ochre dossier. The direct approach had failed. Though more complicated, he would adopt the indirect approach.

Izod Investments was a closely held private company. Harshavardhan held 49 % of the equity. The widow and daughter of his demised partner, Nathan, jointly held another 49 %. Ascot Bank held the remaining 2 %. Relations between Harshavardhan and the family of his demised partner were cordial with no proof of conflict or animosity. However, neither mother nor daughter had shown an active interest in the business of venture capital financing. That was the key to Abhimanyu's ingress into Izod Investments. While an amicable strategic alliance was his first choice, he was not averse to a covert takeover either.

◆

The same afternoon, Abhimanyu's driver parked the Toyota in front of a modern bungalow in East Bangalore. Veronica had called the Nathan residence ahead of time and informed them of Abhimanyu's impending arrival.

Nathan's wife, an attractive woman in her fifties and Nathan's daughter, an Amazonian girl with her hair in a page cut, welcomed Abhimanyu with polite courtesy.

Abhimanyu introduced himself and came straight to the point. "Are you willing to sell to me, the 49,000 shares you together hold in Izod Investments?"

Mother and daughter looked at each other's faces for a while. "Neither of us is interested in managing an investment company," Nathan's daughter said. "After father's death, we wanted to sell our share but did not know how. Mr. Harshavardhan pays us dividends regularly. That is our only source of income."

"My daughter is getting married soon." Nathan's wife pitched in. "We will consider an offer if it is attractive," the daughter said. "We understand that the value of each share is 100 rupees." Mother and daughter looked at each other again.

Abhimanyu did not bother to decipher the non-verbal communication that was exchanged between the two. He assessed that the duo was somewhat naïve when it came to business and finances. He would be fair to them. He had no intention of cheating them.

"If you pay us Rupees fifty lakhs in total, we will sell all our shares to you." Nathan's daughter looked hesitant. "On one condition."

Things were going the way he wanted. Abhimanyu reached for the folder nesting in his valise. He had come fully prepared. A two percent premium above the face value was fair consideration for what he would get in return.

"Please transact with us directly and pay us by cheque," Nathan's daughter said. "We don't want Mr. Harshavardhan to know we are selling out."

"He was Nathan's business partner for twenty years," the mother added.

Things were going better than he had expected. "Harshavardhan will come to know about the transaction when the shares are registered. I cannot stop that. But we don't have to tell him until then." Abhimanyu placed a typewritten document and two cheques for Rupees twenty-five lakhs each on the centre table. "Read the agreement. If you have no objection you can sign it."

The mother-daughter duo signed the agreement. The mother picked up the cheques.

"Do not hesitate to call me if you have any questions." Abhimanyu proffered his visiting card. While he was used to winning in all his business dealings, this one, had been easy. He now owned 49 % of Izod Investments. Ascot Bank owned 2 %; Shetty was his puppet. That gave him voting rights of 51 %, enough to stall Harshavardhan's friendly overture towards Vikrama Ventures.

◆

*October 2, 1986*

Abhimanyu's entry into the cosy office of Izod Investments located in a modern commercial tenement two blocks down from Lakeview Terrace elicited an angry glare from the taciturn Harshavardhan. This was the first of a series of in-camera meetings Abhimanyu had scheduled with Harshavardhan.

"You took advantage of two gullible women," Harshavardhan erupted.

"I compensated them handsomely."

"That is still less than the market price."

"Izod is a privately held company," Abhimanyu said. "Market price has no meaning."

"You know very well that the market price of a privately held company is based on its net worth."

Abhimanyu cursed under his breath. Harshavardhan was one of the toughest cookies he had handled. "I paid them 102 % of face value. It was a fair business transaction with full disclosure and honourable intent."

"Had he been alive, my friend Nathan, would not have allowed this to happen."

"Let me get to the point. Since the capital structure of Izod Investments has changed, your deal with Vikrama Ventures is no longer valid." Abhimanyu pulled out a copy of the merger and acquisition agreement from his valise.

"There is no change in the capital structure, only a transfer in ownership," Harshavardhan said. "You now hold the same 49 % equity that was previously held by Nathan's wife and daughter."

Abhimanyu thrust a legal document in front of Harshavardhan. "As Chairman of the Board, I hold the Power of Attorney for Ascot Bank. In effect, I now control 51 % of Izod Investments versus your 49 %."

"There is no change in the capital structure," Harshavardhan reiterated.

"Have it your way. It is a matter of semantics."

"The merger and acquisition agreement with Vikrama Ventures is valid." Harshavardhan repeated each word distinctly. "Nathan's wife and daughter had given me their approval verbally."

"The agreement is void. There is no clause in it to cover changes in capital structure or ownership." Abhimanyu held out the Xeroxed copy of a *Financial Express* article. "Read for yourself."

Harshavardhan scanned the article and tossed it aside. "The date has been set. There will be no change."

"I will not approve the acquisition without due diligence. The valuation is excessively high given the financial frailty of Vikrama Ventures. I am ordering a reassessment of the deal."

"You have one week until the acquisition date, to conduct any reassessment," Harshavardhan said.

"That will not work. I am aware that Siddhartha is your friend. That is why the valuation of Vikrama Ventures is not fair. The deal is not in the interest of Izod Investments."

"I am aware that Siddhartha, the legitimate son of Vikramadityaji is your enemy. And your half-brother. That is the reason you want to stall the acquisition."

"Wrong," Abhimanyu said. "I do not make emotional choices in business."

"You are using Izod Investments as a pawn to fuel your personal vendetta." Harshavardhan rose to his full height and looked Abhimanyu in the eye.

Abhimanyu did not flinch. "I offer you two choices. One, you agree to postpone the date of acquisition and I undertake a reassessment. If at the end of one month, we both concur on the terms, we have a deal. Two, you insist that the date of the acquisition is set in stone. I disapprove the deal for good, right away. End of the matter."

Harshavardhan sat down. "Let me consult my legal advisor and revert."

Abhimanyu licked his lips with satisfaction. He had outwitted Harshavardhan. Siddhartha would never again cause him any harm. *I have the blackguard by the balls.* One month was sufficient time to unearth data that would substantiate squashing the deal permanently.

•••

Book 4

# October 3, 1986: To Each Their Own

———

# 27.

# Ending the Mad War Dance

Sadhana could barely contain her nervousness, as she busied herself with the morning chores – watering the kitchen garden plants, preparing breakfast, performing her prayer ritual and finally, reading the morning newspaper, as she sipped a tall tumbler of filter coffee.

She had sensed Siddhartha tossing and turning in bed several times during the night. While he had been high strung ever since the tiara theft, his agitation had reached a new high on hearing from Harshavardhan that the deal had encountered an unexpected obstacle. The details were beyond the realm of Sadhana's comprehension. What she gathered was that Abhimanyu was trying to sabotage the Izod deal and Harshavardhan was trying to protect Siddhartha.

The one-time Sadhana had woken up, Siddhartha was sitting at the desk, poring over legal-looking documents with the aid of a torch and a magnifying lens, and muttering to himself. That was when Sadhana had made her resolution. She would put an end to the mad war dance that her vulnerable husband was engaged in, with the formidable Abhimanyu.

Sadhana handpicked an elegant chiffon sari for the historic meeting she had unilaterally scheduled with the regal Gayatri Devi who also had the reputation of being ruthless. She should not appear whining and needy, but operate from a position of strength, Sadhana told herself, as she applied her make-up. When she was brushing her loose let hair in front of the dressing mirror, Siddhartha had woken up. Given his state of mind, her only option was to keep him in the dark about her plan.

"You look lovely." His voice was groggy. "But I am not accompanying you to any social function."

She wanted him to head straight for the bathroom, as he usually did. "I am going to Chamundi Hills with Pallavi. You are not invited, Mr. Atheist."

"That is the best news I have heard in a whole week." He yawned loudly and got up. "No Chamundi Hills for me."

As soon as he had locked himself in the attached bathroom, Sadhana fumbled inside his side of the wardrobe, to locate the keys to the vault.

Siddhartha and Sadhana had stayed put in Panchsheel Villa ever since the completion of Project Tiara, two weeks ago. The bejewelled tiara lay in the old-fashioned vault within the drawing-room on the ground floor.

Going down the stairs, Sadhana unlocked the vault door and switched on the bright fluorescent light. The steel shelves were bare. The safety lockers were empty. Well, except one. Was the state of the vault an authentic reflection of the hollowness within their own lives?

Unlocking the one locker that was not empty, Sadhana extracted an old-fashioned bag with an intricate embroidered pattern; her trembling hands traced the shape of the tiara within, before stuffing the bag into the outsized purse she had chosen for the occasion. Casting a sad look around her, Sadhana started to close the locker door when the lacquered box caught her eye. Why not?

She would play the role of a rich woman one last time. Sadhana threaded the heart-shaped diamond pendant through the chain she wore on her neck and screwed the pear-shaped diamond solitaires through the lobes of her ears. Her eyes moist, she locked the vault and ran up to their bedroom to place the keys back in the wardrobe.

"Goodbye honey." She shouted out to Siddhartha through the bathroom door. "I will be home by six in the evening."

"I hope nothing goes wrong with the Izod deal." Siddhartha's voice had an air of dejection. "The trauma is killing me."

"All the best," she shouted back. "I will pray to Goddess Chamundi."

She was saving Siddhartha from an imminent catastrophe, a fate worse than death, Sadhana told herself, as she drove the blue Maruti towards Gayatri Devi's abode, located at the opposite end of town. If only she had known how prophetic her thoughts were?

When she had parked the car in front of the wrought iron gates of Indigo Castle, the uniformed security guard signalled her to wait, and went into the house. Sadhana switched off the engine. Indigo Castle loomed over her intimidatingly. She could quietly leave and go back home. No one would be the wiser.

The security guard had reappeared. Sadhana got out of the car and followed him through a long winding driveway. A matronly housekeeper welcomed her into a marble-floored foyer. The soothing smell of lavender permeated the air. Sitar music wafted down the stairs. A Tanjore style painting depicting a rare scene from the Mahabharata – Krishna's sister, Subhadra, in a chariot along with paramour Arjuna – adorned the wall.

"I am the daughter-in-law of Lawyer Vikramadityaji," Sadhana introduced herself. "I have come to return something valuable that belongs to Rani Gayatri Devi." She held up her outsized purse.

The matron informed her that Rani Maa did not meet anyone without an appointment and offered to hand over the package.

"I have to give this to her myself." Sadhana made the pretence of retreating. "If you give me an appointment, I will come back on that day."

Requesting Sadhana to take a seat, the matron went up the stairs. Sadhana sat down on an overstuffed pouffe and looked around. The spacious foyer opened out into one of the biggest living rooms she had ever seen. The proverbial opulence of her surroundings – blue and silver wallpaper, leather sofas and ottomans interspersed with ebony and ivory coffee tables, clichéd crystal chandeliers dangling tantalizingly from the high ceiling, objets d'art strewn across the length and breadth – was in sharp contrast to the dilapidated state of their own house, precariously on the brink of an impending collapse.

The overstuffed pouffe felt like a gigantic pincushion. Sadhana stood up. Envy as an emotion was not familiar to her. Yet, a wave of newfound empathy was engulfing her – for the hatred, her husband harboured for his haughty half-brother.

●●●

# 28.

# Emotional Truce

*The girl has spunk.* From her vantage point on the first-floor landing, Gayatri Devi had observed Sadhana's interaction with the portly matron in the foyer below. She had been playing the sitar in a valiant bid to nurse a defiant jet lag. The flight from London had landed at the Bangalore airport in the wee hours of the morning; from there, her personal chauffeur had driven Gayatri Devi to Mysore. She was a wee bit upset that Abhimanyu had not met her at the airport.

Gayatri Devi instructed the matron who came up the stairs, to seat Sadhana in the living room and offer her tea. Retreating into the dressing room to change out of her kaftan, Gayatri Devi wondered about the real purpose of the girl's visit. *I cannot fathom what valuable possession of mine she is here to return.* For no obvious reason, she felt a sense of elation about meeting the girl who had intriguingly introduced herself as 'Vikramaditya's daughter-in-law.'

Until then, Gayatri Devi had never met any member of her husband's first family in person. Having shifted to Bangalore and lived in Manyata Manor her entire married life, she had returned to Mysore, to live in Indigo Castle, only after the death of Vikramaditya, to escape the memories that had threatened to inundate her.

When Gayatri Devi entered the living room, dressed in an elegant crepe sari, Sadhana who was sitting on the edge of a stuffed chair, an oversized purse by her side, got up and reverentially touched Gayatri Devi's feet.

*What a cultured girl.* Gayatri Devi settled down on the burgundy daybed in the centre of the living room and asked Sadhana to draw her chair closer.

"I apologize for arriving at your house unannounced." Sadhana bit her lower lip.

"I am sure whatever it is you want to discuss is important."

"I have been terrified for the last few days." Sadhana's fingers clasped and unclasped the end of her chiffon sari. "Abhimanyuji and my husband are out to get each other."

"I don't interfere in my son's affairs," Gayatri Devi said guardedly. "As a successful businessman, he deals with a million things."

"We are on the verge of going bankrupt. In January, Ascot Bank stopped financing my husband's video business. That was Abhimanyuji's decision."

"Ascot Bank is governed by Reserve Bank guidelines. Neither Abhimanyu nor another director can set policy measures that violate those guidelines. Besides, my son is a noted economist and a director of the board. I can't dictate to him about banking decisions, if that is what you are suggesting."

"That was only the beginning." Sadhana's limpid eyes shone with sincerity. "Whatever is happening now is nothing short of the Kurukshetra[11] war. I do not know all the details, though."

*Kurukshetra!* Gayatri Devi's face formed itself into a frown. *That bad? I do not know the details either.* It was unlike Abhimanyu to keep her in the dark; but she had been away on an extended tour, she consoled herself. She could only hope the repercussions of whatever it was that he was doing would not be severe.

"My husband can no longer hold on to his business. He is in talks with a company called Izod Investments for a takeover." Sadhana's expression was forlorn. "He is terrified that Abhimanyuji is sabotaging that deal."

It was obvious that Sadhana was choosing her words with great care for fear of implicating her husband or making accusations at Abhimanyu or both. "I trust my son unconditionally." Gayatri Devi's gut recoiled under the brunt of the half-truth. She had trusted him unconditionally until a few minutes ago, she consoled herself. "I cannot intervene based on a supposition."

---

[11] the dynastic war in the Mahabharata

"I have great respect for my father-in-law. I am scared that the bad blood between my husband and your son will tarnish Vikramadityaji's reputation."

*I understand you are trying to establish common ground. Your doe-eyed expression does not fool me. Yet, I cannot but admire your approach to resolve this conflict. If you were applying for a managerial position in our business empire, I would hire you immediately.* "You are hiding something from me." Gayatri Devi glanced at the Swiss watch on her left wrist. "You have to tell me the whole truth."

There was a flicker of hesitation on Sadhana's face as she opened her oversized purse, pulled out an old-fashioned cloth bag and placed it on the nearest table. "I beg you. Please stop Abhimanyuji from harming my husband and ruining his business."

*Why did the bag look familiar? What did it contain?* A chill spread through Gayatri Devi's gut.

"I know this is a symbol of your royal heritage." Sadhana took out the tiara from the bag and offered it to Gayatri Devi.

"Did your husband steal it?" Gayatri Devi rasped, taking the tiara. Her chilled gut was now frozen.

"He was going to return it sooner or later. I decided to do it sooner."

The tiara was a trifle light. Gayatri Devi inhaled deeply. She pointed the tiara towards the open window. In the stream of the bright sunlight, the emerald shone a shade lighter than royal green, to her discerning eye. The original tiara was safe. Gayatri Devi rubbed the back of her neck lightly.

"My husband only wanted to make Abhimanyuji understand the pain of suffering. He did not have any other bad intentions," Sadhana said.

Gayatri Devi listened attentively as Sadhana narrated how she and Siddhartha had stealthily obtained the royal tiara.

*It is all Kalpana's fault. I must hold Abhimanyu accountable for his lassitude.* She exhaled deeply. Expecting Kalpana would do something spiteful after finding out Rahul was Abhimanyu's son, Gayatri Devi had lodged the real tiara with the State Bank of India, as collateral for a paltry loan. The tiara was the only vestige of her royal past and she had always taken extra precautions to preserve it.

"We guarded it with our life though." Sadhana folded her hands in a sign of deference. "We were troubled the entire time we had it with us."

218 | Family Secrets

"You did the right thing in returning it," Gayatri Devi said. "An eye for an eye, a tooth for a tooth is an archaic law. Both parties will go blind." As she inserted the tiara back into the bag, amidst the intricately embroidered pattern, the words 'Sulakshana Vikramaditya' caught her eye. Visions of Vikramaditya transporting transcripts in the bag during her court case flooded her memory. She clutched it to her bosom.

"My husband started his business with the money from his father's life insurance policy." Sadhana was choking. "He named it Vikrama Ventures in memory of his father. Abhimanyuji, who has inherited the entire wealth of his father, is somehow out to destroy whatever little we own. I am scared we will be on the streets. You are the only person who can prevent your son and my husband from destroying each other." Sadhana had collapsed at Gayatri Devi's feet.

*I hate tears.* Gayatri Devi pressed the buzzer. The matronly housekeeper appeared. Gayatri Devi watched, as the matron coaxed Sadhana to get up, and made her another cup of tea. In a way, Gayatri Devi envied Sadhana. *I wish I could lie on the floor and sob like that.*

"Rani Maa, please protect the honour of our families." A more composed Sadhana entreated soon after the matron had left.

Gayatri Devi moved her numbed legs and winced at the shock waves going up her spine. The turbulence in her mind was threatening to consume her entire body. How Siddhartha had obtained the tiara no longer mattered. Sadhana's tearful words had touched a part of her heart that she thought never existed. The infallible Gayatri Devi had fallen in her own eyes.

Forty-six years ago, she had unwittingly robbed Siddhartha of his rightful inheritance, so she could secure Abhimanyu's future. That Abhimanyu was now destroying the same Siddhartha, was unthinkable. That she was in the dark on his antics, was unacceptable. She breathed deeply several times, trying to quell the blaze in her gut.

"I am sorry I got emotional." Sitting on the chair sipping tea, Sadhana seemed to be back to her old self, except for the smudged mascara around her eyes. "I just thought, you and I should preserve Vikramadityaji's honour."

Gayatri Devi, who had never ever had a best female friend or sister or a daughter to bond with had the strongest urge to engulf the petite woman in a warm hug, hold her head to her bosom and console her. She stretched out both her hands instead, as if to allow her compassion to flow freely in Sadhana's direction. "I cannot go back and change the decisions made once upon a time. I will however stop my son, if as you say, he is causing you harm. Only if you tell me the whole truth."

"Only if you promise not to involve the police."

"You have my word." Gayatri Devi leaned forward.

Listening to Sadhana narrate how she and her husband had pulled off the diamond heist to pay off their debts, marvelling at their ingenuity and courage, it was with great difficulty, that Gayatri Devi contained her lips from breaking out into an appreciative smile. Siddhartha had inherited his father's intelligence, no doubt; except that he had used it for the wrong purposes. Sadhana was the perfect wife; supportive of her husband, yet with a will of her own.

"I am grateful to you for listening to me." Sadhana removed the diamond studs and pendant she was wearing and placed them in one of the crystal bowls nearby. "This is a token of my repentance."

Gayatri Devi made no move to either accept or return the trinkets. "You have nothing to fear from my son anymore. That is my responsibility. But do not for a moment think I condone your actions. I will tolerate no more hanky-panky from you or your husband," she said sternly.

"Please forgive us. For everything." Sadhana prostrated in front of Gayatri Devi and sheepishly bid a polite goodbye.

When Gayatri Devi picked up the crystal bowl with the trinkets that Sadhana had placed on the ebony table, the Tanjore painting on the wall caught her eye. Waging a mad war dance with Siddhartha, Abhimanyu had entangled himself in the throes of a complex labyrinth, a Chakravyuha[12] of his own making. She prayed that, unlike his namesake from the Mahabharata who had gotten himself killed, her darling son would disentangle himself with his honour intact.

◆

"Cancel my appointments for the rest of the day. Ask Lawyer Shiladitya to come here immediately. Tell him the matter is urgent. Connect me to my son in his Bangalore office." Seated on the burgundy daybed, Gayatri Devi had doled out the string of instructions to Upasana, her executive secretary, who worked from the library of yore, now converted to a full-fledged office within Indigo Castle.

---

[12] military formation to surround enemies

Having moved to Bangalore after marrying Vikramaditya, Gayatri Devi had never crossed paths with Sulakshana who had continued to live in Mysore. Whenever Vikramaditya attended conferences and cocktail parties, it was Gayatri Devi who was by his side. When he was posthumously honoured by the bar council, it was Gayatri Devi and her son, Abhimanyu, who represented him.

Yet, when Vikramaditya died, as irony would have it, when he was staying at Panchsheel Villa – Sulakshana and her son Siddhartha had been at the forefront and taken care of the final rites as per the Hindu tradition. Gayatri Devi and Abhimanyu had stayed back in Bangalore, unwilling to risk the repercussions of meeting the members of his first family – Vikramaditya's four daughters and their families and a plethora of extended family members, several of whom had lived under a single roof within the umbrella of the joint family. Gayatri Devi had to be content with organizing a separate prayer service for Vikramaditya's Bangalore friends, a month after he had passed away.

Upasana came back and informed Gayatri Devi that Abhimanyu was unreachable but she would keep trying to contact him at his office.

Sulakshana had only lived for three or four months after Vikramaditya's death. Like she was reuniting with him in heaven to make up for all the time she had surrendered him on earth to Gayatri Devi. Like she was fully fulfilling the image of the devoted wife she epitomized in the eyes of the Indian society. Around the same time, Gayatri Devi had returned to live at Indigo Castle in Mysore, after officially relinquishing the reins of the Aradhana Conglomerate to Abhimanyu.

Gayatri Devi had never seen pictures of Sulakshana – making her wonder if any even existed. She did not know what Siddhartha looked like. While she had never felt compunction of any sort for usurping their property rights, her diamond-edged heart had momentarily turned into candle-wax after meeting Sadhana, now the face of the first family.

Upasana was back one more time to deliver a fax that had arrived from the lawyer's office. The matron escorted Lawyer Shiladitya into the living room, at the same time.

Gayatri Devi went through the faxed document, which was a copy of her existing will. Even thinking about the transgression committed by Kalpana and Simi caused her blood pressure to rise. Twenty-one years back, she had unequivocally believed that Nayantara was the ideal match for Abhimanyu. But Nayantara's father had turned out to be such a glib deceiver that discarding the alliance had been the right decision at that time. Her thoughts turned to Rahul, the love-child that Abhimanyu and Nayantara had together created. Her heart almost burst from the sheer love it emitted, for the grandson whose existence she had discovered only recently.

Using a red felt pen, Gayatri Devi marked her changes on the faxed document. "Add Rahul Roy, my grandson, as the beneficiary of all property and assets belonging to the trust – personal and business – of which Abhimanyu and I are currently the joint owners. In the event of my death, Rahul will inherit my share and become the joint owner along with Abhimanyu. This Indigo Castle and the royal tiara, which I inherited from my father, I bequeath jointly to Abhimanyu and Rahul, following my death." She handed the red splashed document to Shiladitya. "Make sure you remove all references to Kalpana and Simi. Disinherit them for me."

Shiladitya had made his own notes on the faxed document with a green pen. If he was curious about the identity of the newfound grandson, he said nothing. He did though ask her to consider all contingent scenarios and provide for them.

Gayatri Devi shuddered. "God forbid, in the unlikely event my son does not outlive me, Rahul will inherit Abhimanyu's share. I will not consider the possibility of outliving Rahul under any circumstances. He is only twenty years old."

Shiladitya got up to go into the office, where he would work with Upasana and prepare a draft of the final testament.

"Tomorrow is the first day of Dussehra." Gayatri Devi said. "I want to register the final testament on Vijaya Dashami, the tenth and last day of Dussehra." She would dedicate the rest of the day to reviewing and refining the testament, until she could declare it was flawless and final.

•••

# 29.

# Losers Weepers

I *hope Izod Investments makes a quick decision. The uncertainty is killing me.* Siddhartha dressed with haste after his leisurely stint of morning ablutions in the bathroom. He had turned into a nervous wreck, since Harshavardhan's call a couple of days ago, when he had learnt that Abhimanyu was plotting a strategic alliance with Izod Investments.

"I will not form any kind of business alliance with the enemy." Harshavardhan had sworn his allegiance to Siddhartha. "I called off the meeting and refused his offer outright."

Yet, the news had pushed Siddhartha to the brink of his tether. Vikrama Ventures could be cannibalized, if Abhimanyu, with his financial muscle and limitless power, entered the fray. Siddhartha had engaged in lengthy conversations separately with Joshua and with Harshavardhan ever since, pleading with them to ensure the acquisition deal was not in jeopardy.

*Bless her heart.* Savouring the South-Indian style rice noodles and millet porridge that Sadhana had readied for his breakfast, his sadness melted away for the briefest moment.

Over the last few months, Joshua and Harshavardhan had worked together on the acquisition deal. Financial analysis was complete, legal guidelines had been addressed and the paperwork was lined up. The date for signing the agreement was set to coincide with Vijaya Dashami, the most auspicious day of Dussehra, October 14. On that day, Izod Investments would become the unequivocal owner of Vikrama Ventures. Siddhartha would receive a gross consideration of Rupees eighteen lakhs and allotted shares equivalent to one percent of the new equity as a gesture of goodwill – for permitting Harshavardhan to retain the name.

Siddhartha switched on the radio to listen to the mid-morning news, and settled down in his favourite armchair near the phone, to wait for Harshavardhan's call. *I hope the merger does not fall apart. I do not want to lose Panchsheel Villa.*

Hearing screeching tires outside, followed by a loud rap on the front door, Siddhartha shouted for Laxman to open the door. The rap had given way to incessant knocking, causing his heart to pound in a disturbing unison, but there was no sign of Laxman. He was probably washing the car in the back yard. Siddhartha kicked away a chunk of the crumbled plaster that had fallen from the ceiling and got up.

◆

Three tall uniformed men stood at the door. "Income Tax Enforcement Federation." The tallest of them introduced himself as Nachiket and thrust a search warrant to Siddhartha's nose. "We have orders to search the premises and the people."

*Deep breath.* A stunned Siddhartha skimmed through the warrant. Having grown up with a lawyer for a part-time father – he had learnt that it paid to stay calm so he could exercise caution. He checked the date and the address and ascertained that the warrant was bona fide. "I am a law-abiding citizen. I have never defaulted on my income tax."

"Then you have nothing to worry," Nachiket said.

"My business losses are mounting. Financially I have nothing to hide. I cannot fathom why you are here."

"If you wish, you can call your auditor to be present."

"I wish," Siddhartha said. Joshua was out of the country. "What set off this search?" *Is this a ploy engineered by my father's ignoble son?*

"We have routine orders," Nachiket said. "If you cooperate with us, it will be over fast."

Realizing that he had no choice but to comply with the search, Siddhartha asked the officers for their identification. Looking at the identity papers they produced, he memorized the name and designation of each officer. While their identity appeared genuine, he had to make sure that the officers would not plant any evidence and get him in legal trouble.

Siddhartha yelled for Laxman one more time, and thanked his stars when Laxman came running. Having sought Nachiket's permission, Siddhartha searched all three officers personally, with Laxman's assistance, before permitting them to enter the house.

Nachiket took charge of the situation thereafter. Siddhartha accompanied Nachiket upstairs while Laxman handed over the account statements and related records to the other two officers and stayed back with them on the ground floor.

◆

Squatting on the floor and watching Nachiket nonchalantly ransack the master bedroom, Siddharth was half-glad Sadhana was not home – it had saved her the ignominy of watching a perfect stranger comb through their most personal and intimate belongings.

The garlanded portraits of Vikramaditya and Sulakshana that adorned the bedroom wall stared back at him. With pity? Abhimanyu had used his power and influence to set the Enforcement Federation after him. That was the only explanation for the raid.

Nothing of value had surfaced. Nachiket's face looked dour as they exited the bedroom. Nachiket rapidly searched the remaining rooms on the upper floor and the terrace.

When Siddhartha and Nachiket descended to the ground floor, the other officers had finished ransacking the dining room, the puja room and Laxman's bedroom. They looked disappointed – there was nothing of value anywhere.

"Anna, please tell them we have no money." A cowering Laxman implored Siddhartha.

"We know that." Nachiket held up the account ledgers. "My men tell me the business is kaput."

"Why are you doing this then? Just leave us alone," Siddhartha said.

"I am following orders." Nachiket led his team into the drawing-room. Siddhartha and Laxman followed.

It would all be over once Nachiket opened the drawing-room vault and found the tiara. Siddhartha felt his face turning blue and legs going stiff. He was a law-abiding citizen posing as a con artiste. He would have to tell Nachiket the truth. Since he had intended returning the tiara, he could subvert charges of larceny and plead misdemeanour.

He had to get in touch with Lawyer Iyengar, who had once been his father's junior. He did not want to go to prison. He would have to use the money from the Izod deal to pay off any penalty for the glorified misdemeanour.

"All the cash and jewellery must be here." Jingling the key chain, he had found in Siddhartha's bedroom, Nachiket opened the vault door. Switching on the fluorescent light, he unlocked the safety lockers one after another and shone his torch.

*What happened to the bag containing the tiara?* Siddhartha distinctly remembered seeing it inside the topmost locker the last time he was in there. He looked slyly at Laxman, who gave a slight shrug of the shoulders.

The empty shelves and lockers must have told him a story he did not like. Nachiket pounced on Siddhartha. "Where have you hidden everything?"

"Mr. Nachiket, I have told you the whole truth. You have searched my person and reviewed my ledgers. The entire house is at your disposal. You are welcome to complete the search." *If you find anything valuable, I will be truly delighted.*

Nachiket prodded the corner stool with his foot, trooped out of the vault and started ransacking the rest of the drawing room.

Partly relieved, partly anxious, Siddhartha stood at the bay window and stared outside.

The tiara and the diamond set were both missing. Sadhana had gone to the Chamundi temple; she had probably worn the diamond set. He wondered where she had taken the tiara and what she was doing with it. He was certain she would never wear it. She had said she would return at six o'clock. The enforcement squad would be long gone by then. Design or default, Sadhana had saved them. Even under the dire circumstances, the Shakespearean irony of his situation was not lost on Siddhartha.

◆

Siddhartha had no clue how much time had passed. There was a tap on his shoulder. Nachiket thrust a copy of the Panchnama, a record of the search and observation, into Siddhartha's hands, and stood near him like a hawk monitoring its prey, as Siddhartha read it.

1. There was total cooperation from Siddhartha and his family

2. Siddhartha maintains he is innocent; the squad's findings on the premises agree with his statements

3. No cash, jewellery or other valuables were seized, since none were found

4. The ledgers and statements show huge business losses for Vikrama Ventures

5. Bank account KA04M316 at Ascot Bank, of which Siddhartha is a joint owner with his late father Vikramaditya will be frozen with immediate effect

6. Siddhartha will be responsible for payment of income tax and penalties for the unexplained credits of Rs. 5,00,000/- in Ascot Bank savings account KA04M316

7. The Enforcement Federation will place a lien on Siddhartha's house, the only unencumbered personal asset he owns, until the assessment is over

8. Siddhartha can be arrested if the Federation's investigation establishes an intent for concealment of income

Lien on Panchsheel Villa? Siddhartha shot up like a fired bullet. "Can you please explain points 5 and 6 in the Panchnama?"

"I am not allowed to discuss the reasons of the raid with you."

"Unexplained credits. Is that the reason for the raid?"

"All I can say is that I have come to believe you are innocent."

"Please explain unexplained credits." Siddhartha was keen to find the underlying cause of the day's debacle.

"Sorry, Sir."

"I swear on the life of my dead father; the joint account has not been operated since his death." Siddhartha felt the sadness gush out through his words and permeate the air. "I did not close the bank account for sentimental reasons."

"You are a perfect gentleman." Nachiket's hard stare had softened. "I share this with you in strict confidence. The manager of Ascot Bank alerted the Federation that there were multiple cash deposits into your account."

"Bullshit. Neither I nor my family nor my employees deposited the money."

"The amount was significant. Rupees Five Lakhs."

"I wish I had that much money! My house would not be such a dump then." An aura of dejection engulfed Siddhartha. "Can I see the deposit slips?"

"I am not allowed to show them." Nachiket shook his head. "There were around eighty of them. No name or signature on any of them."

*The whole thing reeks of an Abhimanyu gambit.* "Have you considered that someone else may be behind it?"

"Why would someone else spend five lakh rupees?"

"To get me in trouble? Spoil my name?"

"We are talking real hard-earned money here."

"Money is real but may not always be hard-earned."

"Are you saying you have rich enemies?"

"Yes." Siddhartha refrained from making further accusations for fear of undoing the credibility he had established with Nachiket.

"The best recourse you have is to engage a lawyer and provide proof at the assessment proceedings that you did not make those deposits," Nachiket said.

"Anna is innocent." Laxman folded his hand. "Don't arrest him."

Siddhartha put a consoling arm around Laxman and mussed his hair, grateful to him for articulating his own worst fear.

"You cannot be arrested, I assure you." Nachiket held up the Panchnama. "Based on statements 1 and 2."

"What about the freeze on this house? There is no cause to suspect me. That is what you just said," Siddhartha pleaded.

"That is a standard clause." Nachiket's face clouded. "I do not have the power to waive it."

"This house is all we have." Laxman started weeping.

"The sooner you get a lawyer, the faster the assessment proceedings can be completed," Nachiket said, packing up his files.

◆

The squad was gone. Laxman's anguish was uncontrollable. Siddhartha did not have the energy to pacify him. He was nervous about the mysterious disappearance of the tiara but too fatigued to figure out what may have happened. Income tax authorities had just confiscated Panchsheel Villa, his only valuable possession. Born a loser, was he destined to die a loser? Izod Investments was his only ray of hope. Siddhartha dialled Harshavardhan's number.

"Siddhu, is Sadhana with you?" Harshavardhan sounded anxious.

"No."

"Are you at a place where you can sit down?"

"Yes." Siddhartha ran his tongue over his parched lips to overcome the feeling of his heart being in his mouth.

"Do not panic." Siddhartha heard Harshavardhan say. "I am here to help." Why had darkness enveloped the house? Though, he could see the bright sun through the window, withering the plants in the garden.

"Things have got complicated." Harshavardhan's voice was even. "Abhimanyu is a tyrant. He bought out the share of my partner's family. He now controls 51 % of Izod Investments."

"I am screwed." *My father's ignoble son has debilitated me by a deliberate act of revenge.*

"I know Joshua is away in Nepal." He heard Harshavardhan say. "I will find a way to get in touch with him. Hold your horses for a day or two. Promise me."

The grandfather clock was striking. Siddhartha gripped the armchair. Why was the pendulum not visible? Was it noon or was it midnight?

"I am going into a closed-door meeting with Abhimanyu. Whatever happens, I will not side with the enemy." Harshavardhan stated with his characteristic conviction.

The voices in Siddhartha's head were getting louder and louder. 'Give us our money.' The lenders chanted in unison.

"I will sort things out, in our favour, yours and mine." Harshavardhan sounded reassuring. "I promise."

*The bastard has decimated me.* A big chunk of plaster fell from the ceiling, as if in validation. Why were the walls of the house converging on him? Were they out to trap him?

"Trust me. I am there for you." He heard Harshavardhan say.

Siddhartha put the phone down and stared at the weird pattern formed by the chunks of fallen plaster on the dining room floor. With the best of lawyers, it would take three to five years for an income tax case to come up for hearing. Proceedings were known to last from three to six months. How would he and his family survive during that period? Where would they live? With Vikrama Ventures on the verge of collapse and Izod Investments backing out, he did not have the money to engage Lawyer Iyengar. Should he declare insolvency?

Siddhartha went out of the house and wandered around the vast garden, looking for Laxman.

The mysterious appearance of the five lakh rupees in the bank was an additional liability. Siddhartha dreaded the taxes and penalties that would be levied if the source of the deposits could not be established. That was assuming he was not declared guilty of deliberately concealing income. God forbid, the Income Tax Federation decided otherwise? Siddhartha convulsed. With everything stacked up against him, Siddhartha knew not what other cards the powerful Abhimanyu would play against him.

Siddhartha found Laxman shearing away the tall weeds in the hot afternoon sun. "I have to leave for Bangalore immediately," he said. "Get me a taxi?"

"Don't go." Laxman threw the shears onto the ground, wiped the sweat off his bare torso and clutched at Siddhartha.

Siddhartha held up his palm to shield his face from the scorching sun. "Promise me you will take care of Sadhana."

"Wait for her to return, Anna. You can then take the car."

"Urgent business matter." Siddhartha cajoled Laxman. "Related to the Izod deal."

"Only if you give me the phone number," Laxman negotiated.

When Siddhartha had handed him Harshavardhan's business card, Laxman reluctantly released Siddhartha from his hug, slipped on a shirt and ran out of the gate to fetch a taxi.

Siddhartha walked back into the house and collected the things he would take to Bangalore. The matter was out of his hands. Like any good project manager, he had to activate the contingency plan. In this case, it would be the last resort of a loser.

●●●

# 30.

# Mother Knows Best

Seated in his penthouse cabin in Lakeview Terrace, Abhimanyu popped a floppy disk into his computer and feasted his eyes on the fund flow analysis that Varun had formulated for the venture capital foray with Izod Investments. Abhimanyu almost levitated out of his revolving chair as he tweaked the scenarios and estimated the pile of profits forecast for the coming years. At this rate, Aradhana Conglomerate would reach the revenue milestone of Rupees one hundred crores much sooner than envisioned.

The phone rang just as the clock struck. Abhimanyu hastily saved the Lotus 1-2-3 file. The DCP had promised to call him at four o'clock. The enforcement squad should have found the tiara by now. It would be in his hands shortly. He rubbed his hands in anticipation.

"Rani Maa herself is on the line," the receptionist said. "Her secretary had left several urgent messages when you were out."

Abhimanyu cursed under his breath. Veronica had taken the day off or she would have known what to do. Abhimanyu was aware, Rani Maa had returned from Europe in the wee hours of the morning and headed to Mysore straight from the airport. He had not gone to meet her at the airport, citing that he was busy with the strategic alliance research. The real reason was different. He could not lie to her. She did not yet know about the tiara theft; he would meet her after the raid had yielded the tiara.

"You have to come down immediately," Rani Maa said.

"I have been adding to our wealth while you were on your world tour. Our business portfolio now includes venture capital. We own 49 % of Izod Investments."

"Come now."

"You will love the projected cash flow." Abhimanyu sucked in the saliva that was drooling through his lips. "Are you not jetlagged?"

"I will see you at seven o'clock. That is an order." She had put the phone down.

Why did she sound so grave and disciplinarian? Abhimanyu hit the save button on the computer. Had Rani Maa discovered that the tiara was missing? He dialled Zero to connect to the receptionist and asked her to fetch the driver.

Why had the DCP not called? Abhimanyu tapped on his forehead lightly. He hoped the enforcement squad had found the tiara. When Abhimanyu had met with the DCP at the golf club that morning, he had confirmed that the squad, headed by one of their star performers, would raid Siddhartha's house in Mysore a little after ten o'clock.

Abhimanyu dialled the DCP's private number. There was no response. He dialled Zero yet another time and asked the receptionist to connect him to the DCP's office. He hoped Siddhartha had not pawned off or worse still, sold off the tiara. Not possible, he would have known by now, Abhimanyu consoled himself. Not only was he the president of the Karnataka Gemmology Association, but also his network of contacts would have notified him if that had happened.

The intercom buzzed. The receptionist informed him that the DCP would not be available until the next day. He had however left a message for Abhimanyu, with his secretary. 'Mysore mission complete. Item not found.'

"Dammit," Abhimanyu banged the phone down. What if Siddhartha had sold off the tiara to a jeweller outside the Bangalore-Mysore circuit? Or a private buyer? Or an underground agent? Abhimanyu's network was not wide enough to cover those scenarios.

His bladder was threatening to burst at its seams. Abhimanyu went into the attached bathroom and locked the door. Had Siddhartha hidden the tiara in another place rather than Panchsheel Villa? A bank locker perhaps?

There was no urine stream. Abhimanyu shook his penis vigorously. Siddhartha did not own a locker at the Ascot bank, of that Abhimanyu was sure. If he had, it would have been the ultimate irony.

Abhimanyu looked down. The shrivelled member nuzzling his left hand had stayed dry. He took several deep breaths. Siddhartha was neither a businessman nor a criminal. His tactics were neither scientific nor methodical. Siddhartha's mind worked like that of an artist and a mad one at that. That is why it was so difficult to predict what he had done with the tiara.

Abhimanyu let out a deep sigh of relief when his bladder finally started depleting itself. Watching the clear stream hitting the bowl, another bitter thought struck him. Siddhartha might have a Bangalore address that was not public. Maybe the tiara was in a rented flat or office in some corner of Bangalore.

Abhimanyu shook his contented member forcefully and zipped up his pants. He had to stop speculating. He would wait until he had a chance to talk to the DCP and get the details. The toilet would not flush and the soap dispenser was running dry; Abhimanyu kicked the toilet seat hard so it shut with a loud bang.

The intercom was buzzing when he returned to his desk. The receptionist informed him that the driver had played truant and left for the day. She had contacted the cab company and their earliest available cab was at six o'clock.

It was a three-hour drive from Bangalore to Mysore. 'I will see you at seven o'clock. That is an order.' Rani Maa's words boomeranged between his ears. He could not remember the last time his mother had been angry with him. He was certain she had discovered Kalpana's blunder and his indiscretion. He would drive down to Mysore himself. He would own up his mistake and seek Rani Maa's help to retrieve the tiara.

Abhimanyu picked up his valise and dashed towards the elevator. Life was all about finding solutions to the problems it posed. He was successful because he had perfected the science of surmounting every challenge he encountered. Why should this time be any different?

◆

"Rejection. What you did to Rahul is wrong." Rani Maa placed a single sheet of typewritten paper on her son's lap. "He is the natural heir of Aradhana."

Abhimanyu, who had arrived at Indigo Castle a few minutes after seven, sat next to her on the burgundy daybed. A glass of single malt whiskey awaited him on an ebony table with ivory inlay. Sweet-smelling incense sticks kept mosquitoes at bay. Crystal chandeliers cast a golden hue across the living room.

Abhimanyu's eyes scanned through Rani Maa's final testament. He had no objection to Kalpana and Simi being left out of the will. Just retribution. Following the fiasco, Kalpana had brainwashed Simi into believing that he was a philandering monster. But what had prompted his mother to bring Rahul into the picture? Abhimanyu cringed.

"Where is Rahul?" Rani Maa looked Abhimanyu in the eye.

"Rahul cannot run Aradhana. He is weak. Emotional."

"Is that why you made him disappear?" She sounded irate. "Miraculously?"

Abhimanyu's breathing became heavy. "Rahul has abnormal tendencies."

"So outdated. You disappoint me."

"He has grown up in a foreign country. His tendencies are contrary to our culture."

"Homosexuality transcends cultures," she said.

Abhimanyu could feel his face smouldering. He dug into his valise for his emergency medication. "Who told you Rahul has become a ...?"

"You. Your hostile behaviour. And no one 'becomes' homosexual. Sexuality is an expression of nature. Not an acquired habit. Nor a deliberately cultivated practice."

"I never knew you had such ultra-modern views." He swallowed his medication.

"Acceptance is neither modern nor traditional," She said. "It stems from tolerance."

"You are not angry with Rahul?"

"On the contrary, I commend him. For having the courage to be his true self. For asserting himself against his formidable father."

Abhimanyu swallowed a mouthful of whiskey. His mother was scorning him for rejecting his son. He could not digest that. He berated Rahul inwardly for his offensive life choices.

"Rahul is our own flesh and blood." Rani Maa's mouth had formed an O as if she were blowing him kisses in the air. "Bring him back."

Abhimanyu swirled the whiskey, took a whiff, and rolled the liquid around in his mouth. His inscrutable mother was indefatigable as well.

"You will formally adopt Rahul on Vijaya Dashami day." Rani Maa stated with an air of finality. "Lawyer Shiladitya is drawing up the final documents."

Abhimanyu clenched his teeth. His head was still at war with his heart.

"You have less than ten days to find your son and convince him." Her tone had turned soft as silk. "Apologize. Promise him there will be no coercion. Cajole him."

Making a wry face, Abhimanyu handed the testament back to Rani Maa. And bent down to touch her feet. He would obey his mother. He had always trusted her unconditionally.

"I take that as having your word. That you will bring Rahul back." Rani Maa took her son's hand in her own. "I know it. In your heart, there is only love for your son."

"Tell me what prompted you to take this drastic step." He looked at her.

Gayatri Devi handed him the royal tiara. Her face remained impassive.

"Where did you find this?" Abhimanyu had drained the entire contents of the whiskey glass down his gullet and jumped up.

"It was returned to me. By an aggrieved young woman."

Abhimanyu kneaded the octagonal sapphires of the tiara with his fingers. That young woman was Siddhartha's wife? How had she come to return the tiara in the middle of an income tax raid? Made no sense. "That is why the income tax squad could not find it." He blurted out before he could check himself.

"You sent the tax authorities after him? By filing a false complaint? The lengths you go to for fulfilling your personal vendetta!"

"Guile has to be countered with guile. I had no other recourse."

"I never thought you would be so cruel." Rani Maa's face had turned a deep red.

Rani Maa was his closest ally. He could not bear to be the target of her anger. Abhimanyu kneeled in front of his mother. "I take full ownership for the tiara fiasco. Please forgive my infraction. Kalpana misused her access to the vault without my knowledge. Simi admitted to emotional blackmail." Attempting to vindicate himself, he hoped he did not sound vindictive of his wife and daughter.

"Stop sparring with Siddhartha."

"I have not done anything illegal. Whatever I did was to protect us, prevent our ruin . . ."

"Sadhana is adorable. Siddhartha is your Appa's son." Rani Maa cleared her throat and dabbed her eyes. "I have made a promise. That you will stop wrecking their happiness."

Abhimanyu had never ever seen his mother get emotional. "Don't believe everything that woman said. Did she not tell you how her husband..."?

"She told me everything." Rani Maa raised her hand. "And there is no need for your Brahmastra[13] like tactics. Because Siddhartha is not a cruel criminal; he is like a hapless bird. Besides, he is the son of the great man to whom you and I owe everything we own. In a sense, Siddhartha is the bona fide owner of what you inherited ..."

•••

---

[13] Ancient destructive weapon

# 31.

# The Verdict

December 1, 1939. A cold wintry morning. It was the day of the verdict. Gayatri Devi entered the portals of the court with Governess Agnes and Jeweller Gupta in tow. Deliberately, she had chosen an austere look – a plain khadi sari, a grey shawl around her shoulders, hair pulled back into a tight bun and a pair of plain glasses perched on the bridge of her nose. She wore no jewellery, not even her signature pearls; nor her Swiss watch.

The wall clock read half-past ten. The proceedings would not start for the next hour and a half.

What if we lose the case? What if the Judge is swayed by the chastity card that Krishnakant has consistently played in court? Gayatri Devi had agonized all night. Sleeplessly. And ended up arriving early in court. She settled down at the plaintiff table and pulled out a hardbound copy of *Rebecca,* Daphne Du Maurier's latest. Romantic fiction had been her refuge. During the eight-week separation from the object of her affection.

The courtroom got noisier as spectators began to arrive. Raghu and his father, the face of the Rajvamsh family during the case, walked in with the defendant lawyer Krishnakant, who looked uncomfortable in a pair of trousers he must have worn for the first time.

When her body began to feel like molten lava, Gayatri Devi knew that the object of her affection had arrived and occupied the chair to her right. More salt than pepper in his hair, deeper lines on his forehead, an extra inch around his midriff, had he somehow aged? She had the strongest urge to embrace him, slobber his face with her kisses. She put her book away instead.

Exactly at noon, an orderly announced that the proceedings would begin. The courtroom was as full as always.

*You are the architect of my future.* Gayatri Devi held Vikramaditya's eyes for a moment as he prepared to make his closing statement. *Will we flourish? Or perish?*

"A devoted wife of royal birth-right, Rani Gayatri Devi was willing to continue living within the confines of her husband's joint family even after his death ..." Vikramaditya gave a sweeping look across the courtroom. "Yet her late husband's family mercilessly drove her out of their house. Newly widowed, not even thirty years old, she went back to live with her ailing father and valiantly took care of him, until he passed away. As a daughter, as a wife, as a human being – her behaviour is honourable." His voice had reached a crescendo.

Listening to him with rapt attention, Gayatri Devi started feeling more buoyant.

"Envy is the resentment some people feel when they do not possess the good qualities they desire. Envy is the strongest of negative emotions. People who fall prey to this monster become unhappy, aggressive and vindictive." Vikramaditya cast a glance towards the defendant table.

She could sense the hostile vibes emanating from Raghu and his father; Gayatri Devi winced. Agnes, who sat to her right, touched Gayatri Devi's face lightly with her own fingertips and cracked her knuckles – a gesture to ward off evil vibes.

"As a society, we need to develop a more open mind." Vikramaditya's tone softened audibly. "For, it is shameful the way people are tarnishing the image of my client. She is a single woman who has no one – son, brother, father nor any other male relative – who can help her. She has no choice but to interact with me, her lawyer, directly, which has resulted in rumour-mongering."

For a moment, the attention of everybody in the courtroom trained towards where Gayatri Devi sat. Gupta, who sat to her left, extended his palm over Gayatri Devi's head as if to bless her.

"I appeal to the court to grant a decision in favour of Rani Gayatri Devi. She not only shows restraint and maturity in dealing with a tough situation but also possesses the moral courage to obtain justice through legal recourse," Vikramaditya concluded.

The Judge called upon the defense lawyer to make his closing statement.

Speaking in chaste vernacular, Krishnakant focused on the theme of loyalty. A woman's loyalty to her husband, living or dead was the foundation of her right to inherit properties belonging to his family. 'Dharmecha, Arthecha, Kaamecha, Naathicharami.' According to the wedding vows, a husband and wife promise to stand by each other righteously always and not be unfaithful under any compulsions be they justice, finances, or desire. He pointed out that the foundation of that sacred relationship was at stake based on the testimonials of the neighbours, the staff and family members. It was highly unlikely that all of them were lying. He declared that any woman's right to the property of her dead husband's family had to be rescinded under such circumstances.

Gayatri Devi's roving eye discretely scanned the faces in the courtroom. Going by the frequent nods of approval, Krishnakant seemed to have struck a chord with the audience, despite his faulty diction and halting flow of words. Had he deliberately remained silent on the statement of assets?

The Judge's countenance stayed stoic as he summoned Vikramaditya to deliver the closing summary.

Vikramaditya enumerated the immovable properties and liquid assets owned by the Rajvamsh family and accentuated the vastness of the family's wealth. "This list is fully attested by the court commissioner," he reiterated. "Not to forget that the Rajvamsh family submitted a bogus statement that did not even include fifty per cent of the assets. Their intention, as is blatantly obvious, is to deny my client her rightful share."

Why did Vikramaditya's face look so grave? Gayatri Devi gently stroked her abdomen under the folds of her shawl. She could not wait to tell him what she had discovered that morning.

"Your Honour, I appeal for a decision of epic proportions that will ameliorate the status of women in our society." Vikramaditya rested his case.

The Judge cleared his throat. The decision rested entirely with him.

"I have perused the documentation and photographic evidence put together by Mr. Vikramaditya and listened to the arguments of both sides. I have no doubt that the Rajvamsh family has previously provided false information to this court. The court expresses gratitude to Mr.

Vikramaditya and the court commissioner for furnishing accurate asset details and imposes a fine of Rupees Five Thousand on the Rajvamsh family, which they should deposit with the State Treasury within five days of this verdict. Failure to do so may result in imprisonment of some or all concerned family members."

Gayatri Devi saw Krishnakant stand up. She did not dare to look in the direction of Raghu and his father. If their looks had the power to kill, they would have reduced her to a heap of ash right there, of that she was sure.

"While the plaintiff's claim under The Hindu Women's Right to Properties Act 1937 is legitimate, the court has to consider issues of moral turpitude that has been brought to its notice before announcing the final verdict. On ethical grounds, the court wishes to discuss this matter in private with the plaintiff and her lawyer. Subsequently, the court will communicate the verdict privately to the defense lawyer." The Judge got up from his seat.

The decibel level of the courtroom noise increased exponentially.

◆

Waiting in the anteroom to meet the Judge, Gayatri Devi re-draped her silver-grey shawl. Whatever it was, the verdict was not in her favour. While the possibility had worried her all night, she was not prepared for the eventuality.

The orderly ushered them into the Judge's chamber, the court's sanctum sanctorum and seated them in adjacent chairs facing the Judge across his expansive desk. The Judge's assistant sat at a smaller table on the side. The Judge leaned forward and continued from where he had left off in the courtroom.

"The persona of the husband after his death continues through his wife who is the surviving half. The husband continues to live through the widow so long as the widow is alive. This is the concept of the Hindu law that the Act of 1937 recognized and brought into effect. Under these circumstances, therefore, when the Legislature uses the expression 'the same interest as he himself had' it would include all the bundle of rights possessed by the husband which would devolve on the wife."

Gayatri Devi's hands lightly clutched her abdomen. Abhimanyu – that is what she would call their son – for bringing him into a labyrinthine world. The onerous responsibility of making sure that he did not suffer the same fate as his namesake from the Mahabharata, rested solely on her. Every woman has an inherent craving to become a mother – every social stimulus she had ever received had asserted this. Yet, during the ten years of her childless marriage to Ashoka, she had never missed being a mother. Was she a blot on Indian womanhood? She had often wondered. Now she knew the answer. She was not.

"This is the first case of its kind, up for hearing in the State of Mysore after the Act of 1937 was passed," the Judge continued. "I want to base my first verdict on circumstances that can never be challenged. Unfortunately, doubts have been raised in this case – which the court cannot prove conclusively one way or the other – owing to their moral nature. While the court cannot take them into consideration, it cannot ignore them either."

Vikramaditya was nodding his head vigorously. It was evident that he was worried.

"You are both mature individuals, civilized in your behaviour and with exposure to westernized society," the Judge said. "What is normal interaction for you takes on a different meaning when viewed through the narrow prisms of a highly conservative society. While I maintain neutrality in my personal views and condone the moral aspersions that were cast – I have to desist from awarding Rani Gayatri Devi the same bundle of rights that her husband possessed – in accordance with the premise of the law I just quoted."

Vikramaditya started to make a request for reconsideration. The Judge's hand went up.

"The defendant will be ordered to pay Rani Gayatri Devi a one-time settlement of Rupees Five Thousand as well as reimburse all expenses including lawyer fees incurred for the case." The Judge leaned back in his chair.

*Dreams die first.* Gayatri Devi tugged at her shawl. She had been denied equal rights in the property of her dead husband's family, because of moral turpitude. How would she secure Abhimanyu's future?

At a minimum, could the court award his client ownership rights to one house and an annuity of one thousand rupees a month? Vikramaditya played on the emotions of the Judge and pitched for reconsideration of the settlement. Though amicable, the Judge was not pliable. Negotiations continued. Vikramaditya was tough yet sincere. The Judge eventually conceded marginally, doubling the one-time compensation to Rupees Ten Thousand. "Indian society can be cruel. Even Goddess Sita Devi had to go through an agnee pareeksha[14] to prove her chastity and be accepted by Lord Rama," he declared.

*I am no Sita. Within a year of my husband's death, I am pregnant with another man's child.* Gayatri Devi stared back at the Judge numbly. Rupees Ten Thousand. She would pay off the pawn loan with Brindavan Bank and cover living expenses for a year or two. She needed to establish her business, so she could secure Abhimanyu's future. Losing the case had smashed her plans to smithereens.

"Lord Rama may be a role model for everything pure and perfect," Vikramaditya said. "The act of suspecting his wife even after the agnee pareeksha and then abandoning her is a huge blot on his nobility."

The Judge made a clucking sound. "Lord Rama was the King; he had to set high standards. We cannot take everything stated in the Ramayana literally."

Gayatri Devi was thankful for the plain glasses – her disappointment at losing the case was moistening her eyes. *I cannot give up now. Abhimanyu must inherit the royal tiara. I will not sell it under any circumstances.*

The Judge's assistant had recorded the final verdict. The Judge summoned the defense lawyer. Repeating the final verdict, he presented carbon copies of the transcripts to both parties. "Please arrange to make the full payment of ten thousand rupees to the plaintiff before December 31," he instructed Krishnakant. "And full reimbursement of expenses as per the statement that will be provided by the Plaintiff's lawyer. Also, before December 31."

◆

As Gayatri Devi exited the anteroom, with Vikramaditya a step behind, she could hear Raghu and his father cackling audibly. "You have made your bed. Now lie in it. Your Bahishkaara from our clan is full and final." Triumph danced wildly in their eyes as they continued to blow her curses.

◆

"First and foremost, I apologize for losing the case," Vikramaditya said as soon as they were in the back seat of his car. "I will find a way to make up for it."

---

[14] ordeal of entering the fire

She looked at him intently through the plain glasses. Why was he being so formal? Had the many weeks of separation created a chasm in their relationship? His face looked as innocent as ever. "I am sorry too," she reached for his hand. "This is the first case you have ever lost. I want it to be the last."

"Victory and defeat are two sides of the same coin." His hand caressed her fingers.

Dignity in defeat. The courage to render a heartfelt apology. This man can do no wrong. She tightened her grip on his hand. *All I want is to be a good mother to your son. You must know today.* When the driver stopped the Austin in front of Indigo Castle, Gayatri Devi would not let go of Vikramaditya's hand.

"A house full of people awaits me back home. But I want to be with you." Vikramaditya alighted after her.

The maid served them a hot lunch, after which they retired to the sitting room – their new haven in Indigo Castle – and closed the door.

"How can I make it up to you?" Vikramaditya asked.

"Marry me." Gayatri Devi had occupied the leather swivel chair behind the desk.

"I wish."

"I am serious."

"Seriously? You want to be my second wife?" He sounded frazzled.

"I did not say that."

"You do know my situation. My daughters are married into orthodox families. One of them is a mother. Another one is now in the family way. They may be driven out of their in-law's houses if a scandal erupts." His eyebrows had knitted themselves into a fragile frown.

She wanted to bury his head to her bosom and smother it, so his eyebrows would unknit and regain their original state. "What then is my status? Mistress?"

"You are the love of my life. But I can't leave my wife. What about my daughters?"

Was there a fleeting glimpse of pain on his face? "You don't love your wife then?" She had to know.

"I did not say that. Sulu, I mean Sulakshana runs my house, is a wonderful mother to my children and takes good care of my parents. I would not have been a successful lawyer without her constant presence."

"You have always wanted a son, haven't you?"

"I have never treated my daughters with any disparity. If I had a son, I would treat him as their equal."

"You will have a son." She held his gaze.

"Are you into fortune-telling?" He walked over and knelt next to her.

"Do you know the story of Subhadra?" She swivelled the chair around, pulled out a package from the desk-drawer and unwrapped the tissue to reveal a Tanjore style painting, studded with gold leaf and semi-precious stones.

"Is this a game?"

"This is a scene from Mahabharata." She traced the gems studded on the painting with her fingers. "Subhadra, the half-sister of Lord Krishna, is driving a chariot away from Dwaraka with Arjuna, the valiant Pandava warrior. Belonging to an upper caste family, Subhadra had asserted her right to choose her own husband, against the wishes of members of her family. She was a strong warrior and a courageous woman. Arjuna was already a much-married man. Taking the reins of the chariot was perhaps her way of telling the world that she had neither eloped nor been kidnapped!"

"I only knew her as the mother of Abhimanyu," he said.

"Abhimanyu." She shrugged off the pallu of her sari and thrust her abdomen forward. "Our son will be Abhimanyu."

Vikramaditya stared at the expanse between the hemline of her blouse and the top edge of the sari. "Are you telling me you are pregnant?"

She pulled his face down with her hands and pressed it into her stomach, poising his lips on her belly button. "Touch our son."

"I will marry you." Vikramaditya buried his face deep in the soft ivory flesh of her skin.

Gayatri Devi closed her eyes, conjuring up pretty images of a brand-new future, with her new husband and infant son, in neighbouring Bangalore, a city bigger than Mysore. She would no longer be a blot on Indian womanhood. She would become the ode to motherhood.

"I will never leave Sulu either." Vikramaditya had pried himself free.

Had he really said that? "I am not going to be your second wife," she stated.

"I don't want our child to be illegitimate." He sat perched on the desk facing her, his hair mussed and eyebrows furrowed deeper.

"This is absurd. How can you marry me without divorcing your wife? I had not for a moment thought you were like all those feudalistic chauvinists who celebrate taking on a second wife."

"The court has no framework for granting divorce. Indian laws neither cover bigamy nor divorce. Bigamy is not recognized as a crime or an offence."

She did not detect any emotion there. Was he back to just being a lawyer? Gayatri Devi draped the sari back over her shoulder, with slow deliberation. She had attributed the absence of divorce in the Indian milieu to two factors. One, the unequivocal superiority of the male gender in a typical paternalistic society – where having a wife and a mistress or two wives was a symbol of virility that exalted the man's social status. Two, the economic and social condition of the average woman – stereotypically traditional and unassertive, financially dependent on a man from cradle to grave – be it father, brother, husband or son. It was news to her that there was no legal recourse to protect a marriage nor obtain a divorce!

"What does the great Hindu Marriage Act have to say about it?" Her voice sounded shrill and inimical even to her own ears.

"The Act is silent. Culturally, Hinduism advocates monogamy though."

*I cannot give up my dreams just because the law is silent.* She stared at her own reflection in the mirror on the opposite wall. 'Pioneering woman entrepreneur of the state of Mysore.' The words jumped out at her. The unwritten ode to motherhood jingled in her ears. "A secret second marriage. Neither legal rights nor social status. What do I get out of it?"

"A secure future? For yourself and the baby." His voice was low.

"I will consent to become your second wife on one condition." She ran her fingers across the length of his thigh. She could feel his thigh muscles throb and then flex, the warm flesh turning into cold steel. Panic. Dejection. Ire. Had her emotions sliced through the air between them and engulfed him? ... "You will, will away all your wealth to Abhimanyu." Her tone was no velvet.

"Have you gone mad?" He pushed her away.

"What choice do I have?" She unfurled her bun and shook her hair free, letting it cascade around her shoulders. "You lost my case. You got me pregnant. You will not leave your wife."

"What choice do I have?" Without looking at her, Vikramaditya had walked to the door, and out of it, sans goodbye.

Gayatri Devi sat motionless in the swivel chair. *Unlike me, you have a choice. You can stop seeing me and your life will not change. I can only hope you do not make that choice.* She had succumbed to the temptation of gambling with her future. Had she driven him away with her aggression? She turned her attention to the painting lying on the desk.

Subhadra, mother of the illustrious warrior Abhimanyu, was an inspiration. Often ignored, courageous Subhadra was a prominent female ruler of ancient India. After the devastating destruction of the Kurukshetra war, where many young descendants of the Pandavas, including the valiant Abhimanyu, were killed, Subhadra had gone on to become the guiding force for building a brand-new Indian civilization. By mentoring her grandson to become an able administrator, she had maintained the tradition of dynastic rule.

Gayatri Devi scouted around the sitting room for a spot to hang the painting on the wall. She needed to see the painting at least once every day. To reaffirm her conviction in herself.

Somehow, there was no gnawing feeling in her stomach, that things would go wrong. Vikramaditya knew her predicament. He would take his time to digest the facts and weigh the implications. This was a major turning point for both. They could not allow their decisions to be merely guided by the emotional velocity surrounding their extraordinary situation. As transactional as it sounded, they needed to arrive at their own rationale. *I must be patient. He will come back.*

•••

# 32.

# The Devil and the Deep Blue Sea

December 1, 1939. "You will, will away all your wealth to Abhimanyu."
The words she had uttered trolled his head. Heading back to Panchsheel
Villa, his own house in the western part of Mysore, Vikramaditya's mind
was a cauldron of conflicting emotions. Gayatri's demands were devilishly
brutal. Did she not trust him to take care of her? And their son?

He loosened the knot of his tie and opened his car window. Bold and
beautiful, she was the love of his life. With her, he had experienced true
togetherness. He had once cherished the dream of having a son; he had
then given up the dream. Son or daughter, his heart sang with joy at the
thought of the child they had together conceived. He wanted to protect
her and their unborn child.

Panchsheel Villa, bustling with unbridled festivities as it had for the
last few weeks, welcomed him with a renewed warmth. The huge house
was filled with his daughters and their husbands, Sulakshana's siblings
and their families, and an assortment of uncles and aunts and cousins
and spouses on both sides. The menfolk clustered around the dining table
caught in a deep discussion of the latest happenings of the Second World
War. Vikramaditya pulled a chair and joined them.

Gayatri had trusted him unconditionally. He had thrown her life into
a royal mess. He did not want their child branded 'illegitimate'. A soft
ache occupied Vikramaditya's heart. He could not walk away. Unable
to participate in the surrounding chatter, he had the ominous feeling of
being an alien spectator in his own abode.

Sulakshana and the other womenfolk were amid the elaborate ritual of
serving snacks and coffee to the entire household. His elder daughter was

playing with her baby girl. Vikramaditya stared at the cherubic face of his granddaughter, as his daughter rocked the child, close to her chest.

What would happen to Sulakshana and his daughters? What would he tell them? Would it not be humiliating if they found out about his secret marriage? How could he will away all his wealth to the unborn child? Nothing in life is for the rest of our lives. He would walk away. From Gayatri. From the most fulfilling relationship of his life.

His younger daughter placed a plate of snacks and a cup of coffee on the table. Picking up only the coffee, Vikramaditya excused himself, to go over to the drawing-room that served as his office, and locked himself inside. *It had all been too much for a single day.*

Seated at his desk, savouring the coffee, he stared at the black and white family photograph adorning the pale blue wall opposite him. Surrounded by her four daughters, Sulakshana looked peaceful, almost divine. His concept of self, extended beyond himself. It included his parents, Sulakshana and his four children. He could not forsake his family. He would wade through the rest of his life in the monotony of everyday routine.

Someone was knocking on the door. He did not move. The knock quickly turned into a loud thump. Amidst all the merriment that he did not feel a part of, the solitude he yearned for, seemed unattainable.

◆

Sunday morning, when Vikramaditya returned home from his morning walk, he found the atmosphere in the house unusually sombre. His father, his uncles and one of his brothers-in-law were assembled in the dining room. His mother and Sulakshana sat on a mat near the door, looking forlorn. An elderly aunt was supervising the preparation of breakfast in the adjacent kitchen. No one else was around; most likely, they had been asked to stay on the upper floor.

The Sunday magazine lay open on the dining table, to the page with a prominent picture of Vikramaditya whispering into Gayatri Devi's ears. 'Historic verdict in the case of Rani Gayatri Devi Rajvamsh vs. The Rajvamsh family', read the caption underneath.

Vikramaditya picked up the newspaper. Gayatri Devi looked regal. How could he sever his relationship with her? She had made his life livelier. She was his intellectual equal. She had lost her case because of him, whom she considered her protector. He looked around the room.

The scene had not changed. Why did he feel like a defendant facing the jury? He skimmed through the article amidst the steely silence.

"... The alleged affair between the good-looking couple has caused the royal lady to lose her right to property. It has resulted in the London-returned lawyer to taste his first defeat in over a decade." The reporter had quoted. "The Judge expressed his disappointment that the moral turpitude surrounding the case robbed him of an opportunity to deliver a landmark verdict that would have set a precedent for women's rights in the annals of legal history."

While the reporter had been objective in stating the facts surrounding the case, he had also succeeded in sensationalizing the romance. Vikramaditya put the newspaper down. The imminent volley ensued immediately.

The brother-in-law was the first to erupt. He called Vikramaditya a traitor and a two-headed snake and cursed the day his sister Sulakshana had married him. He had heard several rumours over the past months but hoped they would go away. The more vociferous of Vikramaditya's uncles were next, launching a joint tirade for bringing dishonour to their reputed family. They had heard the rumours too, but chosen not to believe them.

Vikramaditya neither denied nor accepted the allegations. Raising his voice, a notch higher than theirs, he pointed out that this was a high-profile case and there was bound to be gossip. Once the commotion had run its course and emotions were exhausted, Vikramaditya requested only his parents and Sulakshana to meet with him in his office.

Seated on the soft Persian rug, opposite three kindred souls that stared at him earnestly, Vikramaditya made a clean breast of what had transpired. "A few months back, a young widow came to my office. She belongs to a royal family. She is English-educated. The Rajvamsh family, instead of giving her the respect due to a daughter-in-law had kicked her out of the house. She has no real money to make a living. She was taking care of her ailing father and he died recently. While fighting her case in court, love happened."

Watching Sulakshana shed copious tears, Vikramaditya's heart sank deeper and deeper into the unfamiliar terrain of gloom. Her wistful eyes would haunt him to the day of his death. Sulakshana always put the family's interests above her own. She had never uttered an unkind word to anybody. The topics of their conversations may have been limited but the memories of tender moments spent together were many.

His mother implored Vikramaditya not to abandon Sulakshana and their four daughters. Her hands caressed Sulakshana's back all the time to console her.

"I never intended to betray Sulu." He looked tenderly at the trio huddled together before him. Despite coming from modest means and living within the confines of a conservative culture, they had never come in the way of his progress. They were his biggest strength. They would always be his biggest weakness. Vikramaditya could not bring himself to tell them about the child Gayatri Devi was expecting. That would have to wait for another day.

"Sulakshana is the daughter-in-law of this family." Vikramaditya's father, a simple man of modest education, who had remained silent even when the other menfolk had made their outbursts, spoke up for the first time. "We will take care of her until our last breath. Having left her father's house twenty-five years ago, she has made this house her home, and it will remain so for the rest of her life. We should respect that commitment. Vikrama, you have already caused her sorrow with your affair. Please do not make it worse by leaving her. We cannot cause her further injustice."

Erudition had transcended his father's hallmark reticence. Vikramaditya had listened with unquestioning respect. He only had one real choice.

"We cannot show disrespect or dishonour to any woman." His father reclined against the wall. "You will have to marry the royal lady in a quiet ceremony. She has our blessings as long as she lives separately and does not do anything that dishonours our family."

His father had unwittingly solved the great dilemma he faced. Had his father somehow read his mind? A grateful Vikramaditya got up and prostrated at the feet of his parents. *I had never thought the day would come when I would make such a decision.*

◆

Over the next few days, Vikramaditya sensed a subtle shift in the way his daughters treated him; they became distant, even distrusting of him. Each separately requested him to be discrete, gravely concerned that his dalliance would affect their family life. All of them expressed sympathy for their mother. In addition, his eldest daughter had some caustic words of scorn for the other woman, for wrecking their happiness.

Sulakshana continued to take care of him, paying extra attention to make sure his needs were satisfied to perfection, within the joint family. A separate copy of the daily newspaper started appearing for him with his morning cup of coffee. Every meal he ate included at least one of his favourite dishes. His ironed shirts were crisper and his polished shoes shinier – Sulakshana was personally supervising the servants performing these tasks.

Having little in common intellectually, their conversations had always had their own limitations. Not much changed there. Was she more accepting of the situation than he had expected? Or was she in denial? He could not tell.

Vikramaditya registered a testament to transfer the rights of Panchsheel Villa to Sulakshana, with immediate effect. Sulakshana and his parents would continue to live there and run the household with his earnings. His daughters were well settled – he had found them respectable alliances, paid for their weddings, set them up with ample jewellery and silverware, and even presented them a small piece of land each.

Initially, willing away the rest of his wealth had posed a legal challenge, for the simple reason that the child was unborn. Resorting to legal research, Gayatri Devi unearthed a case law where the court of England upheld trusts for unborn children, though their existence was not a fact at the time of inception. Destiny was already favouring Abhimanyu!

Vikramaditya prepared a testament, to hold in a trust created in favour of the unborn child, his entire wealth comprising many acres of lands in the environs of Mysore, a plethora of cash and bank deposits, the portfolio of shares and bonds with Indian and British corporations and most importantly, the palatial mansion under construction in the city of Bangalore. Vikramaditya and Gayatri Devi would be the executors of the trust until Abhimanyu came of age and became the legal owner of all assets belonging to the trust.

◆

January 1, 1940. On his fortieth birthday, the same day that the trust came into existence, Vikramaditya wed Gayatri Devi in a private ceremony, at Indigo Castle. Governess Agnes, Jeweller Gupta and a few other people who had been friends with Gayatri Devi's father, Mr. and

Mrs. Neeladri, and two senior staff members from Vikramaditya's office, were the only invited guests.

Vikramaditya had informed his joint family of the event but refrained from inviting them. Not that any of them had shown any inclination to attend. The entire family was collectively in conscious denial of the alliance.

Sitting in front of the holy fire and obediently performing the rituals dictated by the priest to synchronize with the mantras he chanted, Vikramaditya could not stop throwing appreciative glances at Gayatri Devi sitting to his right, gorgeous in a Banaras silk sari that concealed her pregnancy. The peacock blue of the sari immaculately complemented the brilliant sapphires and the radiant emerald in the golden tiara adorning her forehead.

"Where did you get that tiara?"

"My family has owned it for a century." She smiled mischievously.

"That I know. I mean, was it not given to the bank as collateral?"

"That one is faux," she whispered.

"As in artificial?" His tone harboured mild admonition.

Amidst the hazy fumes emanating from the holy fire and pervading the air with the aroma of saffron and ghee, she acquainted him with the anecdote of the tiara substitution.

*I keep discovering new facets to your personality.* "What you did is tantamount to embezzlement." He frowned.

The priest had called upon the bridal couple to get ready for the Saptapadi.[15]

Standing, Vikramaditya held out his right hand. Gayatri Devi knotted the pallu of her sari to the loose end of his silk uttariya. Repeating the marital vows chanted by the priest, bound by the knotted ends of their apparel, Vikramaditya and Gayatri Devi circled the holy fire seven times, cementing their conjugal union for an entire lifetime, as the traditional music filling the air headed towards an auspicious crescendo.

◆

The first thing that Vikramaditya and Gayatri Devi accomplished as a married couple was to pay off the pawn loan with Brindavan Bank. Clad in a colourful sari with floral patterns, a new mangalsutra around her neck

---

[15] Hindu marriage ritual – literally meaning seven steps

and vermilion powder in the parting of her hair – Gayatri Devi flaunted her newlywed status.

Manager Prithviraj had handed over the blue velvet box with a glum and flaccid face.

"Now that I am taken, he is no longer smitten." Seated in the car, she giggled.

"You could have gone to jail for the tiara deception."

"I cannot part with the relic of my royal heritage. Abhimanyu – our very own Prince Charming – will inherit it. Along with the business empire, I will build for him."

"What if the child you are bearing is a girl?"

"Not possible. It will be a boy. Mother's intuition."

"Should we at least think of a name, just in case it is a girl?"

Removing a ruby ring from her finger, she unhooked the gold chain he wore around his neck and threaded the ring through the chain. Suspending the chain above her belly, she asked him to describe how it was swinging.

"Meaning?" He stared at her staring at the chain and ring with undivided devotion.

"It is swinging from one side to the other." She pointed to the chain. "Our child is a boy. It would swing in a circular motion if the child were a girl."

He never would have believed that she believed in such old wives' tales. Gently, he pried his chain from her fingers and put it back around his neck.

◆

When Vikramaditya stepped into Panchsheel Villa, it was the hour before noon. The menfolk were not around. Neither Sulakshana nor his mother was in the dining room, their haven for that time of the day. Climbing the stairs to go to his room, he saw that the door to the terrace was ajar. Standing in the middle of the terrace in direct sunlight, his mother was braiding Sulakshana's hair. Seated on the terrace swing, his father was reading the Bhagwad Gita.

The time had come to tell them about the second testament he had registered. Setting foot on the terrace, Vikramaditya was gathering his courage to do so, when his mother beckoned him. Sulakshana looked at him with an expression mixed with hope and happiness. His mother whispered to him, that after fifteen years, Sulakshana was pregnant again.

Had he heard right? Vikramaditya sat down on the swing next to his father and gripped the chain. He and Sulakshana had shared a rare intimate moment during the eight weeks he and Gayatri Devi had shared a hiatus. Unthinkable that he had succeeded in getting both women pregnant around the same time.

For the second time within one month, Vikramaditya made yet another clean breast of what more had transpired during the recent past. He tried to keep it brief, but it was no longer simple. "Gayatri is pregnant too. I have willed away everything but Panchsheel Villa to our unborn child."

His mother stared at him, tears streaming down her cheeks. Sulakshana shed no tears. His father closed the Bhagwad Gita and stood up. "This day you have truly let us down."

The wail of their hearts would haunt him to the day of his death. "Forgive me," he said. If only he had known, even a day before, that Sulakshana was expecting his child, he might have changed his decision. Now there was no going back.

He heard his father advising Sulakshana to name the child Siddhartha, the birth name of Gautama Buddha, in the hope that he would be detached from all material things.

Long after Sulakshana and his parents had retreated, Vikramaditya continued to sit on the terrace swing. As the British liked to say, he had robbed Peter to pay Paul. Unknowingly, he had sealed Siddhartha's fate even before he was born.

◆

Gayatri Devi had not erred with her intuition. Neither had the gold chain and ring that had swung over her belly. She gave birth to a radiant and robust baby boy on August 1, 1940. Abhimanyu was born to win. Destiny had ensured this. He would one day take destiny into his own hands.

Vikramaditya's father had not erred with his declaration either. Sulakshana had given birth to a tall and emaciated baby boy, one day after the birth of Abhimanyu. Destiny would always elude Siddhartha.

•••

# 33.

# Destiny's Chosen Child

"The Parliament of India enacted the Hindu Marriage Act much later, sometime in the mid-fifties when Jawaharlal Nehru was the Prime Minister. Provisions for separation and divorce were introduced. And bigamy became illegal." Having narrated the circumstances under which she had thrust the tough choice on Vikramaditya forty-six years ago, Rani Maa looked unusually drained. "I sold several acres of land held under the trust to set up Aradhana. Over the years, I sold the remaining acres, to fund our expansion."

A baffled Abhimanyu stared at the crystal chandelier, as he lay curled on the burgundy daybed in the living room of Indigo Castle. His mind was a melting pot of myriad emotions. His mother was the daughter of the uncrowned prince of Malnad. She had brought him up in an atmosphere of elegant affluence. They had always led a life of abundance. The discovery that she had been on the brink of penury in a distant past was unfathomable.

"I always associated our well-to-do-ness with your royal roots." He could barely hear his own voice. "I assumed Appa had divided his wealth between the two families. In some equitable fashion. After all, he was fair-minded and principled." Abhimanyu closed his eyes. The bright light was causing them to water.

He had never ventured to understand his father's predicament of having two families when the rest of the men around them only had one. Abhimanyu had focused on achievement and success, at academics, and in business. 'ROI' – getting the best return on any investment – be it time or effort or money – had been his mantra. He had been quick to label

Siddhartha a loser and seek revenge. He had never paused to question why his half-brother had resorted to such desperate measures. *I lack empathy. Rahul was right.*

"For your Appa's sake." Rani Maa placed a palm on Abhimanyu's forehead. "Get Siddhartha out of whatever mess you have created."

The touch of her hand, as soothing as it was to his burning skin, would not suppress the volcanoes erupting in his heart. The corporate wars he waged were always with equals. He never resorted to underhand dealings to win business battles. He never treated family and friends as adversaries. He had broken all his rules at once. And pushed Siddhartha, his brother, towards financial insolvency and incarceration. The income tax squad had likely booked a case against him for concealment of income. And placed a lien on his house.

Abhimanyu got up with a jolt and picked up his valise. Whatever catastrophe was brewing, he had to stop it from exploding. "I am going back to Bangalore. To approve the merger of Vikrama Ventures and Izod Investments. Immediately. To meet the DCP and personally admit that I made a mistake. If there are income tax injunctions against Siddhartha, I will get them revoked. If there are liens on his house, I will get them cancelled."

"You have to do what you have to do." Rani Maa walked with Abhimanyu to the door, her gait reluctant. "First things first. Though, I wish you had stayed for supper." She planted a tender kiss on his cheek.

Backing his car towards the winding driveway, seeing his mother in silhouette as she stood outside the front door waving, Abhimanyu's eyes turned misty. She would turn seventy-five on Vijaya Dashami day. He made a mental note to inform Veronica and organize a small party in commemoration of Rani Maa's birthday.

The unlit roads were bereft of people. The mist was hampering visibility. Abhimanyu turned on the wipers. Wealthy parents, academic success, flourishing career – life had bestowed him with everything without the asking. He had grown up with a sense of entitlement, attributing his success to his superior intellect and delighting in his pompous arrogance, claiming it was confidence. Would he have been as successful if he had not inadvertently robbed Siddhartha of his rightful legacy? A haunting sense of scepticism engulfed Abhimanyu.

He was not the master of his own destiny, as he had believed. He was merely destiny's chosen child. The time had come for him to take destiny into his own hands. *Father, please forgive me for wrecking the life of my brother.* Abhimanyu let the single tear roll down his cheek. *I promise to make such amends that shame shall recede and pride shall emerge.*

◆

Mahalaya Amavas – The Great New Moon Day. The last day of the Tarpan period. When Hindus perform spiritual rituals to appease the dead spirits of their ancestors. The monsoon winds wailed and whistled as the jet-black Toyota sped along the Mysore-Bangalore highway in the pitch-dark moonless night.

Abhimanyu's distraught mind that made furious plans to salvage Siddhartha's situation was unaware that the car headlights were not on. Even as the speeding Toyota bumped intermittently on the speed-breakers, placed in strategically awkward spots, huge trucks carrying cargo from Bangalore to Mysore zoomed continually in the opposite direction.

The head-on collision was inevitable. The driver of the car did not stand the slightest chance to survive. The next morning's newspapers would describe it as the spot death of Bangalore's beloved business baron, the owner of the Aradhana empire.

Have we not heard that when a person is dying his entire life passes in front of him in one transient moment? Dreams and disillusionments. Achievements and setbacks. Family and friends. Platitude? Blind belief? Superstition? There is no knowing. No research can reach the inner sanctums of a dying mind.

Yet when Abhimanyu was on the verge of death – in those nanoseconds when he was suspended in the threshold of a rapidly sinking awareness – a slew of thoughts crossed his mind in quick succession.

Remorse. Siddhartha was the legitimate heir to the Vikramaditya fortune. Abhimanyu had robbed Siddhartha of this basic right. For no fault of Siddhartha. Except that Abhimanyu had been born the illegitimate son of Vikramaditya. Paradoxical.

Repentance. Rahul was his son; born from the womb of the exquisite woman he had loved. Rahul had sought acceptance. Abhimanyu had perpetrated rejection. Because he expected flawlessness. But Rahul had chosen authenticity. Rani Maa was right. Rahul's sexual orientation was not his fault. Even if he could never understand his son's lifestyle, Abhimanyu, as a father, should have accepted him for who he was.

*If I can traverse life all over again, I will not make the same mistakes. I will offer my son, unconditional love. I will restore my father's wealth to my brother. If only God gives me the opportunity to fulfil these two wishes!*

The mind went numb, and then stopped functioning. The body went limp, then cold. The soul escaped and merged with the large pool of souls in God's own repository. It would de-merge later to enter the body of little Abhi, who would never know that the soul he possessed belonged to his grandfather Abhimanyu.

●●●

# 34.

# The Contingency Plan

Just as Abhimanyu died amid the whistling and wailing monsoon winds, the imminent catastrophe he was rushing to prevent, was exploding. Siddhartha's journey had been arduous. The taxicab he had hired in Mysore had broken down *en route*, forcing him to trek to a neighbouring town and flag a crowded bus. It was almost nine o'clock when he arrived at his twelfth floor flat in North Bangalore.

He immediately opened the steel almirah in their bedroom, took a bunch of documents and set to work; alternating between reading intensely and writing vigorously. Siddhartha wanted to be the master of his destiny. Abhimanyu had wrecked it all. It was all over. Only *her* God could protect Sadhana from any evil forces that were out to evict her from Panchsheel Villa. Sadhana had supported him at every step of every phase of his tumultuous life. He could not face her this time. If only *her* God had been kind enough not to take away their only daughter? Or at least, give her another child? Why was he invoking God? He had always maintained he did not believe in God, much to the chagrin of Sadhana and before that, the consternation of his mother, when she was alive.

Siddhartha sorted and placed a set of documents in a maroon briefcase and clipped the primary ingredient of his contingency plan – a life insurance policy valued at Rupees sixteen lakhs of which Sadhana was the sole beneficiary – at the top. God, Destiny, Fate – whatever the name, there was a superpower operating much above the realm of the effort of a mere mortal. The day's events had proved that maxim. His mother was right, so was Sadhana. Siddhartha could only heave a sigh, a mixture of regret and relief at his own realization, as he pinned the letter he had written, to the front of his shirt.

Switching off the lights, he walked out of the twelfth floor flat, past the security guard who bowed to him, climbed the single flight of stairs leading to the terrace, locked the terrace door after him and stared at the starless night. Everything was pitch-dark. The story of his life. What a tragic loser he was. He would live up to that image. In the eyes of the world. *Except I will not be there to suffer the humiliation this time.*

Siddhartha plunged into an oblivious bliss as soon as he put his leg across the parapet wall. The body crashed to a thousand pieces. The poor man had no knowledge of his progeny growing in the womb of the wife he loved so much. Nor did he realise that he had died in vain. For life insurance policies did not provide suicide coverage during the early years. His policy would be deemed invalid since he had committed suicide within a year of its commencement. Which meant that Sadhana would not receive any benefits under the policy. Had he found this out, perhaps the good-hearted Siddhartha would not have jumped to his own death? The proof of the project lies in the planning. Even his mantra had failed him.

◆

Driving back to Panchsheel Villa from Chamundi Hills in the blue Maruti car, Sadhana kept looking at her watch in dismay. She hated to keep Siddhartha waiting.

That morning, Sadhana had not lied to Siddhartha. After the rendezvous with Gayatri Devi, she had gone to Chamundi Hills with Doctor Pallavi and her family. Having climbed the one thousand steps to reach the hilltop, she had visited the temple and prayed her heart out. And after a late picnic lunch, lounged around the vantage point until sunset. After returning the stolen tiara and the diamond set, a sense of tranquillity had descended on her.

Sadhana looked forward to the conversation with her loving husband – the reassurance from Gayatri Devi, the matriarch, had infused new hope. A part of her dreaded the conversation with him though – that he might feel hurt that she had not consulted him before taking the matter of returning the tiara into her own hands. No matter what, his eyes would light up when she gave him her news, their news. Pallavi had confirmed that Sadhana was well and truly pregnant. The foetus was six weeks old.

Panchsheel Villa was shrouded in darkness. An eerie feeling began to haunt Sadhana as she entered. The bedroom no longer felt like her sanctum sanctorum. The strewn clothes and the ripped bed made her feel violated. Laxman, amidst tears, gave her a halted narration of the day's goings-on.

Sadhana swiftly changed into a pair of jeans and a kurta. Whatever this was, it had to do with the tiara. Gayatri Devi had the clout to get this income tax case dropped, of that she was confident. After all this was over, they would sell Panchsheel Villa, Sadhana resolved. She would convince Siddhartha. Their baby would be the harbinger of a life bereft of stealth and deceit, envy and rejection. Sadhana decided to pack an overnight case. She had to drive down to Bangalore. Siddhartha needed her.

◆

Gayatri Devi could not stop waving long after Abhimanyu had backed his car into the driveway of Indigo Castle. She was proud of him for realizing his follies and rushing to ameliorate the situation he had advertently created. Yet she felt a gnawing discomfort as she stared at the Tanjore painting of Subhadra and Arjuna on the wall of the foyer.

*I do not want my Abhimanyu to be unwittingly consumed by the Chakravyuha of his own making.* She beckoned the housekeeper and ordered her to unhook the painting. "Send for the watchman. Have him fling it into the woods," she added.

The thought of dinner was repelling. She knew sleep would also elude her. Gayatri Devi settled down on the burgundy day bed in the living room. Her body was in dread of something that the mind refused to comprehend.

It was the middle of the night, when the terrifying news was relayed, heralded by the incessant ring of the telephone. The mind regained perfect control once the details were known. She had to do what she had to do. Wrapping a grey shawl around her shoulders, Gayatri Devi beckoned the chauffeur. Destination – Benson Hospital, Bangalore.

◆

The night was dark and moonless. Laxman by her side, Sadhana eased the car cautiously into the Mysore-Bangalore highway and held her speed steady. The last thing she wanted was to be involved in a road accident. It was past eleven o'clock when they reached Bangalore. A pit of the stomach feeling spread over her as Sadhana veered the car into the road leading to their apartment complex. A stationary ambulance occupied the entire width of the narrow road, the red lights flashing. Sadhana stopped the car.

Getting out of the car, Laxman ran towards the ambulance, gave a shrill scream, and gesticulated wildly. Sadhana followed him zombie-like, and walked straight into the ambulance, to be confronted by Siddhartha's motionless body. The doors of the ambulance closed immediately. The ambulance moved rapidly, siren blaring.

A paramedic thrust a letter into Sadhana's hand and told her it was pinned to the front of her husband's shirt.

> *Sadhana, forgive me, my love. You are the best thing that ever happened to me. In life and in death, you are the one person that I love with my body, my mind and my soul.*
>
> *My grandfather named me Siddhartha after the enlightened master Gautama Buddha. Desire is the root cause of sorrow, he taught me. Today I realize the gravity of his words.*
>
> *Ever since my father's death, the burning desire of obtaining justice for us had consumed me. That same desire has caused my downfall. My business has been ruined and our house may not remain our house anymore.*
>
> *Yet desire is what gives meaning to life. When desire is lost, life becomes listless.*
>
> *I am taking my life out of my own will and volition. I know you are strong, stronger than I am. You will learn to face life alone. Believe me, once I am gone, the bad luck that has pursued us will be gone too.*
>
> *You are the sole beneficiary of my life insurance policy. I hope that the money helps you start life afresh. I wish I could have done more for you. I am sure that your computer education will bring you lucrative job offers and professional success. I pray that your solitary life will be fuller and brighter than the one you have shared with me.*
>
> *Please take care of Laxman in a way you deem fit. Sad that I never told him, I love him as if he were my own son.*

*If the lien on Panchsheel Villa is ever lifted, as the sole surviving owner, you are free to do whatever you want with it.*

*Forgive me, my darling*

*Forever and Always*

*Adieu*

*Siddhartha*

Sadhana looked at her loving husband as if in a trance. Death had given him the peace that life had eluded him. *If only you had waited for a few minutes, you would have found out that our life was about to change, acquire a new meaning, make us chase new dreams.* She placed her head on his ashen face, bathing his cheeks with the copious tears flowing from her eyes.

The ambulance had arrived at Benson Hospital. The doctor's verdict would be a mere formality. Paramedics wheeled Siddhartha's body away. Sadhana fainted.

◆

More sirens in the distance. Flashing lights coming to a halt in the hospital portico. Paramedics rushing out. "Spot death. Business baron Abhimanyu." Loud whispers. Another stretcher wheeling out.

"Two half-brothers, born one day apart, meeting their separate deaths on the same night, one hour apart." The morning newspaper carried twin headlines about the double tragedy. News, as sensational as news could get.

Abhimanyu was dead. So was Siddhartha. Vikramaditya's progeny had been erased. Gayatri Devi sought Sadhana. Her compatriot of sorrow. Hugging Sadhana to her bosom, she cried her heart out. "Come live with me." She invited Sadhana.

●●●

Made in the USA
Middletown, DE
27 October 2020

22855313R00146